RECEIVED JUN - - 2018

Praise for
and *Tat*

... PROPERTY OF
SEATTLE PUBLIC LIBRARY

"A hallucinogenic post-apocalyptic carnival ride—Nikhil Singh has a strange and intriguing mind."

—Lauren Beukes, author of *Broken Monsters*

"Imagine if Lewis Carroll had written five Alice adventures and crammed them into one volume but veering into untried perversions, new drugs, and a beatnik-Gothic vibe. Only out of Africa. William S. Burroughs—only more imaginative."

—Geoff Ryman, author of the hypertext novel *253* and its print version, *253: The Print Remix*

"A wild, marauding vision on acid. Nikhil Singh creates a world that threatens to leave the confines of the page. Brilliantly compelling."

—Irenosen Okojie, author of *Speak Gigantular*

"Savvy, ultra-modern, *Taty* straddles the mediated realities of our own continent and the groundbreaking possibilities of our ongoing universal imaginaries."

—Billy Kahora, managing editor of Kenya's Kwani Trust

RECEIVED

"Finding words to adequately describe Singh's writing is not easy, but let's start with these: radiant, explosive, provocative. These characters and their stories are remarkable. *Taty Went West* is a dizzying ride of a novel that will leave you breathless and wanting to get right back on again."

—Michael Thomas Ford, author of the Shirley Jackson Award finalist, Lambda Literary Award finalist, and Tiptree Award long list title *LILY*

"Nikhil Singh writes a prose as lush and crocodile-infested as the rainforests in the Outzone."

—Mehul Gohil, winner of the 2010 Kwani? "The Kenya I Live In" Short Story Prize

"*Taty Went West* is not your average adventure story, and Taty is a new kind of adventure heroine."

—*New African Magazine*

"There's no one else like Nikhil Singh and their intricate illustrated dark visions of the future. Their individuality stains their work in an eerie and pervasive manner making for an incredible multi-layered experience for the reader."

—*Short Story Day Africa*

TATY WENT WEST

Nikhil Singh

Cover art © 2018 Nikhil Singh
Colors by Carmen Incarnadine
Cover design by Gerald Mohamed III

Copyright © 2018 Nikhil Singh.
All rights reserved. No part of this publication may be reproduced, distributed, or transmitted in any forms or by any means, including photocopying, recording, or other electronic or mechanical methods, without the prior written permission of of the publisher, except in the case of brief quotations embodied in critical reviews and certain other noncommercial uses permitted by copyright law. For permission requests, write to the publisher at the address below:

Published by Rosarium Publishing
P.O. Box 544
Greenbelt, MD 20768-0544
www.rosariumpublishing.com

"When the Traveler turns west, time travel ceases to be travel and becomes instead an inexorable suction, pulling everything into a black hole."

—William S. Burroughs, *The Place of Dead Roads*

PART I

Into the Outzone

1
The Zone

THERE HAD ALWAYS BEEN STORIES of lost cities in the jungle. Descriptions of vast structures hidden behind impenetrable veils of steaming foliage, their once-great plazas and floating pyramids now the haunt of monkeys, shades, and folkloric spiders. Many such places must have existed in the trackless quadrants of the Outzone. Much of the jungle was still unexplored with only two highways leading into the lower portion of the Zone—the old colony, long since abandoned and declared lawless. One of these passages came in over the hot carbon wastes while the other became a coast road.

This tarmac strip hugged the wild shoreline and was the most common point of entry from the cities of the Lowlands. The coast itself was dotted with seedy port towns, the largest of which was Namanga Mori at the farthest tip of the old colony on the threshold of the jungle. Before the colony had broken down, Namanga Mori had been a thriving center of trade, ferrying jungle produce from the deepest regions of the Outzone. Now it was decrepit, populated by smugglers, sleepwalkers, and those who came staggering out of the trees looking for work. The Outzone was a place where people went to escape. It was large enough for anyone to lose themselves in, a feverish sanctuary for those seeking to escape their lives or memory. In this way the jungle became a forest of dead time, a necrotic wonderland, a province of waking coma where time itself had grown sickly and died. Travelers called the Zone "the Land of Strangers": the place where anyone could escape anything and where the lost things lay.

2

Heading West

THE PIGGY BANK BOUGHT HER a bus ticket to nowhere fast. But it felt like nowhere slow. When Taty was on the coach staring out at an unreeling landscape, everything seemed pre-recorded. She was reminded of films she had seen as an infant.

It was claustrophobic aboard the yellow-windowed old coach, surrounded by strangers in the droning dimness. Every driver's announcement was preceded by the intro of that old "If You're Going to San Francisco" song, and the screening facility was broken. The interior was heavy with the stench of sweat and jungle chicken. Taty held her nose for most of the way, disembarking at the edge of the jungle where the road branched out into the Zone. She found herself on the verge where the route left the Lowlands, gazing out at the distant rises of greenery and watching the coach slug away down the highway as she sang the lyrics of her current favorite pop anthem quietly to herself: *Just a girl from a small town running wild* ... To her left foliage-choked valleys winked like lazy eyes within the distant dips and swells. To her right flexed the long golden biceps of the beach. A warm, dark sea swelled and retracted beyond the blurry shore, fuzzing up the air with haze. Fields of rushes shimmered within the curtain of this obscurity, a hairline clinging to the edges of lagoons.

Taty followed the coast road into the Outzone until it got dark and then slept in the wreck of an old car. It was a busted-up shell of a thing crouched in on itself like the husk of a beetle. She had discovered it along the way partially engorged by vines and left the road to investigate. When the back seat was found to be somewhat still intact, she decided to linger. The night was stuffy and sticky. She could at all times hear the sea moving behind the stage curtain of the trees. A lull of singing insects carried in haunting waves through the dense, black heart of the mangrove. Already she was starting to erase things, tapes and memories, tiny little lines of pencil. Erasure came easily to her, and she didn't give it much thought. She had recently turned sixteen, and things were shifting radically. The decision to run away from home had been taken, and it was too late to turn around now. She was stepping lightly into the framework of a brand new universe without so much as looking back. And there was a special kind of strength in this. But it was easy in this gloomy Eden, which was so different from the clear-cut provincialities of the Lowlands. Although she had heard a hundred stories about the Outzone, it was the pop songs that had finally cemented her decision. She had been listening to the *In with the Outzone* album that was on all the radios in the hive that summer. Her favorite holo-pop singer, Coco Carbomb, had recorded most of the music in the Outzone with some local character they called the "witchboy." The pair sang about a wild place filled with crazy parties, pleasure tech, and high adventure. It seemed as good a place to run to as any. When she heard the song about a small-town teen running wild, it struck a chord. She downloaded the song directly to tape and would listen to it on repeat, sullen-faced in the knowledge of what she was about to do.

No one could have suspected her true motives or the strength of her conviction, yet lots of girls her age must have shared the urge to escape the locked-down routines of the Lowlands: the subterranean suburb bunkers, the regimentation, and factory food, all those sky malls. Almost anything that blew out of the lawlessness of the Outzone was quickly elevated to fable in such sterile quarters. But now that she was finally here, the reality of the Zone turned everything she had heard about it to lukewarm gossip. The music, however, lingered, becoming even more potent in its native element. She remembered all those times trapped in the 'burbs, staring out of a bubble window with the volume turned all the way up, fantasizing about the tropical realm that *In with the Outzone* described. It was to these escapist moments that she returned when it finally came time to run. Because, by now, she truly believed that it was in the Zone that she would finally be able to leave behind—and indeed, forget forever—the terrible thing she had done. Even now, so far away from home, she could not even bring herself to think about it. Out in the jungle, strange birds called. Their voices looped out into space, and she imagined that they were speaking to her in an

ancient, long-forgotten language. Calling to her from just beyond the tree line.

Taty awoke before dawn and watched the sun split like a ripe melon over the world. She was listening to tapes on her Walkman® when light started creeping through the meshwork of densely knitted trees. And she felt quiet and still within that spectral light. She clawed off her heavy metal headphones, cut the tape, and listened to the immensity of the wild jungle she had heard so many stories about. Soon she was out on the road again.

The day began to blur as the heat rose. The sound of the sea tantalized her with a promise of coolness, but as much as she searched, no beach path marked the almost-solid walls of jungle. Rather than enter the tangled labyrinth of vegetation, she simply trudged on. By late afternoon the charm of adventure had drained away, and fatigue lay heavy upon her. She spent another mosquito-haunted night in the rough. Her sleep was broken by the distant whooping of dinosaurs. She stayed up till dawn in a haze of fear, stepping back out onto the road as soon as the sun came out. She had been walking for almost two days now, eating stale chocolate cookies and resting now and again on the side of the road. In that time she had seen only two vehicles pass. One was an overloaded jungle chicken rig stacked high with the corpses of man-sized gilas. The lizards were part of the staple diet of the Outzone inhabitants, often referred to as "jungle chicken" due to the flavor of their firm white flesh. A man with a painted face was driving, but he barely glanced at Taty as he passed. The other vehicle was battered beyond description and almost ran her over. Nobody else seemed to want to enter the jungle. And so the road gleamed starkly before her, a sanitary incision across the flank of some inebriated behemoth.

IT WAS APPROACHING LATE AFTERNOON when Taty heard the sound of another car. The light was by now heavy and orange. The sound of the sea had dulled out to a distant ebb. Taty stopped in the middle of the highway and glanced back over her shoulder. Heat waves had become disturbed by the passage of the distant car. These oiled around against the embering light, distorting the sun in their churn. A mounting bass hum suggested that the car was moving fast. Taty stopped and stood, observing the noisy speck approach in a heat-drunk fashion. She was too fatigued to move, or perhaps she assumed that the car would simply barrel by like the others. The hum swelled to an engine roar, and the car didn't so much as slow as stop on a dime. It screeched to a neat, contained halt, its massive bulk vibrating gruffly beside her. She found herself staring at the hot wall of a towering chassis. Dull black paint flaked in parts. The weathering showed sea rust and bullet-pocked metal. Barbed wire had been twined around the heavy bumpers, left to oxidize. A sharp-nosed teddy bear was tangled up in it like a kooky kamikaze.

"Where you going, Sugarplum?" a smoky voice inquired.

Taty glanced up to see a plump, pale woman smoking slyly down at her from the driver's window. One of the smiling woman's hands was draped over the sill, and Taty noticed that it was large and paw-like. The fat fingers terminated in black raptor claws that stroked around constantly, dislodging tiny fragments of paint in slow circulations. Taty gazed back down the highway, lifted an arm in response, and pointed. Her finger seemed to describe an area where the chalky highway tapered out into invisibility, becoming gradually swallowed by the looming mass of the jungle.

"That way."

The woman brushed back a fringe of bottle-black hair, revealing an intricate tattoo. The shocking patterning sprawled out over her rounded cheek and forehead, radiating from her staring kohlrimmed eye. It completely dominated the entire left side of her doll-like face, lending her a schizoid quality. Taty found that there was a strange mystique to the tattoo, a quality that was difficult to place immediately. It captivated her attention, allowing the woman the freedom to inspect her. Sensing that it was perhaps the sort of distraction a predator might employ, Taty snapped up to meet whirlpool eyes. The woman exhaled smoke while she studied the girl.

"Death is very quick. She is also very quiet."

She breathed out more smoke, her statement somehow drawing the various sounds of the jungle into focus: clicking and whirring, distant calls of birds, and the rummaging of animals.

"If we come by this road later, will you still be walking?"

Taty considered this, the dream of her day suddenly intruded upon by an unforeseen gauze of reality.

"I ... I don't know," she murmured.

The passenger door popped open a moment or two later, almost of its own accord. Yet Taty lingered on for long seconds, observing the unspoken offer of a ride in a state of dreamy indifference. She and the massive motor car formed an unmoving tableau against the darkening jungle. Frozen, as though within a film still.

3
The Insect Christ

TATY HAD LEANED HERSELF OUT into the slipstream, staring up at grey and turbulent recessions of cloud. Somewhat bipolar industrial power electronics blared out of the bass-heavy speaker system, flickering between piercing feedback and whispery white noise without any warning. The crucifix was the first thing she had noticed upon entering the car. It dangled heavily from the rearview, swinging like a pendulum. The face of the Jesus figure had been broken off, replaced by the severed head of a large jungle insect. It was a comical—though inexpressibly perverse—image.

LATER THEY WERE SITTING IN a lapsed silence, rocketing through the pre-dusk dimness.

"My brother ..." Taty faltered. "He died."

"That's nice."

"What is it you do?"

"We collect."

Taty glanced sidelong at the fantastic moonscape of the woman's shadow-drenched profile. A long cigarette dangled off gloss-black doll's lips, coiling out a blur of smoke. This blur extended as the day drew on, filling the car and smudging Taty's day.

"Miss Muppet's the name, sister."

Taty fell asleep watching the crucifix. Its swaying lulled her while the world blackened. She awoke dazed, somewhere in the night. Miss Muppet sat like an ancient statue fixed behind the wheel, under-lit and bathed in violent music. Taty scuffed off her sneakers, crawled over onto the vast back seat, and slid instantly into a restless slumber.

She awoke again deeper into the muggy wash of a tropical night. They had stopped on the side of the road, and a troubling stillness filled the car. A dim glinting along the metal of the windows cut slim shapes out of the blackness. She could hear the rumble of the sea and the close clicking of a palm tree. Warmth swelled in ambiguous shapes above and beside her. She found herself drifting in and out of sleep. It was almost too hot to breathe. Something heavy and pale shifted beside her in the blackness, and she found herself mumbling out loud.

"Mommy," she slurred.

The utterance surprised her in a distant, unforeseeable way. It came to her that this was the longest she had been apart from her state-medicated mother. When she was contemplating running away, Taty didn't imagine she would miss her mother at all. Who could miss the housebound ghost that saw imaginary white rabbits in the corners of rooms and often failed to recognize her own daughter? Yet now, in hindsight, Taty's feelings were altogether different. It had been difficult for her growing up with a mother who often appeared to be living in another reality. The robots made sure her mother didn't stray and kept her doped up, but everyone would still worry about her falling through open windows and the like. Despite this, the woman drank heavily, lapsing into chaotic, almost schizoid behavior at the slightest provocation. The various conditions she suffered from and the treatment they necessitated created a constant state of tension. In the last few years, however, Taty's feelings had turned to irritation and even rage. She knew that it wasn't right to feel this way. She made every effort to be charitable and accepting, only to find herself coming up short when her mother started hurling crockery at her or bawling like a baby. Her father, for the most part, absented himself, entrusting his kids to robotic care—a well-worn tradition in the Lowlands. The man always seemed to be away on assignment buried deep in subterranean bases, available only as a hologram or in the form of presents, easy enough to dismiss. The abandonment of her long-suffering mother, however, seemed all of a sudden an invitation to calamity. Taty wondered whether she had made a mistake. Here in the hot darkness beside a stranger, she fantasized about returning home. She began to imagine that the authorities and her family could forgive her for what she had done. The cold fact was that, if anyone in the Lowlands discovered the truth of what had happened to her little brother, she would be medicated alongside her mother. There could never be any acceptance or understanding of her

actions. Not in that machine-hearted wasp hive. The course she had taken was the only one open to her, and she had to be brave about it. The longing she felt for a mother who wasn't always drunk and delusional had been with her for as long as she could remember. But now that the suffocated umbilicus had finally been severed by her own hand, she felt desperate for comfort. The emotional charge drew her reflexively to the stranger. Her eyelids grew heavy before she could contemplate the full import of the situation. Sleep washed down like the sound of the sea, drowning her quickly.

Taty sat up abruptly to find herself alone in the bright white light of morning. She noticed immediately that the crucifix had disappeared. Fresh sea air knifed in through the open windows, gusting hair into her eyes. She scuffed it aside and glanced around. The jungle had fallen away to reveal a vast barren seascape. The highway had elevated, straddling the edge of a bony cliff. This precipice overlooked the wild dark sea. She rubbed her eyes and crawled blearily out onto the windy tarmac. Miss Muppet was nowhere to be seen. Taty peered around before walking to the edge of the cliff and gazing down at the distant rind of the beach. After a moment or two, she could clearly discern a tiny black blot on the grand arc of sand.

There was a path leading to the beach, and Taty followed it down to enormous pristine dunes. She could see the faraway figure of Miss Muppet standing with her back to her and staring out to sea. The dark static figure would disappear for a moment or two each time Taty went down a depression only to reappear when she rose, a little larger than before. For some reason she kept expecting the figure to vanish each time she crested the dune. But it never did. Taty drew close and saw that Miss Muppet was carrying things in her hands. The object in her right hand was sleek and black and turned out to be a six-shooter shotgun with a dangling strap. Her other hand clutched loosely at a couple of dead seagulls she had nailed. Their splattered wings fluttered in the wind, staining her fat knuckles with blood. A bandolier was slung like a chain over her round shoulder. She was moving now, smoking contemplatively, watching the waves from behind dark sunglasses. Talon-tipped toes flexed slowly in the sand, scratching like bird claws. Bobbing in the light surf some meters before her was the carcass of a great white shark. It floated belly-up punctured by a bullet wound. The entry hole had torn open in the trawl, and its guts now spilled out into the water, trailing like ribbons through the foam. The water lapped at the blood, sucking it back out toward the deep. Taty noticed immediately that the insect Christ was now attached to the hardwood butt of the gun. It whipped around in the wind at the end of its beaded string. She jammed her hands into her pockets and came up beside her companion. Together they regarded the corpse.

"Shot a shark," Miss Muppet announced.

Taty nodded.

"Saw the fin, took a shot. Tide washed him in."

"'I see,' said the blind man. 'How can it be? My eyes are blind, but I can see,'" Taty parroted from memory.

"Huh?"

"Nothing, just something my brother and I used to say."

Miss Muppet finished her cigarette in silence. When she was done, she tossed it into the wind.

"Taty?"

Taty looked up.

"Close your eyes."

Taty did as she was bid, and Miss Muppet raised the hand she was using to hold the gulls. She swung her bloody fist into Taty's face, knocking her unconscious. Up on the cliff, a knocking began against the inside of the car's trunk. It was a frantic hammering, the sound of something wanting to be let out. Miss Muppet watched Taty crumple to the sand just as the seagulls had. Some loose feathers followed her cigarette butt down the beach. She crossed slowly back over the dunes and up to the car, flipping the rusted backplate to reveal a complex keypad lock. The knocking ceased abruptly. Hydraulics clanked as pressure seals were released. A steam of icy haze fizzed out into the turgid sea wind, dispelling quickly in the heat. Kinky Hawaiian music wafted out from the interior. Miss Muppet cranked up the heavy lid to reveal a mess of piping and hardware. Ancient monitors winked and hummed within nests of sparking Scooby wire. A pair of small candy-striped deck chairs stood in the center of the cramped space separated by a minuscule coffee table. Two rococo cupids were sprawled across the dirty canvas of the chairs, lacerated by IVs and nasal tubes. Various cumbersome life support machines blinked and beeped all around them. A pair of colorful cocktails balanced precariously on the ringed glass surface of the coffee table. One of the bald babies leered, picking at its nose with a clumsy finger. It was evidently the idiot of the two. The other cupid smiled lasciviously behind enormous electronic goggles, thoughtfully fondling maraschino cherries, paper umbrellas, and pineapple slices. Both seemed magnificently drunk.

"OK! OK! OK!" the goggled Cupid belched. "Another fishie, fishie, fishie ... Or is it a pretty birdy?"

"I'm not sure," Miss Muppet replied.

"Birdy, birdy, birdy," the second Cupid bleebled.

"It's so good to be right—"

"... Again," finished his idiot companion, now surprisingly erudite.

"Yes, yes, again," the goggled Cupid sighed. "Tie it up, then toss it in here with us."

"Pretty birdy."

Miss Muppet fetched out a black sack (standard-issue customs hermetic) and some rope. She lit another cigarette before strolling back down toward the beach.

"Count to 444," she threw over her shoulder.

Lazy Hawaiian slide guitar trailed after her like smoke.

4
Portrait Photography

NUMBER NUN STOOD AT THE foot of the four-poster bed staring down at the dead girl. After a while she stripped the mutilated corpse and carried it all the way down to the graveyard at the back of the house. Her robotic strength allowed her to complete the burial in just under fifteen minutes. Number Nun had, in fact, been specially programmed to complete emergency burials in the field and was able to link the titanium knuckles of her porcelain fingers together to create effective spades. In appearance Number Nun was a saturnine figure cloaked in a black habit that swirled in her wake like an oil slick. Her towering body buzzed beneath this garment with a barely perceptible humming of electronics. Like all the Religio Robots in her range, her face had been sculpted to closely resemble the Virgin Mary of High Renaissance portraiture. Faint seams ran the length of her translucent porcelain body flexing soundlessly as she moved. Intricate machinery was constantly visible, clockworking below the impenetrable cuticle of her shell-like skin case. Glowing cells lit her from within, casting her in a perpetual halo. She had been air-dropped into the jungle some years ago to perform missionary work with the cat people. Work she did with great zeal and efficiency after locating their secret nestworld—a hive, which they kept hidden in cave systems beneath an enormous waterfall. Number Nun's body and programming were such that she could survive the ravages of any wilderness for great periods of time. A nuclear cell gave her a shelf life of over 2,000 years, and she was possessed of incredible fortitude. Her good works had been performed without interruption until Alphonse Guava, the imp pimp, had had her captured and rewired. Now she haunted the imp's house of ill repute, constantly attempting to fulfill her original programming, hopelessly hampered by ceaseless parades of freakish tenants and the mercurial whims of her new master. The pirate programming allowed for all manner of obscenities, and she suffered dreadfully beneath the infernal yoke of Alphonse Guava, perpetually scanning for some method of release from her bondage. Number Nun had in fact just completed the burial when her internal communications system alerted her to an incoming summons. It was evidently time for the monthly group portrait, and all pertinent members of the house were being called down to the frangipani grove to assume their various positions behind the imp. Number Nun duly adjusted her course and glided through the abandoned plantations toward the sprawling gardens, which collared the façade of the old colonial villa.

THEY HAD HIRED THE USUAL vintage equipment. The photographer himself appeared to be a relic from some nineteenth century sideshow. He was hunched in britches beneath his black cape, adjusting antiquated fixtures and complex light meters. It was a bright bustling afternoon, and the gelid light seeped like liquid through the flowering trees congealing in enormous golden slabs across the lawn. This buttery light illuminated the rotting mulch of fallen blooms and the chaotic flight of many clumsy butterflies. The decaying colonial splendor of the house was at its peak when viewed from the perspective of the frangipani grove. A bell tower rose above the grove, creating the atmosphere of a Spanish mission. Other structures emerged against the backdrop of the jungle. The entire sagging mass of the villa rose in a sequence of cream-colored planes much distorted by the unchecked growth of Spanish moss. Unnameable jungle creepers further disguised the true shape and breadth of the structure. The fact that the estate was so deep within the jungle some distance outside Namanga Mori only added to its atmosphere of surreal desolation. Wild fruit had invaded the walls like the overtures of a sexually transmitted disease. Granadilla blossoms formed tiny starbursts of complexity along the high vines, dangling ripe hand grenade-shaped fruit in a suggestive manner. Banana trees lurked like hobos brooding beneath tall French windows. An atmosphere of languid torpidity rose off the many rooftops, dissolving all emotion in a slow heat.

θθθ

A SET HAD BEEN CONSTRUCTED beside the enormous leaf-choked pool. Baby crocodiles lay in the lukewarm water snapping at bugs and fallen cupcakes. Heavy Moroccan rugs cascaded drearily across the magnolia-littered lawn, supporting a plethora of tiny wrought-iron tables. These were laden with English crockery and a nauseating assortment of cakes and pastries. Ashtrays overflowed between bulbous wicker birdcages. The cages were all open, and murderous hatchet-beaked tropical birds minced like waiters through the confectionery. The place was alive with ants and beetles. Black candles guttered, constantly threatening to set fire to the lurid Japanese parasols that decorated the entirety of the monstrous picnic. In the center of this vortex was a throne. And upon this throne coiled the slender suited form of the imp. Alphonse Guava wore a perfectly tailored white suit, tea-stained and trimmed with pale yellow silk. The only thing that gave him away, in fact, were his pointed ears, which tapered up to mischievous peaks above his flaxen hair. That and perhaps his unwholesome smile, which fermented constantly between knife-edge cheekbones, shifting and changing but never completely disappearing. His entourage milled and crowded around him: a pack of suspect flamingos. There was, of course, the zombie, Typhoid Mary, who was possessed of a skinny Frankenstein charm despite the many flies buzzing about the cured appearance of her sloppily stitched skin. Her mouth had been sewn tight with red thread, but still she smiled like a reptile. With her head shaved institution style, her hobnail boots, and long filthy coat, she brooded and hissed to herself, seeming constantly to threaten violence. Someone had painted her name on the back of her coat in fire engine red enamel paint, but she didn't seem to mind. Her eyes had, in any case, been replaced by tiny pink Kewpie dolls' heads. She found her way around mostly by smell or by some unfathomable zombie sense. It was a widely known fact that Alphonse was fond of creating zombies. Many refused his cocktails on that premise. One or two people knew the story of Typhoid Mary before the fall, but it was a subject no one ever brought up. Now the truth of it was all shrouded in mystery—she was seen simply as the muscle of the house. A red sledgehammer protruded from her coat in testament to this. It was an implement she wielded with considerable venom and at Alphonse's smallest whim, so she was understandably given a wide berth at all times.

The Sugar Twins were also in attendance, twining around in the rotting flowers. They were a pair of "Detachable Siamese," and their nubile gender was impossible to pinpoint. They were joined at the hip by kinky adjuncts of bone that dovetailed together and separated according to their own mysterious fancy. Their almond eyes were a succulent silver filmed by membranous eyelids. They lounged semi-naked like angular cats, licking lazily at fallen sweetmeats, stroked occasionally by the wing tip heel of the enthroned Alphonse. Number Nun's diametric opposite, Michelle, was brooding at the far end of the gathering. Ever the outsider, Michelle was an overweight girl somewhere in her late teens and clad in beach tongs, vest, and dingy surf shorts. She was nailed to a large wooden cross, which she dragged around everywhere she went. This situation was unavoidable as her palms and wrists were nailed very solidly to the wood. Some leather was lashed about her throat to help support the weight of the central beam, but still the stigmata seeped whenever she strayed too far from her basic position. The uncomfortable posture had resulted in unwanted weight gain and back problems, but she bore these deformations stoically in the true manner of a self-afflicted martyr. Her lifeless hair was forever drawn back into a clumsy ponytail, and she was in a characteristically foul mood. The heavy cross rested upon her calloused calves, and she shuffled about like some enormous cynical hamster, muttering about things—usually Number Nun.

The characters began arranging themselves as the photographer made his final preparations. Several small zeppelins were tethered to posts, and one could see them gusting above the trees. Pennants had been attached to these aircraft, and the guylines often drifted erratically, catching on teapots and things. Stagehands were present, smoking cigarettes off camera, ready to take action if any last-minute items needed arranging. The photographer had, in fact, just climbed under his black shroud when Number Nun detected a despondent voice calling from the house.

"Alphonse," she said in her well-modulated analogue voice.

"Hmm?"

"Judas is coming."

Alphonse glanced over to the house where a figure could be seen crawling desperately toward the gathering. This was Judas, aide-de-camp to Alphonse, secretary of the house, and general punching bag.

His upper half was battered and his progress further impeded by the junk casing his lower half. Pipes and pig-iron scraps dragged from his twisted spine like an industrial wedding train. Nails protruded from his hips and back, catching in the lawn, dragging Campbell's Soup cans in a pitiful fashion. Yet, despite all this, Judas was always to be found turned out in a spotless white vest, his beard immaculately shaped into a Moorish goatee, his head neatly sheared. Pride tokens dangled from his neck. You could smell his aftershave from several kilometers away.

"Aaaaaaaaalphonse!" he called repeatedly. "Wait for me! Wait for me!"

"Should we wait?" Number Nun asked.

"Have we ever?" smirked the imp.

He waved his hand petulantly at the photographer. A moment of tension ensued, followed by the dramatic eruption of the antique flashboard. Magnesium sparks vomited. Some passing butterflies went up in flames.

"Clickety click," said the photographer, emerging from his cape. "A real Kodak moment."

Everyone was already relaxing out of their poses when Judas finally arrived. Bulky laborers in dungarees and sailor caps had emerged from the woodwork disassembling the previously unseen film lighting, rigging, and backdrops. A stone fountain was carried off, now proven to be cardboard. Sailor types began to sweep away the fallen blossoms, revealing a pristine lawn beneath the artful decay. Rugs were rolled up as the principal characters moved aside, dodging flurrying birds.

"Thanks for the nonexistent effort to alert the photographer to my meager presence, Alphonse," Judas scowled.

Alphonse raised a hand in a princely, somehow utterly unreadable gesture.

"Miss Muppet and the Goo Crew have netted another childbride," the junk-laden sidekick continued unabated. "The Goo Crew sniffed her out from a few clicks out, apparently alerted Miss Muppet, who pulled the old big sister routine and got her in the cookie jar. I'm pretty dazzled those blobs spotted her at all! She was on foot out in the middle of nowhere. I mean ... is she irradiated? Who exactly are the Goo Crew, anyway?"

"Little monster babies," Michelle said.

"They are *authentic* Cupids," Alphonse explained haughtily. "Can sniff out a ghost girl at a thousand clicks."

"Expensive little loaves," he continued, lighting up a slim white cigarillo. "Need constant life support outside their natural habitat."

"That being?"

"Clouds."

"Oh."

"Always liked Miss Muppet," Michelle nodded sagely. "Always knew she was the best."

"Oh, *please*, Michelle!" Number Nun snapped, attempting to dress one of the Sugar Twins in some dungarees. "Yesterday it was the Purple Clown you were praising—you are utterly backward, my child."

"You fucking nun!" Michelle exploded. "If I wasn't nailed to this cross, I'd rip your tits off!"

"Really, Michelle," Alphonse drawled. "You must learn to control your temper—have a piña colada."

He deftly snagged a cocktail from a props tray and passed it to her. She took it with comic difficulty, finding it impossible to drink.

"Well, what do you expect from someone who thinks she's God's illegitimate daughter?" Number Nun muttered drily.

"*Concubine!*" Michelle spluttered. "And He really liked me!"

"Oh, shaddup!" Judas said.

Alphonse leaned down to Judas as though addressing a small dog.

"This little thing Miss Muppet found on the side of the road," he confided. "Is it yummy?"

"Like a French postcard, I think ..."

"You mean, you don't know."

"Don't patronize me!" Judas wailed.

"Miss Muppet does bring in the Juicy Lucys," Michelle said, spilling her cocktail.

"I prefer the Purple Clown," Number Nun smiled.

"Fucking robot," Michelle spat back.

"Oh, please, shaddup!" Judas practically screeched.

"Is she even a she?" Alphonse quizzed.

"Er ... yes, of course, what else?"

"A he."

"Shaddup!"

"Cow," Michelle hissed, still glowering at Number Nun.

"So, where is *it*?" Alphonse asked.

"The Soft House," Judas explained in the official tone he often employed for house affairs and painful anecdotes. "Customs, you know ..."

"Are you *sure*?" Alphonse teased.

"Don't patronize me!" Judas shouted, almost in tears. "I'm very sensitive!"

"Sensitive?" Michelle retorted. "You can't even feel pain!"

"That's the whole *point*, Michelle," Judas began. "As you know, my brain can't receive any pain signals, but it compensates by ... You're not listening to me, are you?"

Typhoid Mary caught a fly between thumb and forefinger and attempted to eat it on some reflexive impulse. Then she remembered that her lips had been sewn shut.

"Well, we've all heard it before, Judas," Alphonse said, blowing a triple succession of near-perfect smoke rings. "Ad nauseam," he added with a cruel twist of his lips.

"But ... I'm ... sensitive ..." Judas said, through gritted teeth.

"Come to Christ," Number Nun muttered.

"... *You*!" Judas blathered, wracked by incommunicable fury.

"Methinks the little pup would rather come *in* Christ," Michelle snickered, taking Number Nun's side in a rare show of solidarity.

"Trolls!" Judas bellowed, purple as a grape.

"Judas," said Alphonse, "make yourself useful. Fetch me a glass of prune juice from the house."

"Get it yourself, *Caligula*!" Judas clattered.

"What was that?" Alphonse grinned, pleased at having elicited a hostile response.

"Nothing!" Judas replied, sensing imminent disaster.

Alphonse clicked his fingers at Typhoid Mary: "Break his kneecaps again."

Out came the sledgehammer.

"This is getting ... monotonous," said Judas wearily, crossed momentarily by the shadow of the falling hammer.

5

The Soft House

THERE HAD ALWAYS BEEN WRESTLERS in jungle country. Some came from disenfranchised tribes and settled along the filthy river settlements, others drifted in from the big cities in the Lowlands. It was difficult to get good gigs and earn decent money in the more developed areas; everyone knew that the real money was to be found in the Outzone. Wrestling, in particular, had a perverse attraction for the suffering and alcohol-wracked. Even the scattered jungle folk seemed to like it better than all the other forlorn forms of traveling entertainment gestating within the Zone. Perhaps the bizarre outfits and fetishistic masks reminded them of their long-departed customs and strange gods, many of whom were apocalyptic and bloodthirsty, speaking of the end of days and of fire from the sky. At any rate, it was comforting for villagers to witness the spectacle of a large ring of banana leaves illuminated by candy-colored light bulbs and traversed by gladiatorial men in tights. These rings would be erected with great pomp despite their shabbiness, patrolled at all times by security guards in sunglasses and handlebar moustaches. More often than not, this "security force" was nothing more than waterfront knife trash picked up in bars and made suddenly civil by the addition of uniform facial hair, green fatigues, and matching eyewear. They did their jobs playing soldier. The wrestling events were accorded more importance than they deserved, but the people enjoyed the heady cocktail of circus extravagance and freshly spilled blood. In those early days the wrestlers were little more than a raggle-taggle caravan—carnival strongmen drifting from village to village staging fights for whomever came. This sideshow existence of theirs went on for some time until an historic event forever altered the role they had played as simple performers.

A particularly vicious robber baron had begun killing old people in an attempt to extort more goods from a long-suffering tribe. The elders were taken in night raids and then held ransom for goods and valuables. Often the hostages were killed anyway, even after the hefty tariffs had been settled. The wrestlers, who were in the area at the time, took umbrage at the treatment of this particular tribe that had always been faithful followers. They decided to arm their waterfront trash guards with submachine guns, explosives, and machetes, pooling their resources in an attempt at a counterstrike. Their tactical strength and capacity for actual violence were more formidable than even they could have anticipated. Within a day they had taken the robber baron's compound and mounted his and many of his closest cohorts' heads on stakes. Drunk on victory, they began to stage a number of successful assaults upon various despotic chieftains and feudal lords along their riverside circuit. The wrestlers fought bare-handed as they did in the ring, sweeping down in a multi-colored blaze once the moustachioed guards had laid waste to the majority of the opposition with mortar fire and machine guns. They began to gain a tremendous amount of praise and respect from the people along the river. Scattered military emplacements started to defect to the wrestlers, who were far more effective and less corrupt than the official forces left behind in the Outzone. The wrestlers swelled in power. They were opposed on several occasions but within time became the recognized authority in the lawless Zone. The wrestlers themselves had by now become a sort of elite group surrounded at all times by legions of uniformed moustache men with machine guns. Their masks and costumes became more and more intricate as a hierarchy began to develop within their numbers. Some speculated that they staged secret bouts to compete for positions of power. Whatever the case, the wrestlers maintained their original nomadic configuration, moving in heavy convoys through the jungle territories and down the river, laying down whatever law they saw fit. They were not unfair, but they did become more inflexible over time. People soon came to fear their stranglehold of power. The wrestlers' coup de grâce was to establish a roving border around the Outzone—one that flexed and shifted like a membrane. And anyone or anything coming in or going out had to pass through border posts that, although not entirely corrupt, were amenable to "specialty tariffs" and "first views" by speculative smugglers with large amounts of nontraceable cash. To aid mobility these stations often took the form of specially designed jumping castles referred to collectively as "the Soft House."

θθθ

THE AFTERNOON HAD TURNED SUNNY and balmy. A breeze gushed in from the sea, rippling up the enormous fields of cane like fingers through hair. This was old plantation land long abandoned and given over to anarchy. Alphonse Guava had the midget juice up the banana-colored jalopy and take him out to the Soft House after lunchtime cocktails. The clanking vehicle was a turn-of-the-century relic mounted on bicycle wheels. These spindly wheels had undergone extensive balloon tire modifications to handle the rough roads outside the known maps of the territory. Alphonse had won the car off a gambler on a steamboat some years before and kept it in good condition—mostly out of spite. The in-house cigar smoking circus midget who loved tinkering had managed to track down a manual or two detailing parts and set about making his own replacements in the forge. He had little else to do except smoke those repulsive stogies of his, so it soon became something of a pet project. Alphonse, tickled by his dedication, decked the little fellow out in aviator goggles, leather skullcaps, and elegant pairs of driving gloves. The car was noisy, difficult to handle, and broke down almost on an hourly basis. Yet, despite these numerous failings, it was used more often than the deluxe-finned Caddy or the Star Bright V8. Even the Speedster saw less mileage than the cranky yellow car. The midget had a large gramophone welded to the back and tacked it out with gyroscopes, so that it could play across almost any terrain. They were listening to old Al Bowlly records en route to the Soft House, quaffing Martinis splashed out of chrome shakers. Typhoid Mary was perched on the back seat grinning at nothing, lost in a zombie world all her own. Judas was also in the back with his bloody legs and junk trailing behind the car in something of a "just married" motif. He was sulking, staring at the sky through chunky sunglasses, chain smoking, and petulantly ignoring the blood seeping from his freshly mangled knees. Campbell's Tomato Soup cans bounced ridiculously behind him, constantly threatening to catch in the wheels and jerk him overboard. Alphonse was in the front slowly getting sloshed. All his times with the midget seemed to be grand ones. Even the most trivial were a cause for cocktails. His white suit had, in fact, already gathered one or two fresh stains along the way.

A checkpoint appeared some distance down the dirt road. Three soldiers with handlebar moustaches and mirrored sunglasses were manning the candy stripe blockade. Bossa nova blared deafeningly from a tinny radio inside the watchman's shack. One of the soldiers paced the road with a machine gun. The other two were a small distance into the cane, viciously beating a purple clown. The clown had been tied to a chair, and one of his teeth was traveling slowly down his violet-powdered cheek on a snail trail of blood. The soldier on the road waved for the jalopy to stop. The midget shifted the cigar in his mouth, gunned the engine, and ran the soldier down. There came a crunch, squeal, and clatter as the vehicle trundled over the figure. This was followed by the sound of the blockade being destroyed by the barreling jalopy. Alphonse barely seemed to register the entire episode, so intent was he on refreshing his drink. The two soldiers in the cane paused for a moment to witness the death of their comrade. They observed the car drive off with perplexed expressions before returning to their battery of the clown.

The jalopy crested the ridge of a sugar cane rise, and a huge lime green jumping castle emerged into view. It was nestled in an open field, and its translucent bulk quivered like an enormous jelly dessert against the sky. It was at least six stories high, and various towers sprouted and swayed in the offshore breezes. The sunlight shone down a weird beach-ball light that embered in multiform shadows. Figures and furniture could be seen bouncing around inside the castle moving like protoplasmic motes beneath a microscope. Soldiers performed aerobic exercises in the cane, syncopating to leotard-clad girls on battered television sets. These and other small devices were powered by a squadron of deflated pygmies manning several bicycle-powered generators. Hundreds had clearly died keeping the soldiers fit.

"You think they would have pillaged enough gold fillings to erect a proper barracks by now," Judas muttered blackly at the jumping castle.

"Small mercies, Judas," Alphonse grinned. "'The Hard House' would sound a little too bouncy, don't you think?"

"Oh, fucking cackle," Judas quacked bitterly as they drew up to the front of the quivering structure.

Alphonse hopped out, passing between the two surly heavies who guarded the labial entrance to the lime green castle. The others waited in the car. The midget maxed out the volume on his gramophone system, and their music clashed uncomfortably with the energetic beats pumping out of the soldiers' aerobics programs. Some of the soldiers were thrown off by the dissonance, and this afforded the midget no end of pleasure.

MELANCHOLIC BOSSA NOVA BLASTED THROUGHOUT the entirety of the Soft House. It bled from plastic intercoms, warping in the weird metallic acoustics. The lobby had a dreary bureaucratic atmosphere despite the shiny transparent walls and constant squeakage. A large wooden desk occupied the center of the globular chamber, and a wrestler in a waspish black-and-yellow leather mask was installed behind it. Filing cabinets creaked dangerously against the flexible walls. Sunlight filtered through the giant bubble bath of a building, lighting everything up with sugary luminescence. Audio spillage from adjoining vacuoles also added to the confusion. Interrogations were being carried out behind one or two membranes of clear jelly green. Long corridors flexed like the intestinal networks of cartoon animals. Soldiers were passing through these passages in a comical anti-gravity sort of hopping. Some of the chambers had been filled to capacity with water, and nasty looking sharks bobbed inside them. Rubber airlock valves separated these rooms, further intensifying the oversized beach ball motif. The wrestler regarded Alphonse critically, evaluating him in a couple of glances.

"Picking up or dropping off?" he barked.

"I've got a sack waiting for me in customs, Tower Three," Alphonse answered in a drunken, yet well-modulated drawl.

"Know the way?"

"Sure."

"Carrying any sharp objects? Scissors? Knives? Needles?"

"Only my rapier-like wit."

The wrestler observed him for several seconds without a trace of amusement.

"We shoot people for that sort of talk, you know," he muttered.

Alphonse withdrew a silencer-tipped pistol and shot the wrestler twice in the face. The yellow-and-black mask split with red, and the heavy wrestler slumped across the desk. Alphonse replaced the pistol in its cream leather shoulder holster wordlessly, uncapped the nearest beach ball airlock, and stalked off down a flexible corridor.

ⱻⱻⱻ

OUT IN THE CAR, JUDAS was leaning against the door smoking his forty-sixth cigarette of the day. He watched Alphonse moving through the membranous structure while the midget rolled a joint and Typhoid Mary caught flies.

"He pop him?" the midget asked with a grin.

"Yes. Fuck it."

"Don't worry, you can pay me later," the midget snickered, lighting up off a hula-hula Zippo.

Inside, Alphonse was slowly making his way through the sunlit Soft House. He had to adopt a curious half-height shuffle across the bendy see-through floors. The squeaky noises this created slowly amplified themselves to absurd proportions within the shiny tracts. The bossa nova music also seemed to swell in volume the farther he penetrated, reaching a monstrous, distorted din toward the central regions. Sharks at times navigated beyond the plastic of his corridor, and he grinned playfully at them. At one point he passed a vending machine. It was rattling dangerously around, and Alphonse sidestepped it gingerly. Other rooms passed above and below, viewed through a complexity of translucent obstructions. He ascended a wobbly tower. At the top was a wildly waving chamber, wherein were placed a mangle of black customs sacks. These hermetic sacks had been secured with heavy shipping rope, which he proceeded to inspect and poke with alacrity. Outside the plastic walls, the sky and field seesawed around hysterically.

Alphonse continued to separate the sacks until he came upon his name typed on a tag around the neck of a particularly large sack. He dragged the cumbersome sack free, clinging to ropes to avoid slipping across the swaying room. He undid the clasp and peered through the aperture. Inside was the little girl Miss Muppet had delivered. She was sleeping, naked and curled in a fetal form, packed in an abundance of goose feathers to prevent damage. Alphonse resealed the hermetic sack and heaved it toward a rubber valve in the corner of the room. A crazy tubule could be glimpsed beyond the seal, spiraling down through the mazy innards of the Soft House. Alphonse popped the valve, pushed the sack in, and watched it swirl away through the pipes of the jumping castle. After a few moments he followed, sucking down the tube like a bug down a drain. After several rollercoaster minutes both popped out of a postal chute almost directly in front of the jalopy, landing on a vast pile of abandoned letters and mail.

6

Crocodile and Sno-Globes

THE WEIGHTY TWILIGHT OF THE jungle was just beginning to glaze the house of Alphonse Guava. The mauve sky deepened like fluid lashed by stripes of vivid yellow. Few of the lights had been turned on yet, and the majority of the house was sunk in a sort of subaqueous gloom. The light was particularly dim in one of the quiet bedchambers in the upper west wing. There was a bilious rococo quality to the decorative features of the chamber: lace curtains, porcelain knickknacks, heavy mahogany furniture, and sepia floral print wallpaper. The overall mood of the room was cloying, the inescapability of a grandmother's attic. A long French window was the only light source, and this was overgrown with creepers. The tendrils meshed tightly beyond the lightly frosted glass emitting a pellucid underwater light into the chamber—sunshine seen from below the surface of a still pond. The air was motionless, almost pressurized. A Victorian rocking horse grinned beside one of the walls, facing into the cool green light. The only discernible sounds were the faint regular breathing of a young girl sleeping and very distant birds. Vintage dolls littered the floor. The farthest, dimmest end of the room was literally a wall of dolls. This overwhelming collection stretched from floor to ceiling, and hundreds of glass eyes glinted in the wan light. A curtained four-poster bed had been placed in the center of the room, and Taty lay asleep in it. Someone had dressed her in a white vintage nightgown, and only her head and neck were visible above the old linen coverings. In the dimness of the far end just below the wall of dolls, it was vaguely possible to discern the form of a large crocodile. The reptile lay comatose, its nictitating lids licking slowly together and apart in the half-light. Alphonse Guava was seated in a high-backed chair just below the tall window. His hands were steepled, and he watched Taty sleep, waiting patiently for her to stir. The light faded gradually, creating antiquated purple shadows and an atmosphere of gathering oppression. Taty began to awaken slowly in this dimness.

"Mommy ..." she found herself mumbling.

She turned her head, blinking in the greenish light, gazing dreamily at the silhouette of Alphonse.

"Am I swimming into focus, yet?" Alphonse smiled.

"Is this heaven?" she slurred, thinking she was perhaps dead.

"Depends."

"I'm so sleepy ..."

"You should be. Miss Muppet drugged you."

Taty frowned and then yawned like a kitten.

"I liked her," she tut-tutted.

"She emits a certain pheromone. It makes her impossible to dislike."

"Oh. Kind of like a bug?"

"Exactly like a bug."

Taty shifted under the covers. She attempted to raise her arm only to find it attached to one of the posts by means of a rusty chain. She wiggled a bare foot to discover that it too had been secured.

"I'm tied to this bed," she announced blankly.

"Chained, Cupcake. Chained."

"I like the rough stuff," Taty joked, flicking at a chain.

"We all do," Alphonse replied quietly.

She stared at him, unsure of her ground. He rose slowly out of the chair and circled slowly toward the bed. The crocodile, sensing movement, reacted slightly. Taty did not even notice it, so intent was she on the approach of the dark figure.

"Are you going to rape me now?" she asked in an unreal dreamy fashion.

"No," he replied seriously. "Actually, I need you for some things."

"I ... I don't fuck well," she stammered. "I'm virginal ..."

"It works better if you are a virgin," he whispered, his face swamped by shadows. He was quite close to her now, and she could smell the tea and alcohol on his soiled suit. She peered deep into the shadow of his face, attempting to understand his intentions. A flicker of movement caught her eye, and she noticed the crocodile. As with everything, she reacted with slow fascination rather than fear—as though it were all a dream. She glanced back at Alphonse as he lingered beside a bedpost, somewhat distracted.

"What are you going to do with me?" Taty asked with an intense childlike curiosity.

Alphonse seemed to wake from his momentary reverie as if suddenly realizing that she was there. He drifted to the far end of the bed, his voice taking on a business-like tone.

"I want you to come and work for me," he began. "I pay well, can give you a bed, toys, whatever ... I'll even feed you; you look like you could use some food."

"What do I have to do, exactly?" she pressed.

"It's ... complex," he sighed, wandering over to the rocking horse.

She watched as he mounted the horse, facing the window, his back to her. He was much too large for the child's toy, and it creaked dangerously. Despite this, the imp continued to rock back and forth, staring out of the window. When he finally did speak, his voice carried an almost religious fervor.

"You see, a while ago some people rediscovered their souls," he mused, staring into the light, haloed by illuminated dust motes.

"They brought them out of the cupboard, so to speak," he continued. "Shook them around and began to see their envelopes— the sno-globes that encase us all—our invisibilities ..."

He rocked faster, clearly inspired by whatever he was saying.

"Some saw fantastic colors and intricate shifting formations within the sno-globes," he rambled. "A doctor, Dr. Dali, discovered that these sno-globes were something like our emotions— sensations and mental emanations rendered visible—he saw people as paintings of light!"

"So you're saying I'm a sno-globe?" Taty frowned.

Alphonse turned to peer at her over his shoulder.

"Not just any sno-globe, my little sweetmeat," he grinned toothily. "Tinkerbells like you are rare as rubies."

He dismounted and rocked sideways, staring at her.

"See, when most people are receptors, you are, in fact, a transmitter ..."

"I'm like a radio?" she asked blankly.

He drifted closer now.

"You are double stereo psychic television, baby!" he giggled. "You can be tuned to create specific sensations and emotions within people—just the sight of you playing tennis in the right color skirt, if amplified correctly, could be enough to kill a person!"

"I can't play tennis."

He brushed aside her remark and continued circumnavigating the bed.

"Each pigeon will be different, my dear," he elucidated. "For one happy Frank it may simply be tennis in a peach ball gown, for another you might be called upon to—oh, I don't know—weld red screws to the underside of an antique unicycle at midnight ... upside down!"

He cackled a little at his flight of fancy while she just stared expressionlessly at him, tugging at her chains.

"Each person reacts differently to different stimuli," he continued. "Each has their own private path to paradise ... we find it, and you just lead them up it—for a nominal fee, of course."

He leaned in close to her at this point and rubbed his cold nose against hers. She flinched slightly from the clamminess of it but was otherwise unafraid.

"You can be taught to kindle soul-pleasure more intense than a thousand orgasms," he hissed brutally before pulling back.

She gazed up at him while he allowed for a dramatic pause.

"But if I can do anything ..." she mused thoughtfully, "why just use me for pleasure?"

"My business *is* pleasure," Alphonse uttered in a rehearsed fashion.

"A little limiting, don't you think?" she taunted.

"Limitation is a limitless source of amusement to me," he grinned.

They stared at one another, sensing a possible friendship. Something in Taty was drawn to the flightiness of the living Joker card she saw smiling in the darkness before her. And whatever it was, it seemed far more concrete than the empty highways she had wandered.

"Think of the wonderful, wonderful degradation," he teased.

She found herself mirroring his ridiculous smile.

"OK," Taty acquiesced. "But I want a lollipop," she added with a playful laugh.

Alphonse clapped his hands together in glee. And in the darkness beyond, the crocodile stirred, crossing the room in three giant strides.

7

The Nebula Shell Sea Hotel

THREE BATTERED MANTA RAY KITES billowed against a turbulent grey sky. A monsoon was threatening to break over Namanga Mori, and the air was juicy with ionic interference. Three men in black polo necks and sunglasses smoked bananadine roll-ups on the crepuscular rooftops of the Nebula Shell Sea Hotel. They had the kites rigged up to the little fingers of their left hands, reciting incantations to each other in dead languages while they tangled up the sky. The corpse of a zebra had been strung up on the television aerials some weeks before, but the parrots had pecked it to pieces. Now its guts hung like laundry fluttering down the bricks of the old hotel, gathering flies, moths, and inexplicably large beetles of the type the natives ground up for medicine. The hotel itself was a benchmark relic of the downtown waterfront district. It was located in the septic end of the city where grimy warrens of microwave tenements cascaded drearily down to a gutted boardwalk. The streetlights gleamed like vulture-stripped ribs while neon soaked in hazy pockets along the strip. Fast food clotted up the air vents. Rotting piers lay like skeletal remains in the hot heaving sea. Jungle vagrants stalked these labyrinthine piers relentlessly with spears and spiritual disorders, sometimes moving in packs like starving hyenas. The air was pierced by the ululations of paranoid schizophrenics caught in torment beneath the boardwalk supports. The sky was rancid with rising effluvium, and the sound of waves swarmed along the waterfront. Its drone muffled the buzz of the city chaos, strangling it down to a barely acceptable ruckus. The decaying hulk of the Nebula Shell Sea stood overlooking this grim beachfront, looming like a tombstone—all sallow light, death trap elevators, stringers in crash helmets hanging off fire escapes, ancient telephone booths, filthy checkerboard floors, and stained walls. Enormous electric blue monitor lizards nested in the tangle of wild palms outside the entrance. You had to watch for them at night as they sometimes made dashes for anyone they felt they could drag up into the trees. Children and skinny working girls were especially vulnerable to attack. Their corpses were occasionally found bundled among the leaves and coconuts. Bones clustered in the gutters and dropped to the pavement at odd times. Above the portico of the hotel was a beaten retro chic sign from another era. It read SHELL SEA HOTEL in carved stone. Above this legend, formed out of lurid green neon tubing, was the word NEBULA. The neon pulsed with a hallucinogenic throbbing, making the hotel easy to find no matter what high you happened to be on at the time. It pulsed like a beacon for the vagrants of the strip, shining over the dingy streets—a lighthouse for all the mind-animals and sinking people.

Romeo the Dealer was down in the lobby of the Shell Sea. He stood, a razor-thin silhouette, zipped up into tight shiny leathers, corded muscles shifting like mercury beneath his fish-pale skin. He had a doughy complexion glazed with light perspiration from the tropical heat. His short peroxide hair was spiky with static. Enormous bug-eye shades disguised half his clean-shaven face. He had never been seen to smile and had no lips to speak of, in any case. His mouth was a postal slit from which words dropped like glass. He was waiting, checking his rubberized wristwatch at intervals. Movements that afforded rapid glimpses of the ray gun he jockeyed in a nylon fast-grab shoulder holster. A bandolier of loaded syringes hung close beneath his opposing arm. He tapped bright white tennis shoes on the pavement and clenched studded black cut-off gloves. He seldom shifted position but remained somehow animated—never still. Somewhere within Romeo was an internal dynamo that was spinning so fast it was hardly seen to move. This made him exude a certain cold charge, a gravitational field, that caused most people to steer clear of him. Many weren't sure if he was even human. He shifted position after a few minutes of watch checking, pulling out a yo-yo to kill time while waiting for the midget.

The midget, meanwhile, had just pulled off the jungle flyover and entered the bridge-stricken streets of the warehouse district. The long black sedan was his car of choice when visiting the city, and he wore a miniature chauffeur's uniform with brass buttons when driving it. A popular single from *In with the Outzone* was blaring out of the radio, and the familiarity of the tune comforted

Taty. The speaker system was rich with analogue crackling while she quietly sang the verses of "Robot in a Red Dress" along with Coco Carbomb to soothe her nerves. Number Nun had the front passenger seat, her faintly glowing face reflected against the windscreen in a ghostly play of light. Taty had the back seat all to herself because the Sugar Twins were in the trunk. They were curled up on a very cramped mattress—the bones of their hips dovetailed like a car and caravan—watching cartoons on a tiny television. The greenish glow of the tube illuminated the cramped and bucking insides of the trunk. It caught like oil on their matching gold lamé catsuits, ermine jackets, and platinum Cleopatra wigs. It also caught in their dazed silver eyes in which were reflected the crazed antics of animated cats and mice. On the back seat Taty was adjusting her skirt. She was perpetually stealing glimpses of her reflection in the shiny windows, quite proud of the ensemble she had managed to put together for the evening. Alphonse had let her run riot in the walk-in wardrobes because he was throwing a pool party and couldn't have her looking like "a stray." So she set about prettying up something supreme for the do and also, more importantly, for her first jaunt as a ghost girl. This was her first real job, and she was excited. After much deliberation she had picked out a Paisley print polyester mini with long puffed sleeves, high collar, and low cuffs. The patterning was faded gold with emerald highlights and copper trim. It fitted her like a glove, and Number Nun had had her hair treated and blow-waved to neaten her up for business hours. She had chosen flat gold slip-ons and huge tan sunglasses to complete the ensemble. The smooth metallic soles flapped lightly against her feet when she walked, and she loved the bird-like sound they made. A slim gold ankle bracelet glittered in the shadows below, and she would occasionally lift up her foot to study it. Her face was so pancaked she felt like a boiled sweet or a character in a Japanese play. Metallic green eye shadow caught her reflection each time she turned her head, and the car was filled with the scent of the rich perfume she had selected.

She had been at the house for a week now, living in one of the high bedrooms, avoiding crocodiles, and watching cartoon reels in the private cinema. They gave her vanilla ice cream on demand, and twice a night she was made to go for treatments in the psychic Jennerator. The "Jennie" was a huge, old thing. It resembled a tanning bed and was said to boost one's psychic abilities. Copper pipes ran out of it, and the whole shebang was covered in flashing lights. Alphonse was fond of saying that he "snapped it up wholesale" from Dr. Dali when the mad scientist went underground. But that meant nothing to Taty, who hated the thing with a passion. She came out of the Jennie each night with a bulging headache and the tingly feeling of having been fried lightly in oil. Her dreams thereafter were wild and cluttered with visions of psychedelic talking panthers and mountains of candyfloss. On Friday they got her Barbied up, and she was down at the pool with the others when the guests started crawling out of the woodwork. She was introduced to strange men with damp handshakes—tuxedo vipers who whispered things in Alphonse's pointy ears without taking their eyes off her. Introductions were also made to traveling musicians and a trio of thin tribe girls with stringy jungle braids though Taty could sense that she herself was the wafer in the sundae. She managed to escape at one point, sneaking behind one of the ice sculptures with an hors d'oeuvres platter before Number Nun sniffed her out and told her it was time to get to work. Within minutes she was in the back of a sedan heading for her first appointment.

"Is it true that the Shell Sea Hotel is made entirely of sea shells?" Taty yelled over the blaring radio.

Number Nun glanced disapprovingly at her via the rearview mirror.

"Not entirely, my little sinner," the Nun replied.

Taty went back to examining the shadow-infested warehouses and low squalid buildings of Namanga Mori's downtown districts. They flashed beyond the tinted glass, describing an immensity of desolation that numbed her somewhere deep inside. The monsoon broke as they entered the waterfront areas. Storm gutters vomited, and the gleaming tarmac steamed through its oil painting sheen of colors. Figures staggered like puppets in these solid sheets of roaring water. Sugary neon lit up the wet clustered air, and drunken sailors screamed like monkeys from high red windows. Taty saw cannibals with bones in their noses crouched beneath umbrellas and roving pods of moustachioed soldiers. Giant rusted billboards heaved past, glowing in the rain, gilded with moth-choked bulbs and swirly script. The midget eventually started laughing at something no one else understood. He lit up a cigar, dousing the cabin with bluish smoke. You could hear the Sugar Twins being tossed around each time they turned a corner.

The monsoon stopped abruptly. The sedan pulled up into the palm-infested courtyard of the Nebula Shell Sea, and the whole world looked like it had just stepped out of a washing machine. The neon of the hotel was especially vivid and fizzy in Taty's eyes. Romeo detached like a bat and swooped down out of the shadows, popping the trunk. Number Nun stepped out imperiously, lifting her habit above the wet tar, her naked porcelain feet lighting up the puddles like a cheap religious painting. She let Taty out while Romeo hefted the twins from the back. They hung lasciviously off him as he approached Taty to introduce himself.

"I'm Romeo—"

"The Dealer!" the midget butted in, finishing his sentence with a cackling cough.

"I'm—" Taty began.

"Working," Number Nun interjected primly. "Now hush, Childbride."

Romeo regarded her seriously, and Taty could see that he was almost always serious, even with the Sugar Twins draped like absurd fur coats around his lean shoulders.

"Well, sisters," he announced expressionlessly, "let's get it on."

IT MUST HAVE LOOKED COMICAL, the sight of them all squeezed together into the rat trap elevator.

"Noticed you singing along as you exited the sedan," Romeo remarked to Taty. "Like that 'Robot in a Red Dress' number, do you?"

"Coco is my fave," Taty admitted.

"It was recorded right here in the Shell Sea," he confided. "I was the sound engineer."

"Wow!"

She felt a feeling of success warm her. This emotion was, in part, a tribute to the claustrophobic life she had left behind. As they ascended, Taty recalled being trapped in her room, overplaying "Robot in a Red Dress" to drown out her mother's wails and daydreaming about an outside world she thought herself forever barred from. But she had beaten the odds and made it into the inner games of the Zone, standing at ground zero of the music that drew her here. She caught herself smiling, but as Romeo cut the mechanism between floors and jerked aside the rusted grate, the nervousness returned. The personal prestige she had by now accorded the Nebula Shell Sea came with its own pressures: Could she live up to what was expected of her? Romeo uncapped a hidden airlock, and they disembarked onto a high, secret thirteenth floor, entering into a maze of dingy corridors all lined with worn red velvet. Some of the hotel doors were chinked, and Taty caught glimpses of strange scenes. One of the rooms was piled high with acoustic guitars. The broken instruments made dunes of themselves in the otherwise barren space. Another room contained men in scuba gear, berets, and white goatees playing ferocious games of ping-pong against one another. Another room was occupied by tribal figures in grass skirts dancing around a fire of paperbacks. These savages wore oversized tiki masks and were feeding cheap novels to the flames without pause. Number Nun put a firm hand on Taty's shoulder, nudging her on each time she loitered to look.

Romeo unlocked a sliding metal shutter and ushered them all into a spacious concrete chamber. The lights were down, and costume racks clustered cattle-like in the spaces. The backstage atmosphere was further enhanced by the many props and stacked racks of lighting equipment. Taty sensed immediately that she should be quiet as though a performance were being enacted just beyond a nearby, as yet unseen, curtain. And as she tiptoed deeper in, following after the gliding figure of Number Nun, she eventually saw the illuminated "stage." It was the only light source in the ambiguous chamber: a long aquarium window that looked into a shabby, yet well-lit, hotel room. Number Nun ghosted close toward the one-way glass, speaking to Romeo in hushed tones.

"Is that an astronaut?" Taty heard her ask.

She drew alongside Number Nun and peered into a faded red room hung with framed prints of tropical flowers. Old wallpaper bulged with damp, sagging from the upper areas along the ceiling skirting. A bed had been wedged in the corner beneath a tiny window. A Formica-topped dresser brooded opposite, decked with a large beaded lampshade. Two diffuse spotlights had been placed on either side of the mirror glass on the inside of the room. They faced in and washed the space with a surgical glare. The hotel room was a staged tableau reminiscent of an old record cover. Dust roved— a thousand stars in the light orbiting the incongruous figure of an astronaut. The astronaut himself stood beside the bed clad in a bulky spacesuit fitted with numerous snug straps and attachments. The suit had once been white but was now soiled by the city. Parts of it were singed by extreme heat exposure. A gold visor disguised the face of the astronaut, and pipes ran from the heavy helmet to a back-borne life support system.

"He told Martha he piloted a lunar module around the moon," Romeo whispered to Number Nun, plugging in a series of cables. "Now I think he just plays chess in the park."

He moved quietly toward a bank of levers, leaving the light of the window.

"He still wears the suit?" Number Nun muttered drily after him.

The Sugar Twins had by now slunk up to the window. They nuzzled the glass like cats, the plastic strands of their wigs trailing in the foggy areas their breath created. The mechanical corneas of Number Nun's eyes flowered open with a subdued hum. A quicksilver patina gleamed within her porcelain skull punctuated by the internalized flickering of many tiny glowing panels. Her spectral filter activated, shifting her vision. It caused the room beyond the glass to appear all of a sudden translucent and wavy to her. Objects were encased in a sort of X-ray jelly, rendering them somewhat immaterial. The skeletal system of the astronaut flexed beneath a glassy chrysalis of suit and flesh. The internal structure of the bed shone like an undersea sponge. Each image quivered, flickering like the flaws on old celluloid. A parade of quasi-bacterial forms suddenly crossed her line of sight, passing through the room as though it were just one bubble within a vast matrix of bubbles. Energy signatures fluttered like tapeworms, flexing and freezing in the air. A ghost was even discernible beside the tiny bathroom's entrance. It sat heavy as damage; the shade of some elderly gentleman in a vintage suit repeating movements like old videotape phasing in and out of existence. Number Nun ignored all these extraneous details, focusing instead on the astronaut. A sno-globe of swirling emanations encapsulated him, forming an entrancing sphere. The energies at work in this sphere were more than just unique to the astronaut. In effect they *were* the astronaut— fizzing in filaments, flooding rivulets about his body mirage like sap through vines. Various bulges of color and textured energy build-up mirrored shifting emotional states, slicking around him like oil on water. Number Nun's vision locked into a portion of the sno-globe running parallel to the astronaut's lower back. Sensory data fluttered and collapsed in her artificial mind, causing her to zoom in on a strange ganglion of energy that throbbed and pulsated behind the astronaut's spine.

"I see his trip switch," she announced to the Sugar Twins.

Taty glanced at the twins, realizing that they served some mysterious function beyond ornamentation. She wondered what this was, observing with interest.

"It's in the lower spinal atmosphere," Number Nun informed them. "Four and a quarter fingers west of the ventral narthex adjoined to his sum-jism by a tiny clutch of diamond ecto."

Number Nun turned to face the twins, who stared rapturously at the astronaut.

"Do you see how to trip it?" she asked.

Taty craned closer, clinging to Number Nun's robes like a nervous child. She saw that the twins' eyes had milked over and that their bodies were convulsing lightly. Their vision had also apparently altered though the processes at work were chemical and the outward effects more dramatic than those of Number Nun. There was, in fact, a marked difference in the way they saw the room, attuned as they were to a different set of spectral frequencies. There was also an X-ray quality to their vision though the resolution was far sharper than Number Nun's. The objects in the scope of their vision were diamond-edged and appeared to shimmer with neon aura hazes; internal structures glowed as though viewed through packages of garish syrup and crystallized sugar. Instead of the ghostly microbial forms that clotted Number Nun's synthetic filters, the twins saw bursts of fibrous electricity and fast-forward time reflections cascading like chimes through space. Their perception of the astronaut's sno-globe was also glittery and constellated—a gravitational spinning of tightly meshed and idiosyncratic energies. The Sugar Twins moved their heads in a synchronized fashion, bee-stung lips leaking milky drool, focusing on the area Number Nun had indicated. After a while they seemed to find what it was she was describing and took several moments to study the anomaly, nodding their heads in response to supernatural stimuli. Then suddenly without warning, their eyes became silvery again, and they stopped shaking. Number Nun daubed at their mouths with a napkin while they flexed their waists. Taty saw the jutting bones of their hips dislodge with a slippery click. They fell apart and immediately flanked Romeo. One began to whisper intently into his left ear while the other whispered into his right. Taty couldn't make out what it was they were saying, but it sounded like the rushed twittering of birds or snakes. Romeo nodded every so often, ballpointing notes onto a stack of lumo Post-its. When the twins had ceased their sibilant whispering they seemed somehow to deactivate, lapsing back into the luxuriant aloofness that was their natural state. They drifted to the door bumping into things, huddled in their ermine furs, not even bothering to reconnect at the hip. Romeo thumbed through the pad of scribbled notes and turned to Number Nun.

"You can take them down to the diner for a milkshake and fries," he announced in a tone of confirmation. "I've got it gift-wrapped."

Number Nun shot Taty a sharp look and gently dislodged the girl's clutched fingers from her cassock.

"Back in a tic-tic," she said before sweeping off.

She ushered the Sugar Twins into the corridor outside, and Taty watched the metal shutter close, feeling suddenly abandoned and unsure of her situation. She fidgeted with her dress in the darkness, occasionally lifting her feet to click the soles of her slip-ons together. Romeo was too busy rummaging in drawers to register her nervousness though he was used to a certain level of discomfort in fresh blood and made a point of practicing his own particular brand of bedside manner. He put a cold hand on her shoulder.

"Don't fret, Cupcake," he whispered supportively. "It's a little like drowning goldfish—everything you need is already there; all you got to do is shake it up."

Taty nodded nervously while he returned to his preparations, her eyes glued to the astronaut in the other room.

8
In the Shadow of the Moon

THE ASTRONAUT LOITERED IN THE corner of the room.
His reflective visor regarded the long mirror, which he knew to be
a window. An infinity mirror was created between his visor and
the one-way glass, but nobody was around to see it. Although the
spotlights faced him directly, his visor cut the bite out of them. It
allowed him to face into the bright white glare. The room was stifling
from the heat of the lights, but a climate control unit in his suit
eradicated any discomfort he might have experienced. The sound
of the astronaut's breathing emanated from a low-fidelity speaker
on his chest plate. A vintage radio also crackled in the corner of the
room, which had been professionally soundproofed, so that these
were the only sounds. They were magnified and drawn into focus by
a magnetic echo-proof field, creating a sense of staged tension. The
sudden sound of a door mechanism broke the pregnant stillness. The
astronaut turned heavily to see a sturdy white fire door swing open.
Taty entered the room as cautiously as a deer, peeking around the
jamb before tiptoeing in. She wore a navy blue Olympic swimming
costume with a matching swimming cap. She was also drenched and
breathing heavily as though she had just swum a lengthy marathon.
Romeo had quickly improvised this illusion by hosing her down with
lukewarm water while forcing her to jog on the spot. Impenetrable
blue goggles and a flesh-tone nose plug completed her ensemble. It
was obvious that she was nervous, switching her weight from foot
to foot as though she needed the bathroom. The movement created
puddles everywhere, but she didn't seem to notice. Her bare legs
were goose pimpled despite the heat. The astronaut observed her
with an unreadable and intense stillness. His measured mechanical
breathing filled the sound-dampened hotel room. Taty clumsily
daubed her finger to a concealed earpiece, checking that it was in
place. A tiny wire ran from the tiny device to a miniature radio pack
at the small of her back. Romeo suddenly appeared in the doorway.

He pushed a massive airport cargo trolley over the threshold. A vintage fridge had been loaded onto the trolley. It clinked heavily as he navigated past obstructions to the center of the room, an outdated golf bag slung over his shoulder. He handed the bag to Taty before deftly depositing the heavily loaded fridge onto the floor. Once this task was accomplished he wheeled the trolley out, locking the door behind him. Taty and the astronaut were left alone to regard one another like mismatched gladiators. Her fingers were clenching and unclenching on the golf bag's strap as his distorted breathing quickened slightly.

Romeo got backstage to find Number Nun already at the one-way glass surveying the proceedings. Her eyes had irised open, and she was once again employing her spectral filter. Romeo took his place at a bank of controls and removed an intercom from a wall bracket. He thumbed the device on and winced as a wash of feedback whined from a small speaker. Taty jumped in the harsh lights, slapping her hand reflexively to her ear. Romeo muttered something to himself, quickly adjusting the sound levels to a comfortable volume.

"Sorry about that," Romeo's small telephonic voice spoke into her ear.

Taty nodded in the general direction of the mirror.

"OK, show the spaceman what's in the fridge," Romeo commanded.

Taty set the golf bag down on the wet linoleum floor and padded over to the fridge. The astronaut's helmet swiveled, following her across the room. She opened the fridge to reveal an interior stacked to capacity with unmarked milk bottles. A cold white light ratcheted on inside, and the astronaut saw that each bottle had been filled with a different type of paint. There were many bright colors, each held separately in gleaming glass bottles. The loaded rainbow of them all reflected hungrily in the astronaut's visor.

"Right," Romeo's voice crackled in her ear. "Now close the door and get the axe out of the golf bag."

Taty shut the heavy fridge door and walked over to where she had dropped the golf bag. She withdrew a bright red fire axe from the bag without taking her goggled eyes from the stationary figure of the spaceman.

In the darkness of the observation chamber, Romeo shot a glance at Number Nun and deactivated the microphone.

"Her readouts are tipping the scales," he whispered. "Where did you find her?"

"They found her out on the road," Number Nun replied thoughtfully. "I don't know where she comes from."

Romeo thumbed the line open and spoke quietly into the intercom.

"Now, when you hear the music, do like I said," he ordered.

He glanced up to see Taty nod beyond the mirror.

She was clutching the axe with slippery fingers, water dripping off her chin and wrists, chewing her lips in nervous anticipation. Number Nun surveyed the scene in spectral mode. Taty's sno-globe was radically different to the energy body of the astronaut. It had a weirdly mutable shape that altered textures and color like a cuttlefish, spiking with occasional geometric peaks and swelling to three times its size in irregular pulses. These swellings continually interfered with the energy fields and ghostly forms around her, creating strange disturbances.

"Her globe's responded rather incredibly to the Jennerator," Number Nun remarked.

Romeo tapped a counter with a pale finger, his face underlit by tiny green LEDs.

"I can see that," he nodded. "We ready to get it on?"

Number Nun nodded slowly without taking her eyes from the unfolding scene beyond the glass. Romeo reached down and started up an antique Nagra tape machine. The buttery hiss and crackle of analogue tape spooled out into the room. It blared from submerged speaker systems, creating a din within the bright room. Taty flinched as a burst of maniacal cartoon music jangled alarmingly into the hotel room at a deafening volume.

"Let's go!" Romeo snapped in her ear.

Taty hesitated for a moment before crossing the cigarette-burned carpet and swinging the axe wildly at the fridge. Her first blow was mistimed, and it glanced off clumsily, scraping a lashing of white paint from the metal. Her second strike was more pronounced, and the entire fridge clattered and shook. She could sense the astronaut's breathing gathering in intensity as she heaved blow after blow at the denting surface of the appliance. The crash of the axe must have been loud, but it was dissolved against the torrent of sound. As the soundtrack became increasingly animated, she began to hack at the fridge with all her might, feeling the casing begin to buckle and split. Behind the mirror Number Nun was focusing in on the energy formation she had pointed out to the twins—the ganglion-like "trip switch" in the lower spinal area of the astronaut's sno-globe. The trip switch had begun to swell and shine in response to Taty's actions. It throbbed with an eerie internal light. The astronaut had subconsciously begun to sway in time with this throbbing. His motions indicated that he was entering into some form of trance. He clutched the edge of the bed at one point seeming almost to fall. Taty's energy body had also begun to morph in response to her actions. Several emanations softened as they spiked out from her sno-globe. The energies exuded themselves, transmuting into long filaments of questing energy. These tendrils reached magnetically out of her, seeking the peculiar light emanating from the astronaut's trip switch. As Taty's hacking became more and more brutal, the filaments intertwined, lacing together to create a crackling tentacle that waved blindly in the air between them. Romeo was watching Number Nun closely, waiting for a signal. And when Number Nun saw that the tentacle was fully formed, she nodded to Romeo who immediately took the intercom.

"Open the fridge," he commanded.

Taty dropped the axe, nearly severing one of her toes. She jerked open the damaged door, and a river of multicolored paint ejaculated from the half-destroyed fridge. At this moment of climax, Number Nun observed Taty's tentacle of ghostly energy flicker like a muscular snake. It swirled in the air before arrowing deep into the sno-globe of the astronaut. There it wrapped deftly around the trip-switch and squeezed, leeching the strange light from the trip switch as though pulping a ripe fruit. The action produced dramatic consequences. Number Nun observed as the entire sno-globe of the astronaut bloated like a rapidly inflated balloon. A mechanical scream shrieked from the chest speaker of the spaceman, and he collapsed heavily to the floor. The theft of the astronaut's trip switch light seemed to settle Taty's energy body. It ebbed heavily back into cohesion like a globule of colored oil in water, somehow soothed.

Taty froze in panic staring at the fallen figure. Sweat and chlorinated water glistened on her as the vivid paint flowed out around her bare feet. She tore the goggles off and splashed through the rainbow tide, falling to her knees in front of the astronaut. The cartoon music died abruptly in a garble of tape, leaving behind the nullified hiss of powerful speakers.

"Are you alive?" Taty shouted at her reflection in the gold visor.

The astronaut moved weakly in the paint, and she tried to assist him. Lashes of green, purple, yellow, and red splashed over her arms and legs as they slipped about, settling heavily against the bed. After a moment, the astronaut's voice emerged from his chest amid convulsive electronic respiration. And while he spoke, Taty sought his face only to find her own distraught and distorted image caught in the visor. Fluid dripped off her and onto the heat-proof mirror glass. Her breathing was jagged as the astronaut spoke.

"When you pass into the shadow of the moon, you see a darkness that no man can truly imagine. There, in the outer darkness, the stars are like white fire shotgunned across infinity ... And you finally know how alone you truly are and how far you have gone from the world."

The door crashed open, and Romeo entered, followed by the swooping figure of Number Nun.

"Get her out of here," Romeo muttered, surveying the damage.

Number Nun pulled the struggling, paint-smeared girl off the astronaut and then dragged her, kicking and screaming, out of the room.

9
Milkshakes at the Dead Duck

THE DEAD DUCK DINER CAPSULED a corner just two fingers short of the waterfront. It gleamed like the wet fin of some imaginary car, all sleazy chrome against the fast-forward decay of the esplanade. Festooned with rotisserie jungle chicken, pink-on-green neon, and loud checkerboard trim, it bubbled with all the indigestible traffic from the strip. You name the parasite, and their umbilical leavings would be smeared along the linoleum countertops: robo-jox, the bitchdoctors, all the sailor drek, cyborg love bunnies, bible jerkjumpers, jewel shifters, soldier camp dropouts, alien trannies, cannibal hobo freak shows, keyboard cowboys, jungle mummies, the whole carnival sucked through the place like a vacuum cleaner and gathered like gunk in the filters. The Dead Duck never closed. It was a shower drain for clandestine information, functioning as a sort of dysfunctional, somewhat diseased nerve center. All the little Namanga grapevines had their roots in the milk booths, and everyone on the knock came by at some point to bleed their personal underground for the latest word on the wall. The spacious cartoon booths clustered around the space age windows upholstered in bright lime and banana-colored leather. Cherry red Formica tables radiated out from a central grill and milk bar sucked as sweets between the puffy lips of the leather booths while ghettotech grind squirted like poisonous toothpaste from the glowing jukebox. It scratched a nerve-hop beneath the psychotic veins of conversation, creating a buzzy atmosphere of noise and anarchy. Number Nun had taken Taty to a powder blue booth at the far end where the Sugar Twins were already installed picking at fries with purple ketchup. Taty was wrapped in a huge cachou-pink towel, still in her swimming costume and marbled irreparably in lurid paint. Rainbow flakes of color chipped off her bare limbs and feet each time she moved while her wet hair dripped down onto the counter, creating contaminated puddles out of the spilled ketchup.

She slouched on the massive crescent booth, staring wistfully into a glass of napkins. Rollerskating waitresses whizzed past at breakneck speed, shattering her reverie at times. Some nearby sailors were pawing the Sugar Twins, catcalling incessantly, buying round after round of milkshakes, which they proceeded to hurl at the wall. A poor little nervous wreck of a redhead was mopping at a heart-wrenching rate, but nothing she could do would calm the storm. Cherries, chocolate syrup, and double-mint cream covered the wall behind her like modern art. The Sugar Twins didn't seem to notice the commotion or the hands on them and pecked up fry after fry as if they were working on an assembly line. Taty glanced up at one point and noticed that Number Nun was studying her thoughtfully. "So, how was it for you?" the robot Madonna asked quietly.

Taty sighed, "I feel like I drank a whole bottle of peach shampoo."

"Good girl," Number Nun nodded.

She reached into her cassock and withdrew an electric blue lollipop, which she handed ceremoniously to Taty.

"You've earned it," Number Nun smiled, patting Taty's head.

"Are you being serious?" Taty frowned, staring blankly at the garish lollipop in her hand.

Number Nun seemed confused.

"Alphonse told me that it was what you wanted," she flustered.

"Don't be such a robot," Taty muttered, unwrapping the lollipop and jamming it into her cheek.

"I'm afraid I can't help it," Number Nun answered quite primly.

Taty glanced sideways at her as another bowl of fries arrived. A fresh volley of milkshakes exploded against the wall, eliciting a wail from the cleaner and a chorus of raucous laughter from the sailors.

"Forget it; it's yummy," Taty slurped, tugging at Number Nun's sleeve.

Her lips had already begun to turn bright blue from the sucker. She sighed, curled her paint-smeared legs up on the couch, and plonked her head onto Number Nun's lap.

"This sno-globing is hard work!" Taty exclaimed, staring up past the edge of the table at Number Nun's chin. Number Nun peered down at her.

"They programmed me to prevent you from escaping," Number Nun said. "But I can deactivate myself if you want to run away."

Taty cracked the lollipop between her teeth, feeling the sherbet fizz up in her mouth.

"But this is all so much fun, why would I want to escape?" she lisped through a mouthful.

Number Nun raised an eyebrow in exasperation.

"You are very stupid, Childbride," she muttered, turning her head away.

"I'm not stupid!" Taty yelled up at her.

Number Nun ignored her, fussing over some aspect of the Sugar Twins' behavior or appearance.

Taty sullenly sucked at the candy, feeling it dissolve. She bared her teeth up at Number Nun's chin, imagining them to be a blinding cobalt blue. After a while she settled down, twirling her rainbow-scaled feet in the air.

"I just don't have anywhere to go," she mouthed to herself.

"Why don't you just go home?" Number Nun snipped, passing down a napkin for Taty's stained mouth.

"How did you hear—what? Oh," Taty trailed off, pushing aside the proffered napkin.

She glared at all the mold, cutlery graffiti, and ancient bubble gum fossilized beneath the diner table, irritated that Number Nun had overheard her talking to herself.

"Wherever you go, there you are!" Taty snapped up at the porcelain chin.

Number Nun ignored her until it was time to leave.

THEY RETURNED TO THE NEBULA Shell Sea Hotel every night after that, getting into the groove of what was soon to become a strenuous grind. Taty would wake up around noon and wander down to the pool where she would come to life slowly, listening to tapes on her Walkman®. There would always be leftover breakfast in the kitchens, usually paper-thin jungle chicken steaks, fresh purple cornbread, and bowls and bowls of weird fruit gathered from the surrounding jungle. Sometimes there would be other people at the pool—house regulars or strangers who had stayed because they were too inebriated to leave the night before. Yet, despite this traffic, nobody ever really spoke to Taty. She barely saw Alphonse though, when she did, they would chat amiably and he would show her some new and secret part of his kingdom. He seemed to be busy almost all the time and not particularly interested in spending time with "the stray" as he had begun to call her. Sometimes the house would hold a high tea in the frangipani grove, and the silent servants would set out table after table of pastries. People would drift from the villa like sleepwalkers, drowsily nibbling cakes in the syrupy sunshine while an old record player fuzzed out antique LPs. The days were a blur. Taty would vegetate in the pool or watch cartoons in the private cinema till Number Nun found her, usually in the late afternoon. The android Madonna would take her down to the basement and stick her in the Jennie where Taty would spend about an hour getting baked and seeing funny lights and colors fizz before her eyes. She was always woozy afterward, vomiting and passing out. But these effects would soon pass. Number Nun would carry her up to one of the big bathrooms and bathe her in cool water to get her back "into herself." She would brew Taty medicinal tea from local plants before hosing her down with bizarre solutions that glowed in the dark. Taty would then get dressed for the evening. If there was a party or some event, she would ritz it up in the labyrinthine walk-in closets. But more often than not it was just a ghost girl session in the Shell Sea, and her costume would depend on the work required. Romeo would dress her according to what the Sugar Twins had "seen" in the pigeon's sno-globe, and each night was different. Some of the outfits were utterly absurd: green ball gowns made entirely of balloons and full-body gelatine casing. Other times she would be called upon to be a librarian or an air hostess. Romeo seemed to have a never -ending supply of costumes and props and displayed an inhuman ability to improvise under pressure. Somehow, however absurd the requirements, he would always manage to get her spruced up so she would be able to juice the pigeon's trip switch. He told her that it was easy with her, though, because she had so much natural ability it made stage management "glaze on a cake that had already been baked." After a while it became a mind-numbing routine, and she would beg for a day off. They would often grant her that, and she would spend the day listlessly wandering around the house or nagging the midget for a ride into town.

θθθ

JUDAS SMOKED A PARTICULARLY PUNGENT strain of purple-headed space-spice, and it was he who got Taty stoned for the first time. It was an attempt at corruption on his part, and Number Nun became particularly annoyed, banning Taty from the spice. She still managed to sneak down to the old plantation area on occasion where Judas would hotbox an old greenhouse in the middle of the night. They would get plastered, and Judas would bitch about everyone in the house, the city, and the universe in general. Taty spaced out during these bitch sessions lying on the piles of leaves, staring out at the dark banana trees, listening to Coco Carbomb at high volume. It was obvious that Judas disliked the girl though he was the type that required an audience and anyone would do at a pinch. He prattled on for hours. His legs were mangled beyond repair, but he seemed not to notice. Alphonse, Michelle, and the midget would tie junk to him when he slept, and his bridal train of soup cans and metal parts got bigger every day. Number Nun would occasionally take pity on him and slice off some of the heavier items with her laser fingernails.

Taty eventually ended up locked in her room when Number Nun found out she was smoking semi-regularly. She threw a tantrum, and Number Nun explained that space-spice conflicted with the Jennie sessions and that it was in her programming to maximize the effects of the treatment. When Taty was finally allowed out, she sulked by the flower-clotted pool, getting more and more bored as the days began to run into each other. Each night would see her drinking milkshakes at the Dead Duck with Number Nun and the Sugar Twins, recovering from her latest escapade in psychic theatricality. They sometimes waited for Romeo, who would join them after arranging an army of maids to clean up the rooms. Romeo had become famous for his ability to find discreet cleaning ladies over his years of sno-globing. He even ran a small domestic agency on the side that catered to all manner of businesses on the strip. Romeo the Dealer, as Taty soon discovered, had a lot of things cooking on the side. He and Number Nun would talk shop whenever he came into the Dead Duck after hours arranging the week ahead in schedules. Sometimes it would take ages for them to leave. They would often reach the house just before daybreak. The whole thing bored Taty stiff, and she preferred to chat to the safer denizens of the diner, becoming known as a regular, ordering round after round of milkshakes. She liked to mix discordant flavors—bubble gum and vanilla or chocolate and lemon sorbet. Once she asked her favorite rollerskating waitress, Cherry Cola, to have a whole slice of banana cream pie blended into a pineapple shake. Whenever she thought back on that period in later years, it was often the milkshakes that she remembered best.

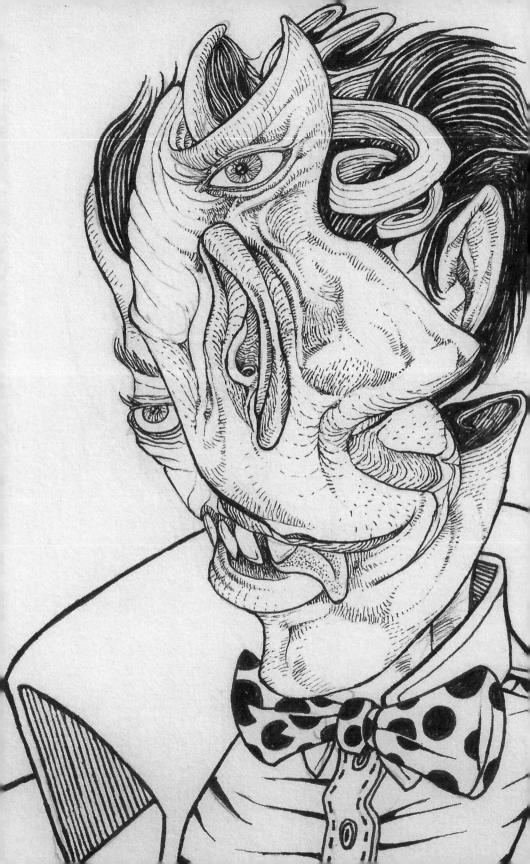

10
Checkmate at the Clock Shop

MEANWHILE, IN ANOTHER DIMENSION, THE Clock Shop seemed to hover against an undefined glacial space like a photorealistic addition to an otherwise abstract painting. The wasteland in which it existed resembled a gassy tundra, which seemed to flutter constantly into celluloid insubstantiality. The nullifying scape lay between—and somehow outside—the idea of night and day as though bathed in the effulgence of an alien star. The dense skies were pure white, and images would occasionally flash across them as though projected from some distant source. Static-rimmed holes carouseled in the air, sucking nearby cloud-like formations of drifting milky liquid into themselves. Gelatinous creatures creaked across these skies, inverting occasionally in the manner of stop motion seedpods, bursting fast-forward storm showers of tentacles and tendrils before snapping inside out again.

The Clock Shop itself was constructed in the style of a cozy Swiss chalet. It had been designed and erected in this forlorn and desolate dimension by Dr. Dali, functioning as a sanctuary where the good doctor could allow himself to indulge the more catastrophic of his experiments. He was, of course, supervised closely by the envoys of certain powerful cabals, who retained vested interests in the potentially devastating effects of many of his projects. The structure cast a lonely nostalgic silhouette against an incomprehensible horizon—a line which constantly distorted like the melting wax of a lava lamp warping one's sense of distance. A quaint wooden signpost had been spiked into the soft crystalline substance before the chalet. It read "THE CLOCK SHOP" in hand-chiseled calligraphy.

The interior of the Clock Shop was disproportionate to the petite Swiss chalet glimpsed from the glassy waste. It was a quirk of this particular reality—an inversion of displaced masses—an alien aspect that Dr. Dali had been able masterfully to incorporate into his design. Nobody could ever say for certain how many hidey-holes an individual like Dr. Dali had stashed throughout his personal subway of realities. The man shuffled universes like playing cards. His motives were unknown, his brilliance disturbing. Various powerful organizations consulted him and hired him for clandestine tasks. He was an easy man to reach despite his secrecy. He displayed an interest in the world perhaps as much as he displayed for other worlds. Who could even say which world he came from?

DR. DALI SAT, LEGS CROSSED, in a vast vault. The cavernous chamber was set with gigantic machines and resonated with a deep humming. The metal juggernauts closely resembled the turbines used to draw power from large antiquated dams. These titanic machines stood at intervals of several hundred meters, disappearing into a receding perspective on either side. The ceiling could not be seen, and the walls arched up into a void of lunar darkness. Pylons crackled with bluish electricity between the machines while distant pistons clanged endlessly in the void. The table at which Dr. Dali sat had been set with a smoked-glass chessboard, and a game was in progress. A high spotlight lit the table, distinguishing it from its industrial surroundings. In appearance Dr. Dali was small, slim, and wiry. He sported a lab coat stained with luminescent residue and various splatters, tailored green tweed beneath. The odd thing about the doctor, however, was the condition of his head and face. Due to some fantastic accident, his cranium had phased into a mode of existence that lay somewhere beyond the three dimensional. His head bore a vague resemblance to certain Cubist paintings except that it was a shifting fugue of features. These unmoored fragments fluxed and repositioned themselves according to some brain-bending alien logic. His perceptive faculties had not changed with the accident, though, and when questioned about his predicament, he would sigh and explain that his head had simply begun to function in a state of reality that most would be perceived as "conceptual." Beyond this he would not go and was sometimes known to wear scarves, hats, and bulging sunglasses at meetings—accessories that seemed to float and skim on a Rubik's Cube of eyes, eyebrows, nasal profiles, and tidal cheekbones. But in the sanctity of the Clock Shop, his head was bare, and the ghost of a smile quivered and slunk across and over and through his amorphous cloud of a skull. Opposite him, across the chessboard, was a squat ginger-haired man attired in the manner of a "Dad" from a 1950s television sitcom. He smoked a pipe, wore a cardigan, and even sported golf shoes. A nametag on his chest read "Mister Million No. 789678367." In the background could be glimpsed other Mister Millions, all identical save for their attire, which differed according to their various tasks. Some wore lab coats and worked at consoles embedded into the titanic machines. Others were dressed in engineers' overalls like garage attendants or Formula One racing mechanics. They all roved like clones attending to various activities. The chess game was not going well for Mister Million—if that was even his real name.

"This will be the quintillionth time I've won," Dr. Dali quipped, his voice emerging from a mouth that swam like a fish into a fluttering nostril. The nostril submerged beneath a hairline, and the hairline broke like a wave into the area where his chin should have been. An eye drifted, moon-like, over this, turning flat abruptly like an image on a television screen. Staring at his face, one often got the impression that it had become flat and two-dimensional like something printed onto paper. But this visual quirk did not ever last long, and holographic effects were often known to occur soon after this perception. People had suffered intense migraines after speaking to the doctor for longer than a few minutes. Mister Million, however, was made of sterner stuff. When one spoke, all the other Mister Millions spoke in tandem. The reality of a mass of identical figures speaking the same words at once tended to create staggering choruses over distance. Mister Million was often forced to resort to a quiet whisper, which was amplified by his multitudinous existence. Sometimes this created problems, especially when one of the Millions was already using his mouth or engaged in strenuous activity. "One of my many multitudinous disabilities," Mister Million would explain modestly when teased. Despite these difficulties, the consciousness of the many Millions was singular and seemed to rove between them displaying the kind of single-mindedness you might see in a swarm of bees. It made the doctor wonder what Mister Million did when he was "alone." Thoughts like this amused him greatly.

"I'm sure you exaggerate, doctor," the army of ginger-haired figures replied synchronously.

The gargantuan space created a phased delay in their speech, so that although the sentence was uttered at the same instant, it became subtly fractured in its delivery, mushy at the edges, frayed like an old rag doll. Dr. Dali had pondered fixing this little sonic problem only to discover that he enjoyed the dissonance. The presence of Mister Million in his sanctuary was against his wishes. He was there as an agent of outside powers, and it was a presence the doctor tolerated for various reasons though it was clear that he preferred his own company. Mister Million wasn't a bad sort for an interdimensional agent of mysterious origin and offered his plural services as a private staff (no doubt to learn as much as possible about the doctor's devices from first-hand experience). The doctor set him to work on various devices, limiting his access and challenging him to countless games of chess in an attempt to belittle him. Mister Million took it all in his stride(s), and the pair evolved into the protagonists of their own private and rather absurd buddy movie.

The chess game progressed rapidly, approaching another bloodthirsty finale. The rhythm of it was, however, rudely interrupted by the sudden clanking and booming of one of the titanic machines. Green light flashed and flickered behind a porthole set into the black metal as a curtain of emerald electricity discharged from the glass. It illuminated several nearby Mister Millions in a charge of blinding color, incinerating one of them in an instant. The cloud of fizzing energy billowed about the vault like a charm of hysterical hummingbirds, dissipating into the bluish lightning of the pylons. The enormous mechanism abruptly powered down rather like a washing machine that had just completed an arduous cycle. A distant egg timer pinged, and a big red light shifted to green. Dr. Dali had turned to observe the action over his shoulder, and it seemed that he was smiling though it was difficult to tell.

"Has the interdimensional flytrap caught something?" Mister Million's voices asked.

Some of the more damaged Mister Millions nearby spoke in smoke-scorched hisses, which added a gravelly undertone to the sentence. Dr. Dali swiveled in his seat, and this time it was clear that he was indeed smiling.

"Well, that is the thing with deep-sea fishing, isn't it, old chap?" the doctor sniggered. "It's all in the wrist."

Mister Million, by now used to Dr. Dali's absurd deflections, simply nodded, realizing that he wasn't going to get much more out of him. To his surprise the doctor began to elucidate upon the occurrence.

"Be a good chap and telephone Mister Sister," he asked his opponent, moving a rook across the board.

In a distant office cubicle within the hive of the Clock Shop, a suited Mister Million began placing a telephone call on an antique rotary dialer.

"Get me extension 000088776786567246728653347," the Millions said, displaying the officious telephone manner of an entire switchboard of civil servants.

"It's an order for the good fellow," the doctor continued as his opponent waited for a connection, slyly placing the enemy king in check.

"Vice is nice," Mister Million muttered in a wave of sonic interference. "I wasn't aware that you were undertaking consignments for petty criminals."

"Oh, we all have our vices," Dr. Dali sneered.

He observed Mister Million counter his check before quickly snapping him up into a neat little checkmate. Mister Million sighed, a sound reminiscent of a low tide ocean, leaning back into his chair. It always took an age for long-distance calls to connect out here.

"What should I tell Mister Sister?" the voices asked as the chess player lit his pipe.

"Why, tell him his symbiote is all done and ready, of course," the doctor grinned enigmatically.

11
Pillow Talk with the Nun

NUMBER NUN'S PORCELAIN BODY WAS modeled on the statuary and paintings of the Renaissance period. The forms of these android Madonnas were designed with Botticelli's *Venus* as a primary physical reference in order to create an angelic appearance. The beauty of a sentient and spiritually virtuous statue of course attracted unwarranted attention from the upper echelons of the various sex trades. Rogue scientists were employed to devise methods to capture said robots, and the enslavement of a Missionary Model became something of a status symbol among the more eclectic and resourceful degenerates on the planet. When Alphonse first heard about a Religio-Robot being deployed to minister to the cat tribes, he set his mind to adding a metal Madonna to his collection of stolen treasures. He hired the best robo-wreckers on the river to capture the android in specially designed containment fields before trucking her off to a rogue weapons developer for reprogramming. An underground chop shop on the waterfront was able to fit her with synthetic genitalia and program in certain pleasure modes copied from synth-geisha models. Thus was Number Nun corrupted and adapted for the amusement of the imp who often employed her for his own personal and perverse indulgences.

The bedchamber of Alphonse Guava was spacious, globular, and dominated by curved tinted windows that arced up from the floor to create an expansive bubble skylight. This greenish glass encapsulated three quarters of the room and overlooked central courtyards, sun-bleached terracotta roofing, and the missionary bell tower that stood adjacent to the chamber across a wide gulf. A crescent balcony splayed out beyond the large observation windows overflowing with tropical blossoms in large ceramic urns. Vines boiled out of these pots, crawling up the walls and lacing the glass in a mesh work of greenery, which attracted and housed all manner of insects. It was an intentional feature and made perfect sense when one considered

the contents of the bedchamber. Some of the windows were chinked, and a warm fragrant breeze breathed in over the heavy vines. The room inside was hot and humid, the muggy air thick with the stench of chlorophyll and reptiles—conditions that seemed not to bother the imp in the slightest. In fact, Alphonse seemed to thrive off the claustrophobic heat and fecal intimacy of the jungle. The walls that were left between the monumental windows of the room had been papered in a lush photographic leaf print blending out into the vistas beyond the glass. The furnishings were sparse and of black wood. Large vivariums and aquarium tanks were stacked around the periphery of the chamber, and many translucent pipes and life-support systems ran out of them, chugging and bubbling quietly away to themselves. Some of the glass enclosures contained large orchids, but most housed various specimens of rare reptiles. Fat dwarf pythons and iguanas explored the shaggy cream-colored carpet in spastic convolutions. Giant chameleons roosted in the manner of gargoyles, their prehensile tongues occasionally darting down like fleshy lightning as they supped upon the bugs clustered around the windows of the balcony garden. Providing feed for the many reptiles was, in fact, the primary reason for attracting such a large number of insects. Alphonse had cultivated specific blooms that, aside from their ornamental functions, served to draw large iridescent beetles, succulent night moths, and bumblebees in droves. The tanks were all left open, and the creatures could leave their enclosures when they chose to feed, hiding among the blooms of the balcony, growing fat on the bounty that had been provided for them.

A large circular sunken bed occupied the center of the chamber, and it faced an imperious white-and-gold writing bureau. This ornate piece of furniture stood on a small elevation, facing a tinted jungle view. An oval monitor was attached to the desktop beside a vanity mirror of equal proportions. Papers, cosmetics, and a selection of small luxurious pistols were disarrayed upon the surface of the bureau. Number Nun and Alphonse were on the bed. She was unclothed, balanced on her hands and knees, while Alphonse grappled her from behind, engaging in intercourse with her newly-installed genitalia. The sunlight refracted through her translucent skin casing, blurrily illuminating the clockwork parts that operated within her in a golden haze. Faintly glowing mechanisms ran in seams along her internal structure, giving her form a holographic jellyfish quality when she turned in the heavy sunlight. Despite the vigorous thrusting of the imp, she seemed rather bored by the entire event which, truth be told, was something of a regular pastime for Alphonse who enjoyed immensely the desecration of the Madonna's image.

"So, how is my new Tinkerbell working out?" he panted at one point.

"She's the business, all right," Number Nun replied over her shoulder.

"Well, that's just peachy," Alphonse grinned, returning to his exertions with renewed alacrity.

"There is another matter that I need to bring to your attention," she mentioned.

"My psychic intuition tells me that it concerns Mister Sister," he breathed raggedly.

"Yes," she answered. "Right again."

Her midriff split abruptly along a seam. The seam was hermetically sealed and circled her naturally, following the line of her hips and abdomen. Her glassy vertebrae expanded, and the spinal column unfurled, telescoping like an articulated snake. Her upper half moved at the tip of this extension, drifting to the bureau like the head of an anthropomorphic plastic flower. Her lower half remained where it was while the rest of her busied itself at the desk. Alphonse, by now accustomed to the secretarial flightiness of Number Nun, gripped the disembodied hips and continued to thrust into the kneeling lower half. Number Nun's torso wafted over the surface of the bureau with a low hydraulic hum while she sorted through a pile of letters. She eventually located a violet-scented, violet-colored envelope and extracted the sheet of paper sequestered within.

"Apparently Mister Sister has acquired something from Dr. Dali," she said, detachedly scanning the florid quill scrawls with disdain.

"It's something which he claims will put you out of business," she added. "He's invited you over to gloat."

"Ah, Dr. Dali and his fabulous Clock Shop!" Alphonse thrusted mercilessly. "What new and terrible joy has the good doctor birthed into this black world?"

"Shall I RSVP?" she asked, swiveling in the air to face him.

Alphonse ejaculated dramatically and fell backward across

the sheet-twisted bed, accidentally crushing a blue-headed gecko beneath a carving knife of a shoulder blade. In the drowsy light, naked and glazed with tropical perspiration, it was possible to witness his inhumanity a little more clearly than usual. His powder-white skin gleamed under the gold glare, and tiny spiracles suckled in the fashion of miniature navels along the sides of his torso, quivering open and closed as he breathed. His genitalia were also unusually formed, and he carried no scrotum or testicles. His member seemed rather to extend from his girlish hips like a threatening barbed tentacle. The rose-thorn barbs along the edges of his sexual organ were legendary, of course, and it was widely known that he could not indulge in sexual congress without irreparably damaging the other party. There were stories of lovers he had torn apart, but these were few and far between. Despite his various wicked streaks, he was not particularly fond of mutilating people in acts of lust. Perhaps it was the crude nature of the screaming, the baseness of accidental bleeding, and general physical resistance, which failed to appeal to his delicate sensibilities. Alphonse, after all, favored slow spiritual corruption over casual annihilation when it came to love play, and it was a peccadillo that had caused him much sexual frustration. In this matter Number Nun saw it as her duty to appease the physical needs of the imp and thus avoid the rare but occasional mutilation of waifs and strays. He could not damage her bulletproof porcelain body, and her pirate programming would allow her to satisfy his alien appetites no end. She watched him slip out of her with a clinical disinterest as her lower half rose and walked across the chamber to rejoin the rest of her body. After clicking smoothly back into cohesion, a small glassy capsule of fluid could be glimpsed moving through the tubes of her pelvic region. Various robotic relays and devices manipulated the capsule upward into her frosted glass belly. A navel port squelched open, and the capsule was delivered smoothly into the palm of her hand. Number Nun knelt down and opened a small metallic fridge, upon which was printed the legend: "PERM BANK." A gush of icy gas flooded out, creating a small silvery cloud for an instant. She placed the capsule among other similar containers and sealed the airlock. Alphonse lay like a speared marlin staring at a progression of livid white ants along the ceiling. He clicked his fingers, and Number Nun placed a cigarette in his mouth, lighting it with one of her laser fingernails.

"Well, why not?" he exhaled thoughtfully. "Tell the fat man that Judas, Mary, and I will join him for cocktails by the pool."

Number Nun had by now crossed to the edge of the room and was buttoning herself back into her long, black cassock. She nodded to him, and an autodial sound emitted from the communications array in her face. Mister Sister was on the line within moments.

12
Selling the Symbiote

MISTER SISTER OCCUPIED AN OLD abandoned seaside resort beside a wild stretch of coastland, a run-down property he had added to and developed over the years. Rows of ornamental palms had gone completely wild, ballooning between tangled mango trees. A white-walled, tinted-window comfort zone had been erected on a cliff facing the sea. At one time this complex must have been chic and breezy with its spacious atriums, glassy balconies, and rambling kidney-shaped terraces. Now hundreds of rooms stagnated, their walls extended into the nearby mangroves, festering with ruin. You had to enter the complex through a white tile mezzanine arched over with broken pavilions of filthy tinted glass. Everything outside the scope of renovation had long since fallen into disrepair. Cheap brick walls had been constructed where modifications were necessary or on chaotic whims, lending the place a shabby patchwork appearance. Piles of disused bricks lay in stacks. An abandoned cement mixer housed a small nest of quails. Mister Sister's "Buddhist Punks" haunted the hotel—slim gutter psychopaths perversely clad in the robes of monks, sporting spiked or intricately shaved heads, and hefting machine guns. They slunk around the stained corridors, metal accessories glinting in their sour faces, sharpening kukri knives against banisters or smoking hashish through the cured finger bones of their many victims. Tattered pennants fluttered from holiday poster palm trees, catching against the severed heads that dangled from them like rotting coconuts. The filleted carcasses of giant lizards were suspended upside down above guttering fires, undergoing preparation for the smoked jungle chicken stores. A wide procession of stairs led up to the main piazza where a decaying arch gave way to wide air-conditioned passages hung with oversized photographic prints and large canvases. Mister Sister liked to think of himself as something of an art collector, and his ruined luxury resort was a maze of cluttered sculpture gardens and storage areas.

A wide variety of lackluster paintings overloaded the curving walls plundered from museums and galleries throughout the Lowlands. The stolen canvases were of the abstract variety indicating the taste (or lack thereof) of the "Big Buddha." Large squares dominated by zesty splashes of luminous yellow or enamel-red grids sparred for attention with navy blue table cloth-like panoramas. It was enough to evoke a snarl or two from the imp, whose sensibilities were about as rococo as one could imagine. A large mirrored elevator ferried visitors up past the extensive sex slave suites where the resort earned its keep, past living quarters and lounges to the pool deck. Alphonse, Judas, and Typhoid Mary followed a topless girl in a grass hula-hula skirt out of this elevator onto the sprawling top level of the hotel complex. The girl had attempted to place flower garlands around their necks at the gate, but Alphonse had refused coldly. Judas also squabbled in irritation, but Mary did not even seem to notice as the woven frangipani flowers were draped around her stitched throat. A recent disagreement had rewarded Judas with splints and bandages on all his fingers. The legend "I AM A PRUNE" had been scrawled onto his forehead with lumo paint. Unable to remove it, he sulked like some strange seal, dragging his cargo of junk behind him as he crawled dextrously, avoiding his own reflection. He batted about in this manner, a maligned platypus, ignoring his wounds and cursing each and every thing that tickled his wrath—of which there were many.

The most overwhelming feature of the pool deck was obviously the pool: a flat ice cube blue expanse that melted into the horizon as part of an elaborate architectural illusion—a recent addition by Mister Sister. The overall effect in relation to the ruined resort was, however, tacky and unavoidably nouveau riche—an accessory mined from the unreality of a glossy periodical and transplanted into a fecund nightmare. There was a sound of heavy machinery clanking as a large guard robot swiveled noisily to scan the visitors. It stood about eight feet high and was easily as wide as a small car, balanced on a pair of girder-heavy hydraulic legs. Its parts were stained, rusted, and bullet-pocked. Yet, all the internal mechanisms seemed to be in operation. Yellow-and-red panels flaked, hinting at an original paint job now plastered over with ornamental insignia, innumerable stickers, and graffiti. Painted flames decorated the lower casing of its legs while fighter jet shark teeth bisected the

long snout-like chassis. The clanks and squeals of its motors were dangerously loud, indicating that certain mechanisms were in dire need of lubrication. Machine guns and multiple rocket launchers spiked in pods from the heavy plating while scanners and cameras roved in a paranoid fashion beneath its hood. The mech operator sat beside the robot in mirrored sunglasses, eyeing the new visitors strategically. Next to him was a deck chair upon which was berthed an obese blue-skinned native in Bermuda shorts, straw hat, and a floral print shirt. He drank pineapple beer, his eyes hidden behind aviator sunglasses, a samurai sword balanced across his belly within easy reach. Across the pool was another grotesquely corpulent character: the fat man himself, Mister Sister. Mister Sister had an Asian physiology and bore an uncanny likeness to those laughing Buddhas one often spied in the niches of seedy Chinese restaurants. It was a resemblance he exploited by dressing in richly brocaded Oriental robes and a Mandarin's cap. Even his ears had been stretched to match the image of a fat jolly Buddha. Yet, there was something recklessly off-kilter about this spectacle, something in the eyes and mouth: a gluttonous disregard for social propriety. He was the kind of character who was always invading an individual's personal space—someone who could never breathe quietly.

"The imp itself!" Mister Sister squealed in falsetto, air kissing the immobile cheeks of Alphonse Guava.

"What the fuck do you want?" Alphonse smiled politely.

Mister Sister threw his hands up dramatically, smiling across at the pale impish countenance.

"Now, now," he chided. "Claws in, tits out, wot wot! No need to be uncivil on such a sunny day. Some watermelon?"

"I warned you not to bother me again," Alphonse announced silkily. "Now I'm going to have to get Typhoid Mary to fillet you."

Mister Sister ignored this display of aggression, glancing down at Judas.

"Nice doggie ... I mean, prune," he coochi-cooed.

"Don't look to me for sympathy," Judas muttered, glaring at the pool in barely contained disgust.

"Kill him, Mary," Alphonse ordered.

Typhoid Mary slung out her sledgehammer, and the various Buddhist Punks reached for their machine guns as the robot went into attack mode. Mister Sister batted his long false eyelashes and pressed his hands together in an attitude of mock pleading. He even went down on one knee.

"Five minutes' grace?" he play-begged with a lascivious smile.

Alphonse beamed frostily down at the kneeling Buddha while everyone else waited to kill each other.

"Only for your grandmother's sake," he relented diplomatically. "She was such a wonderful specimen."

"I'm going to fucking cry!" Judas screeched.

Typhoid Mary replaced her hammer, deftly snagging a wasp out of the air and pressing it to her sealed mouth. It stung her sewn lips several times before she once again realized that she was unable to open her mouth. She crushed it as Mister Sister led them around the ostentatious pool toward a series of tables laden with metal trays of watermelon. Saffron-robed Buddhist Punks in sunglasses lounged around oiling themselves and their guns, jockeying vast cockatoo Mohawks, which rippled colorfully in the breeze.

"See," Mister Sister began in a conversational tone, "Dr. Dali has been busy tinkering with the concept of a holistic interconnectedness between clocks and quasi-dimensional reality ..."

"We could just eat him," Judas offered helpfully.

"... Apparently he's discovered something quite remarkable," the fat little caricature prattled on, completely unfazed. "According to his calculations there exists between nanoseconds an infinitely tiny space, a vacuole that acts as a loophole to different dimensions."

"Same pimp, different holes," Judas barked. "Break *his* kneecaps for a change!"

"I'm sorry, Sister," Alphonse broke in as they reached the tables. "I should have warned you beforehand of my intense prejudice against pseudoscientific monologues. You see, my mother died in a particularly incoherent one ... Mary?"

"The point being," Mister Sister interjected, ignoring the ominous hissing of Typhoid Mary, "that Dr. Dali, in his infinite schism of wisdom, has devised a sort of interdimensional Venus Flytrap that enables him to capture foreign specimens ..."

"*Foreign* specimens?" Judas repeated with a look of utter disbelief.

"*Interdimensional* foreign specimens." Mister Sister winked coyly. "And I have one that should put you out of business double quick."

He swished theatrically on his pointed slippers, pointing up at the ancient lifeguard station, which rose above the pool area like a dismal erection. It was an imposing decayed tower topped by a turgid dome of fractured glass and overrun by flowering fruit vines. Yet, it was what was clinging to the dome that drew their attention.

"I give you ..." Mister Sister paused melodramatically, then intoned, "the Symbiote!" A figure crawled and crept like a gecko along the outer walls of the lifeguard station. It resembled a lanky teenage boy except that it was possessed of slick green skin similar to that of a tree frog. The amphibious resemblance did not end there. The arms and legs of the being were double-, if not triple-jointed, and possessed of a rubbery flexibility. An extra elbow and knee joint lent the legs and arms a vague "z" shape when they flexed. When the creature stopped moving, these limbs folded up like wet origami and it assumed a sickening sort of yogic position not unlike that of a grasshopper. Another dramatic feature of the thing was its long antennae, which quivered in spasms upon its head. The antennae themselves were gigantic and feathery like a moth's, fluttering spastically against surfaces. The eyes of the symbiote were disproportionate, bulbous, and reflective. Nictitating membranes licked across their surfaces while complex sets of mandibles operated below. Someone had dressed the thing in loud neon surf shorts, whether for a joke or modesty it was hard to tell. Mister Sister clapped his hands together twice, and the symbiote responded by leaping nimbly down to the deck. It landed with a sickening bending of limbs and scuttled over to the faux deity, squatting on the edge of the water while the fat man petted it. The nearby Buddhist Punks found much amusement in the antics of the creature. One even ran up and placed a cheap pair of mirrored orange sunglasses on its insect face. The symbiote twitched, spat, and chittered mindlessly in the ludicrous eyewear, eliciting uncontrollable giggling from the gun-toting youths. Judas, who had flinched wildly at the landing of the symbiote, now stared at the thing in disbelief.

"What the fuck is that and how do we kill it?" he called out.

"This is my symb," Mister Sister explained with churlish satisfaction. "A rare bird indeed, even in its native dimension, for despite the rather froggy façade, our friend here can evoke a sensual bliss unparalleled on this plane."

He attempted to pinch the nonexistent cheek of the alien

only to cause it to flutter and gibber in panic. Perhaps it thought that he was attempting to injure its eyes for it reacted in fear, flapping amphibiously into the pool where it sank like a stone. It lay unmoving at the bottom of the deep end, an exotic and hideous statue, blinking its huge black eyes up at them.

"Aside from tapping the sensory pits to create lifelike illusions and slave driving the pleasure cortex," Mister Sister continued smugly, "the symb can also deliver a state of almost perpetual orgasm."

"So?" Judas spat. "We have plenty of auntie-empaths and ghost girls who can also butter toast without coming off like a Billy Burroughs vomit comet ... is that ectoplasm it's oozing? Jesus!"

"True, true," Mister Sister cooed. "But all of your rather, let's face it, archaic modi operandi depend on troublesome staging and require many players working simultaneously off each other."

He drifted to a table, hacking distractedly at a bright red melon while he spoke. Alphonse had, meanwhile, stepped to the pool's edge and was regarding the monstrosity at the bottom. The poolcleaning device motored around, and the symbiote batted at it as one would a fly.

"The symb here is a one-bug show," Mister Sister continued, sucking at ragged slivers of watermelon. "It jockeys an ovipositor instead of a cock rocket because it isn't quite male—more a sort of aphid."

"An ectoplasmic aphid with an egg dick!" Judas chortled. "And you expect this to sell?"

Mister Sister shrugged schoolgirlishly.

"It's true," he giggled. "Getting it on with buddy buggy can't be all tea roses and peach flambés ... I mean, all that ooze and whatnot, disgusting!"

He paused dramatically, spitting some seeds out of his smile before approaching Alphonse to deliver what he considered the coup de grâce.

"But it's worth every froggy pump, my fine-feathered philanderers," he hissed in grandiose fashion. "Because every time the symb gets down and doggy, he ejaculates a tiny sentient symbiote into his partner—a tiny little baby symb, which bonds with the host—symbiotically, of course ..."

Alphonse glanced up from the pool, reaching for his cigarettes.

"Internal parasites don't make for very good cherries on top," he quipped, lighting up a menthol as slim as a chopstick.

"Au contraire, Alphonse! Au contraire," Mister Sister leered slyly.

He placed his hand softly on Alphonse's shoulder and leaned in close to the pointed ear of the imp.

"You see, when the baby symb has crawled up the spine and nestled at the base of the skull, it begins to grow," he whispered in an exaggerated mockery of confidence.

"Not as big as its daddy here, of course, but just as potent," he smirked. "And when the symbiote locks in, everything becomes intensely sexual for the lucky host. Something about the way the bug interfaces with the spinal and cortex systems. The host can orgasm just by tasting something yummy ... like strawberry ice cream, for example. Can you imagine it? Even the bad things will become good! An orgasm a lifetime long!"

"How much ... did you say?" Judas eyebrowed.

The symbiote abruptly surfaced, took hold of the pool's edge, and launched itself acrobatically into the air. They watched as it sailed over their heads, landing clumsily on the lifeguard dome and scuttling around it like a bewildered insect. The robot tracked it like a giant noisy toy, its guns adjusting and fixing on the symbiote with many hums and whirrs.

"We love you, you housefly from heaven you!" Judas yoohooed.

"So, what's the drawback?" Alphonse asked.

Mister Sister removed his hand from Alphonse's shoulder and backed away a few steps, clearing his throat.

"Um, well, yes. The drawback," he coughed. "There is always one, isn't there? What price perfection, as that poet said ..."

They all watched as he procrastinated.

"Well, the host has to eat a minimum of 130 carrots a day," he let slip as encouragingly as he could.

"But ... why?" Judas asked in something like amazement.

"Oh, I don't know," Mister Sister flustered. "I suppose there must be some unknown carroty nutrient that the little buggers desperately need! We've tried other orange vegetables and extracts and things, but it seems like only those will do. ... Carrots have secrets, too!"

"Oh, please," Alphonse snapped. "This is like some sort of absurd attempt to justify health food franchises. I think we should just perform a little pest control and annihilate you all now."

"Let's not be too hasty ..." Judas piped up.

Mister Sister smiled poutily, not at all taken in by Alphonse's aggressive posturing.

"Oh, Al, you are such a *doll*," he smooched. "You may fool the help, but as one skin trader to another, I know that you are just fizzing up with curiosity!"

He leaned in closer, running a pudgy finger quickly down one of Alphonse's scalpel cheekbones.

"You want to see how the green boy operates," he teased. "Say it ain't so ..."

Alphonse remained silent, meeting Mister Sister's gaze for a moment before staring back up at the alien. A low chuckle bubbled up from somewhere in the depths of Mister Sister. It built to an extended smear of mockery, which utterly defaced the air between them.

"I could just dance!" Mister Sister exclaimed, turning away from Alphonse in a vaguely dismissive way.

"Music, my little Buddhist Punks!" he trilled.

Some of the nearby Mohawks began firing their machine guns into the air, creating a dismal racket. Mister Sister danced away through the gun smoke. He activated an enormous rhinestone ghetto blaster, which began vomiting a chaotic native rave track. Some of the Buddhist Punks began dancing alongside him, firing their guns in time with the hard beats pumping out of the woofers. Alphonse stalked away wordlessly. Typhoid Mary followed him to the elevator, spooked and panicked by the gunfire. She clutched her hammer and dragged Judas along with a free hand, lugging him as though he were a cooler bag of beer. They piled into the elevator, slammed the door, and descended quickly, leaving the noise behind.

"Why didn't you just kill them all and take the bug?" Judas exploded.

"The Big Buddha has a point," Alphonse murmured. "He's shown an enormous amount of initiative and will no doubt corner a huge market."

The imp sighed sharply, pulling out a small silver six-shooter and polishing it on his jacket as though sorry that he was unable to put it to immediate use.

"I can't just kill him now," he muttered. "I have to outdo him first; my delicate sensibilities just won't have it any other way."

"You and your fucking sensibilities!" Judas belched sarcastically. "Did you see that thing?"

Alphonse leaned back against the wall of the elevator, ignoring Judas entirely, withdrawn and lost in thought. He remained like that all the way home.

13
Things Fall Apart

TATY SNUCK OUT TO THE abandoned planter shack in the late afternoon. She wandered barefoot through the ruined plantations listening to "Siamese Inside," a new Coco Carbomb track. Her Walkman® had a satellite tracker, so whenever the pop singer released a new song the machine would catch the pirate transmission and write it directly to cassette. She had the new tape on repeat in her oversized headphones while a heavy gold light played in the fuzzy heads of distant trees. The door of the shack was ajar, and a dreary little fire spluttered some distance into the banana groves. An old jungle Indian she often saw down in the plantations was boiling a can of beans in the coals. She threw him a little unreciprocated wave and went into the shack. She found Judas babbling to himself about little green men and feverishly packing dirt-crusted carrots into old fruit crates. He was struggling to hide these crates beneath a table and had chewed off his splints to aid his endeavors. He was using his fingers despite the horrible fact that some were definitely bending the wrong way. The neon words on his forehead were by now hopelessly smeared. Taty rolled a fat joint, lay on the banana leaves, and proceeded to get stoned. She was desperately trying to listen to her new favorite song under the influence, but the pitch of Judas's ravings had crescendoed to a raucous din that invaded the heavy casing and overtaxed volume of her radar headphones. Now that she thought of it, his maniacal attitude seemed to fit perfectly into the charged atmosphere of the house that day. Final preparations were underway for some massive party, and she remembered being grateful that she would be in town even though the prospect of another night working the dingy underworld of the Shell Sea depressed her. It was the first time she began seriously to court the idea of leaving. She had some trade-worthy valuables she'd nipped here and there and, by now, knew her way about. She had even made one or two friends who would help her get out of town. But the lassitude of the house had her under its heavy sugar blanket spell. It was just all so easy on the estate: routine, creature comforts, and food on demand. She had a nice room, which she had gotten used to, a cinema that no one else seemed to exploit, and the pool to which she was hopelessly attached. Sure, there were the weirdos, crazy parties, and the crocodiles, but the prospect of the road seemed raw and intense in comparison. She snuggled down into the leaves trying to relax, but a niggling feeling of doubt had infected her mind, growing to absurd proportions beneath the lens of space-spice and Judas's insane raving.

She left when she couldn't take Judas's noise anymore and headed back to the house in a luminescent daze. Number Nun would be scanning around for her soon in any case. Dusk smoldered in the abandoned plantations, and the evening trees were alive with the din of frogs and insects. It was dark by the time she reached the frangipani grove—that sullen claustrophobic immensity of darkness that drowned the jungle at night. Servants were stringing paper lanterns up in the gardens, and cars were already starting to arrive, swooping up the long drive. The pool lights had been switched on, and they threw kaleidoscopic water patterns against the flank of the mission bell tower. She glimpsed Michelle sneaking through this swirling light across the poolside patio. She appeared to be talking to herself in a secretive and surreptitious way that was entirely out of character. It was only when Taty emerged into the light that she saw Michelle was on a communications headset of some sort. Taty waved in her direction, but Michelle seemed disproportionately agitated to be caught talking on the set that Alphonse had tacked to her cross at one point when her inability to operate a phone became a headache for everyone. The device was operable by vocal command and a couple of press studs located near her stigmata. Taty watched Michelle scrabble for one of these studs when she noticed that she was being observed. She scuttled off like a hermit crab, dragging her cross into the watery shadows, vanishing down a half-lit passage. Taty frowned in the gathering gloom of the tree line. Something was definitely afoot.

DURING HER FIRST WEEK AT the house, Taty had discovered a large bathroom on the fourth floor. It was used infrequently by the denizens of the house and was quite grimy in the corners. The large chamber had a short tiled corridor cul-de-sac, which had been fitted with a showerhead and drain. A large vine-eaten window gazed out into the blackness of the back gardens. The room was in the old part of the house, and there were still no light fittings in place. She had to carry up one of the hurricane lanterns from the pool area when she wanted to shower. Sometimes she would sit in the tiled cul-de-sac for hours obliterating the rest of the world in a never-ending gush of steamy recycled water. She wanted to escape into this private shower zone of hers for a little while before Number Nun found her, but there were too many people in the corridors. A spotlight from a chamber down the passage was throwing white light into the bathroom, destroying the feeling of isolation and solitude. She bathed instead in the en suite of an uninhabited room, pulled on her emerald disco catsuit, and ran into Number Nun on the way back to her room.

"Childbride, I've been scanning for you," Number Nun said, taking her aside as a couple of inebriated guests drifted past.

"What's going on?" Taty asked. "These people are everywhere."

"I'm not exactly sure myself," Number Nun frowned. "I think it has something to do with Mister Sister though I can't say for certain. In any case, I can't come to town with you; I have some things to do here."

On any other night, this announcement would have given Taty a sense of liberation, but tonight the presence of Number Nun would have been a reassurance. She took hold of Number Nun's sleeve.

"Please come," she whined.

"Stop it, Childbride," Number Nun chided, removing her hand. "And don't think I can't tell that you are loaded on reefer."

"It was just a little J!" Taty complained, now sulky at the prospect of going into town alone.

"Pull yourself together now," Number Nun ordered. "The car will pick you up in half an hour, so just do your job and then wait for me in the Dead Duck."

Taty glanced around, sensing some deeper disturbance in the fabric of the house.

"Is this even a party?" she asked nervously.

"I've told you already, I don't know what's happening," Number Nun reiterated. "Nobody seems to know except Alphonse, and he isn't anywhere to be found."

She bundled Taty off after giving her precise instructions about where and when to meet the midget. Taty complied uneasily, feeling more and more unsettled by the way the night was progressing. Outside, large cars were beginning to clutter up the driveway as a drunken stranger began to scream obscenities from the dark flower groves. Taty did her makeup to the sound of distant thumping music, feeling depression descend upon her like white noise, fuzzing everything else out behind its static.

The midget was unusually surly on the ride into town. Taty had taken Number Nun's usual place in the front seat and insisted that they listen to her tapes as they zoomed down the long foliage-choked road into town. She had already played the same song three times in a row, and you could tell it was starting to get on his nerves. He chewed his cigar aggressively at each chorus, taking the corners like a maniac. She watched the undergrowth flurry by in the headlights dissolving out into the primordial darkness of the jungle.

"So, do you know what's going down back at the house or what?" Taty asked, halfway in.

The midget glanced sideways at her before finally ejecting the tape and loading in that old "If You're Going to San Francisco" song.

"Boss got a bee in the bonnet," the midget muttered enigmatically.

Taty stared blankly at him.

"A bee?" she muttered in irritation.

"Alien honey for alien bees!" he snapped back, turning the volume all the way up and thus eradicating the possibility of any further conversation.

THE MIDGET DEPOSITED HER ON the drive of the Nebula Shell Sea and screeched off into the night before the door was even closed. Taty scuttled briskly up the steps, terrified by stories of the girl-snatching monitor lizards in the palm trees. The sallow light in the stained marble arcades of the hotel further intensified her depressed mood. She avoided the scary rattrap elevator as usual and headed for the stairs. She passed by the vagrants, junkies, and scuba gear beatniks with her headphones at full volume. Some waved to her, shouting, "Hey, Taty! Hey, little ghost!," and she waved back without smiling. She had become a Shell Sea regular now, and the thought added lead sinkers to her each time she crossed the dirty checkerboard floors onto the cigarette-burned carpets of the corridors. She could feel the weight of the place dragging her down. The fact that she was on a stoner comedown further amplified the sense of cosmic inertia, causing her to slouch and bump against things. Some crazy deep-sea fisherman had left a rotting swordfish on one of the fire escapes, and it smelled like death itself: the end of times finally come.

She ran into Romeo exiting an elevator. He was with Karolina K-Star, the war correspondent. Karolina had been a ghost girl for Alphonse until she started landing journo gigs with glossies out in the Lowlands. She had spent hours in the Dead Duck with her little dog, Gizmo, writing diaries in tattered notebooks. Romeo was able to arrange some kind of deal with a small underground press that circulated subversive pamphlets, and the *Life on Planet K-Star* diaries went into print. They sold like hot cakes in the distant Lowland cities, especially among teenage girls who wanted to know everything about what it was like to be a ghostie in the Outzone. Pretty soon Karolina had landed a dime novel publisher, and a film crew was deployed to Namanga Mori to shoot a television movie of her diaries. The crew was robbed blind in the first week, and shooting canceled when the wrestlers "confiscated" all their equipment. Glossies still ran her columns, though, and dubbed her a "teenage war correspondent" because she chose to stay and "report" from the Outzone. In actual fact it was the only place she knew; she felt uncomfortable out in civilized society. She and Taty had met at one of Alphonse's parties. They'd shared a joint behind the orchid house and spent an hour or two snapping Polaroids of sleeping peacocks in the dim glare of handheld flashlights. Now they hugged hello outside the elevator, and Taty noticed that Romeo and Karolina were both dressed in black and carrying video equipment.

"What's going down?" Taty fished.

"Listen, Cupcake," Romeo said. "I have to help K-Star shoot a deployment of soldiers for a news network. I left your costume backstage."

"But what do I have to do to jump the trigger?" Taty frowned, annoyed that all the comfortable routines of her day had been turned upside down.

"The pigeon's a regular," Romeo answered briskly. "She'll explain what you need to do. Listen, I'm sorry, but we have to split if we want to catch these 'staches in the act."

"What's going on?" Taty pressed.

"I think there's some new glue in the stew," K-Star confided after a moment's hesitation. "Massive deployments all over the city and big bad bubbles on the vice vine," she added, taking into account the fact that her friend was hanging on to every morsel of news.

"Hectic electric!" Taty goggled.

"Yeah. So, me and Romeo are gonna go grab some all-seeing eye candy and get it out on the wire before the boil blows."

"Can I come with?" Taty asked brightly.

K-Star shot Romeo a look, and Romeo placed a cold palm on Taty's shoulder.

"Not tonight. Alphonse still has you on contract, so best go upstairs and get your sno-globe on."

"Besides, it's dangerous," K-Star shrugged.

"Danger is my middle name!" Taty protested, practically stamping her foot.

"Your middle name is Munchkin," Karolina winked, pinching her cheek. "Later, alligator."

They swept off down the passage, ninja style, leaving Taty feeling despondent and useless like she was missing all the fun.

TATY UNROLLED THE METAL SHUTTER leading to the backstage area. The sullen glow of the adjacent room outlined props and cables in half-tone, amplifying the shadowy recesses. She discovered a cheap flannel nightgown draped over a canvas chair along with a printout, a pink plastic hairbrush, and a quarter-cup of nut oil. The nightgown was powder blue with a smiling teddy bear embossed on the front— one of those throwaway items you could imagine skid row mothers picking up at charity shops. The message on the printout read: "Grease your hair with oil—not too much—so that it appears not to have been washed for several days / carry hairbrush but do not use / enter barefoot / wear nightgown nothing else—pigeon will tell you what to do." Taty sighed miserably, wandering over to the long mirror window to survey the scene. In the room beyond the halogen spotlights lay darkness, and the only illumination came from an amber reading light on the bedside table. The lamp created a cozy glow that seemed somehow out of place in the shabby hotel room. A woman in her mid- to late fifties was seated on the bed, clutching a wand with a tinfoil star at its end, staring sadly into the light through a pair of thick spectacles. She was dressed in a sort of shabby peach ball gown topped off by a tarnished tiara. Her hair was a premature white, and everyday clothes could be glimpsed tucked under the bed along with a handbag. Taty left the glass and greased her hair in the large dormitory bathrooms adjoining the backstage area. She disobeyed the note, however, and kept her underwear on beneath the gown.

Taty entered the room, dangling the tacky hairbrush between her oily fingers. The woman started, ogling Taty over her shoulder as though she were a burglar.

"Romeo the Dealer says you're a regular," Taty announced. "He said you'll tell me what I'm supposed to do."

The woman continued to glare at her through thick spectacles as though dealing with a foreign waiter whose language she could not entirely comprehend. Taty found herself drifting to the window, already bored.

"Are you all right?" the woman inquired. "You seem distracted," she added when Taty didn't answer immediately.

"Huh? Oh, sorry," Taty mumbled, subconsciously counting the pulses of the neon sign outside the window.

"I guess I'm a little tired," she sighed, dragging her attention back to the matter at hand.

"You look exhausted," the woman said. "Why don't you sit down for a moment before we begin?"

A clatter of distant gunfire came out of the night, echoing down the dark streets and filtering through the half-chinked window.

"Sounds like machine guns," Taty observed, perking up slightly.

"They seem very far away," the woman responded off-handedly. "Why don't you sit down?"

It was clear that the woman wanted her to sit on the bed next to her, but Taty, feeling rebellious, took the small plastic chair beside the window. She slouched against the wall, swinging the chair recklessly on its hind legs and staring morosely down at the city. Cars screeched across a nearby alley, escaping like birds into the night. There was another speckling of gunshots over by the waterfront. The woman turned to face her, and they sat for a moment listening to the city.

"So, what's the matter?" the woman asked in a not unfriendly fashion. "Why don't you talk to me about it? I don't mind a little talk."

Taty studied her for a moment. The woman had apparently

relaxed and was now fiddling with her wand. In the cozy light with her tiara and ball gown, she had acquired the benign aspect of a character out of a bedtime story. Except for the thick glasses, of course, which obscured her intentions in a vaguely disturbing way. Taty rubbed her eyes and frowned.

"I'm just tired of all this, I guess," she moped. "I mean, you're a regular sno-glober, you know what I do."

The woman nodded patiently, staring into the lampshade while Taty continued.

"I've been up and at it for almost two months now!" she complained, flicking specks of grime out at the rooftops. "Every day in and out of this crummy hotel, all these berets, all these lollipops. I need a holiday ..."

"Did you run away from home?"

"No. I walked away," Taty muttered confrontationally.

"I see," the woman replied.

"No one noticed," Taty murmured, turning back to the light-punctured night, lost in thought.

"You see, my brother, he died ..." she said quietly, almost to herself.

"I'm sorry to hear that," the woman said.

"He wasn't supposed to die, it was ... we were ... Anyway, I left, and then Alphonse Guava found me and set me up with this job."

"Do you like your job?"

"I don't know," Taty replied after a while. "It's changing something ... something inside me." She cleared her throat, frowning down at her stomach as though sensing disturbances within it.

"It's milkshaking," she said. "It feels like a milkshake, like how a milkshake looks, you know, when it's mixing. That's how it feels, in my tummy. Like a dream of something ... I don't know."

She swung her bare feet in weary irritation, tapping a repetitive beat against the sill with the handle of the hairbrush.

"So, what's your deal?" Taty asked, changing the subject. "What's with the wand?"

"I'm your fairy godmother," the woman answered quite seriously.

Taty's swinging feet skipped a beat as she tried to decide whether or not she was supposed to play along.

"If I could grant you a wish, what would you wish for?" the woman asked suggestively.

After so many weeks Taty had grown tired of the games the people in the hotel played, the secret games with the intricate rules that she was somehow just expected to know. Tonight felt different, though. There was all the chaos in the street and no Romeo in the booth to tell her what script to follow.

"I wish I could just ... just burn the Zone and all its perverts to the ground!" Taty snapped.

The woman surprised her by waving her wand three times in the air and muttering some sort of incantation. Somehow this infuriated Taty even more, and she could begin to feel tears of frustration welling up behind her eyes.

"Look, what do you want from me?" she gritted. "If you don't want anything then I want to go!"

"Don't cry, little baby," the woman hushed sympathetically.

"Don't pretend to be nice to me," Taty protested, a hot tear of anger spilling down her cheek. "Just tell me what you want!"

The woman now seemed quite embarrassed that she was not being indulged. She shifted uncomfortably on the bed, adjusting her tiara and smoothing down her shabby gown.

"What do you want?" Taty squealed, now standing and pawing tears from her face.

"I only wanted you to take off that nightgown and brush your hair ..." the woman faltered in a small broken voice.

Taty stared at her for a moment before bursting into tears. She screamed with fury, flung the hairbrush at the woman, and stormed out.

She jangled down the fire escape in a dream of rage. Out in the night she could hear more gunshots. All of a sudden the sordid reality of what she had been doing for the last two months seemed to occur to her, and without Number Nun to cushion the blow, she felt lost and abandoned. She passed barefoot through the flytrap lobby and fled across many monsoon puddles, too upset to worry about the threat of girl-stealing monitor lizards. She crossed wet streets and ran all the way to the Dead Duck. Kenzo Cold-Eyes, the private eye, was at the Duck's cigarette vending machine and spotted Taty coming across the pavement, clearly agitated. He was a Dead Duck regular and knew Taty from the diner. Needless to say, he was concerned to see her in such a state and decided to find out whether he could be of any assistance. In appearance the middle-aged Kenzo Cold-Eyes dressed the part of an airbrushed Philip Marlowe who had strayed from his genre one too many times—a caricature lifted from the cover of a cheap paperback: trench coat, perpetual neon -rimmed sunglasses, and white cowboy hat. His personality was much the same, and he seemed a refugee from the film of his own life now cast adrift on the ugly shore of reality. He cut through the crowd of wet neon freaks and low-lighters as Taty entered the Dead Duck. She collapsed into a nearby booth and put her forehead onto the countertop breathing raggedly from her exertions. The detective sat opposite her and knocked on the tabletop to get her attention.

"Little Miss Taty!" he called above the jukebox's fleshy electro-grind and the raucous babble of voices. "A-OK down there? Raining rainbows on planet Taty?"

He had an almost indecipherable accent garnered from the many B-Grade movies he had swiped his syntax from. He also spoke in a broken abstracted form of English that lent him a comical aspect—a characteristic accentuated by the mutated Chandleresque image he cut.

"I can't breathe with all these sno-globes!" she sobbed, her face buried in her arms.

He placed a worried hand on her shaky shoulder and then patted her back, unsure of how to soothe her.

"Zoot down four dials, baby! I'll be jinglin' Romeo the Dealer ten ten on your command?"

She shook off his hand and sat with her face on the table. He shrugged to himself, looking around, bewildered. Just then, Cherry Cola, the rollerskating waitress, skidded to a halt beside them, cartoon-like in her tiny candy pink uniform. Cachou-colored Marilyn hair floated like a dream around her lip-glossed face, and she was blowing big pink bubbles in the middle of it. She set down a massive strawberry milkshake and slid in next to Taty, wrapping an arm around her.

"You chill out now, Cookie, and drink this shake," Cherry Cola popped and chewed.

Taty snuggled into her friend, calming down a little, staring at the galactic swirls of syrup in the shake, thinking of her sno-globe and the similar patterning she had seen within herself.

"That fucking motel! Mister Kenzo Cold-Eyes!" Cherry Cola bitched, stroking Taty's head with her flamingo-colored nails. "I tell you, it's a beatnik rattrap filled with carny narcs, tax collectors, and alien sex fiends!"

Kenzo Cold-Eyes nodded sadly in agreement, energetically chewing on a plastic toothpick.

"Last week only I see a fucking astronaut pissing on the dumpster outside!" Cherry Cola continued with wide eyes. "This district is turning to custard and trifle, I swear ..."

At that moment a gang of five Buddhist Punks exploded into the diner firing machine guns into the air. The bullets tore the ceiling to shreds, and bits of mildewed plaster rained down on everyone. There was the sound of neon signs shattering and chrome denting as people ducked for cover. Cherry Cola threw herself over Taty while Kenzo Cold-Eyes went for the snub-nosed ray gun he kept under his coat. He drew it, quickly concealing the firearm beneath a napkin just as the firing ceased. Three of the Buddhist Punks mounted tables, kicking condiments everywhere and shrieking with their blue-stained tongues out. They brandished firearms to the blaring jukebox music, staring down some of the harder customers who probably also had weapons ready under their napkins.

"Give us all your carrot cake!" one of them commanded in a clicking jungle twang.

The countergirl, Sunshine, exchanged a befuddled look with Raoul, the fry chef. Another Buddhist Punk lugged a massive old suitcase onto the counter, scattering plates every which way.

"I said, give us all your carrot cake!" the one on the table repeated viciously.

"You sure you don't want the chocolate cheesecake?" Raoul piped up from behind the stoves. "It's much fresher."

The one with the suitcase raised his machine gun and blew a few holes in Raoul. Sunshine screamed and plastered herself into a corner as the kitchen was suddenly redecorated with blood. Nobody liked Raoul much—he was a cheapskate and a pervert—but this was really taking things a bit too far. You could see certain customers getting ready to square off with the Buddhists on general principles. Cherry Cola was muttering abuse under her breath, and Taty could see hands going for guns under tables. Sunshine glanced at the corpse in the kitchen, came to her senses, and grabbed the glass-bubbled carrot cake off its pedestal. She hurled it venomously into the open suitcase and hovered, red-eyed and chest heaving, while the Punks raided the muffin counter.

"Carrot cake?" Cherry Cola mouthed at Kenzo Cold-Eyes. "What the fuck?"

Kenzo Cold-Eyes leaned in over the table.

"Whole weekend down the wire," he hissed. "Downtown jungle border silo say Big Buddha loco in Acapulco on carrot-to-carrot-related products downside by closing up cold storage!"

"Like I said: custard and trifle," Cherry Cola whispered back bitterly.

"Now, give us all your carrot juice!" the Buddhist Punk on the table demanded, kicking a syrup dispenser into the wall for added effect.

"We look like the kind of joint that serves carrot juice?" Sunshine shouted back.

"Well, what other carrot dishes you got on the menu?" the one with the suitcase slurred all low and disinterested.

Sunshine was about to answer when a black van screeched around the corner, skidding to a halt across the street. The doors slammed open, and five moustachioed soldiers swarmed out followed by a pair of wrestlers in colorful masks and costumes. One wore a cape of ostrich feathers, and the other was braced into a skin-tight getup of kneepads and electric blue Spandex. The Buddhist Punks went for the door while everyone in the joint rushed to the windows for ringside seats. Everyone except Taty, who curled up under the table with her head on her knees. The soldiers took down the first Buddhist Punk out the door with their rifle butts, but the second came out shooting. Two of the soldiers caught the spray, and you could see their mirrored sunglasses fly up into the streetlight glare while they jerked around like puppets. One of the Buddhist Punks saw an opening and cut down the street, sucking into an alleyway while the soldiers fired short submachine gun bursts in after him. The remaining pair of Punks had taken cover behind a copper Buick, firing around the sides. It seemed as though they were well and truly pinned, though, forced to fire blind. Some of the patrons of the Dead Duck were laughing and throwing ketchup bottles out the door at the Punks while the soldiers took up offensive positions across the street. Somebody pumped up the jukebox volume, and you could see the wrestlers flexing their biceps in the van, oiling up for the final takedown once the Buddhist Punks had finally exhausted their ammo. For a verse or two off the juke, it looked like it was tickets for the Punks until a deafening clamping was heard approaching from the esplanade off-ramp. Mister Sister's military robot abruptly sailed through the air, having hopped several meters from the shadows. It landed so hard that it cracked the tarmac and rattled all the cars. Some windows even broke. Gunpods locked along its flanks, and it discharged a volley that utterly annihilated the armored van with the wrestlers inside. The rate of fire was so intense that blue cones of swirling flame could be seen butterflying out of the ventilated barrels as the van was chewed up like an old beer can and mangled into the wall of bricks behind it. The soldiers had started running but another short volley popped them all over the street like water balloons. The Buddhist Punks were laughing on the pavement, shooting into the air for kicks while the van wreck caught fire. Plateglass shop fronts collapsed in on themselves, and someone started yelling that the Buick's tank might blow. The Buddhist Punks scampered up the robot's legs, crawling atop its bullet-pocked blast shields like cats. They found the cushioned quad of soldier niches and buckled up. This accomplished, they screeched victoriously, holding onto the stirrups as the gaudy machine crouched in on its powerful hydraulics. Within moments the robot had launched itself into the air like a many-tonned grasshopper. It sailed over several streetlights and crunched half a car on landing. The wiry drugged-up Punks rode the lurching robot off a bridge as sirens began to wail down the street. Cherry Cola skated back over broken crockery and spilled shakes to find Taty still crying under the table. Kenzo Cold-Eyes was at the window, re-holstering his ray gun, his mind racing with mental calculations.

"Come on, Baby," Cherry Cola cooed, helping Taty up. "I'm gonna get you a ride back out to the jungle."

"Bad show," Kenzo Cold-Eyes clucked, shaking his head like a schoolteacher while surveying the damage. "Blow town time almost, I think," he nodded, lighting up a cigarette.

He offered the soft pack to the girls, and Cherry Cola extracted one while Taty shook her downturned head, clinging to her friend's arm.

"Custard and trifle can only mean one thing, Mister Kenzo Cold-Eyes," Cherry Cola puffed, unlacing her skates. "Party time."

"Party time, you for me, say?"

"Party time number one, Baby."

14
Aftermath

THERE WAS A SMALL CHAPEL on the grounds of Alphonse Guava's property. It was a part of the old estate, and the imp maintained it purely for aesthetic reasons. He enjoyed the quietude of the place in the afternoons and the degradation of Number Nun upon its altar. He even liked the light beneath the quaint stained glass. The blasphemous episodes within the chapel troubled Number Nun greatly, but she was, of course, powerless to stop them and endured their torments in the name of her synthetic savior. She would regularly drag Taty in and force her to pray for forgiveness for her sins—an activity that Taty detested. In the late afternoons the sun would strike the chapel from the left side, throwing shafts of dusty honey light across the altar and into the shadowy nave, illuminating the structure like the hull of an old galleon.

The deactivated body of Number Nun lay half-naked upon the antique altar, a puppet with hacked strings. Her inert form was suffused with late afternoon sunshine, lower half exposed, the inner glow of her parts, and clockwork mechanisms dim and still. She appeared, in fact, for all intents and purposes, dead. The android operating systems had been shut down, and she now showed no more life than a mannequin—yet another life-sized effigy of the blessed Virgin. The sunlight lit her glassy hips and thighs, illuminating her mechanical workings and the messy residues caught within her mangled synthetic genitalia. Many people had evidently been at her in the night, and the playflesh was ruined beyond repair. The Sugar Twins were draped like cats along the aisle. One was sleeping, and the other was on its stomach, purring. They wore matching red velvet jumpsuits, which complemented perfectly the crimson lines of kohl around their metallic eyes. The sleeping twin had bundled itself into a heavy white cape coiled upon the wine red carpet. The twin who was awake studied the flotation of glowing dust motes with feline attentiveness, moving its head very slowly back and forth. The chapel was a mess of champagne bottles and cigarette butts. Broken things gleamed in and among the heaps of confetti. Soiled party streamers were tangled across the sacred imagery, dangling down into space like Christmas decorations. A window had been smashed and colored glass twinkled across overturned pews. Suddenly, the lucid twin stopped moving its head. A small object had caught its attention. It lay discarded in the darkness beneath the lectern, flashing intermittently. The twin flipped, padding over to the lectern on long pale feet. It went down, reached under, and scooped out the thing it had seen, tasting it quickly. The object was about the size of a small key and resembled a translucent mechanical baby squid. Tiny see-through tendrils flopped pathetically about, questing this way and that. They were adjoined to a glassy central node within which pulsed a faint but steady red light. It was obviously some vital part of Number Nun that had either been removed or come loose before, during, or after her rape. The Sugar Twin stroked the part lightly with its finger, and the tendrils flayed delicately against the crescent of the nail much like a minute anemone. The twin picked up the object and sauntered over to the prone figure of Number Nun, who lay propped on her back, legs apart like a glass spider. Her crystalline head hung off the edge of the altar, caught in the heavy light. Little rainbows flickered throughout her cranial networks, and from this perspective it was easy to see the tiny aperture that lay just above and between her blank eyes glittering like the vacant socket of a third eye. The Sugar Twin loitered, dreamily observing the tiny mechanical octopoid wriggle across its palm. Finally, the twin tweaked up the mechanism and plugged it back into Number Nun's forehead. The tendrils immediately extended, slithering throughout the translucent skull as the device clicked itself snugly into place. The red pulsing switched to blue, and her mechanisms began powering, charging the silent air with a delicate hum. Lights flickered on throughout her body, and her eyes irised open. She sat up in full combat readiness.

"How long have I been deactivated?" she asked reflexively. The sound of her electronic default voice disturbed the silence of the chapel, frightening the birds out of the rafters.

She was shocked to find that certain areas of her memory core had been tampered with, creating fuzzy grey holes in her perception of reality. Almost two days were missing. She performed a quick

internal scan and discovered that a small hole had been drilled into her skull.

Number Nun stalked furiously up to the house with the Sugar Twins trailing in her wake. They became distracted by something in the grove at one point and loitered in the sunshine while she moved on across the savaged lawn. The wake of orgiastic celebrations had defiled the grounds. She saw a white limousine crushed like a menthol cigarette into an old fig tree. Tables and couches had been overturned throughout the lawns, and party detritus was strewn everywhere, blotching the greenery with flotsam and jetsam. There were inert figures lurking in the flowerbeds, some still moving slowly against each other. The sound of an electric guitar thrashed and wailed from somewhere inside the house.

The interior of the villa was even more of a catastrophe. Broken vases and mangled furniture cascaded across vast expanses of ruined carpeting. Crockery lay crushed among rotting food while iguanas and insects drank from the fallen bowls of punch. A trio of unconscious go-go girls had been stuffed into a closet in the pantry. She passed a Buddhist Punk in the hall. The youth was writhing and gibbering feverishly on the stone tiles. He kept banging his limbs sickeningly against the walls with his exertions, drenched in greasy sweat and tangled up in his robes. A massy greenish hump jutted from the nape of his neck like a tumor, and this seemed to be the primary source of his physical grief. Number Nun moved away performing a quick audio scan, scrubbing under the distant insistent noise of the electric guitar. She discovered the sound of a film being projected in the private cinema and headed toward it.

Michelle sat in the cinema with the house lights up, muttering into a barely noticeable headset. She was running her favorite reel—a heavily solarized and hand-tinted cut-up of Cecil B. DeMille's *The Ten Commandments*—while she chattered away. Whoever had desecrated the celluloid had done a choice job creating little obscene animations throughout the film using glowing scratch marks and dosing all the characters with flickering slashes of digital color. The footage had been so pixelated with 8-bit tones that it sometimes resembled snippets of an old Atari videogame. A couple of refugees from the previous night's chaos were rutting in one of the back rows, but Michelle ignored them. The distant overdrive guitar was much more discernible in the cinema, sifting down from one of the upstairs rooms. Number Nun appeared in the entranceway and called down to Michelle.

"Have you seen Judas?" she demanded.

Michelle ignored her, remaining frozen in place, crucified against the kaleidoscopic mess of the screen.

"What happened last night?" Number Nun snapped. "Was Mister Sister here? Why was I unplugged?"

Michelle ground her teeth, desperately wishing that Number Nun would leave her alone. A small sheen of sweat had broken out across her forehead as she surreptitiously turned up the volume of the film while hissing quietly into the tiny mic.

"No! I've been crucified, you idiot!" she whispered ferociously while trying not to move her lips. "I can't just hide the communications device! I knocked out her periphery tracer with the dentist's drill last night, so she can't scan for any hardware and electronics in her vicinity. I couldn't do more; she has safety mechanisms ... Fuck, she might see if I move now ... Wait ... Wait!"

"Well?" Number Nun called from the door.

Michelle remained frozen and unresponsive, too nerve-wracked even to turn her head.

"Never mind, you filthy heathen," Number Nun muttered, sweeping up a flight of stairs.

She passed through opulent trashed surrounds: courtyards cluttered with comatose bodies and pilfered mattresses, ivy-trellised koi ponds poisoned with rum coco, and bodily fluids. Marble statues had been spray painted black, and a leopard lay dead in one of the bedrooms. She saw screened gazebos charred beyond repair by accidental fires and a bathtub full of cocktail scampi. At one point she passed another anguished Buddhist Punk who was struggling with a hump on his back. This one was crawling painfully across a large rug, puking carrots at irregular intervals. Number Nun passed other random survivors, all writhing in exhausted but somehow orgiastic pleasure. And it seemed to her as though their pleasure centers could not be deactivated despite the obvious fatigue of their bodies. More greenish humps disfigured these Boschean figures. Some seemed to be more vibrantly colored than the others, the virulent green of their humps leeching into their flesh. The bodies of these advanced cases were all slightly warped. Jointed insect-like patterns were developing within their clammy flesh, subtly altering them. The solid wall of discordant guitar noise had by now intensified, and Number Nun was able to pinpoint its source of origin. She moved up stairs and down corridors toward it, pausing outside the disused room. A familiar sound of breathing had caught the attention of her spectrograph sensor, and she tuned into it, entering the long dusty dance studio. Large windows flooded the space in the cold glow of twilight that reflected in the expansive ballet mirrors lining the far wall of the chamber. A large gloomy pavilion brooded in the darkest corner. It seemed part of some long-abandoned carnival float, the relic of a long-forgotten Mardi Gras. A large crocodile waddled around the base, gurgling up at something on the roof of the structure.

"Childbride!" Number Nun called. "Come down from there at once."

There was a scuffling, and after a few seconds, Taty's bewildered face emerged over the edge of the roof. She was scruffy and dirty, still wearing the tattered remains of the cheap flannel nightgown, wrapped in some old stage cloth she had discovered atop the pavilion.

"Where have you been?" Taty shouted, bursting into tears.

"Childbride, stop sniffling and come down from there at once."

"But the monster will eat me!"

Number Nun deftly grabbed the crocodile by the tail and swung it aside one-handedly. The surprised reptile tumbled and skidded across the room, crashing into a large ballet mirror. It hissed and snapped but did not come any closer. Number Nun stood directly beneath Taty.

"Jump," Number Nun commanded.

Taty hesitated, struggling out of the stage cloth. She gripped the edge of the float, faltered, and then dropped neatly into Number Nun's outstretched arms. The android was about to set her down, but Taty clung fast, refusing to be released, sobbing into the black cassock. Number Nun crossed back into the corridors with her as though carrying a doll. She bore Taty up through the house, and the screaming noise of the guitar grew steadily louder.

"I couldn't find Cherry Cola," Taty sniffed.

"Cherry Cola?" Number Nun frowned. "The waitress from the Dead Duck? What is she doing here? What happened these last two nights, Childbride?"

Taty started crying again, blowing her nose in her nightgown. Number Nun paused, realizing that a detour would be necessary.

"We are near your room," she said. "We might as well get you some fresh clothes."

The room had survived surprisingly unscathed, and Number Nun was finally able to detach Taty from her and get her out of the wretched nightgown.

"Cherry Cola brought me here from town," Taty sniveled, wriggling into a pair of skinny white jeans. "But when we got here it was just terrible!"

She rummaged around for a T-shirt and her favorite black jersey while guitar noise thrashed and fed far off in the background.

"The carrot-stealing monks were here with the Big Buddha and this green alien boy who ... it was so disgusting!"

She paused to take a deep breath, shaking on the edge of the bed. Number Nun wet a towel with warm water and began to wipe the grime off Taty's face and neck.

"There were these rituals they were doing ..." Taty whispered, her eyes red and unfocused. "They were wearing robes, and they had black candles, and people's heads were ... their heads were just lying there! On the floor! Like cabbages! And there were all these funny patterns drawn on the floors in white paint and rat poison ... They were all ... they were all getting with the monster boy! And then they caught us, and they wanted me to make it with him, too. But I ran away into the secret passages ... Then the crocodiles got loose!"

She buried her head in Number Nun's robes, breathing raggedly.

"Where was Romeo the Dealer?" Number Nun asked.

"He was out filming with K-Star. I didn't see them after ..." came Taty's muffled voice.

Number Nun took her firmly by the shoulders.

"Listen, Childbride. It's not safe here anymore," she said. "Put some shoes on and let's get moving."

Taty nodded, and Number Nun could see that the muscles along her neck were tense and bunched. She helped her dress and then led her by the hand up the stairs to the master chamber of Alphonse Guava.

The white-and-gold bunker doors were firmly shut. The shrieking instrument emanated from within along with an inhuman jabbering and screaming. Taty was hiding behind Number Nun, trying to pull her away from the doors.

"Don't go in there!" she kept shouting frantically.

Number Nun ignored her and began hammering on the lead-reinforced double doors.

"Alphonse!" she called in an electronically amplified voice, which cut instantly through the guitar's frequencies and caused Taty to clap her hands to her ears.

"That hurt!" she squealed.

Number Nun calculated her options for a nanosecond before extending her left hand and microwaving the lock's electronics. The door began to open on its auto-hinge, and the scene within was slowly revealed. A mess of broken tanks littered the soiled white shag. Pipes spurted liquid from smashed life support systems while reptiles roamed free, antagonizing one another. The noise was immense, staggering. All the glass was rattling violently. Some of the windows had even shattered. Alphonse was on the sheet-twisted satin of the bed clad in the ruins of a pink suit. He was writhing and gibbering in a paroxysm of ecstatic agony, a chitinous hump surfacing from his torn collar. Taty stared in horror as Alphonse gorged himself on the small mountains of baby carrots around him. After each spluttered swallow he seemed to calm slightly only to surge back into palsy moments later. A massive arena-quality sound stack had been moved into the room. It occupied an uncomfortable amount of space with its black bulk and cables, making the room seem so much more constricted than before. A haggard youth in a torn green jumper, black skeleton tights, and a plastic Mickey Mouse ear cap stood before the tunnel-like woofers. He was wired for sound, slashing mindlessly at a glitter-pink telecaster, making the whole world shake with each frantic emission. Taty watched him sway recklessly in the stereo field, palms pressed desperately to her ears. The output was such that his lank straw-colored hair fluffed out each time the speakers belched. The shouts of Number Nun were barely discernible within this sonic chaos despite her frequency cutters. Her appeals to Alphonse quickly ran dry when she realized just how far gone he was. She muted her sonic input and shifted to spectral vision. Reptile energy-bodies mangled like frog spawn in the waves of sound. She tuned her vision to Alphonse's writhing form, focusing in on the odious hump that plagued him so. The X-ray aspect of her vision detected a miniature symb straddling Alphonse Guava's upper spine. The green homunculus was even clutching at the tendons attached to his skull like reins as it attempted to settle against his bone. Somehow the creature seemed to realize that it was being observed and turned to face Number Nun through the ghostly layers of flesh. Alphonse's head mirrored its reaction in delay, turning to face her. She was disturbed to see how many of Alphonse's facial characteristics the symbiote had adopted, creating a nightmarish, little caricature of him blemished by antennae and mandible extrusions—an obscene little biological self-portrait, which he now carried beneath his skin and close to his bones. His own face was a distorted wreck, drooling and sightless. Number Nun gathered Taty up like a rag doll and strode back out through the aftermath, carrying her close.

"We have to find Romeo the Dealer," Number Nun told her when the guitar noise had faded sufficiently, so that she could hear her speak. "He's the only one who can get us out of jungle country."

A hot-pink ray gun bolt unexpectedly ate a glowing hole out of a nearby Doric column. The blast momentarily lit everything the color of watermelons in the sun, and Taty saw electric-blue retinal mirages flicker in the aftermath.

"Stay away!" shouted a ragged voice—a voice to which Taty immediately responded.

She scrabbled from Number Nun's bosom and ran down into the white marble courtyard beyond the pillars. The sunken square into which she stumbled was bright lushly illuminated by glass skylights. Potted palms saturated the corners in leafiness. A fountain dominated the area, and a statue of the Venus de Milo (perversely depicted with arms) occupied the center of it, gushing water from its headless neck. Cherry Cola was splashing in the water, handcuffed wrist-to-wrist with the statue. She had been badly beaten and sported a succulent purple eye as well as various ugly bruises. Her candy uniform was torn at the shoulder, and she clutched a walkie-talkie in her upraised fist. Her other hand brandished an oversized chrome ray gun still smoking from its latest report. The courtyard was strewn with the remains of crocodiles, Buddhist Punks, and party-harders who had attempted to approach her during the night. Some still flailed limply, leaking alien fluids and greenish malformations. It was impossible to say how long Cherry Cola had been cuffed to the statue, but she looked to be in pretty bad shape. She started crying dry, heaving sobs when she saw Taty, dropping the ray gun in relief.

Number Nun snapped off the statue's hand at the wrist, freeing Cherry Cola's upraised arm instantly. The rollerskating waitress collapsed into the water, clutching her ligatured limb while Number Nun pincered off the cuffs with her laser fingernails.

"We need to leave this house immediately," Number Nun reiterated.

Cherry Cola nodded as Taty helped her out of the fountain.

"I got this walkie-talkie off a dead man," she coughed. "I managed to find Kenzo Cold-Eye's frequency about an hour or two ago."

"Is he coming?" Number Nun asked.

"He said he'd be here by nightfall," she winced, leaning on the android for support as they limped through desecrated boudoirs and partially flooded conservatories.

"Let's wait for him in the frangipani grove," Number Nun suggested. "That way we can see things coming."

She glanced down and saw that Taty was crying. The expression on her face was frozen and mask-like, yet hot tears leaked down her cheeks, collecting at her lips.

"Alphonse is gone," she whispered.

15
The Surgery Ship

KENZO COLD-EYES DROVE A souped-up space cruiser with a blue-glitter paint job and stingray fins. You could see him coming a mile away any time of the day. The car had a massive carrying capacity, and the back cabin had been fitted with a semicircular white couch, mini-bar, and television. He would occasionally supplement his income by hiring himself out as a limo service for those who could afford it. Everybody who was anybody in the Namanga party circuit knew Kenzo Cold-Eyes. He was often hired to follow errant spouses with a telephoto lens and a notepad or to transport visiting celebrities. When he finally arrived at the house of Alphonse Guava, he had the Pink Samurai with him. Number Nun tried the limo's television, but the channel reception was fried. As much as they tuned about for news, all they could pick up was an old soap opera broadcast on every public access channel. A mirror ball spun a tactless party shimmer over the grim passengers huddled in the back while Kenzo Cold-Eyes gunned the car down a dark jungle road. Foliage swept ghostly blurs through the yellow headlights, catching in the eyes of animals. The occasional grass hut flashed past, but these structures grew sparse as the jungle became denser and less inhabited. The front section of the cruiser sported two luxurious cream couches, well-spaced. Kenzo Cold-Eyes had the wheel, of course, blasting indecipherable arcade game jingles into his loopy cigarette smoke. The Pink Samurai rode shotgun, an enormous pair of military-issue night vision goggles obscuring half his swarthy face. He scanned the darkness outside in drunken sweeps, the light glinting off his gold teeth and candy-colored armor. Number Nun occupied the back along with Taty, Cherry Cola, and the twins. Cherry Cola was sobbing hard, her head on Taty's lap, refusing to speak about her experiences in the house. Subdued strip lighting illuminated them from below in a muted aquarium shimmer, creating a chic cocktail bar effect that was now thoroughly out of place. Number Nun was attempting to retune the television with optically projected, infrared beams. In times of crises, the wrestlers were known to jam all transmission, so the TV blackout was not entirely unexpected. Yet, against all odds, Number Nun still persisted in the hopes of uncovering rebel transmissions hidden within the noise.

"Not far so closely! Hit deep jungle so bang on in," Kenzo ColdEyes announced. "Three-day jungle deep from Outer Necropolis—City safe as cans in a cannery! Uncanned! Uncanny! Short-full days only so long, I say—total chaos! Everybody frogfucking!"

Cherry Cola let out a pitiful whine when she heard this.

"They made me do it with the green boy," she whimpered from the depths of Taty's arms.

Number Nun snapped to attention, instantly activating her eye filters. She scanned the girls with her spectral vision and quickly noticed an anomaly at the base of Cherry Cola's spine. A baby symbiote was hiding like a child behind the tree stump of her coccyx. It noticed Number Nun and stared back at her through the shifting bone and glassy layers of flesh, its face already beginning to mimic the rollerskating waitress's like a crudely manufactured finger puppet.

"There's one of those things inside you," Number Nun said.

Cherry Cola began to panic and scream, begging the android to remove it.

"Leave her alone!" Taty shouted. "Stop frightening her!"

Number Nun turned to Kenzo Cold-Eyes, adopting a confidential tone.

"We need to head back into Namanga Mori," she muttered. "We have to get her to Daddy Bast's chop shop and slice this thing out of her."

"Daddy Bast central zone number one." Kenzo Cold-Eyes squinted fatalistically. "Ground zero-zero."

"According to my estimations, it will take five hours for the parasite to reach her brain stem," Number Nun insisted. "We have to try to save her."

Taty's attempts to restrain and comfort Cherry Cola fell apart without warning. The afflicted girl began screaming uncontrollably, thrashing about like an injured animal. Taty clung to her, pale and terrified. Number Nun flipped back the tip of her right index finger, revealing a hypodermic needle. She jabbed it into Cherry Cola's neck, and the rollerskating waitress immediately fell limp, cluttering to the carpet like a mannequin. Kenzo Cold-Eyes slowed, pulling over onto a muddy verge. He cut the engine, and the arcade game music died, leaving them with the ragged sound of Taty's frantic breathing.

"What did you do to her?" Taty shrieked, regarding the fallen form in horror.

Number Nun brandished the syringe in irritation.

"Quiet, Childbride. Or I will put you to sleep as well."

Taty shrank to the far end of the cabin, squatting numbly beside Cherry Cola's inert form.

"Die maybe we turn back," Kenzo Cold-Eyes stated matter-of-factly.

"Don't be ridiculous," Number Nun tut-tutted.

The detective lit a fresh cigarette while the Pink Samurai scanned the trees outside. Soon they had turned around and were heading back into the city.

Upturned cars lay burning in the streets. The inner quadrants of Namanga Mori had transformed overnight into a sort of deserted war zone bristling with craters and pockets of flaming debris. The passengers scanned furtively about while driving. Kenzo Cold-Eyes had his ray gun out on the dash, and the Pink Samurai was anxiously fingering the hilt of a rhinestone-encrusted shotgun. Distant gunfire followed them around every street corner. The esplanade was less altered than they had anticipated. Despite the rubble and the damage, stragglers still loitered on the strip. Lights burned in the windows of the Nebula Shell Sea, and there were people on the street. Some of the windows of the Dead Duck had been obliterated, but music still jangled from the juke, creating an unexpected atmosphere of festivity among the patrons on the pavement. Cherry Cola had woken up and was leaning groggily against the sill, cuddled up in Taty's arms, watching the lights with narcoleptic fascination.

"Thank fuck the duck is still diving," she slurred with pride.

"Not so bad so low it seems though, you know," Kenzo Cold-Eyes reported.

"It's just a power shift," Number Nun stated. "Things will resume a sort of normality very soon."

"Is the Big Buddha taking over?" Taty asked, still shaken up about the demise of Alphonse.

"It looks that way," the android confirmed.

The Pink Samurai unexpectedly jumped from the slow-moving vehicle, slamming the door behind him. They watched him stagger into the Dead Duck like a big pink cockroach.

"Don't stop till we reach Daddy Bast's," Number Nun said to Kenzo Cold-Eyes. "We need to find Romeo the Dealer when we are done—he's the only one who can get us out of town."

THE ENTRANCE TO THE WHARVES was a region of cluttered shanty shacks housing all manner of disenfranchised zonesters and maritime dregs. Massive rotten warehouses loomed and receded in the headlights. Sailor types mingled with the occasional blue-skinned jungle hoodlum, clogging up doorways, smoking space-spice, and playing antique games of chance with bird bones and hood ornaments. Strange orchestras of organ-grinders drifted like lepers, emitting a haunting xylophonic ruckus wherever they went. They arrived at the inner dockyards where monstrous piers reached into the creeping breakers. Decrepit vessels and abandoned freighters clung to these ghostly structures, harking back to a time when the town was still a thriving and legitimate seaport. The farthest and longest pier was abandoned save for a vintage cruise liner anchored about halfway down. The vessel was monumental, a rusted hulk twinkling with many tiny pinpricks of light and topped by triple funnels that loomed like fins against the gloomy cloud banks. They passed through a small maze of crates and through the wreckage of a barricade where disenfranchised tribal families nested in shabby encampments. The drive down to the pier beyond was, however, smooth and unobstructed. A wide metal gangplank creaked against the stone of the pier, watched over by blue men in beaded gowns. These men huddled beside the water, toasting mutated fish in the fire of an old garbage can. Their knives glinted in the oncoming headlights, creating long shadows against the barnacled flanks of the old ship. And it was only when they drew closer that Taty noticed the many mangy hyenas all tethered to leashes licking at human femurs. Some had patterns shaved into their scrawny flanks while the fur of others had been bleached and dyed improbable colors. A sign above the gangplank read: DADDY BAST'S VOODOO SURGERY in hand-scrawled script. They came to a halt, and Number Nun exited the cruiser addressing the blue guards in a sibilant jungle tongue. They seemed to recognize her and smiled out of the half-dark. She exchanged pleasantries with them before leaning back in through the window.

"Daddy Bast will help you," she assured Cherry Cola.

She opened the door and scooped out the drugged waitress as though she were a flimsy toy. Too afflicted to protest, the usually feisty girl simply clung on as she was ferried up the plank toward a gaping hatch. Taty went with them, grabbing onto Number Nun's garments, too afraid to remain in the car. The Sugar Twins also followed suit, trailing like dazed pets. Kenzo Cold-Eyes wasn't particularly happy at being left to wait alone in the car, but his good conscience kept him from voicing displeasure. He simply watched them as they were swallowed into the side of the wounded ship, neurotically checking his watch and the dwindling charge status of his blaster.

THE INTERIOR OF THE SURGERY ship was dim and encrusted by a hivework of shrines. Dark cubbyholes engulfed almost every corridor and cranny, each dedicated to the effigies of disturbing deities. Candles glowed out of this darkness, illuminating sacrificial birds, wooden carvings of cigarette smoking gods and pterodactyl hearts festooned with nails and personal tokens. Patients were clustered throughout the constricted metal passages either dying on makeshift gurneys or leaning against bulkheads, their limbs and faces obscured by leaf fiber bandages. Bioluminescent algae tubes glowed at intervals, throwing out a cool green light illuminating a warren of physical catastrophe. The sounds of chanting and jungle drumming were everywhere roving through the metallic corridors, creating dissonance. The nurses were all clad in ritualistic dinosaur leather aprons and strap swatches, their faces obscured by suffocating masks from which gurgling tubes overflowed. Their disturbing appearance seemed at odds with their role as nurses. Tanks on their backs fed gas and fluid to their faces via the pipes while they limped painfully through the darkness on poised metal-foot braces. These rickety spring-loaded contraptions, which kept the nurses perpetually en pointe, mimicked the legs of large cassowary-like river birds, lending each a sinister swagger. Some pushed wheelbarrows of stained home-welded medical equipment through dripping holds while others engaged in various ceremonial activities with the more seriously injured patients. Glitchy holograms of beaked dinosaurs roamed the halls around them, eliciting waves of adulation and chanting from afflicted worshippers lighting up the corridors. The metallic ringing wails of the wounded penetrated deeply into Taty, causing her to grit her teeth and clap her palms over her ears. She stumbled through this Hadean madhouse on a sort of autopilot, terrified at the prospect of being separated from the others. The small caravan clattered down iron stairwells and along unilluminated shafts until a dismal reception booth eventually loomed out of the darkness. It was a flame-licked niche swathed in flower garlands and carvings of jungle spirits. A nurse was stationed within, locked into a face brace and collared cruelly to a post. She was sorting through a pile of severed limbs, her bare arms spotted with blood and biological secretions. A drip was attached to her inner thigh, slowly feeding phosphorescent-green fluid into her veins. She smiled sweetly enough when she saw Number Nun, though.

"Haven't seen you down in the soup for a while," she giggled through stainless-steel facial clasps.

"Where's Big Daddy, Sabrina? I have a waitress with some sort of alien internal parasite."

"Fucking symbiotes," the nurse spat left and right. "Nothing but symbiotes for the last few days. Daddy told us Mister Sister's introduced some form of interdimensional contagion into the city."

She peered at Cherry Cola, her face distorted by the punishing brace.

"Has it taken her over, yet?" she inquired in a clinical manner.

"Still crawling up inside the lower spine, eating out pain arrays, virtually undetectable."

"Yeah, Big Daddy will wanna see her. We've only been getting vickie-victims in the late stages, so this could help. Take Cinderella down to the wait pit, and I'll get the panther on the horn."

The wait pit was a long mess room that had been converted into a waiting area. Taty and Number Nun sat on uncomfortable makeshift wooden benches for some time with Cherry Cola lying across their laps. The twins had drifted back to the deck somewhere along the way. All around the wait pit, blue men in heavily beaded capes restrained hunch-ridden symbiote sufferers in various stages of transformation. Their pitiful sounds were almost unendurable, and fluid covered the floor, seeping through grilles into the gutters.

"So, what's up with the nurses?" Taty asked Number Nun, her nose pinched firmly shut. "Why they got up all pony style?"

"Daddy Bast enslaves and breaks those who seek to study under him. It's part of his priestly duties," Number Nun recited in a somewhat rehearsed fashion. "If they are subservient enough, he slowly transforms their bodies and bequeaths powers to them, so that they may help him in his work."

"What a creep," Taty muttered.

"Oh, he's not like that at all," Number Nun replied quietly.

A blue-skinned nurse in lace-up stilettos and restrictive body strapping approached them through the blood and broken bodies. Clutched in her hand was the head of a flamingo, its serpentine neck twined about her bony arm like a fat rope.

"Big Daddy will grace you now," she rasped in a husky jungle twang, anointing each of their foreheads with a smear of bird blood.

The "operating theater" was sealed with a large circular hatch in the floor. A metal ladder descended into the bowels of the vessel, and the nurse and Number Nun preceded Taty down into the gloom. Cherry Cola was lowered in on a gurney through a separate trapdoor. The chamber had originally been a storage area for liquid cargo, and the interior walls lay smooth between tracks of heavy bolting. It was very dark within, and tiny lamps guttered sporadically. The floor was littered with human organs, and the stench was intense. Shark-sized tadpoles hung upside down from the ceiling suspended from meat hooks embedded in their whiplash tails. Some of these beasts had been slit open, and their whitish entrails butterflied down to the metal surfaces in intricate arrays. A butcher's block took center stage, illuminated by infrared bulbs. They could see Cherry Cola cranking down like a radioactive angel alighting neatly on this chopping block. The chains holding her gurney released and then slithered back up into darkness. The light caught like quicksilver in the eyes of an enormous cat, an apparition that lurked beside the table, observing them as they descended. Taty was almost too frightened to carry on once she had seen the creature, but Number Nun reassured her with a touch of her hand. Together, they approached the pool of red light, slipping and sliding in long puddles of coagulating blood. As they drew nearer, the panther seemed to rise on its hind legs, attaining the height of a tall man. Large eyes glistened and glinted lamp yellow above a semi-humanoid face. The cat priest was smiling, long whiskers draped like an elegant moustache, the light absorbing into his sleek black fur. He drew on a heavy velvet cape, swaddling his body in its regal folds. The blue nurse with the flamingo head preceded them, kneeling in supplication before the cat priest, her forehead pressed into the cold blood at his feet. They watched as he withdrew a leash, attaching it to the slim collar around her throat. He pulled the leash gruffly, and she jerked up to her knees, remaining at his side like a docile pet.

"It's been forever since I've seen you in the confessional booth," Number Nun said in an almost friendly fashion, her face and hands glowing like ice in the darkness.

"You are such a charming appliance," the cat smiled back. "Even brought us a baby symbiote to play with—come up to the dining table and watch Daddy get his hands dirty."

They clustered around the chopping block where Cherry Cola lay on her stomach. The girl was shaking with fright, her skin lathered over in a creamy layer of sweat. Daddy Bast leaned his heavy triangular head over her and sniffed deeply several times. The muscles in his thick neck rippled as he moved, and Taty could easily discern the glint of ivory teeth protruding from between cleft lips.

"Can you smell it?" Number Nun asked quietly.

The cat priest glanced up and winked unnervingly.

"Yes," he purred. "Nurse, anesthetize her."

The nurse suddenly lurched up, baring tiny needle-like fangs, which she sank into Cherry Cola's thigh. Cherry Cola screamed, spasmed, and then lay still. Taty let out a sharp yell and rushed reflexively to her friend's aid, only to be firmly restrained by Number Nun. The nurse withdrew her fangs, licked venom from the wound, and then sank back to her bruised knees. Taty observed as she then reached beneath the butcher's block to fetch a rope-bound bottle for the cat. Number Nun, meanwhile, had leaned over and was unbuttoning Cherry Cola's uniform, slowly baring her slick back and defiled cotton panties. A tattoo of crossed cola bottles beneath a heart-shaped red cherry adorned her lower hips, creating an amusing parody of the classic skull and crossbones. Daddy Bast uncorked the bottle, releasing a cloud of noxious green fumes. He took a mouthful, gargled deeply, and then spewed it all over Cherry Cola's exposed back. Taty grimaced in disgust, hiding behind Number Nun as the cat man began to undergo some form of suppressed fit, his large yellow eyeballs rolling back to show their intricately veined undersides. His heavy paws sank down onto the skin above the tattoo, their fur becoming instantly matted by the fluid. Claws retracted and elongated in syncopation with his deep bass purring. He began kneading and massaging her flesh in heavy languid strokes, growling pleasurably. At one point his clawed fingers seemed to slide and fold bloodlessly into her wet skin. They trawled around the tattoo, sinking deeper into her body. He began to probe around her insides, hissing and spitting to himself like an old radio. After a moment he froze, almost as though his claws had snagged on something. Taty became rigid with discomfort, imagining one of those barbed claws tagging on tender muscles or some vulnerable organ. The cat tensed and gradually began to pull the symbiote out of the tattoo. The little green monstrosity arose cleanly through the skin, emerging from the red cherry and crossed cola bottles like some cheap special effect. It was hissing and spitting from its tiny malformed Cherry Cola face, throwing up lewd finger gestures and scuttling helplessly in the claw grip of Daddy Bast. Cherry Cola was raised up from the hips as the thing attempted to hold onto her spine with its twisted feet. But then, with a final yank, it was extricated and thrust into a large jam jar. Cherry Cola fell back, her skin miraculously unbroken. A palpable sensation of physical relief seemed to breathe off her prone body, and this instantly reassured Taty. She gazed up in awe as Daddy Bast raised the jam jar into the light. He shook it around playfully, grinning at the mandibled homunculus with a mouthful of tusk-like teeth. Number Nun also began to examine the imprisoned creature, flicking her eye modes to and fro as she performed various forms of visual analysis.

"What is it exactly?" she asked the cat priest.

"Some sort of thing no doubt," he answered flippantly.

"They say these parasites are transmitted through inter-dimensional intercourse," Number Nun said. "Spread from a single source; some anomaly Dr. Dali brought through from beyond."

"That was the situation about three days ago, yes," he replied, placing the jam jar on the butcher's block.

"What do you mean?"

"After three days the host begins to change. The original

personality is absorbed and replaced with that of a foreign hivemind. The physical body begins to alter to match the makeup of the symbiote, and we are left with a grotesque personalized mutant—a caricature of the former self imbued with an alien consciousness. At the end of the third day, the host is transformed entirely into a large version of this thing here. These newly formed hybrids can reproduce in the same manner as the original symbiote."

"Can anything stop the transformation?"

"Large doses of carrot juice halt the process for an indefinite period of time, triggering chemical imbalances in the brain. Transformation is inevitable, though."

"You mean ..."

"Yes. Dr. Dali, in his infinite capacity for perverse annihilation, has succeeded in raping the future. A now unstoppable epidemic blossoms among the sodomites and whore folk of Namanga Mori. Soon they will all be green and rubbery monstrosities rubbing themselves up against the barge pole of their former existence. They will cry out for satisfaction from satisfaction itself until all the slum regions and luxury villas are eaten alive and stripped of their populace by these appetite-sick deviants. Until we are all drowning in the filth of another world."

The cat priest let loose a stream of slippery, coughing chuckles before skulking back onto all fours and padding into the far shadows of the echoing chamber. The velvet cape trawled off, soaking into the ooze that guttered all around. The nurse followed in the manner of an obedient child, crawling on all fours, her abandoned leash trailing behind her like a broken tail. Number Nun buttoned up Cherry Cola and hoisted her over a shoulder.

"Let's get back to the Shell Sea," she said decisively. "We need to find Romeo the Dealer and then head back into the jungle."

16
Robot-on-Robot Action

KENZO COLD-EYES WAS LISTENING to freshly transmitted Coco Carbomb remix tapes on his sunglasses' wireless, running a cable down to the car's speaker system while watching the blue men huddled around the fire. They had stripped the massive fish down to its bones and were now throwing scraps of its head to the laughing hyenas. There was a spot of blood on one of his pristine white leather loafers, and he wondered where it had come from. He was about to remove it when, without warning, the men seemed to freeze, pricking their ears in accord. One of them doused the fire with a bucket. As the light went out, Kenzo Cold-Eyes noticed distant glimmerings at the entrance to the pier. The hyenas became excited, sensing danger. They began frothing in the darkness, tugging at their chains. The men fanned out silently, their beads and machetes glinting in the moonlight. Long black horns began to exude stickily from their foreheads as they went into some kind of danger mode. Kenzo Cold-Eyes killed the tape, fumbling for the telescopic night goggles that the Pink Samurai had accidentally left behind. He found the apparatus and quickly buckled it over his sunglasses (which he never removed). He pulled his white cowboy hat low and focused in. He sighted a line of backlit Buddhist Punks advancing up the pier like gunslingers, swords drawn. Behind this unbroken advance he could make out a raised gaudy palanquin festooned with colorful paper lanterns. Mister Sister reclined on the many cushions of the palanquin, absently playing with several severed heads. Kenzo Cold-Eyes zoomed in closer to discover that one of the heads belonged to Typhoid Mary.

"Oh, my dog ..." he flustered.

The detective disembarked quickly, ray gun in hand, goggles glinting, skirting round to crouch behind the trunk of his cruiser. He extracted his walkie-talkie and held it close to his face, radioing in to the ship.

θθθ

NUMBER NUN BORE THE UNCONSCIOUS Cherry Cola along a passage while Taty trailed behind now vaguely fascinated by the goings-on in the surgery ship. The Sugar Twins brought up the rear, having reappeared out of nowhere. They were close to the upper deck when they heard the voice of Kenzo Cold-Eyes crackling from deep within the folds of the nun's cassock. The android immediately set Cherry Cola down upon the flower garlands of a nearby wooden altar, rifling around for the communications device.

"What's the matter?" she answered.

"Big Buddha!" came the garbled transmission. "Head of Mary lap luster! Off cuts! For real!"

"Jump off the end of the pier," Number Nun told him after a microsecond of deliberation. "I'm on my way up."

Kenzo Cold-Eyes squinted at the approaching mob. He calculated his chances before fleeing toward the distant end of the pier, his grey trench coat flapping comically behind him as he clutched on to his hat. Number Nun slid the walkie-talkie past sensors in her head until a tiny light flashed green. She then took Taty's hand and knelt down to face her.

"Listen to me now, Childbride," she told her seriously. "I have scanned this walkie-talkie's frequency, so that you will be able to communicate with me via my internal communications array. I want you to keep it, wait here, and listen for my holy instruction."

Taty began to protest, but Number Nun quieted her with a wave of her hand.

"OK, fine," Taty sulked.

Number Nun nodded briskly before marching up a nearby flight of stairs. She activated her internal voice system and called Kenzo Cold-Eyes.

"Are you wet, yet?" she mind-asked without moving her lips.

Kenzo Cold-Eyes stood before broken rails, poised gingerly above the end of the pier. Rotting timbers formed a sheer drop of several meters down to a boiling crash of greasy waves wherein milkshaked a myriad of fish skeletons, trash, and broken tires.

"My eyes may like the cold, but my trench coat doesn't," he replied, in a rare display of eloquence.

"I have enough little girls to look after," she snipped. "Jump and I will come and find you."

The detective cast one last loving look at his distant car before re-holstering his ray gun and withdrawing a pair of red nose plugs. The armed mass was almost at the ship now, and there was clearly no turning back. He plugged his nose and leapt out into space, his flailing form vanishing instantly into the maelstrom.

NUMBER NUN EMERGED ONTO THE upper deck and skirted to the ocean side of the ship. Some nurses and blue men with machetes clustered at the opposite railings facing out onto the pier. There was a buzz in the air, and figures skittered about preparing the ship for some form of attack. Number Nun glimpsed the approaching mob, made some calculations, and then gazed out beyond the far railings. The ship faced into a sullen churn. Spiked buoys drifted among the wreckage of long-beached vessels. Some small rocky islands receded, speckled with malignant hunting birds. She stripped off her cassock, and the light of her unclothed body illuminated the deck around her in a bluish glow. She flipped neatly off the side and entered the swell like a crossbow bolt, lighting up the oily water around her. She swam lithely through the murk, skirting drifting pillars of bone-tangled weed and the jumbled husks of fallen boats and cars. The monolithic architecture of the old pier stretched off into gloomy distances, and so she finned down, catching a ride in the riptides that swept alongside it and out to sea.

"Well, Mister Kenzo Cold-Eyes," she spoke in mind-radio. "Have you drowned, yet?"

Kenzo Cold-Eyes had by now managed to pull himself from the filthy froth. He was clinging to slimy columns of rotten wood like a wharf rat while breakers pounded to and fro. The network of pier supports created a rotten cathedral behind him, funneling wind and spray in erratic lukewarm blasts that kept threatening to dislodge him from his perch. He had somehow managed to hold onto his walkie-talkie and was now yelling into it above the crash of the waters.

"They tell tall tales tadpoles! Doom to swimsters! Chum bait chompers!"

Number Nun weaved in and out of the dark supports, lighting

up the gloom like a phosphorescent bluebottle. She noticed large clouds of dense jelly clustered around the sediment-caked bottoms of some of the supports. Monstrous comma-shaped tadpole creatures spawned in this ooze, flickering like microscopic bacteria among partially digested human skeletons and scuba gear. The jelly was, in fact, a veritable tapioca of lost fishing gear and body parts, denoting the gruesome end for many a drunken sailor. Number Nun changed frequencies.

"Childbride?" she called.

A crackling transmission emitted in her head, followed by Taty's excited voice.

"There are nurses with spearguns!"

"Don't irritate anybody, Childbride. I'm going to kill the Buddha and his men. Soon we'll be back in church."

"I hate going to church."

"You are an atrocious little sinner, Childbride. But my programming compels me to protect and nurture you. Try to make an effort now."

"Jesus can eat my—"

Number Nun disengaged the transmission before any serious blasphemies were committed. In doing so, she noticed a pair of tadpoles swimming sharkishly in her wake. She paused to electrocute them before continuing on to the end of the pier.

THE RANKS OF BUDDHIST PUNKS stopped just before the surgery ship. A line of armed guards flanked the entrance to the gangplank, restraining their hyenas and waiting for the signal to attack. The palanquin was jostled to the front, crawling over the heads of the Punks like an enormous gaudy beetle. Mister Sister leered benevolently from this cushiony platform, his hands bloodied from the heads on his lap. He gazed down, addressing the many horned blue men who protected the ship.

"Oh, my beautiful blue bucks!" he crowed to them. "You cordmuscled remnants of a savage cyan South! I wish you and your Big Daddy no harm. Not that a poor fat deity such as myself could ever ..."

He was cut off by the amplified whisper of Daddy Bast, who had appeared on an upper deck, a microphone stand held delicately before him by a nubile slave. Several leather-bound nurses strained murderously against the leashes he had coiled in his paws, their vampire fangs bared.

"Come now. You are nothing but a perfumed thug!" the cat priest smiled. "A sodomite with galactic leanings and genocidal intent. What could you possibly wish from Daddy Bast? A cure for your foolish infection of reality?"

"Oh, gosh. Never!" Mister Sister chuckled uproariously. "I want to see it all frogged up and fancy-free! I wouldn't dream of interfering with your mumbo-jumbs ... Why, I'll even throw you victims to cut up and probe! I don't want a cure, I just want to see it all turn to slime ..."

"Very noble," Daddy Bast interrupted again. "But you still haven't told me what it is that you want."

"Well ... there is that troublesome Number Nun. I think she means to gut me for castrating her Lord and Master. My spies tell me she is on board?"

NUMBER NUN HAD MEANWHILE ASCENDED into the thrashing breakers at the end of the pier. She rose from the dirty foam like a glowing skittle scanning for the detective among the dismal colonnades of support beams. She located him and knifed through the surge, crab-climbing up slippery concrete to where he clung. The tips of her breasts had unplugged, revealing nipple-shaped mouthpieces through which she could redirect any number of nourishing substances, including air. Devices realigned within her glassy chest cavity, unfurling clear tubing, piping airflow from her internal oxygen supply to bladders contained within her translucent breasts. She peeled Kenzo Cold-Eyes from the slippery timber and pushed his gagging mouth to her scuba nipples before launching back into the heaving surf. She swam along the side of the old pier with the detective clutched to her bosom like an overgrown baby, torrential bubbles whirling away in their spiral slipstream.

"WE ARE ALL RATHER FOND of Number Nun here," Daddy Bast spoke into the microphone, his whispery voice echoing down to the pier from a bank of converted foghorns.

"She performed most benevolent missionary work in the jungle before that imp reprogrammed her dogma drive for carnal interface."

"Oh, come now. Let me squash her!" Mister Sister squealed petulantly. "I won't be able to sleep peacefully until she's rusting in a ditch! I don't want a war with you, Big Daddy, I would hate to exterminate such beautiful bodyguards and rape all your patients ..."

Daddy Bast paused to consider the intolerable tenacity of the faux Buddha and his minions. He summoned a kneeling nurse with a flick of his claw.

"Fetch me Number Nun and her brood."

The nurse licked his hand and scampered down a trapdoor like a hunting spider.

RUSTED "DANGER! KILLER TADPOLES" SIGNS creaked along the trash-strewn beach while racks of barbed wire receded like monstrous tapeworms. Weathered deck chairs were scattered down the strand, occupied by spooky hairless sunbathers. These pale bloated figures only emerged to sunbathe at night. They sprawled out on filthy towels among the flotsam and jetsam of the contaminated shore, blinking at one another like brain-damaged mollusks. A faint glow appeared in the sluggish lap of waves, coagulating slowly into the form of Number Nun. She strode out of the surf, dragging a coughing and spluttering Kenzo Cold-Eyes across the sand. She deposited him unceremoniously on a rickety deck chair and watched as he vomited a large quantity of radioactive seawater.

"I'll be along shortly," she snipped. "And remember, heathen—you now owe your life to the Blessed Virgin."

He waved his arm in irritation as she stalked off across the shoreline. The sunbathers observed their exchange with poached-egg eyes, oblivious to what had just taken place. Like slugs, they seemed to exist in a slower dimension of time, unaware of events that had transpired too quickly. Number Nun flicked her head as she crossed the beach, powering down her internal lighting. She became instantly shadowy and insubstantial in her crystalline nudity, barely visible in the muggy darkness of the beach. Only her eyes gleamed faintly like tiny quicksilver almonds. Cloaked in shadows like this, she padded soundlessly back toward the massive structures of the pier, preparing herself for a violent confrontation.

θθθ

A PAIR OF NURSES HERDED Taty and the Sugar Twins onto the deck at knifepoint. Another dragged the comatose figure of Cherry Cola up a flight of constricted stairs. They presented the four of them to the cat and then sank back to their knees.

"Little one say Number Nun is in the sea," the nurses whispered to Daddy Bast.

"Is that true, my little pup?" The cat smiled toothily down at Taty.

She wordlessly extended the walkie-talkie, and Daddy Bast scooped it up.

NUMBER NUN ENTERED INTO THE maze of crates, which cluttered the dockyards leading up to the pier. She slunk like a glass ghost past rusted cranes and winches along the narrow channels created by closely packed metal containers. A tinny voice came through her head.

"Blessed be the bored, my pretty little appliance," Daddy Bast spoke directly into her electronic radio mind.

Number Nun's face remained lightless, soundless, and expressionless as she answered, more of a mannequin than ever.

"God made every screw in this body," she replied drily. "Even now He watches over your shoulder like a parrot in a pirate movie."

"You've been spending too much time with transsexuals. They have given you bad karma. Now the Buddha wants your diamond ass."

Mister Sister had by now grown thoroughly impatient. He smashed Typhoid Mary's head against the swirled pillars of the palanquin like a sulky child.

"What's going on up there?" he ranted. "I want that toy Nun, or I'll slaughter you all!"

"Did you hear that?" Daddy Bast purred with amusement. "His Worship appears to be throwing some form of tyrannical tantrum!"

"It's a rather strange effect hearing him across the pier and through the walkie-talkie," Number Nun answered snidely. "I can calculate the delay in transmission down to 0.02 seconds—very high-quality piece of equipment."

She moved past a large dumpster and the car-sized hulk of

folded machinery that lay beside it. The open pier stretched out before her, and she crept up to the railing. She was feeling somewhat handicapped by her newly acquired inability to scan for peripheral hardware and resolved to fix the damaged circuitry as soon as she was back at the Nebula Shell Sea. Romeo the Dealer would have the necessary parts, and a quick installation would take very little time.

"I'm not sure I want to sacrifice my ship for an appliance," the cat man confided to her. "Even though our time in the jungle was very special for me."

A tiny red LED lit up in the depths of the car-sized hulk of folded machinery that now lay behind her. The light illuminated a tacky decal for Oriental vanilla milk, which one of the Buddhist Punks had planted upon the battle robot in a fit of childish sentimentality. The folded robot scanned the area before it in a sort of antiquated videogame vision comprised of saturated shadowless shapes. The statuesque form of the nude Number Nun was clearly visible among the boxes and bins painted a pixelated white-blue against the surrounding red-black of inert forms. A cartoonish target blinked on, settling instantly over her and sticking like glue.

"I've never felt less like a jaguar than I did then," Daddy Bast admitted with uncharacteristic sentimentality.

"You are a filthy sinner and in need of spiritual cleansing," Number Nun stated matter-of-factly.

Unbeknown to either of them, Kenzo Cold-Eyes was listening in from the beach, his dripping walkie-talkie clasped to his ear. He shook his wet head, covered the mouthpiece, and turned to one of the sunbathing slug people.

"Robot bitch!" he muttered conversationally, eliciting many drooling noncomprehensive stares.

Mister Sister had meanwhile received a transmission from his camouflaged battle droid. A garble of digital noise erupted quietly from an electronic earring, causing his pudgy face to light up with an almost gastronomic bliss. He raised an ornamental flower, which was, in fact, a communications device, to his lips.

"Do you have the Nun?" he breathed wetly into the petals.

"Target acquired," came the monosyllabic bass-heavy video-game voice.

"It is a shame that you are so rude," Daddy Bast said. "One day you will meet your match."

"Not today," Number Nun replied curtly.

The battle robot suddenly activated without warning. It burst apart with a loud hissing and clanking, unfolding like industrial origami. Floodlights lit up along its front, lighting up Number Nun and her surrounding area in a harsh white glare. She was bathed in vicious machine fire before she even had time to turn. Her arms shattered like glass, and a leg was instantly severed. The rain of metal riddled her face and torso, hurling her against the metal railing. The rate of fire intensified, and she was cut in half. Her head and upper torso spun over the twisted railing and out into the dark waves below, and the firing ceased. A haze of smoke drifted, glowing supernaturally in the vivid floodlights. The giant robot clumped over to where her leg and hips spasmed weakly on the bullet-pocked concrete. It squashed these like bugs, throwing vast pillars of blinding light around when it moved. Down on the pier, Mister Sister was squealing with delight, clapping his fat blood-crusted hands together like a demonic toddler. Taty had, of course, seen the lights suddenly illuminate the pier and ocean in an arc of whiteness. And like everybody else aboard, she had also heard the thunder of the machine guns. She had watched Number Nun being torn apart with a numb fascination of horror, the feeling of being caught in a dream from which she would soon wake. Now, of course, she did wake and began to scream. But her screams died abruptly, cutting short as though someone had pulled her plug. She stood staring out into nothing, paralyzed with shock. Daddy Bast lifted the walkie-talkie to his face again.

"Well, I hate to say I told you so," he smirked.

The ravaged limbless torso of Number Nun had been caught in the riptides and was now being trawled out to sea. A vaguely annoyed expression haunted her cracked face.

"I don't think you hate to say it at all," she replied tartly.

Taty flicked her tear-streaked face up to the cat in a display of tragic helplessness. He eyed her with a little smile and a wink, and she wasn't sure how to react to this at all.

"Religion is the Devil's greatest triumph, my little broken doll," he announced theatrically. "Perhaps you could convert some lobsters while you mull that over. Meanwhile, I bid you adieu."

He handed the walkie-talkie to Taty who began weeping into it, barely able to form sentences, she was so distraught.

"Oh, stop crying, Childbride," Number Nun snapped. "It's so undignified."

"Who's going to take care of me now?" Taty sobbed.

"Life is uncertain, death is sure—sin is the cause, Christ is the cure."

Down on the beach, the eavesdropping Kenzo Cold-Eyes could restrain himself no longer.

"This your kinder comfort to drop on abandoned child, like this?" he protested.

Daddy Bast squatted down, staring into Taty's wet face with his Halloween-orange eyes. She began sobbing again, terrified by the enormous slitted orbs. He extended a paw to her and opened it, palm up. A bright orange pill lay on the hard, calloused pads of his black paw.

"Eat this," he gruffed. "It will lock your spinal corridor and kill any parasites before they get a chance to climb."

"No, please!" she pleaded. "I don't want to get with the monster boy! Please!"

Daddy Bast pressed the pill into her trembling hands and then rose. He drifted toward a hatch, dragging his nurses behind him.

"Throw these kittens to Mister Sister," he muttered over his shoulder. "I have no place for strays on my ship."

Taty began screaming, clutching the walkie-talkie to her breast as she was dragged forcibly down the gangplank. Cherry Cola was also manhandled in the same way, tugged down the ramps like a sack of rice. The Sugar Twins sauntered down ahead, unmolested by the ship's crew. They slunk aboard the palanquin and cuddled up to Mister Sister, who stroked them in triumph, utterly delighted with himself. Taty was hefted onto the gory cushions at his painted feet while Cherry Cola was deposited in a heap beside her. The Punks began to relax and chatter as the confrontational energy dissipated. The lantern-heavy palanquin turned, and they all drifted back toward the darkness of the docks, escorted by the massive killer robot. Down on the beach, Kenzo Cold-Eyes slumped into a deck chair and watched the floodlight pillars play across a galaxy of decrepit crates. He observed the distant caravan of Punks with utter glumness, swigging from a hip flask, which he had the good sense to carry with him at all times.

"Jump a pier to frying pan fire on your command for this?" he spat into the walkie-talkie. "For shame, those poor girls!"

Deep below the heavy waves, Number Nun had begun to glow again. She swirled out to sea like a luminous skittle oblivious to the world above.

"I'm busy praying," she replied testily. "Go away."

With that she cut transmission and submitted entirely to the great surge of water, which would now deliver her to the measureless expanses of the ocean. Kenzo Cold-Eyes slouched fatalistically among the mollusk bathers, too depressed to call Taty for he could certainly offer her no assistance now. He tried not to think of the helpless little girl curled in a fetal ball at the ogre's feet now lost to a world of panic. Taty clutched the walkie-talkie close to her racing heart as the palanquin lurched like a boat, quickly eating the orange pill that the cat priest had bequeathed to her as a parting gift. The future had suddenly died, and she was now trapped inside its unimaginable corpse. She began to cry again and found that she could not stop.

17
Soul Gun

FLAMING CARS ADORNED THE STREETS in an almost decorative fashion. Gangs of looters roamed the wreckage, pecking at things like carrion birds. Party music still thumped from the Dead Duck, and drunken strangers were dancing in the streets. A group of sailors was harassing a grinning symbiote, kicking it out across the road and jeering. The symbiote was still swaddled in the remnants of Buddhist robes and possessed a vaguely human face now disfigured by insectile appendages. Its body was a deep emerald green split by carapace joints and crab-like casing. It smiled stupidly with a mouth full of loose human teeth, its newly formed mandibles flicking out from caved-in cheeks. Romeo the Dealer was approaching from the inner city, eyeing the gang warily. He was talking on his army-issue walkie-talkie, ray gun dangling within easy reach.

"Romeo Delta Tango Foxtrot," he signed, scanning this way and that. "It's out on the midnight wire—Number Nun gunned down at the docks."

"I think you should maybe blow town," Karolina K-Star answered from a safe location.

The sailors had placed a generic red-and-white lifesaver around the symbiote's neck and were dousing it with diesel. He watched coldly as they set it on fire.

"No, I'm going to stick around for a while," he answered.

The symbiote was miraculously unaffected by the flames. Its remaining human parts crisped up like bacon, but the symbiote formations remained, impervious to the heat. The lifesaver warped, and the robes went up in flames. Yawning spaces appeared in its green body as the organic burned away, revealing a spindly inhuman frame fraught with distortions. The would-be lynch mob had gone suddenly silent, backing away as the symbiote turned to face them. It was fondling its ovipositor with a clumsy affection, flaming like a torch. It began to wander about grinning insanely, accidentally setting fire to things. The lynch mob dissolved while the symbiote clattered down a nearby alley lighting up all the walls.

"How could I leave when things are just starting to get interesting?" Romeo said before signing off.

THE LOBBY OF THE SHELL Sea was in a dire state. The clerk hefted an AK-47, listening to an old wireless splutter out panicky news reports about the burgeoning chaos. Stragglers in seersucker suits argued with hobos in the corridors. Some partially developed symbiote sufferers were writhing in the pot plants, kicking over things and spilling abandoned bottles of grog. A fully developed symbiote clung to the ceiling, licking at the light bulb with a long human tongue. Romeo paid very little attention to any of this and went straight up to the thirteenth floor. He kept an apartment beyond the backstage area, and it could only be reached by a secret doorway sequestered in the back of a musty old closet. He pushed past the dusty old stage costumes, cranked open the door, and ascended into a dim space illuminated by giant bay windows. Bright blue-and-yellow neon throbbed rhythmically through the glass, illuminating a ludicrous clutter of equipment. Parrots and toucans chittered in giant wicker cages, creating a constant burble of conversation. The irregular flashes just barely illuminated a coated figure hidden in the shadows. A large pistol gleamed in its trembling malformed hands. Romeo bustled about talking to himself, oblivious to the stranger.

"One ... and then another ... then ..." he muttered, switching on a colored lamp.

The kaleidoscopic light illuminated the half-insect face of Judas trembling in the depth of a movie director's canvas chair. Antennae flickered sickeningly in the half-light, causing Romeo to stop in his tracks.

"Fuck me, Mary," Romeo whispered, shocked by Judas's transmutation.

The scrap metal had been stripped from him, and he was dressed in a shabby raincoat and a pair of striped pyjama pants. Metal bracing lined his legs, but it was obvious that his transformation into an alien being had somehow restored his ability to walk. He smiled sheepishly at Romeo.

"Out selling pleasure to little boys in spike heels?" he giggled,

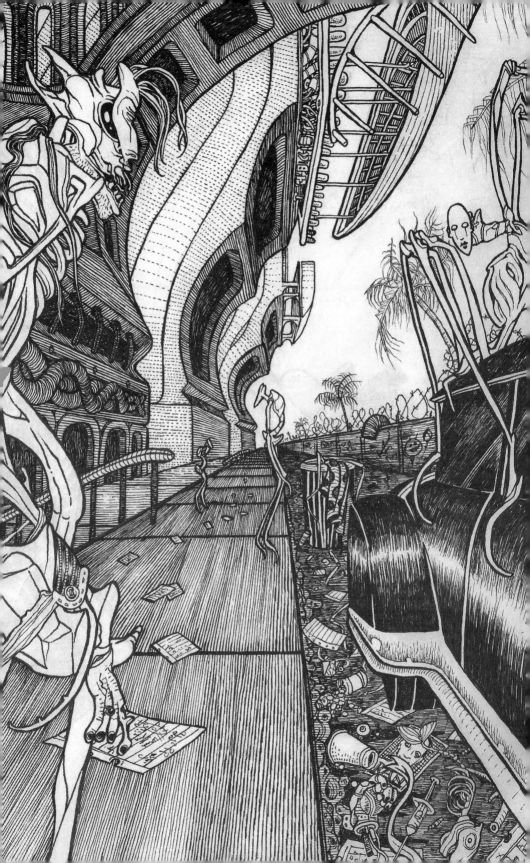

leveling the oversized blaster at the Dealer.

Judas slouched, squirming slightly with discomfort. His broken skin was greenish and frog-like in its slickness. He was also lathered in sweat, a perspiration that caught and clotted in the many fine facets of his newly forming carapace. His goatee still remained, though, stained a hideous orange from excessive carrot consumption. Romeo could just make out his eyes, which had turned the shiny black of an insect's.

"Where's my money, Judas?" Romeo asked, leaning against a bank of hardware.

"Ah!" Judas smiled, displaying a set of emerging mandibles. "As you may have noticed, I hold in my hand a pistol."

"Really? I thought it was a cigarette lighter."

"Oh, it is no ordinary gun, I can assure you," Judas slurped. "It is a Soul Gun, and it fires cloud bullets—etheric projectiles which injure not the body but the sno-globe. Why, even after the body is gone, the cloud bullets ensure that the soul is damaged for a good many incarnations."

"Quite," Romeo smoked, unimpressed.

"It's fascinating, really," Judas mused, trailing off for a moment. "You know ... my *predicament*," he hinted lasciviously.

"I thought that I had achieved some sort of sexual nirvana— which, of course, I had! Endless heaven ... Oh, how I longed for some human pain after the first day."

He paused for a moment, scratching at the base of one of his flickering antennae. A piece of his scalp slipped off. He looked at it with disgust, brushing it beneath a chair with his foot before rambling on.

"When the pain came, though ... Ah, even the pain was joy. Tears spilled in utter and absolute pleasure. All above were the stars, each one an angel with a permanent erection. The night was a slavering cunt—wide open, cold, and quivering. Each tear was drool ... Sexsweat Sundays ..."

He seemed to trail off again, not quite sure of himself, lost in the thrill of confession. Romeo observed his degenerative state with icy interest.

"Now, of course, it becomes the antithesis. An agony. It wrenches apart my collarbones. It rearranges my ribcage. I look in the mirror and see it sliding barbed wire tongues into my mouth. This was my first experience of pain! Why, even as I speak to you now, I am shaking with ecstasy."

Judas seemed to gather himself together, holding up the shiny gun with renewed vigor.

"Need I say more?" he smiled. "Now, give me a fucking carrot before I ventilate your soul."

Romeo the Dealer stubbed out the black cigarette and folded his arms.

"I'm sorry, Judas, but you should have done your homework. I'm a Canaanite, one of the last of the Painbreed. I don't have a soul, so that hair dryer is useless."

There was a long awkward silence before Judas slumped down, panting wetly. Everybody knew that Romeo never lied. The Soul Gun sank uselessly.

"Typical," Judas muttered with an all-consuming bitterness.

"Really, you should have come to me as a friend," the Dealer smirked. "I could give you a couple of carrots, but tell me, will it really make a difference to your 'predicament?'"

"Yes."

"Junkie mentality."

With incredible swiftness Romeo snagged a carrot from a shelf and tossed it to the wooden floorboards. Judas lost all composure in a heartbeat, descending upon the root vegetable with an almost predatory savagery. He devoured it in seconds, and Romeo the Dealer watched as the green in Judas's shelled skin paled and flickered momentarily toward a flesh tone of sorts. A moment of human clarity descended upon him, and he seemed suddenly to realize the depth of his affliction as though for the first time. Romeo watched him with detached interest, lighting up another black cigarette. They exchanged a glance in which Judas conceded that Romeo had made his point. He began to drag himself painfully off the floor and back into the chair. By the time he was seated, he was green again.

"You guys are finished, you know," Romeo announced blithely. "Too revolutionary, always wanting to corner the market."

He cracked a can of cola and took a swig, flopping into a nearby dentist's chair.

"Take me," he bantered on. "Supply and demand. It's best. Besides, the Soft House has had enough of this extraterrestrial vice shit. They've assigned a special project to you from the military strike force outside the Zone. His name is Bronski Glass."

"We'll just ... bribe him, I guess?"

"Sorry. No pleasure center. He's had his brain amputated."

"Amputated? Does he like Mozart?"

"It's like a bad joke," Romeo swigged. "No, wait ... it is a bad joke," he added with deadpan alacrity.

"He's also been working with a mole, slowly scoping out the imp's weaknesses."

"What?" Judas exclaimed. "Who sold us out?"

"Michelle, of course," Romeo smoked. "I think it was even her idea to approach Mister Sister and sticky tape some sort of alliance between the Buddha and Bronski Glass. Why, I'm pretty sure it was her who even gave them the bright idea of offering frogfuck freebies to you boys to get you all roped and soaped."

"If that wench wasn't already crucified!" Judas gritted. "Maybe she really is God's daughter ... Traitor, runs in the family, I suppose ..."

"Mister Sister may be unaware of the extent of her dealings with Bronski Glass. I think she is going to play the Big Buddha the same way. Might be some leverage if you're looking to get square for the greenies."

Judas sighed phlegmatically and stared out at the neon. Membranes licked over his oversized eyes, catching in the pellucid light.

"Getting square isn't going to change the fact that I'm completely frogged up," he admitted miserably.

Something like a smile twisted his stained goatee.

"I suppose you have to admire Michelle's gall bladder," he sniggered. "She's the little crucifixion that could."

"So, what will you do?" Romeo asked.

"I'm running out of track," Judas flumped. "I stockpiled enough carrots to get myself here and threaten someone. Look how that all worked out. Maybe I'll head down to the beach, work on my moon tan. What else is there?"

"Not much, I suppose."

"Oh, well."

Judas raised the Soul Gun to the side of his head and smiled blackly.

"Pow," he said, pulling the trigger.

PART II

The Land of Strangers

18
Dreaming of Icebergs

BRONSKI GLASS SAT IN AN office on one of the upper floors of the Soft House. Late afternoon sun refracted through the structure, bathing him in a sugary green light. The sound of aerobics programs filtered through the plastic walls, their beats clashing with the loud bossa nova transmissions. The office next door to Bronski's was filled to capacity with seawater. Saline environments of varying size and function existed within the wrestlers' castles, all hermetically sealed to localize the water and maintain any wildlife contained therein. Nobody really talked about these areas as they were said to play an obscure role in some of the top-level wrestler games. A trapped man-o'-war wafted about this particular chamber, electrocuting goldfish. In other offices upper-echelon wrestlers performed menial bureaucratic duties at their desks. A desk, chairs, and three brimming filing cabinets bounced around—the higher you got, the more unstable the jumping castle became. Towers would billow around with the wind, and their chambers were always quaking. Bronski Glass wore a pale suit and tie. His skin was almost exactly the same hue as his bloodless suit and gave him a peculiar monochromatic quality. Scar tissue rubbled his forehead in a nougat of reconfigured skin—a clear indication of drastic, possibly experimental, surgery. He had super soldier written all over him despite the whole lounge lizard Frankenstein look. Bitter fruit of a hundred cabals, fate had now found the genetically augmented commando dispatched to the jungle on unsavory and certainly clandestine business. A dog tag read his name, and he was smoking four cigarettes at once. The crucified Michelle was kneeling between his legs, performing fellatio, her wooden cross bobbing comically about as she moved. The top of it occasionally smacked against his face, but he remained unfazed by the blows. Her oral efforts seemed to impress him even less, and he stared absently at the jellyfish in the room next door, waiting for her to finish. The fact that the walls were transparent and everyone could see in also didn't seem to bother him. His eyes had that war veteran glint to them that distinguished those who had seen too much and thought too little. He was now seeing icebergs floating on a dark sea. The masses of glacial ice trembled in the grainy black-and-white film, drifting like leviathans across icy Northern waves. Michelle looked up in irritation.

"Where the fuck is your mind?" she snapped.

"I have a movie projector in my skull," he answered in a voice utterly devoid of feeling. "It's a very small one."

She stared at him in non-comprehension, squinting in annoyance.

"The only reel it has loaded contains footage of icebergs, and this is constantly projected onto the back of my eyeballs. It's supposed to 'nullify' me."

"Jesus, what a drag."

"Are you finished down there?"

"Bronski, baby, do you have any idea what Mister Sister will do to my bod if he finds out that I'm snitching for you and blowing you into the bargain?"

"But I didn't ask for blowjobs. Only information."

"But I'm putting myself in harm's way for you! Don't you realize that?"

"No."

"I was going to ask if you have a brain, only to realize that you most certainly do not!"

She returned to her task with renewed determination, bobbing up and down like a jack-in-the-box, the top of the cross narrowly missing his nose. Bronski Glass's eyes slowly became unfocused, and the muted sound of a film projector could be heard leaking out of his ears. Icebergs flickered across black water, turning in the swell like mountains of polystyrene. He took the four cigarettes from his thin-lipped mouth and exhaled a great flag of patriotic smoke.

"You reported that Mister Sister has taken up residence in the house of Alphonse Guava?"

Michelle began to speak between mouthfuls, babbling with excitement at all her great and secret plans.

"Oh, it's just for a little while. Mister Sister wants to rub Al's face in it. Jesus, you should see Alphonse! Sister's keeping him from greening out by supplying him with carrots, but it's just a matter of time now. When Alphonse is frogged up something supreme, Mister Sister will start getting the 'noids thinking that everyone is plotting against him; it's totally inevitable. We'll wait till he's ripe to pop and then instigate some shit between his outfit and Daddy Bast, sit back, and watch the fireworks! Oh, baby! We are in command! Now that the fucking Nun is lost at sea, nothing can stop us. Fuck, I wish I could have seen her getting munched by that droid!"

"Who is Daddy Bast again?"

Michelle whipped her head up, speechless for a moment.

"Oh God, my Dad above!" she exploded. "You literal numbskull! How many times? I'm sick and tired of blowing guys with no brains! Honestly! Men."

He stared blankly down at her.

"Could you tell me when you are finished, please? Bronski really has to use the head."

19
Antidote Girl

THE HOUSE OF ALPHONSE GUAVA was in a disastrous state. No one had cleaned up since the symbiote orgy, and the remains of food and drink had rotted to mulch across all the floors. Most of the bodies had been dragged out and dumped in the trees. Their stench was a constant backdrop to the atmosphere of dismal chaos that now prevailed. Symbiotes squatted everywhere in advanced forms of transformation. They looked like statues erected at ancient temples with limbs as thin as beaten metal. They swarmed slowly over the walls—gigantic grasshoppers, involved in absurd half-remembered human activities. Most simply stood like sculptures in the sun, soaking up the heat like blotting paper. Mister Sister had had many of the walls spray painted with red and toxic yellow paint. Almost all the lower-floor windows had been destroyed. The lovely atmosphere of the colonial plantation house had been ruined, desecrated. Mister Sister was floating in the pool on an enormous throne-shaped lilo. These days he was almost always grinning in abject satisfaction. His victory over the imp had softened his demeanor, and there were fewer beheadings than his Punks had previously known. He had also gained weight, his hairless body taking on the dimensions of a massive baby. To further augment this perverse image, he had his body rubbed daily with talcum powder and wore a giant diaper into which he would defecate. He took great pleasure in being changed by his slaves and often bawled for no reason. To complicate things, he had himself injected with hormones that eventually caused him to lactate. Milk oozed from his large pink nipples, and he loved to have the Sugar Twins snuggle up to him and suckle on his breasts. They lay beside him on the lilo doing just that, clad in matching Spandex swimsuits that showed off their nubile forms to superb effect. They seemed to thrive on his milk and needed no coaxing to partake of it. Their fickle shift of loyalties was no surprise, and Taty could not bring herself to hate them, as much as she tried.

They simply weren't human enough to hate. The battle droid had been parked in the frangipani grove and had not seen any action since that fateful night at the docks. A half-formed Buddhist Punk writhed orgiastically on the pool deck completing the final stages of his symbiote transformation. Taty sat sullenly at the edge of the pool dangling her legs in the blue, staring at the sun-dappled water in a mesmerized fashion. She was in her habitual bikini, big straw hat, and oversized sunglasses. The flowers she wore in her hair were Venus flytraps. They snapped at passing mosquitoes, making tiny popping noises as they opened and closed. The walkie-talkie, which she now kept with her at all times, was clipped to the elastic of her bikini briefs. She had started smoking cigarettes, a habit picked up from some of the less homicidal Buddhist Punks. One dangled listlessly off her lip as she observed a drowning insect with detachment. A machine gun lay beside her within easy reach. She had found it on one of the corpses and accessorized it with glittery stickers and pictures of kittens. Now it never left her side. One of her favorite pastimes was scavenging the estate for ammunition, and she had built up a substantial stock, which she kept well-hidden. Mister Sister was watching her with a lazy smile, his almond eyes screwed up into knife slits against the sunshine.

"Look at her, my little kitties," Mister Sister sang to the Sugar Twins.

"So many symbs and still no hump ... She must be antidote girl!"

He burst into high-pitched, somewhat maniacal giggles, and Taty glared at him. She threw the cigarette into the pool, grabbed her machine gun, and stormed off. She passed through ruined rooms and halls, stopping in the courtyard where she had found Cherry Cola handcuffed all those weeks ago. It was hard thinking of Cherry Cola after what had happened. She could still hear her screaming when they cut her head off. Baby crocodiles frolicked in the water of the fountain, tangling themselves in the large half-dead lotus blossoms. She could hear music in the distance—old Les Baxter records trailing out from Alphonse's high room, a memory of better days. A symbiote lurched over the terra-cotta roofing, dislodging some tiles, which crashed through the shattered skylights. It stopped to leer at her, and she recognized it instantly. The symbiotes were all unique, containing the seed of their host's facial and bodily characteristics. This one she knew and hated. She glared at it until it clambered off like a massive tree frog, disappearing over an antiquated storm gutter. Taty sat down on the edge of the fountain and unclipped the walkie-talkie from her bikini briefs. She switched it on and tuned up with a warble of static.

"Where are you now?" she spoke into it, swinging her legs.

Somewhere in the middle of the ocean, the half-destroyed torso of Number Nun drifted. Sunny tropical blues dappled her. Tiny fish flickered in her chest cavity while monstrous jellyfish the size of houses wafted below, glittering with refracted light.

"My navigational array is broken," Number Nun pointed out, vaguely irritated. "I've told you this before."

Taty fiddled with her nails.

"Oh. Yeah. Forgot 'bout that."

There was a hiss of open-ended static, and she could hear the low-fidelity churn of the sea outside Number Nun's cracked head. "Whatcha doin'?" she asked.

"Childbride, you know very well that I am doing absolutely nothing! Now, leave me alone to pray. Go bother somebody else!"

The call cut off abruptly, and white noise erupted from the speaker. Taty stared at it for a moment before switching it off. She clipped it back to her briefs and gazed listlessly down at the baby crocodiles. After a while she wandered off, humming along to the distant music.

COCO CARBOMB HAD RELEASED A song about the symbiote invasion from some undisclosed location in the Zone. The track was called "Insex" and languidly reflected the unstoppable degeneration of the Outzone's population. Taty found an old reel-to-reel and was able to copy the song to a giant spindle of tape. She stretched the song out as an experiment after she had played it to death—"dragging" it and slowing the song down in high fidelity, creating an epic and virtually incomprehensible nine-hour version. She edited this "remix" with scissors and sticky tree resin one hot afternoon and fed the product back to her Walkman® on playback, completely destroying the reel-to-reel in the process. She would listen to parts of her extended version every afternoon on the massive radar earphones around sunset when it was time to retreat to the bell tower. A whitewashed spiral staircase ran up to the belfry, and small windows had been poked into the walls along its length. These apertures gazed out onto vistas of the steaming jungle, which stretched out beyond the house. Towering palm trees swayed drunkenly against the galactic cheese melt of sunset, and the silhouettes of monkeys gamboled in the highest branches. Taty was a creature of habit, and any form of routine soothed her. So, every afternoon she would scavenge candy bars, green coconuts, and bottles of fizz pop, which she would then carry up to the top of the bell tower. The spiral stairs opened up into an airy space cluttered with junk. She had hidden a folding ladder behind some crates and used it to gain entrance to a trapdoor in the ceiling. This trap led directly into the belfry, a domed chamber that had over the weeks become her lair. She would shoulder her machine gun and take the packets in her teeth while she climbed, pulling the ladder in after her. The large brass bell had long since fallen, cracking the boards. She would painstakingly roll this gigantic device over the trapdoor to ensure her privacy. Each of the four walls of the belfry had a large hole cut out of it. These balcony windows afforded stereoscopic views of the house and jungle. From this elevated perspective Taty could see almost anything coming, and the height gave her a sense of security. A sleeping bag lay crumpled in the corner beside a pile of old fashion magazines and holiday brochures that she had discovered in drawers throughout the house. A bowl of green mangoes lay on the ancient wooden boards. Coconut shells covered the floor, picked clean and filled with bric-a-brac. Candy bar wrappers clustered in one corner, chased around by the hot breezes. A large box of lollipops took pride of place near the sleeping bag, a picnic hamper of ammunition within easy reach.

Taty sat on the whitewashed balustrades of the belfry as she did every evening, bathed in red-gold light, swigging from a bottle of fizz pop. She would sit watching the sun set behind the jungle and observe the large flocks of flamingos and parrots squall, screaming across the Western skies. She was busy doing this one evening when she spotted the symbiote from the rooftop inching slowly up the tower like some monstrous gecko. She hated how it followed her around like it had some claim to her. She unhitched her machine gun and fired a short burst at it, shattering the silence of dusk. The bullets dislodged the creature, and it dropped to the trees below. Michelle, who was poolside almost directly below the opposite side of the bell tower, nearly jumped out of her skin. She turned in exasperation to Mister Sister, who still floated upon his lilo throne attended to by young male slaves.

"What the fuck does she do up there all night?"

"Oh, who gives a kidney what that little cockroach does?" Mister Sister muttered. "Even the symbs won't touch her anymore—little Miss Pariah."

He leaned up off the lilo in a sudden fit of childish rage.

"Pariah!" he bellowed up to the tower. "I should feed you to the crocs! You hear me, you little brat?"

Taty heard but paid no mind, making faces at them when she thought they weren't looking.

THE NIGHTS WERE FULL OF bats swarming past the tower in high-frequency clouds. Giant clumsy moths would also tumble in like origami constructions sucking back out into the darkness before she had time to study their ornate wings. The raftered ceiling of the belfry was awash with golden orb spiders. The creatures had decorated the old bell supports with a fairy lace of webs, giving her something magical to gaze at before she fell asleep. She would light candles in glass jars and watch the flames flicker drowsily in the moist breezes rising off the jungle. Sometimes it would rain for days, and she would snuggle up in a battered fur jacket scrounged from the walk-in closets. The white fur had been in a pristine state when she found it, but after weeks of continuous use, the garment had grown grungy and pelted like the skin of a stray Persian cat. Now it was the hot season, and she was always in her bikini, day or night. It seemed pointless to wear anything else. She sat cross-legged on her sleeping bag, gnawing green mangoes, hideously bored, watching the flytraps in her hair eat mosquitoes. Her mind was a blank, and she would accentuate this blankness by smoking cigarettes, one after the other. She found she liked tobacco, the way it cured her brain like a hock of smoked ham. She missed space-spice but was too paranoid to get stoned. Every now and then, her mind would drift back to the nightmare of what had happened, and she would wake in a shaking sweat, clutching for her machine gun.

There had been weird rituals in which she'd been dosed with drugs and had woken up in the basement covered in alien slime. She told herself that she couldn't remember what had happened, but she could still feel the carapace scraping against her back when she slept. The interlocking shells of the symb had felt like rough glazed ceramic on her skin, its jointed form making creaky bamboo noises when it moved. The sibilant chittering it had emitted now filled her dreams like an ocean of toads, and she could never completely erase the burned electric wire stench of its body. At least now she could say she lost her virginity to an alien, but who was there to impress? The world was one long heat spell of bad memories and scavenged ammunition. The Punks had left her alone after the first rape, waiting for her to change, laughing and teaching her how to smoke cigarettes to ease the pain. Taty had cried a lot then but stopped dead when Cherry Cola was executed for spitting Mister Sister's milk back into his face. Taty remembered getting very sick the day after being raped by the symbiote. A fever descended, and she became delirious, seeing kaleidoscopic visions and glimpsing people's sno-globes against a backdrop of thrashing energy. They put her in a hammock by the pool and made fun of her while she passed in and out of consciousness. At one point she suffered from severe diarrhea and voided herself every few hours in one of the outside bathrooms. After one of these episodes, she found herself feeling inexplicably better. She looked back into the toilet bowl and saw a dead baby symb staring sightlessly up from the soiled water wearing a mockery of her own face. The second time they tied her to a bed and stood watching, grumbling over their cigarettes, making sure the symb impregnated her properly. Another fever descended, though this time not so bad. She was rid of the baby symbiote within a day. The Buddhist Punks didn't touch her after that. They thought she was cursed—or somehow special. They stayed out of her way, and she was not manhandled like the other girls who had the misfortune of finding themselves trapped in the fallen house of the imp. She kept a low profile and was eventually ignored—the silent household pet with a secret. The symbiotes with whom she had spawned began to follow her around. Their behavior was out of keeping with the general mindlessness of the other symbs, and the sight of them disgusted her. When she found the machine gun some of the Punks even gave her ammunition, trying to tempt her into coming out looting with them. But she kept her massive radar headphones on and listened to tapes at full volume, ignoring their calls, keeping out of everyone's way and stealing candy bars whenever she could.

θθθ

THE NIGHTS WERE RARELY QUIET. From her tower she would hear the screams and pistol shots. The ruckus of debauched celebration rose up along with the stench of the many bodies, choking the night and making it impossible to sleep. Most nights she would stay up smoking, eating coconuts, and paging mindlessly through fashion magazines while the world went mad around her. Sometimes she would lean on the balustrade facing the house and look out across the courtyards to the lighted bedchamber of Alphonse Guava. She watched him through binoculars moving like a green ghost in his ruined room. The chamber was by now an unholy mess. Shattered aquarium glass and the rotting corpses of reptile pets had destroyed the white shag. A lava lamp threw psychedelic patterns on the walls, illuminating the destruction and decay in twisting enchantments of light. Alphonse himself stood at his desk, gaunt and withered, bent and broken. His skin was a minty shade of green, and he had been fighting off transformation for a long time. Yet, even with his impish constitution, the battle for preservation had taken its toll. Antennae drooped over his blackening eyes, and his pale hair was a lank and tangled mess. He wore a soiled suit and operated a juicer with slow movements. He was dicing carrots and placing them into the mixer flask. When it was full to capacity, he juiced the roots to a frothy orange gunk and withdrew a massive syringe. Taty watched as he filled the syringe with freshly squeezed carrot juice and tied a silk tie around his arm. He injected the contents of the syringe into his veins and shuddered horribly, grabbing at the desk. His skin flickered like a cuttlefish shifting from green to orange to ivory. It settled on this pale tint for a few moments before gradually washing back to green again. He would always sit on the edge of the bed after one of these episodes, exuding an air of terrible defeat. It was a painful thing to watch, and Taty would often set down her binoculars at this point, anesthetizing herself with an endless chain of cigarettes.

IT WAS VERY LATE, AND the peculiar stillness of the night hung about the jungle. A few candles still guttered in the belfry, creating swarms of contorted shadows. Taty was curled in her sleeping bag, staring out at the stars. At some point she lifted her walkie-talkie to her lips.

"Hello?" she whispered.

She waited awhile, listening to the sea of crackling static and the monumental quietness of the jungle.

"Come in, Number Nun ..."

She eventually gave up and fell asleep. She woke in the night as she often did, holding the communications device to her breast and speaking in her sleep.

"Mommy ... Mommy ..."

THE WEEKS SEEMED TO RUN into each other like melted sugar, crystallizing indecipherably. She quickly lost all sense of time. One day she was sitting in the cinema watching old cartoons and eating leftover scraps of jungle chicken. She was still wearing the puffy fur jacket and bikini, machine gun across her lap, walkie-talkie jutting from a pocket. Despite the deafening volume of the maniacal cartoons, she had on her enormous headphones and was frying her brain with "dragged" versions of her favorite songs. The cinema was also a wreck with seats uprooted and broken champagne bottles laying smashed everywhere. A huge boa constrictor had slithered in from the jungle and was exploring the projectionist's booth. Michelle suddenly appeared in the doorway. She stared down at Taty for a moment, calculating things in her head.

"Hey, little girl," she called, receiving no sign that she had been heard.

She called again, louder this time, and Taty turned her head, staring blankly up at Michelle.

"Little girl!"

Taty pulled her headphones down around her neck and waited sullenly for Michelle to let her know what all the fuss was about.

"Yeah, you," Michelle scowled. "Listen, Alphonse told me he wants to see you."

Taty continued to stare without saying anything.

"Now, you little brat! This is still his house, you know."

Taty rose, shouldering her machine gun. She plodded up to the door, kicking debris out of the way.

Taty rose, shouldering her machine gun. She plodded up to the door, kicking debris out of the way.

"Do you have to carry that fucking popgun around with you

everywhere?" Michelle muttered. "Mister Sister and his Punks might find it cute, but I think it's ridiculous the way you shoot at bugs and shit all the time."

"It's mine, I found it."

Taty brushed past her and headed down the hall. Michelle suddenly hesitated as an idea occurred to her. She turned and called out.

"Listen, little girl ..."

Taty glanced over her shoulder to witness Michelle suddenly manifest what she considered to be a friendly "how-to-talk-to-a-child" face.

"Listen, little girl," she smiled, all of a sudden adopting the approach of a dirty old man at a playground. "I have a whole box of candy, really special candy in my room ... And I'll give it all to you if you just tell me what Alphonse says."

Taty simply stared at her.

"Well, what do you say, huh?" Michelle pushed, struggling to maintain her somewhat horrific smile.

"OK," Taty answered flatly.

"Good girl," Michelle beamed, showing teeth that had not seen a brush since her crucifixion. "You just come up to my room after, and I'll be waiting with all that candy, OK?"

Taty continued to stare at her in suspicious non-comprehension. In the end she simply walked off without a word.

"OK! Great!" Michelle called after her, with all the vim and vigor of a high school cheerleader.

ALPHONSE GUAVA SAT AT HIS desk in a ruined white suit and decopattern britches. His skin was a sort of pea green split by the intricate ridges and grooves of a newly developing exoskeleton. His eyes had swelled to bulbous globular proportions and were now filmed over with silvery cataracts. Feathery antennae sprouted from his forehead like peacock feathers, and these fluttered about of their own accord caressing and exploring peripheral objects lightly. His pointed ears had finally fallen off, leaving disturbing spiral holes in their wake. The desk at which he sat was a mess of hastily scribbled notes and carrot stubs. The well-worn juicer was close at hand while orange-stained syringes overflowed from a massive black garbage bin. They spilled over into the smashed ruin of his precious "PERM BANK," which had long since been gutted of its carefully collected contents. Mister Sister had raided it using the pearly exudate contained within the many glass capsules to butter expensive croissants which he had delivered every day from a baker in Namanga Mori. Upon Alphonse's bed was piled a mountain of carrots. He didn't sleep anymore anyway and had no use for the circular bed. He had thrown the reptile corpses out of the window in order to make the room semi-presentable for visitors, but the stains remained, irreparable and dark, lacing the fresh juice smells of the chamber with an underlying stench of Mesozoic morbidity. He held before him a small card of paper and pivoted a geometry compass between thumb and forefinger, using the needle to print something across the card in Braille. He had to write in reverse, and it took him several minutes to complete even though it was only one word. When he was finished, he placed the card inside a small suede handbag within which could be glimpsed neatly folded papers, a brick of cash, and a pink cassette tape in a box. It wasn't long before his private doorbell rang, announcing Taty's arrival. He pressed a small glass button and watched the heavy doors open. She stood at the threshold, and for a moment they simply regarded each other in silence. When last they had exchanged words, the symbiotes had not even existed. Now they were trapped in another reality, a new dimension, that had been corrupted entirely by the insinuations of another world. She entered barefoot, glancing at the carrots, avoiding shards of glass.

"That's one, big salad," she remarked, leaning her machine gun against a battered filtration unit.

Alphonse smiled broadly despite his wretched state.

"If I take my time, it'll last me to the weekend," he quipped.

She sidestepped the rotting tail of an iguana, which Alphonse had somehow managed to overlook, and slouched on the edge of the bed, spilling a small avalanche of carrots down onto the shag.

"What's up, Doc?"

She met his gaze, unabashed, and he eventually stood up, hobbling over to the window where he leaned on the sill and lit a slim white cigarette.

"You can't stay here anymore, Cupcake," he announced.

She stared at him, nullified by this unexpected rejection.

"I'm OK," she mumbled after a few moments of pregnant silence.

He blew out a thin cloud and gazed down at the wreckage of his house, still smiling like an injured jester.

"It's going all the way down, baby blue. You need to scram before something comes along and eats you up."

"I tried to run away a few weeks ago, but they stopped me."

"Don't worry, I'll help you to get out," he nodded confidentially. "Anyway, I want you to do something for me."

He was perhaps expecting rebellion, but she answered without hesitation, clear-eyed and sincere.

"OK."

"I'm going to give you a card," he explained carefully. "I want you to take this card to the Outer Necropolis and deliver it to a secret postbox within the Floating Pyramids."

"You want me to be a postman?"

"Yes, exactly that."

There was a pause, and he examined her face, uncertain of her answer.

"OK," she answered quietly. "Is that it?"

He regarded her with a sardonic smile, unable to help himself from picking at her passivity much as one would pick at a scab.

"You seem angry with me," he teased.

She looked away, hunched like a bedraggled squirrel in her mangy fur.

"You let the monsters do things to me," she eventually spoke up. "Was it fun?"

She blinked at him, unable to understand his reaction for a moment.

"No, it was horrible," she murmured darkly. "You let Number Nun get shot. Everybody is dead because of you."

He sniggered without the slightest hint of reproach—and it was at times like this that she could see his inhumanity outlined in a sharp and unforgiving clarity.

"I suppose," he admitted. "But at least I had a ball doing it."

"Look at you! You're turning green! You have bug lashes!"

"Yes, I'm en route to a slimy alien hell. I'm trapped in this decaying body, imprisoned in my own house by my own worst enemy, forced to degrade myself daily with root vegetables. But ... my God, you have no idea how pleasurable it all is! Even my worst nightmare is absolute unquantifiable ecstasy. You just can't understand. You're only a little stray."

"I suppose."

He hobbled back to the desk and tossed her the lavender-colored suede handbag. She caught it clumsily, spilling more carrots.

"There's a secret tunnel that will get you off the grounds," he told her. "Everything you need to know is on the pink cassette. Leave maybe an hour or so before dawn."

"OK."

"And put some clothes on; you won't be coming back."

He turned dismissively, busying himself with papers on his desk. She rose, lugged up her machine gun, and hesitated for a moment beside the door.

"You really don't care about me, do you?" she asked quietly. "You're just saving me, so I can deliver your letter."

He burst into raucous chuckles, swinging madly in his chair.

"Why on earth should I care about you?" he laughed gaily.

She lingered on hopelessly for a moment before finally giving up and drifting back down the hall. His eerie laughter followed her through the passages, poking in at her through open windows.

MICHELLE WAS WAITING FOR HER in one of the courtyards. She loped after Taty, struggling to balance under the weight of her cross.

"Little girl!" she called.

Taty took one look at her and scampered down the nearest corridor. Michelle followed in pursuit, her cross bouncing absurdly.

"Come back here! Come back, you little bitch!"

Taty turned and sprayed machine gun fire along the walls and ceiling, scaring a pair of toucans, which flew screaming down the passages. Michelle dived for cover, landing badly, unable to use her arms. She wriggled on the tiles like a clubbed seal, thrashing about in a cluster of pot plants.

"Traitor!" she screeched, her round face red and distorted with rage. "Traitorous little skag! I'll have your head, you little cunt! You just wait till my boyfriend hears about this! I'll kill you! I'll kill you! I'll fucking kill you!"

The screams receded as Taty fled. She ran and ran and didn't stop running until the big brass bell had been rolled safely over the trap and she could collapse panting onto her sleeping bag.

20
The Lost Quarter

TATY SNUCK BACK INTO THE house before sunset and pilfered the mid-thigh horizontal-pleated black silk dress that she had been eyeing for some time now. It was not the sort of garment you went jungle bashing in, and it clashed amusingly with the lace-up combat boots that she was planning to use for her escape, but she saw this as her last opportunity to take it and was determined to look good when she left the house. She missed all the lush pool parties Alphonse had thrown and the crazy dress-ups she had indulged in. So her closet raid was laced with an unexpected and intense nostalgia for the large strange house, which she knew she would never see again. She had planned to be frugal in the walk-ins but quickly spotted ruffled high-collar satin shirts with asymmetrical quilted sleeves and a pair of pink crocodile skin tights that she simply *had* to have. The shoe racks tormented her, but it was ridiculous to entertain notions of taking Victorian knee-highs, patent pumps, or glass platforms beyond the tree line. She had to settle for a pair of shiny silver plimsolls, strappy black sandals, and a good supply of ballet slippers because they were easy to store. A world was dying and with it, all its treasures. Now, all she could do was watch the ship sink from her lifeboat, packing what she could into the small battered brown suitcase she had discovered in one of the attics. The item was an old belted affair plastered with "FRAGILE" stickers and assorted holiday decals. She liked the sensation of liberation that it gave her and swiped it immediately. She was becoming excited about leaving and wanted to treat the escape like a vacation—a vacation from which she would never return. She even managed to barricade herself into one of the more secluded bathrooms and take a hot shower—a luxury she had not afforded herself in weeks. She was afraid of running into Michelle, who she was sure would have her beheaded. But Michelle seemed to have left the house. She met with little resistance. Lugging the suitcase up the belfry ladder was, in fact, the most challenging episode. She took what ammunition she felt she could carry and stuffed the pockets of her newly acquired fur jacket with candy bars. She put on the dress at midnight, brushed her hair, and paced around until morning, smoking cigarettes and waiting for things to quiet down. She was now feeling enthusiastic about her trip but still avoided looking over to Alphonse's window. She was hurt by what he had said, and her pride kept her from making any private farewells. The sentimentality of the gesture would probably be lost on him anyway, and she would have to deal with his making fun of her. Within the lavender handbag she discovered hand-drawn maps crammed with diagrams, notes on the backs of cocktail napkins, and other absurdly conspiratorial documents. She weighed the pink cassette on her palm, curious as to what lay encoded on its magnetic tape. The "letter," which she had promised to deliver, was, in fact, nothing more than the Braille card, and she wondered what significance it might have to prompt such a vast undertaking. The journey to the Outer Necropolis was a long and hazardous one. Perhaps Alphonse had been lying. Perhaps he did care about her welfare after all and was simply unable to admit it, concocting this ridiculous ploy to get her to safety without losing face. This sort of practical joke was not beneath him. She weighed all these things in her mind, smoking cigarettes in her designer dress, watching the jungle, and biding her time in the hours before dawn.

WHEN IT CAME TIME TO leave, she bade farewell to her nest and climbed down, moving quietly into the plantation before inserting the tape into her Walkman®. She donned her large headphones and listened to the burr and crackle of vintage recording equipment. She could hear the room ambience of Alphonse's chamber as well as the background noises of morning birds, which had been captured so deliciously by the ribbon microphone. When he began to speak, his voice was low, rambling, and confidential. She listened carefully to his fluted ethereal voice and followed the florid instructions he gave to the letter. From the darkness of the gardens, she could glimpse the light of his distant window, and at times she would see his shadow moving like a specter against the glow. It was eerie seeing this faraway image of him and hearing his velvety voice so close to her ears. It was the sort of unnatural disassociation he would have

liked, and she felt an inexplicable pang of sadness to be leaving him there.

"When all the Punks have sunk down into their sick and desolate dreams, I want you to descend from your tower like a princess in a fairy tale [*faint chuckling*]. Go to the stone fountain in the old garden down past the lower terraces where our poor little Typhoid Mary was beheaded."

Taty passed like a ghost through the run-down plantation, entering into the tangled undergrowth of the ancient garden. Here, when she was sure she was alone, she switched on a small handheld flashlight. The hiss and burr of jungle insects had subsided at this time of night, and the air was suffused with a peculiar quietness. The large fountain loomed out of the glare, its stone lip brown with dried blood. It occurred to her that the architecture of the fount was antiquated as though part of another structure entirely.

"The fountain has always been dry and empty," Alphonse said, the sounds of morning framing his voice strangely against the night.

"The jungle people say it was used to collect the blood of sacrificed animals in ancient times. We just used it for garden parties and watched animals rut in it, pouring champagne down its worn spout. Sordid, really ... Anyway, behind the structure are the old storm drains."

Taty stood over the creeper-infested metal grate, a recent addition to a stone pipe which seemed to descend directly down into the rich earth. She shone her flashlight past the bars down into dripping darkness, finding nothing but the slippery walls of the receding pipe.

"Lift the grate and you will find a rung ladder set into the side of the drain. Go all the way down."

Taty paused the tape and raised the heavy grate. Pushing aside heavy curtains of vinery, she discovered a set of metal rungs vanishing down into blackness. She had brought a length of silk rope with her and tied one end of this around the handle of her suitcase. She tied the other end around her right ankle and slowly lowered the heavy case down until the cord went tight. She pulled her machine gun on, balancing precariously with one leg down the hole, hiking her haute couture dress up in a scrunch around her tummy. She was sure the descent would be a disaster as the case was pretty heavy. But after a few rungs she got into the swing of things. The stonework cloistered around her, slowly narrowing into a constrictive flue. This eventually opened out into an immense space filled with watery sounds and the chattering of many bats. She clung to what had now become a ladder suspended in utter darkness, struggling to shine the flashlight around her. She saw that the ladder had emerged from a ceiling of ancient masonry and dropped into pitch dark. Heavy columns stretched downward from the ceiling, but the beam could not radiate far enough for her to see where they led. The reverberations told her that the space was gigantic. She clutched the small rubber flashlight in her teeth, examining the ceiling for a moment; it was carved with strange designs of dancing human skeletons and curious depictions of reptilian beings who stood upright on two legs. There were also simplified motifs of a large temple structure rising into clouds and rays of fire shooting from the sky. She began slowly to lower herself into the enormous gulf, the circle of the beam growing wider and dimmer as she moved away from the ceiling. She saw that the tiny hole from which she had emerged was, in fact, the pupil of a large stone eye. Enormous stone faces raised their countenances in silent screams, looking out from the shadows, scaled with centuries of lime. It took some time to reach the bottom: a square platform of mossy flagstones. There Taty rested for a moment, unfurling her dress and sitting on her suitcase to have a cigarette. She played with the beam of her flashlight in the twists of smoke, discovering an open area of tiny geometric flagstone islands between which gurgled inlets of pure jungle water. Large pale crabs wafted like disembodied hands in the clear liquid, gazing into the light with red-and-gold eyestalks. She could only just make out the semicircular wall of the vast cavern across the many platforms—a carved plane dotted with the yawning holes of archways; openings that appeared to vein deeper into a larger complex of passages and chambers. She untied the rope, grabbed the handle of her suitcase, and picked her way cautiously across the tiny platform islands until she had reached the wall. A clumsy green arrow made of card had been taped to a lintel, pointing out one of the many archways. It seemed obvious that this was the way Alphonse intended her to go. She traversed the passage beyond, un-pausing the tape as she walked.

"The Lost Quarter," Alphonse announced. "Some say it stretches all the way out to the Outer Necropolis. Nobody has made that crossing, though: too many holes, too much wreckage, too many wrong turns. A universe of dead ends. The old stones break and sink deeper in places. They crumble into the God-awful cracks an earthquake must have once made. We used to play golf down there in the good old days. Can't tell you how many balls we lost ..."

Taty emerged into a deserted plaza roofed over with high vaulting. In the beam of her flashlight, she spotted several dejected golf flags receding into gloom, their ends spiked into crudely drilled holes.

"Follow the map I gave you to the eighteenth hole," Alphonse said, prompting her to pause the tape and rummage in the suede handbag. She dug up a sordid excuse for a golf green overview, tattooed in ballpoint on the back of a lipsticked napkin. She used this to navigate in the netherworld, stumbling over fallen pillars and past cracked motifs, lugging the suitcase while attempting to keep her dress from being damaged. It was cold, and she had to put on her fur, pausing beneath a relief depicting intricate pyramids on the moon. It was some time later that she finally came out onto another dark terrace whereupon she espied a filthy yellow flag with the numeral "18" scrawled upon it in what looked like dried blood. She stopped to rest, sinking back down onto her suitcase to dredge out a candy bar and light another cigarette. She played the tape while she smoked, listening to Alphonse's voice in the dark.

"Just behind this hole you will find a wide gallery of steps leading down to the aqueducts. You will find my speedboat tethered to a stone jaguar I like to call Boris ..."

She finished her cigarette, crossed the expanse, and clambered down slippery stone steps until she reached the edge of a wide Stygian canal. Huge snakes slithered out of the light, and crocodiles sank with soft expulsions of bubbles. She staggered around the edge of the canal, shining her flashlight this way and that until the beam alighted on a massive effigy of a snarling cat. Someone had rather tastelessly draped a leopard-print blanket about its shoulders, lending it the appearance of a kitsch souvenir postcard. A long-abandoned picnic hamper lay upended beside it, and empty ginger beer bottles and pâté tins spilled out over the stones. Taty directed the flashlight beam at the water and, sure enough, tethered to one of the massive paws was a sleek wooden speedboat with brass trimmings. She froze as the light caressed the shadowy figure of a tall man. He stood just behind the jaguar, unmoving and grinning insanely in the sallow light. The figure was dark-skinned, yet pale

NIKHIL SINGH

as though drained of blood, clad in a beret, mime tights, and a red-and-white-striped shirt. His paleness was accentuated by a layer of chalky dust that had been rubbed into his skin. When Taty stopped shaking and the man still hadn't moved, she realized that she was in no immediate danger. The figure remained quite still as though awaiting some form of command. She pressed play, and Alphonse cackled lightly in her ear.

"You've probably never driven a speedboat before. But that's, of course, the reason we have zombie chauffeurs. Don't be afraid of old Paw Paw. He only eats crocodile cocks and canned quail eggs ..."

Taty pulled off her headphones and cautiously approached the zombie.

"Paw Paw?" she whispered.

The zombie detached itself from the armpit of the stone beast. It broke cobwebs as it shifted, releasing clouds of dust into the subterranean gloom. He had obviously been stationary for a long time, and when he spoke, moths flew from his mouth.

"Taxi to the Louvre?" he inquired in a thick French accent.

"Huh?"

"La Tour Eiffel?"

She pressed play, hoping for guidance.

"Ask him to take you into town," Alphonse suggested. "Ignore anything he might say about baguettes [*faint sniggering*]."

"Bonsoir, mon enfant!" the milk-eyed zombie grinned.

"I need a ride into town?"

"Mais oui!"

He took her suitcase and led her to the speedboat, staggering stiffly like a dusty marionette. When he had drawn the vessel in, she climbed primly aboard and sat in one of the cream leather seats with her automatic weapon across her lap. She felt like a Hollywood star in hell and began to wish she had brought a camera with a killer flash. A large headlight had been mounted on the stern, and Paw Paw ignited this, illuminating a stone channel skirted by monolithic ruins. The size of it all shocked her—this huge world she had been stumbling in unknowingly, blinded by darkness. The canal was a relatively narrow thoroughfare but just one of many such aqueducts. And all these fed into a distant central canal the breadth of a large river. Arched temples and tattered palaces cluttered the spaces between the waterways, hinting at monumental forms cloaked within the chocolate shadows. At one stage this place must have been a grandiose wonderland—a sort of tropical Shangri-La inhabited by creatures of fables. Now, of course, it was simply a huge seashell, the collective husk of a forgotten era. And what else was there to do in such places but play golf and stage desolate picnics? It was a dead world. The moth developing within the chrysalis had perished, leaving an intricate corpse for lonely scavengers—a universe as impossible to re-enter as a dream upon waking. Paw Paw pushed them off the edge, and they drifted into still waters. Stalactites reached down from high vaulted ceilings, dropping pearls of jungle water into the broken ziggurats. Crocodiles wafted lazily in their wake, hoping that Taty would fall off the side.

"Ah, la Seine!" Paw Paw shouted exuberantly, his voice echoing dismally into the avenues of the sunken city.

"Les cafés! Les arbres! Along the banks of tourist!"

His voice rang and collided, scaring clouds of bats that volleyed off between the buildings. Taty squinted up at the zombie, wondering why he was so ecstatic. Paw Paw simply coasted along, oblivious, lost in a sepia-tinted, inexplicable vision of Paris on a sunny afternoon. In this sustained delusion of his, he piloted a freshly-painted gondola across the caramel waters of the Seine with the sun on his face. Autumnal trees shadowed men on bicycles who ferried baguettes, cheese, and great bushels of grapes beneath their hairy Gallic arms. The air was alive with the sound of accordions. The men's moustaches flicked merrily as they weaved their bicycles between women in Chanel dresses who waved long paintbrushes in synchronized dance routines, leaping like penguins into the Seine. Cinematic couples argued in riverside cafés while thousands of would-be Picassos smoked in doorways, all waving in syncopation as Paw Paw trawled past. Taty watched the zombie warily, oblivious to the all-consuming continental hallucinations with which the imp had poisoned his dead mind. For, unbeknown to Taty, Paw Paw was one of the earlier products of the Jennerator, a fanciful experiment in good cheer and brainwashing. Sullen drippings and the scuffling of predators underscored the sound of his rowing. A small fridge had been set into the seat, and she regarded it with sudden hunger. Inside, she discovered a plate of moldy cling-wrapped sandwiches placed beside a meaty human skull. Some bottles of ginger beer clinked against a box of liqueur chocolates. Taty extracted the chocolate box but quickly hurled it overboard when a horde of huge black beetles swarmed out of it. A crocodile snapped the box up before it even hit the water. She found a tube of caviar and sucked on it, cracking open a bottle of ginger beer and lighting up a cigarette. Paw Paw had by now begun to sing "Non, Je Ne Regrette Rien" at the top of his voice. The sound spilled out into the lost city, dissolving into a scary mush of reverb as the aqueduct widened to join the grand central canal.

LARGE STEPPED PYRAMIDS GHOSTED PAST in the headlight. The zombie and Taty picked up speed in the central canal, and Paw Paw widened the beam, so that the decaying districts passed by like a theatrical frieze. Large pillars towered from the still dark water, dissolving into the patchwork facets of a distant ceiling. In the buttery knife of the light, it became a children's miniature, the backdrop of a shadow puppet play. They weaved in wide arcs between the towers as bats warped collectively through the roving glare. They entered what must have been the downtown district of the forgotten citadel. Narrow harbors and oddly coordinated geometric quays wafted by like pieces in a board game. Taty lounged with her ginger beer watching it all slip past, talking on her walkie-talkie with her boots up on the skirting. She was finally leaving the inertia of the house and all the twisted kaleidoscopic dreams festering within its walls. The sudden sensation of liberation was intoxicating, and she felt as though she were waking from a thousand-year sleep.

"Yeah, so I'm outta here," she told Number Nun.

Number Nun nodded to herself, twirling in sunny waters trawled in the wake of surfacing whales. Long remoras had attached themselves to her limbless body, and they trailed from her back and stomach like silvery belts. The vivid fish within her had multiplied, and a polyp-infested anemone locomoted merrily against the inside of her ribs. The creatures did not seem to bother or degrade her mechanisms, and she tolerated them with a sort of benign divinity, occasionally spurting them with wisps of synthesized protein issued from mechanisms within her breasts.

"It's a miracle, Childbride. You must thank the Blessed Virgin for sparing your miserable existence."

"Yeah, it's great."

"I really thought they would have spiked your head on the gates by now."

"Well, I hid in the watchtower."

"Good. I am pleased that you are finally learning to take care of yourself."

The city had started to thin out, giving way to an enormous cave system. Jagged peninsulas lay in the gloomy water like the bones of giants. Far above, the vaulted ceiling melted into candle wax formations of water-distorted limestone. The headlight juggled, conjuring disorienting shadows from the twisted nodes of rock. Up ahead, Taty could make out a slit of whiteness that grew steadily larger as they buffeted out across open water. The end of the cavern was cleft by a massive crevice. This rift was overhung with vegetation, within which could be glimpsed the angular forms of dangling pterodactyls. The light of dawn filtered through these immense curtains of greenery, diffusing across the dark subterranean lake in a haze of silver. The wan illumination caught on Taty's face as they drew closer to the crevice, and she could smell the approaching jungle, rich and overwhelming after the mortifying austerity of the Lost Quarter.

"I guess I am learning how to take care of myself," she smiled into the light, observing the backlit greenery with a feeling of tremendous liberation.

"So, what are your plans?" Number Nun asked.

"Well, I'm heading into town. Alphonse wants me to go to the terminal and catch a bus to the Outer Necropolis."

"Why? What does that imp expect you to do there?"

"He wants me to deliver a letter."

Number Nun processed this. The whales had moved farther afield, and she watched them recede into the crystalline depths still turning like skittles in their churn.

"The letter is a card with lots of needlepoint dots," Number Nun stated matter-of-factly.

"Uh huh."

"It is a Death Jinx."

"Hectic."

"You see, something was left over from all those lost and ruined cities. Something very precious to the old reptile people. One of their gods, in fact."

"A god?"

"A dead god."

"How does a god die?"

"Well, they don't, my dear. Heathen gods never die. The cursed things always find some way to live on no matter what I do ... Who knows what this god was like before it ... changed. Now it has no face, and so they call it 'Devoid.' It inhabits the Outer Necropolis, living down in the pits and passages. The letter is meant for this dead god."

"How does a god without a face read a letter?"

"The needlepoints are Braille, and they spell out a name. You see, they just couldn't let dead gods lie, these foolish sinners. They had to find a way to communicate with it. My guess is that Mister Sister's name is on the card. Alphonse, in his infernal way, has somehow managed to gain favors from this savage jungle god. In any case, Devoid will eat the sno-globe of the person whose name is on that card. And this will be so much worse than death. So much worse."

"So Alphonse will have the last laugh!" Taty cheered.

"Alphonse will always have the last laugh, Childbride. But don't be too happy for him for his laugh can only signal ruin and debasement. He is an abomination. A true house cat of the horned one."

"I suppose he wasn't very nice to me."

"He violated you, as he did me. The only difference is that I am a precision instrument and you are a sno-globe. Lost little girls ought not to be treated like precision instruments."

"I kind of ... I kind of liked him."

"Pheromones. They make him impossible to dislike. Your childish crush was his silver puppet string."

"I do *not* have a crush on Alphonse!"

"I must go. I see a narwhal."

Number Nun cut off abruptly, leaving Taty in a state of extreme annoyance. She threw the walkie-talkie to the bottom of the boat in a huff and would have probably thrown a tantrum were it not for the grandiose spectacle of the approaching crevice. She quickly pulled on oversized sunglasses as the boat buffeted into the churn of current squeezing through the channel. The cusp of the creeper cave passed overhead like the arch of a cathedral, and the dawn light caught them in a blaze of paleness. Mist and haze uncoiled as the speedboat knifed out of the darkness, entering onto the wide, brown expanse of the river with no name. Dense jungle lay on either side of the broad body of water, saturated with morning mist and pierced with shafts of pellucid light. The river with no name was the largest in the Zone and fed down from the high escarpment of jungle plateaus, widening into an enormous delta of flat swamp and black mud mangroves on its way to the sea. Trade routes had been established all along the various settlements on the river, and disused passages to Namanga Mori still existed in the swamp. They picked up speed, and the wind skirled up Taty's hair. She pulled her fur against the morning chill and struggled to light a cigarette. The view from the speedboat was spectacular, and she could see dawn breaking like some enormous cosmic egg spilling its mess over the tangled panorama of the jungle. Pterodactyls wheeled in this glowing penumbra while flocks of flamingos loitered, haunting the fog-bound tree line like an army of spindly strangers. Far away down the vista of churning water, she could glimpse the ghostly hulks of bathing brontosauruses. They shambled like bluish dumpster trucks at the shore, occasionally letting out long whale-like moans that traveled mournfully out across the distances. She attempted to enjoy this scenic journey down the river but remained annoyed at what Number Nun had intimated before she signed off. It was the sort of irritating thing that became like a fungal rash of the mind—impossible to avoid scratching and just as impossible to cure.

THE SPEEDBOAT WAS FAST, AND they quickly reached the flat marshlands of black mud where the anacondas kept their lonely breeding grounds. It was the hot season, and the swamp was muggy and oppressive despite the earliness of the hour. Taty was regretting not having brought her bikini. She had left it behind in some fit of closure and was now drinking cold ginger beer in the claustrophobic heat and cursing her foolishness. Large flies and gangs of mosquitoes rose up off the stinking black mud plains, causing her to smoke another few cigarettes in exasperation. Soon she was sticky and irritable, stripped down to her cotton briefs after packing away the fragile dress for fear of ruining it. The landscape was deserted, and Paw Paw was brain-dead in Paris, so she remained shamelessly semi-naked, brooding beside the fridge and keeping a sharp eye out for danger. Large glinting flats shimmered beneath the naked eye of the rising sun, speckled with clumps of reeds and rushes that sprouted here and there like tufts of green hair. The buzz of insects was irritating, and noxious fumes caused her to grimace and complain under her breath. After an hour or so, she desperately wanted to bathe or swim, to wash the cloying swamp off. The reality of having left the comforts of the house seemed suddenly to crash upon her, and Taty became listless, faced with the prospect of the hot black world she now traveled across alone with no one for company but the dead man steering the boat.

ISLANDS APPEARED IN THE SWAMP—dark brooding masses, emerging from the watery wastes like the beached corpses of ocean behemoths. She watched these archipelagos wheel by in the morning sunlight, grim and uninhabitable, choked with tentacled masses of vegetation. Soon these islands clustered together to form landmasses, and they began to rejoin the jungle. Inlets appeared at the edge of the waterlogged tree line, and Paw Paw unexpectedly angled for one, cutting the engine down to a low chug. And then, almost like waking from a dream, Taty found herself skimming down a long corridor of greenery. The shade and coolness of the closely tangled plants was delicious after their exposure out on the delta, and Taty scooped bottlefuls of clear water to splash over herself. When she was done, she lay drip-drying and satisfied on the couch sucking caviar and watching the jungle glide by. The channel was so narrow and the edges of the forest so close that leaves brushed the sides of the boat on either side. Branches knitted overhead, creating a pleasant dappling of green light. Monkeys gibbered from the trees, passing above the boat in caravans. Taty snagged a malice fruit from a vine and sat picking shiny black seeds from the yellow flesh as they glided along. It grew quieter in the trees, and the temperature dropped. When she was dry she squirmed back into the dress and brushed out her hair still determined to remain as presentable as possible. The channel began to widen, and after an hour or so, it fed into an estuary. Across the silty water she could see the hazy skyline of Namanga Mori, the low buildings jutting like broken teeth against an asphalt sky. A heavy concrete bridge spanned the estuary just before it met the sea, and Taty could glimpse the riverside jetties and barge ports of the industrial district. She recognized the area and realized that once they landed it would only be a half-hour's walk to the esplanade and the vicinity of the Nebula Shell Sea. The bus terminal was downtown on the far side of the strip, and she got the notion that she would pass by the hotel for old time's sake, maybe say hello to Romeo before leaving town. After all, it had been months since she had been in the city. An entire lifetime had passed.

IT WAS HIGH NOON WHEN she reached the Nebula Shell Sea, and a blinding sun beat down on the empty streets. She was shocked to find the city unpopulated. It was something she could feel before she even disembarked—the sensation of a vast deserted space. It was strange, even surreal, to feel this after her trip through the Lost Quarter. Almost as though the dead cities were extending their borders—which in a way, they were. She considered getting back aboard the boat, but Paw Paw had already begun jetting back on some zombie autopilot. She watched the speedboat recede, left alone on the small concrete jetty with a feeling of intense abandonment. Here she was at square one, on the road again yet bereft of childish wonder and the indestructibility that came with it. The city may have been unpeopled, but it certainly wasn't unpopulated. The symbs infested it like a plague. They were everywhere, dangling upside down from highway overpasses like man-size locusts, clinging to buildings, squatting in the street. Left to their own devices the beings had begun to revert to the mineral stillness of their native sphere. Many did not move at all, standing like green metal statues, hot to the touch and apparently lifeless. The more recently transformed moved slowly, following her with their eyes and heads but rarely changing position. She was almost universally ignored. The entire city had taken on their character: malformed, frozen, and hideously unnatural. Human conflict had left gaping wounds in the fabric of the city, yet there were no bodies. These had all been either cleared or undergone transmutation. Some buildings were shattered completely while others had restaurants where meals had been abandoned half-eaten. Namanga Mori had become a ghost town. She lugged her suitcase through these streets with her machine gun held out before her like a wand. Her teeth were chattering with fear, and she had to bite down to keep from losing control entirely. There was a horrible silence in the city, a silence made pregnant by the consciousness of thousands of alien life-forms. Now she stared up at the wreckage of the Nebula Shell Sea. Windows had been broken, and parts of it were gutted by fire. Pages of a novel spilled down the street, catching in plants and gutters. A pile of acoustic guitars lay smashed beneath one of the windows. Someone had cut down all the palm trees, and the place suddenly resembled a film set from some tawdry low-budget period piece. Despite her fear, Taty was forced to make frequent rest stops. The case was heavy, and she was dripping with sweat from the noonday sun. She stopped outside the hotel and sat on her suitcase lighting a cigarette and swabbing perspiration from her brow. The heat had a way of muffling sounds, so she did not hear the soldiers approaching until one shouted across to her. She jumped up in fright, her machine gun trembling in her hands. A squadron of soldiers in green uniforms, mirrored sunglasses, and moustaches were standing in the street. They had evidently been out on patrol and now stood watching her with long black flamethrowers cradled in their gloved hands. The napalm tanks they all wore gave them the incongruous appearance of scuba divers, and pilot flames danced at the heads of their weapons.

"I said, what are you eyeballing out here?" the soldier repeated.

Taty tried to speak but found that her mouth had gone completely dry. Her legs were also numb, and she had started to quake. The soldiers had their flamethrowers trained on her, and she was terrified that her trembling finger would accidentally pull the trigger.

"This campsite has been flagged a bug-fuck zone!" the lead soldier shouted across at her. "You shouldn't be out here. What are you—a frog fondler?"

Taty started stammering only to be cut off by another soldier.

"Release that peashooter!"

She quickly dropped the machine gun, and three of the soldiers approached her, grabbing her by the hair and arms. She squealed in resistance as large hands ducked her head down, pulling open the back of her dress. She felt the delicate material rip against the hard rubber gloves and struggled uselessly until she was panting in exertion.

"She jockeying no bug hump," one of the soldiers reported after meticulously inspecting her naked back.

The lead soldier grabbed her face and yanked it up into the sun.

She coughed and spluttered, blinking up into the terrified reflection of her own face dancing like twin moons in the mirrored eyewear.

"How come you not greening out, little girl? How did you squeeze through the cheese?"

"I … please, Daddy Bast gave me meds to lock up my spine, so I can't—they can't change me."

The soldier rubbed his unshaven face and considered this for a moment. Her arms were pinned back painfully, and she was dangling from their grasp, pulled up onto the tips of her toes. She could see soldiers lighting cigarettes off their flamethrowers in the street. They were examining the glitter decals and kitten stickers on her machine gun in amusement.

"So, the cat gave you a magic pill, and the bug boys steered clear of you?"

"No, they still … they still got with me, I just can't—they can't change me …"

She had started to cry now and was almost babbling.

"She's clean of the green," another soldier muttered, slapping her quaking thigh.

"We're evacuating the city," the lead soldier informed her. "You'll have to come with us."

"But I'm fine, really; I'm OK, I've got my machine gun. You can just leave me here, please. I'm OK. I've got to catch a bus. I'll be late."

She gazed pleadingly into the soldier's unshaven face, blinking back tears in the harsh sun. The other soldiers loitered in the street, occasionally torching things with their flamethrowers. The lead moustachio stared at her for several moments before turning to one of the stragglers.

"Pablo!" he yelled. "Get in that hotel and find us a room with a clean double bed."

The soldier on the street nodded and trotted up the steps of the Shell Sea. Taty watched in mute fascination, unable for a moment to fathom why he was being sent inside. The lead soldier took hold of her face again, pulling it up, so that she could again see herself in his sunglasses.

"If you can ride the bugs, you can ride the whole rodeo, Chiquita. Get her in there and get her clothes off."

One of the soldiers in the street cheered, firing Taty's gun into the air. She began to screech and howl, clawing violently at the soldiers' faces as they pulled her back up the steps of the hotel—steps she had so often climbed in the dreary routines of another life. She was dragged, kicking and screaming, out of the blinding high noon and into a terrible deformation of her past life. The hotel was utterly deserted, and their passage through these halls of memory was like a claustrophobic dream. Empty rooms yawned around her, peopled by symbiotes and the detritus of a fallen world. It looked like a film set of the Nebula Shell Sea, but it was not even that anymore. She had crossed the river with no name and the delta but had not yet left the Lost Quarter. The dead cities had spread like a disease, infecting even the past.

21
The Terminal

THE CENTRAL BUS STATION OF Namanga Mori had been converted into a refugee exit point. It had once been a somewhat grand place but had suffered the rigor of desertion. Its colonial architecture now wasted in the squalor of a fallen town. Dusty marble and filthy filigree had long since given way to tacky jungle chicken stands and trinket arcades. But now even these mercantile enterprises had fallen beneath the overwhelming chaos of the symbiote infestation. The yawning halls and atriums were packed with people desperate to leave the city. Figures clamored hither and thither, clutching all manner of belongings. The scene had become a menagerie of wicker fowl cages, suitcases, trunks, rolled rugs, and dismantled furniture. A blaze of late afternoon sun fell through the large skylights and batteries of dirty windows, catching the masses from above. A sea of illuminated dust swarmed amid heads, old wood, and memorial plaques, lending an atmosphere of worry and displacement to the scene. Soldiers and wrestlers were herding refugees with rifles and cattle prods occasionally barking orders at one another. Checkpoints had been set up at intervals throughout the large sprawl of tiled corridors and chambers, and officials were frisking individuals for any sign of symbiotic contamination. Those with humps or greenish broken skin were taken to an abandoned parking lot and sprayed with flamethrowers. The symbs, which were invulnerable to heat, lay twitching and writhing amid a clutter of charred body parts and smoking bones. The more fully formed symbiotes simply crawled away, creeping back into the city like wounded insects. The screams of the burning could be heard over the bustling chaos inside. Voices announced gibberish over megaphones, and tinny bossa nova played over all of this, much like air freshener sprayed copiously to disguise the stench of rotting corpses. Vintage coaches clustered in the gothic lots, choked with passengers, guided by garbled commands and verbal abuse. These buses departed occasionally, grinding down swoops of concrete, pregnant with mournful passengers.

Taty dragged her suitcase wearily through the mob. She sported a black eye, bruised cheekbone, and split lip. She was also limping badly. The couture dress had been utterly destroyed by the soldiers, so she had been forced to change into whatever was at the top of her case: a tiny pair of blue denim shorts and the KAMIKAZE KUPCAKE T-shirt she'd carried with her from the Lowlands. Her machine gun was gone forever, and she snuggled her fur jacket protectively around herself, headphones scarfed around her neck, too whacked out to cry. Although she was in a tremendous amount of pain, she pushed resolutely on, a blood-stained cigarette spindling off her puffy lip. Her mouth and throat burned, but she kept lighting cigarettes as though the tar would erase the flavors of rape forever. Eventually she stopped moving, jostled by passing strangers, staring at the buses in growing confusion. After a moment's deliberation she decided to approach the nearest one. It was filling rapidly, fed from several crazy queues, which had evidently been congregating for hours. Trivial arguments erupted all around her while she navigated her way to the driver's window and began to bash numbly on the glass. The driver waved her off, engaged in an argument with a large woman in purple robes. Taty persisted, and he eventually opened the Plexiglas partition.

"What is it?" he grumbled. "You need medical attention?"

"I need to get to the Outer Necropolis," she shouted above the din.

He looked at her as though she were crazy, noting her wounds and perhaps fearing some potential form of insanity.

"What do you want out there in the jungle? There's nothing but crocs and contamination out there. None of the coaches are going that way. We're all heading to the Lowlands."

"I need to get to the Pyramids!" Taty shrieked.

The driver rubbed his jaw, regarding her now with concern. The woman in robes was pawing at him, but he shrugged her off and leaned out the window.

"You got family out there or something?" he asked, rubbing his jaw.

Taty hesitated for a moment before answering.

"Yes ... my brother's out there. I need to ... I need to save him."

"Jesus, girl. Well, I guess the best thing is to double back down to lot thirteen and ask the supply route boys. They're doing some runs in the hot zone—it's a ways off from the Outer Necs but better than nothing, I reckon. They might take you, I dunno ..."

He shrugged and pointed out the direction she should take. Taty thanked him and headed that way, leaving him to his argument. Red arrows were painted onto the walls, indicating paths to each part of the station. There were also mad spaghetti maps of the terminal posted everywhere, so it was relatively easy to find her way despite the chaos. She crossed thoroughfares and hobbled down wide flights of concrete stairs, pushing her way through the crowds. She eventually penetrated the outer lots, which were located on a sub-level. The crowds thinned out as she entered large, gloomy open-air spaces that reeked of machinery. Long barbed wire walls enclosed the yards, and she had to walk carefully to avoid tripping over rusted machine parts and clumps of unchecked weeds. A thin drizzle began to fall as she skirted the shells of buses and large refueling dumps, heading for the yellow glare of rainy floodlights. Lot thirteen was a rambling hangar with filthy tin walls and oversized exit ramps. Two coaches lay in a corner beside a neat pile of military equipment. The seats had been torn from the buses to make space for the hardware, arranged in rows along the floor of the hangar. There was the flavor of an art installation about it—a cinema without walls or a screen. Some drivers were standing beside the equipment, talking with a large wrestler in a bright white-and-blue leotard with matching cape and mask. Across the hangar, a squad of soldiers loitered, smoking cigarettes and comparing moustaches. The sight of the soldiers made her feel immediately nauseous, but she took a deep breath—emerging into the sallow glare of the hangar. She approached the gaggle of drivers, shooting nervous glances across at the soldiers, who were now staring at her. The drivers had also stopped to watch, prompting the wrestler to turn around.

"You!" he barked at Taty. "What are you doing here?"

She froze at the sound of his voice, and one of the drivers took pity on her.

"You aren't allowed here, little girl," the driver called. "You have to go back to the central hall—all the Lowland coaches depart from there."

"Please, can you help me?" she pleaded, dragging her case across the greasy concrete. "I need to get to the Outer Necropolis, my brother's dying out there and needs my help."

"Those are now forbidden zones," the wrestler declared. "You are to report back to the hall and take a coach to the Lowlands just like everybody else."

"But—"

"Are you refusing to evacuate?" the wrestler asked, folding his arms across his chest.

Taty hesitated, looking to the driver who had spoken for assistance. He shot her a sympathetic glance but said nothing. The wrestler was about to speak when one of the soldiers hailed him from across the floor. The squad had begun to mobilize, gathering up their guns and tying their shoelaces.

"Command!" the soldier yelled, holding up a walkie-talkie. "We have a truck of morph zombies inbound on the banana boat—Lucho says to double-double down to the Kentucky frizzler and catch some steel rain for the ringside tickers."

The wrestler suddenly seemed to forget about Taty. He turned to the drivers, adjusting his cape and leotard with military precision.

"You have your orders," he snapped. "Try not to breathe in the fumes."

He trotted off imperiously, following the departing soldiers out into rainy darkness. When he was sure the wrestler was out of earshot, the driver turned to Taty.

"Listen, little girl. We don't operate in the Outer Necs, but some of the truckers are still doing runs. You can try them."

He pointed out into the night, and she nodded numbly, lighting another cigarette.

"If I was you I'd forget about going out there," one of the drivers told her, in a fatherly sort of way.

"Yeah," another piped. "Let the soldiers deal with the lost children."

"I don't fucking think so!" Taty exploded, staggering back across the lot in disgust.

They stared at her in surprise, shocked by her sudden rudeness.

"It's a pleasure!" one of them called sarcastically.

She ignored them, emerging into what had now become rain. The steaming forms of several rigs lay across the dark yards, and she headed resolutely for them. As she drew closer she could make out some of their external details. Most had chrome plating seared by use and travel. Some had flames painted along their cabs while others sported jungle skulls and spiked bumper guards. Machinegun pods had been mounted along the customized rims, and the majority of the external piping had been reinforced with steel plating to survive the attacks of cargo bandits around the Zone. A tarp had been erected in the shadow of one of the larger rigs, and she could just make out two robust figures smoking by the light of a moth-haunted hurricane lamp. The truckers were a curious breed, sporting waist-length beards and woodcutter flannels. Large woolly jackets disguised ponderous bellies and utility belts laden with the implements of the road. One turned to the other and pointed to Taty.

"Look what we have here, Allen. Looks like a little hitchhiker."

"Shit, Jerry," his partner nodded solemnly. "She looks like a song man."

He held a hand to his mouth and called out at her.

"Hey, little girl! You look like a song man!"

Taty staggered into the shade of the tarp, shaking rain from her hair and letting her heavy case down with a wince.

"Got a little trouble with your eye and lip, though, huh?" Jerry said. "A little too much of the fucked-up mascara."

"I need a ride out to the Pyramids," Taty said. "Can you help me, please?"

"Told you she was a hitcher, man. There aren't that many hitchers around anymore; you're a dying breed. Say—you want some dooby?"

He held out a large joint, which she refused.

"Some joe?" he offered, waving a battered canteen.

She eyed it for a moment, and he took this as a sign to pop the top and pour out a paper cup.

"Can you help me, please?" she sniffed, pawing rain from her damaged face.

He held out the cup of steaming coffee and smiled, showing all the cracks around his eyes.

"Go on, little song, drink up now."

She accepted the cup with undisguised gratitude, swallowing it all in one gulp. It scalded her damaged mouth but was so good it almost made her cry. She realized that she had not had anything to eat or drink since the caviar and ginger beers, and for a moment it felt as though she had taken some form of hard drug. The kindness of the truckers was disorienting, and she stopped for a moment, her internal mechanisms of survival faltering like a clock.

"Better get that face job looked at as well, sister."

"Please, can you help me?" she pleaded.

"Well, we're off the clock, man, but Uncle Bill and Kerouac are heading out that way in an hour or so. Maybe you should give them a try."

"Cancel that, Allen. Kerouac pulled a freight job in the liminal zone. He trucked out a few hours ago. Roster's shot to hell, man. It's all these ass-fucking bug boys messing with the order of things."

"Yeah, try Uncle Bill. His is the big red dragon rig down by the garbage release. Just bang on the cab and tell him Allen and Jerry sent you."

"Thanks. You guys totally rock."

"Just keep on trucking, little song."

SHE HAD TO CROSS INTO another lot, an area occluded by acrid yellow smoke and gushing steam. A mess of coolant pipes had ruptured, creating sulphuric fog that obscured the entire area and caught in her nose and throat. Floodlights lit this haze from above, causing it to glow in places. The rain had stopped as suddenly as it had started, and she passed by rows of wet, towering trucks until the very end of the line. There, she came upon the ornate dragonboat truck that the bearded men had described. It emerged from the rift like a creature of fable, horned and scaled with red metal. The rig itself was a hefty sixteen-wheeler customized for war and radiation with a wide spacious cab. The chassis had been cloaked by what looked like a bulletproof carnival float forged out of metal and scarlet trim. Filthy ribbons trailed from its many aerials. Greenish eye decals had been plastered over the quad of headlights, creating a staring dragon's face bisected by a pig-iron grille and buoyed up by a meter-high bumper ram. Large blue-headed lizards clung to the crimson flanks, soaking up the heat, which radiated out through the metal. She could hear twisting flute and zither wafting from a sound system within the beast and called up the collapsible steps.

"Uncle Bill?"

Something moved in the shadowy cabin, and she called out again. But when Uncle Bill appeared, it was from behind her out of the cloying smoke wearing a white panama hat. He was thin, angular, and bespectacled, perhaps in his late sixties. He wore a bedraggled but impeccably cut cream suit. The tie and collar had been loosened, revealing a heavily-lined sunburned neck. The red neck lent him a somewhat reptilian appearance compounded by his expressionless mouth and lens-magnified eyes. Taty saw that he was leveling a small ornamental pistol at her, and she stumbled back awkwardly, unsure how to react.

"Are you with the Mexicans?" he inquired in a looping drawl.

"Allen and Jerry sent me."

He re-holstered the pistol quickly as though embarrassed by it. "Forgive me. I have some unresolved differences with the current militia and must remain on guard at all times."

"I need a ride out to the Pyramids. Can you take me, please?"

He regarded her with his watery blue eyes, summing up her appearance and weighing the request in his mind. To his credit he did not interrogate her further about what business she might have in such a strange locale.

"I suppose I could. It will take several days, though. The main roads are infested, and I must circumvent the border posts if I am to deliver my cargo."

"I don't mind. I just need to get out there, and no one else will take me."

He stared at her for a moment before summoning her up the steps. Taty left her case at the foot of the stairs and followed him up to a battered airlock.

"Take a gander," he drawled, fiddling with the hydraulic seal. "My arrangements are … somewhat unusual—perhaps you won't want to travel with me after all."

The airlock opened with a clank and a hiss, revealing an almost unbelievable interior. A vintage French Quarter apartment had been somehow miniaturized and adapted to fit the confines of the larger than average cab. Small potted palms and antique furniture had been bolted painstakingly through the deco wallpaper and into the metal hull. A wireless blared flute music while an old lace lampshade illuminated the boudoir in a soft rosy glow. The floor had been tiled in checkerboard monochrome, and a red velvet chaise longue floated behind a mahogany coffee table and a wicker chair. An oil painting of a desiccated mummy brooded beside a coat-and-hat stand. Steps adjoined the driver's cabin, a spacious area that floated behind a large bubble dome of tinted glass. Yet, despite the uniqueness of the décor and the size of the truck, it was the symbiote she noticed first. The creature sat in the corner like a sculpture tittering to itself, more animated than its fellow beings in the city.

"Is that thing your friend?" Taty asked, confused by the presence of the creature.

"No," he answered, moving past her and folding primly down into the chair. "It is a portal to another world."

She watched from the doorway as he attached a cigarette to a long ivory holder, his back to the symb.

"So, you're a bug fucker," she stated blankly.

He lit the cigarette and crossed his legs, relaxing back into the creaking wicker weave.

"Well, that's one way of putting it, I suppose."

"How come you're not greening out?" she asked, eyeing the symbiote with suspicion.

"Well, I went down to the Voodoo Surgery and took my medicine like a good little boy."

"Yeah, the cat gave me a pill, too."

"If the Soft House had its way, I would be up against a wall. But no one else will run uranium into the diamond zone."

He turned his lined lizard-like face and regarded the symbiote with a surprising softness.

"The wrestlers allow me my 'symbiotic explorations' while they still have need of me. As long as I am not seen, of course. Willing interaction with the symbiotes is still regarded as a transgression punishable by death. It is, after all, an invasion."

"It's not an invasion," Taty sighed, sinking to her haunches against the wall. "It's just a stupid joke the Big Buddha is playing."

"Most invasions start out as a joke."

They sat in silence, and Taty found herself overcome by sudden fatigue. The weariness came in a shocking wave, but still she stared nervously at the creature as though expecting an unseen hammer to drop. Smoking quietly in the shadows, Uncle Bill watched her watching the symb. Her head began to nod, and she was asleep within minutes. He observed as she curled gradually to the tiled floor a bedraggled little animal. When he finished his cigarette, he brought up her suitcase and covered her with a thin cotton throw, sealing the airlock behind him.

22
Voyeur of the Protoverse

THE LONG RUSHING HIGHWAY LAY illuminated in the catastrophic red-and-green floodlights. Taty had awoken in the rattling darkness of the dragon rig and crawled up into the noisy pod of the cabin. There she discovered Uncle Bill strapped into one of two crash couches underlit by greenish panel displays. Marie Laforêt's "Marie-douceur, Marie-colère" had been locked into an analogue tape reel and was blasting on a loop, thundering the glass dome with an infernal drone of mantras. To either side of the road was a sort of cracked desert sucking out into the terminal blackness of the wasteland. The jungle had finally fallen away, and they had risen on the high hot highway leading into the carbon wastes. The floodlights painted burning cars and the flashing forms of dead bodies strewn like bacteria along the endless expanse of tarmac. Vast rifts of smoke descended from the carbon flats howling in spectral forms through the gulf, torn to violent spirals in the slipstream. Symbiotes squatted along the side of the road fornicating with corpses and scampering out into the wilderness like insects. Packs of laughing hyenas were also on the loose, tearing corpses to shreds and spitting at the interdimensional aliens. At one point the dragon rig passed a convoy of armored trucks and tanks trundling down the line, inbound for Namanga Mori. The situation in the Outzone had evidently become untenable, and all manner of power exchanges were taking place throughout the onset of the "invasion." Yet, despite the truly apocalyptic visions that assailed them on the road, the pair did not exchange many words that first night. Barbed-wire tumbleweed skittered off into the dusty expanses catching on flesh and metal, playing havoc with the hyenas, who often became entangled and severely wounded in their struggle to escape. The front of the truck ground on ferociously through the drifts of yellowish smoke. Its lights seared the air while things caught and disintegrated under its spiked bumpers, screaming as they were ripped apart. Uncle Bill gunned the rig ever faster through this nightmare until the casings shook and the engines roared and blustered. Behind him in the sallow light of the quaking lampshade, was the symb. It squatted on the battened-down chaise longue clacking its mandibles and gibbering to itself. Uncle Bill was hunched, a white mantis before the wheel, juiced on bennies and locked onto the road. He seemed barely able to contain an urge to crash, and the sweat glinted like specks of quartz along his brow. When he finally spoke, it was in a low and dangerous voice barely audible beneath the blood fever of music and machinery.

"When a traveler turns west, all time travel ceases to be travel and instead becomes an inexorable suction—pulling everything into a black hole."

Taty had stumbled back into the lounge at some point. Every-thing was shaking like a house in an earthquake. Her suitcase was sliding across the floor while all the furniture remained absurdly in place. Even the delicate legs of the coffee table had been screwed tightly to the tiles, and the effect of stillness within chaos was unsettling. Uncle Bill was focused intently on the road, crushing long lines of human corpses and tearing hyenas to pieces in a sort of dream of speed. She dragged her case to the airlock and discovered a small sleeping compartment beyond. The cramped chamber had been fitted with a narrow cot and an electric light. Paranoid hieroglyphs covered the walls in crazy felt-tip patterns, and she had to hold fast to the walls to avoid being tossed about. Another oval door led to a stainless steel toilet/shower cubicle. Her private parts ached, and she scooped handfuls of warm stinging water, washing herself out and swallowing some painkillers she found in the well-stocked medicine cabinet. Going to the toilet would be painful, and she would limp for a few days; but she resolved to survive. She showered as best she could in the shaking metal cupboard, clinging to the sink and staring at her face in the chipped shaving mirror. A cold anger had started in her sleep and was now sending out tiny roots seeking purchase in her mind and attempting to grow. Unsure of its purpose, she concentrated on survival. She discovered plasters and made a jagged, somewhat artistic pattern along the left side of her face after disinfecting her cuts and bruises with Mercurochrome. A black felt-tip marker was rolling around, and she scrawled the words RAPE ROCKER across her face in a fit

of morbid spontaneity. The deafening noise and music of the truck was starting to agree with her, wiping away her pain with the balm of distance and annihilation. She noticed that the facial wounds dominated the left side of her face and was suddenly reminded of Miss Muppet's tattoo. There was something of that woman's icy glint in her now—a hardness around her eyes and mouth compounded by dried blood and damage. It was the Outzone itself, she realized. It was creeping into her and claiming her as it did all who ventured into it. With its terrible rites of passage, it was transforming her into something other. Her reflection disturbed her, and she lit up a cigarette, sucking on the red lollipop simultaneously, crawling back to the cabin to watch the highway with Uncle Bill. From the jangled darkness the symbiote watched, too, twittering like some damaged bird. The night passed in whirlwinds, delivering them through a barrage of seemingly ceaseless devastation.

HIGH NOON ON THE CARBON wastes. The arrow-straight highway cut through a smoking plane of volcanic ash rich with quicksilver and toppling into mirages on all sides. They had stopped some hours ago, and she had watched Uncle Bill collapse into the wicker chair with an iced mint julep and a handful of pink pills. She left him to his devices and wandered a few kilometers down the hot road in a spell of dazed listlessness. The red dragon shimmered some distance behind her laden with armored cargo tanks, reduced to a quivering red flame against the stark baking flatlands. The sweat poured off her body in rivulets, burning in her cuts. She had her drenched T-shirt off after ten meters, wrapped in a makeshift turban around her headphones and sunglasses. She staggered on topless, wearing nothing but denim shorts and strappy sandals, Walkman® chugging tape at her hips. She was exploring more panoramic corners of the ever-expanding *In with the Outzone* album. A new song called "The Healing Power of Hate" had her in a daze, and she rewound it each time it ended, unable to listen to anything else that day. The highway was deserted in both directions as far as the eye could see. They had left the carnage of the Low Zone behind and finally entered into the pure nullity of the Highlands. The scorched plain was cracked like a dish separated into countless carbonized plates that ground slowly against each other like ceramic dishes. The glassy sound of all these fragments created a jingly dissonance beneath the muted quality of the heat. The turbulence of lava moved like red paste between and beneath these plates much like blood between the scales of a reptile. The heat rising off the dizzying scape was extreme, almost unimaginable. Some symbiotes had made it out to the carbon waste drawn by the temperatures, roving far and wide into scarred emptiness where they stopped and then stood without moving. She could see them spiked in the lava, superheated to a glittery emerald. They didn't move in the slightest now, all facing the same direction like the grotesque effigies of some ancient and malignant cult, somehow at peace within the slow grind of the lava. The hiss of steam release and perpetual cracking was like the churning of a billion soda pop bottles. The hugeness of it all drove a spike deep into the heart of her growing anger, tempering her newly forming hate like a knife. And it was as though she was confronting the shifting yet utterly immoveable nature of material reality itself when she stood in that heat. What Number Nun said to her on the boat had also fermented in this acid bath of emotion. Had she been under a spell to have feelings for the imp? He had, after all, delivered her into nothing short of hell. She drained the dregs from a bottle of fizzy pop and hurled it into the wasteland. It created a puff of flame upon landing, and she watched mesmerized as it burned. She loitered there in the oven of herself, too heat-drugged to think properly. There were ugly teeth marks around her breasts and plum-purple bruises along her stomach. These wounds stung in her running perspiration, distracting her with spiky thoughts of revenge. The stench of carbon was dense on the open road, reminding her of burning pencils and subsequently of long-buried primary school memories—the detritus of a past life. She had thought all those memories successfully submerged, but now they were coming back, released from suspension by the alchemy of trauma. They rose like little poison bubbles fizzing on the surface of her mind. Taty limped back to the dragon when she could stand it no longer.

MODESTY CAUSED HER TO WRIGGLE back into the sticky shirt as she drew closer to the truck. The steel-reinforced wheels stood just over her height, dwarfing her. She clambered up the burning drop ladder and cracked the airlock. A heavy magnetic humming emanated from within the cabin, causing the hairs on her body to prickle. Objects were inexplicably suspended in the air, buoyed up by a flux of unnatural reversions. Paperbacks, flowers, and glasses wafted in circular gradients, orbiting the peculiar spectacle of Uncle Bill and the symb. Uncle Bill stood in shirtsleeves with his back to Taty, struggling as though caught in a heavy ocean current. He was engaged in some manner of sexual congress with the creature, which had a bridle of meat hooks and chains around its head. He had penetrated the symbiote and was using the bridle to pull its body into a sickeningly arched shape—an activity that caused it to hover in the air. It was as though he had activated a latent ability of the alien using his very own body as a makeshift yogic key. The limbs of the symbiote had stiffened, extending outward like a thorny flower in bloom. Each bent the wrong way, creating a fascinating geometric shape in the space before him. Uncle Bill had forced the symb to enter into a state where its faceted alien body had begun to vibrate at an intense, escalating frequency. There was an atomic violence in this phase shift, and Taty had the impression the thing might detonate any second, creating a puncture in the fabric of reality itself. It was an instability that Uncle Bill was holding in place by the sheer force of his will. A harsh diamond of light emanated from the symbiote's back, shining directly up into Uncle Bill's face. He obscured the source of this light, and Taty hovered at the threshold, uncertain whether or not to leave.

"Sorry," she fumbled. "I didn't mean to—"

"Come and look at this," he commanded, his voice strained and thin as though it cost an enormous effort to speak.

She crossed the cab, her hair rising in anemones as the strands fell in tune with ruptured magnetic fields, gusting about in a frenzy of poltergeist activity. She began to feel dizzy and sick from the gravitational distortions. Her organs felt as though they were gnashing like teeth within her moving in opposite directions. Yet she continued, overcome by a desire to witness the source of the luminosity. Within a few steps of the pair, she felt as though she were wading through thick fluid and had to lean into the invisible surge to keep her balance. Her ears popped with pressure, and she fought the urge to throw up, certain that the vomit would simply flag around her head like some repulsive sail. Slowly, the obscured light source was revealed. The torso of the symbiote had flattened, its spine inventing a sort of intricate ziplock. This aperture had opened, uncovering a fleshy portal. This opening was much like a window in a dark room despite the brightness of the cabin. It was clearly an alien light, the effulgence of a stellar body that luminesced at a foreign frequency. The opened symbiote had created a vortex of energies, buoying up its origami-folded body and emitting a miasma of light and quantum anomalies that played along the inside walls of the cab in a race of vivid water reflections, making Taty dizzier and dizzier with each step. The strange glare shone full force into Uncle Bill's face, pushing his skin back like a man in the wake of a nuclear blast. She drew close to him and peeked over the lip of the biological portal, feeling somehow that she was standing at the edge of a monumental cliff.

Directional velocity blasted her hair back and puffed open her cheeks like a furnace blast. She felt tremendous heat and threw her hand before her face in protection, gazing wide-eyed through her fingers. What she saw beyond the fluttering green porthole of flesh was a vast illuminated space—a window into a glaring nebula of seemingly limitless proportions. Yet, despite its apparent airiness, the space beyond appeared to be comprised entirely of dense liquid. At first she guessed that it might be some watery occlusion caused by the symbiote's porthole body, but she soon realized that what she was seeing was an airless universe comprised entirely of dense protoplasmic fluid. Gargantuan cellular formations turned like clouds in the superheated medium, lending it a microbial aspect. These constellations of semi-organic matter formed out of complex lattices of clear cells—giving them the crystalline appearance of frog spawn on a galactic scale. Tiny black figures floated within each cell, and Uncle Bill motioned to a hovering telescope with a nod of his head. She plucked the instrument out of the air and focused in shakily on the cells, realizing quickly that—contained within each—was a symbiote. The beings floated in suspension as motionless as smelted metal idols. Their brethren in the lava mimicked these straight-backed postures, haunted by some residual memory of this sphere.

"What the hell is this place?" Taty exclaimed in awe.

"It's their Protoverse," Uncle Bill heaved. "The umbilical dimension from whence the symbiotes sprang."

"It's so hot in there! And big!"

"It is an entire Protoverse."

The effort of speaking seemed to be too much for him, and he lost his grip on the bridle. The device slipped a few inches, and the symbiote fell out of its shape, quivering violently. One of its arms knocked Taty back against the wall, and Uncle Bill had to strain to keep it in formation. Sweat leaked out of his strained red face, and he spoke through gritted teeth.

"Been holding it open too long, going to have to refold now."

He eased the arched spine of the symb back and suddenly snatched the bridle off. The creature snapped back into shape like some grotesque rubber band flopping to the floor and licking its eyes with a distended tongue. The lights and humming died instantly. All the levitating objects dropped to the floor. Uncle Bill collapsed to the Persian rug in a panting mess, his trousers collecting around his ankles. Taty staggered up and helped him onto the chaise longue. He struggled pathetically, trying to pull his pants up and breathing raggedly. His face and neck were badly burned from the alien light, and his eyes were rolling and watery.

"Getting harder and harder to hold 'em open," he wheezed.

"What do you want to open up the bugs for?" she snapped. "Who cares where they come from?"

He gazed at her, panting from his exertions.

"Well, between you and me, young Missy, Uncle Bill here is planning a little trip. If I could just get the schism wide enough to somersault through ..."

"But there's a whole Protoverse of them in there!"

He smiled eerily and reached out a shaking hand, stroking the head of his symb with something like affection.

TATY SLEPT IN UNCLE BILL'S bunk while he drove, crawling from fitful nightmares to find the sun baking in through the bubble dome of the driver's cockpit. It heated up the cab like a baker's oven, and she awoke heat-drugged, drenched, and stupefied. She eyed the walkie-talkie, but the thought of relating what had happened to Number Nun overwhelmed her. She couldn't face it no matter how much she missed the android Madonna and so pushed it from her mind, staggering up into the mind-numbing heat. Uncle Bill didn't seem to sleep. When she questioned him about his insomnia, he explained that he would often collapse into a deep sleep after three days of uninterrupted wakefulness. He claimed that he would then sleep for another three days without waking. For some reason three days was his limit either way. She was grateful for this peculiar habit and annexed his cot, badly in need of rest. He was sympathetic, offering her small amounts of morphine to help her sleep and antiseptics with which to bathe her wounds.

After the second day the carbon flats grew cooler, and the flatlands threw up globulous formations of twisted rock. There were no symbiotes this far out, and the region remained lifeless and barren, riddled with top-heavy mesas formed out of solidified lava. The road soon dipped, leaving the elevated hot zones and traveling back down toward the jungle. It sank in twisting curves between high ravines of sulphur-marbled rock while the temperature dropped back down to tolerable levels. Humidity breathed up from the distant woodland, bringing with it the lush smell of chlorophyll and water. Verdant pockets of greenery split from the rocks at intervals, announcing the onset of the jungle. The rock became black and craggy as they descended, and trickles of water began to seep from the towering escarpments. The high road itself was all but disused. Its battered condition bore testament to the desolation. The worn macadam was pocked and cratered. Large fragments of rock had tumbled over the many years, biting ragged holes into the fabric of the road. Uncle Bill drove like an overmedicated maniac, chasing a red and sinking sun down into the ragged gullies. Taty was oddly calm throughout this suicide rollercoaster, observing numbly as he cornered with reckless abandon and danced the rig over crevices like a raging spirit.

At dusk, they rounded a ridge, and the world opened up like a magnificent oyster. A virtually limitless expanse of jungle spread below, carpeting the world as far as the eye could see in an overabundance of growth and fecundity. Uncle Bill threw on the air brakes, and they shrieked to a dusty halt at the edge of the world. He unstrapped, and they cracked the airlock while the engine ticked and hissed, descending to road level, savoring the cool breezes gusting up off the vast canopy of trees. Taty went and sat on the edge of the monolithic drop, swinging her legs in the dying light, feeling rested and lightheaded from the shift in altitude. Uncle Bill smoked by the truck staring out at a great wild expanse, and she wondered if he really wanted to exchange this majestic world for a suffocating realm of amniotic fluid. He was certainly a strange one, Uncle Bill—a real explorer. Something of a gentleman. She realized then that she would be sad to leave him. She would have liked to be able to say goodbye to him before he made his departure into the Protoverse. She had no doubt that he would one day enter that boiling cosm with his pants around his ankles, and it made her laugh to think about it. But then the seriousness of his obsessions would always extinguish her mirth, making her morbid and restless. They were similar, the pair of them, both cosmonauts of the unknown. She gazed down across the broad sweep of jungle and could just make out the dim and distant geometries of the Floating Pyramids. They were suspended in silhouettes—black triangles against a bloody sun. Where would this pointless journey of hers end? Beyond the billowing canopy, the ancient Pyramids beckoned, summoning her to an audience with the god of an ancient civilization.

Uncle Bill slept that night, the symbiote chained to his bunk like some strange hound. The coolness relaxed Taty, too. The pain of her wounds had subsided, and so she climbed to the roof of the towering rig, where she sat among machine-gun pods and sleeping searchlights, thinking. Her head had cleared somewhat, and she did not even feel like lighting a cigarette. The urge to smother her mind had dissipated as soon as they left the heat-stricken erasure of the carbon waste. An internal border had been crossed, and she now felt prepared to face her stark new reality. And so she simply sat there, staring out at the billowing mass of the jungle, pondering what lay ahead. She had been so intent on escaping the city she had not seen where it was she was headed until now: the very deep of the jungle, its silent ancient heart wherein lingered a dead god of the coma cities. Long-dead cities dwarfed by the immensity of growth that cradled them: the big green, the steaming heart of creation itself. The vastness of the jungle had consumed her, and she had no choice but to accept its sleepy annihilation. The House of Alphonse Guava had anesthetized her with the combined narcotics of luxury and trauma, and she had accepted any method of escape without considering the consequences. Now she was awake, sitting at the grave of her own childhood, throwing dead flowers at who she used to be. A candle of hate had replaced the lamp of wonder—and this flame was not enough to warm her. Something was still left undone.

θθθ

UNCLE BILL WAS CHIPPER THE next day. He awoke, took a long shower, and changed into a three-piece candy-stripe suit with a canary yellow tie. Taty awoke blearily to the smell of frying onions and found him outside cooking vegetables and cured jungle chicken. They ate quickly and were soon on the road again. He was in high spirits after clearing the burning carbon flats and was singing heartily along to an old tune by Dan Russo and his Oriole Orchestra—something about "taking off his skin," which made Taty raise an eyebrow. The road wound down the rock faces and soon re-entered the jungle, carving a straight line through murky entanglements and rising steam. She drifted back into the lounge, digging around listlessly, discovering a hefty trunk full of old typewriters. One in particular caught her attention. It was a large brassy affair with dots and peculiar language modes instead of standard lettering. She picked up the machine and hefted it into the passenger crash couch, where she sprawled with it across her lap.

"What's that you got there?" he inquired breezily, tapping his gnarly fingers to the music.

"This sure is one strange ticker-tacker."

"Ah, the old Betsy. She's a typewriter for the blind. We used to use that baby to circulate subversive documents in the old days. Helped train our bodies to converse in other, more tactile languages. I also used to make fast cash writing detective pamphlets for the blind. The hospitals were always in short supply ..."

Taty snapped a key absently, gazing thoughtfully at the antique machine.

"So, this typewriter types in Braille?" she asked quietly.

"Braille? Sure. There are also some code and cipher transcription settings."

He glanced at her sideways, suddenly sensing a conspiratorial undercurrent.

"Are you thinking of writing something in Braille?"

"I think I am," she answered without expression.

23
The Pyramids

A GOLDEN MOON HAD EMERGED in the wisps of cloud, painting thousands of trees against the oil deep of night. The light illuminated recessions of pyramids floating eerily above the moon-washed jungle. That such large monolithic structures of stone could levitate in fixed positions had baffled visitors since time immemorial. The Pyramids simply remained where they had been for thousands of years, cutting clean-edged shadows out of the milky spray of stars. There were no machines at work or evidence of quantum disruption as with the symbiotic portal. Whatever system of power held the structures in place was discreet and long lasting. The pyramids hovered at intervals, some larger than others, mapping out an epic swastika-like formation above a vast necropolis of tree-infested ruins. Rope ladders dangled from some of the pyramids, hoisted aloft by enterprising scavengers or passing explorers. Most of these had either rotted or fallen away by now, and those that remained were twined with creepers and colonized by vines. Some rope bridges even connected the pyramids in tentative man-made cobwebs, allowing access to some of the harder-to-reach constructions. Eroded plazas and broken colonnades sprawled in glimpses between the moon-gold haze of trees slashed to geometry by the pyramid moon shadows. The highway cut through the Necropolis following the ancient avenues of the city's architecture. Taty watched from the windows as they cruised by, passing occasionally into the inky shadows of the Pyramids. She would look up then into the darkness of the passing shapes. They loomed against the stars like the tangram of an ancient jigsaw, filling her mind with an unearthly silence. Uncle Bill had doused all the lights, and they drove by the ghostly moon glow, which was vivid and luminescent against the pale stone. She was all packed and ready to step off and tapped her fingers restlessly against the dash, suddenly terrified at the prospect of being left out here alone.

"You sure about this, Kiddo?" Uncle Bill asked quietly.

She looked at him and saw herself. His expression of concern seemed identical to the one she must have been wearing while trying to talk him out of entering the Protoverse. The synchronicity made her giggle with nervous tension and instantly settled any doubts she might have had.

"I gotta," she smiled in absolute fear.

He nodded grimly and drove on. They stopped presently beneath an overhang of crumbling arches, and Uncle Bill killed the engine. Silence hit them like a wall. He went to fetch something from the back, and she cracked the airlock, lugging her case down to the ancient paving of the avenue. Out on the road she could hear the sound of rope ladders squeaking faintly in the hushed breezes. The sound highlighted the unnatural balloon-like buoyancy of the floating masonry. The usual chorus of night insects and frogs was distant, seething at the edge of perception like white noise on a faraway radio. Creatures seemed to avoid the Necropolis though the place resonated with vitality despite its lack of habitation. It was completely unlike the Lost Quarter, which, although paradoxically infested with creatures, felt utterly lifeless and bereft of energy. It was the presence of the god, she realized. It haunted these ruins, transmuting their obvious dilapidation into something sacred. The thought of this unseen deity chilled her to the bone, and she began to entertain very serious second thoughts about allowing herself to become stranded here. Uncle Bill emerged from the cab and climbed down the ladder. He had some parting gifts with him. One was a rolled-up thermal sleeping bag, and the other was a chromium six-gun in a hip holster. The belt upon which the holster was affixed acted as a bandolier and held up to a hundred bullets. He made her buckle it on and gave her an additional box of ammo, which she tucked under her arm as if it were a carton of pastries. Then he shook her hand solemnly and climbed back up into the cabin. The roar of engines made her jump, and she watched the massive rig rumble off into the yawning dreamscape of broken shapes moving farther and farther away into the luminous night. She stood there for almost half an hour and could still hear it grinding like a mosquito in the corner of a room. She saw its lights go on when it passed back into the jungle, a tiny smudge of color against an enormity of gold-tinted blackness. And then she was alone.

θθθ

T
ATY WANDERED THROUGH THE MOON-BRIGHT ruins clutching the six-shooter and shaking with fear. She cursed herself, broke down into tears, and finally ascended to a numb mental plateau where nothing mattered anymore. The dam wall had broken, and she was still alive, swept away but intact. She picked her way across gloomy courtyards and down long creeper-infested passages hung with luminous moonflowers. Damaged platforms and long dry aqueducts drifted by grainy in the celluloid shimmer of the lunar glow. She began to feel secure that no large predator was going to jump out at her from any shadowy crevice. The Necropolis was truly barren of all animal life. She re-holstered the revolver and drifted as though in some dream. While crossing a bridge over a long-dry canal, she stopped to pull her headphones on and pressed play on the pink tape. Alphonse's voice blossomed out of that vivid night still with her like some pesky and troublesome spirit.

"Still alive ... Well, if you are hearing this then you must be. Something tells me you will survive. I can't help feeling optimistic about you. You have that survivor look about you, don't you?"

The moon passed behind floating structures, creating disorienting shadows, and she fumbled for her flashlight, switching the tape off for a moment. She withdrew the map he had given her: an old aerial atlas scribbled over with lipstick and ballpoint pen. Peculiarly Gnostic doodles converged to create the swastika shape of the scattered pyramids. Over these had been transcribed barely legible notes cramped together in intricate masses. It was impossible to derive anything but her position from such a document, and so she gave up attempting to decode the notes, which she suspected he had placed there simply to confuse and disorient her.

T
ATY DECIDED TO CAMP IN the lee of a towering statue when her suitcase became too heavy to bear. The wide lap of the giant stone figure was swamped with ghostly vines, the wreaths of which created a small shielded grotto beneath its thighs. It seemed fine from without, but when she was inside she felt vulnerable and distraught. Eventually, she simply disguised her case beneath some vegetation, pulled on her fur, and struck out for the nearest rope ladder. She

carried the sleeping bag on her back with the intention of camping on one of the Floating Pyramids. The ladders creaked down from the stars, and she felt certain that somehow she would be safer in the structures above. Stopping every now and then to reorient herself in relation to the statue beneath which she had hidden her things, she took hold of a ladder and began to pull herself up to the hovering mass of stone. As the Pyramids went, this was one of the smaller ones, only a couple of stories high and suspended on a lower gradient than some of the heftier structures. Even so, it was difficult going, and she became overwhelmed by a sensation that the stone pyramid would suddenly drop, squishing her like an ant. She gradually squirmed her way up higher and higher until she was finally able to take hold of a narrow ledge and pull herself up onto the structure. Below her stretched the spectacle of the moon-drenched city, and she climbed carefully up large moss-eaten steps, gazing out into the illuminated night. She came upon dark doorways that led into the pyramid itself but was not tempted in the slightest to enter. Instead, she climbed steadily on until she had crested the pinnacle and stood on the narrow platform at the very top. The silence of the city further amplified the inherent sense of dreaminess, and from her vantage point the soft-edged buildings crumbled like nougat in the spectral light becoming soft and pliable in their paleness. Dark stone cubes hovered in the spaces before her, extending out into aerial distances like the falling dice of giants. And receding into these staggering geometries were the other pyramids, breathtakingly grandiose and level, settled on invisible planes as though constructed atop sheets of invisible glass. She had thought to sleep on the small pyramid but in the end felt too exposed. She eventually curled up in a niche halfway down the side and snuggled into the depth of her sleeping bag, six-gun close at hand. After lying still for several moments, she realized that the pyramid was swaying very slightly. It was not unpleasant—almost like being aboard a boat of some kind. She rummaged for the walkie-talkie but again hesitated too long. She simply felt too ashamed to face the porcelain Madonna. Instead, she drew out the Braille card that Alphonse had given her. She studied it by the light of a match for several seconds before setting it alight. When it was halfway burned, she released it and watched as it tumbled off the edge like a strange short-lived butterfly of fire. In the darkness she could feel another scrap of paper buried deep within her pocket. She ran her fingers over the Braille that had been typed upon its surface in an almost loving fashion. The sensation of stroking it soothed her, and she was soon asleep.

TATY AWOKE JUST BEFORE DAWN and watched a pale sun slowly sweep the shadows from the ruins. The magic of the moon had long since departed, and morning found the ruins gloomy and oppressive. She had a nagging sense that she was not alone even though the ruins seemed utterly deserted. She unfurled from her niche, rolled up her sleeping bag, and slowly inched herself down the rope ladder. Water had collected in the stone carvings, and she lapped some of it before retrieving her suitcase. A steamy mist hung in ghostly scarves throughout the citadel, drifting in tentacled masses between the broken buildings. She warily navigated this penumbra, unable to shake the feeling of being watched, consulting the lipstick-smeared map on occasion to clarify her bearings.

It was around noon when she became aware of a heavy grinding sound—a sound she was steadily drawing closer to. The mist had fallen away with the onset of the sun, and it had grown humid in the maze of stone. She was passing through a series of sunken unroofed corridors when she decided to stop for a moment to rest. She sat on the nearest stone head and chewed on a strip of salt-cured jungle chicken, listening to the mysterious sound, attempting to visualize what might be causing it. It was a dull shrieking of stone against stone, which came and went as though something massive were quarrying into a cliff face at regular intervals. The odd skittering of the sound of falling rubble added to this image. She pondered on it, and when she felt sufficiently rested, she continued on down the channel, arriving eventually at a wide case of stone steps, leading up to an open space. She emerged onto a large plaza the size of several sports fields and immediately saw the cause of the sound emanating from across the gulf. A large pyramid loomed like a UFO above a series of intricate, stepped towers that clustered at the opposite end of the plaza. This pyramid was skirted by a recession of massive floating cubes fashioned of a black stone not unlike obsidian. Yet, for some reason, one of the cubes had fallen out of alignment. The disparate levitation had pushed it off kilter by degrees over time. This deviation had eventually caused the cube to collide with the side of the pyramid and gnash into it over the centuries. The weighty structures ground together like teeth, creating disturbing acoustics as they gradually wore away at one another. The continuous attrition had created gaping chasms in the structure of each, and the continuous fall of dust and small chunks of dislodged material tumbled to the towers below, coating them in debris, giving them the appearance of stalagmites in a lime cavern. Taty recalled a partially indecipherable note about this pyramid on the map and drew out the tattered document. She spotted the site on the map and quickly realized that the postbox of the god lay just beyond the plaza somewhere below the encrusted towers.

THE AREA BETWEEN THE CLOSELY packed towers was rippled with dunes of powdered stone from the structures above. These rose in creamy scallops between the ancient buildings, creating the surreal impression of an indoor beach. The shrieking noise above was deafening. The air was tense as though at any moment everything would come crashing down. This perpetual dread added to the sacrosanct aspect of the area, marking it as the abode of something sacred and inhuman—a forbidden area. The rotund towers spiraled up above Taty as she trudged across crumbly dunes into the labyrinthine channels between. The dust had accumulated over hundreds—if not thousands—of years, and its volume rose steadily as she penetrated farther into the matrix of passages. She discovered that the powdery residue formed a large mound almost directly beneath the grinding, contained within a sort of courtyard clearing deep within the tower maze. This accumulation had created a steep hillock in the center of a courtyard area bordered on all sides by the cornered bases of towers and shadowed by the movements of the great pyramid. Fine curtains of freshly crushed dust wafted down like ash with each grinding, gathering on everything and coating the area in an unnerving uniformity of color. Everything was grey. And even she was becoming grey beneath the windfall. Specks of falling dust clung to her, making her cough and wipe her eyes. She had read the notes carefully, listened to the tape, and knew exactly what to do.

She passed like a ghost through this grey place and quite easily discovered the colonnaded niche described on the tape. The secluded area had been built to nestle in the shadowy space between three large pillars. Ragged bamboo shelved the sanctuary, the racks heavily laden with richly ornamented human skulls. The bones were bleached a spotless white, filigreed with fine metal, and mounted with large jungle jewels, one apiece. Alphonse had explained that only children could be sacrificed to the dead god and that these sacrifices could only be performed by those wishing to send a letter. The process was tricky because the sno-globes of the sacrificial victims had to be concentrated and trapped within the jewels before they were ritually beheaded. These impregnated soul-heavy jewels, once set in the skull of each victim, could then be substituted for a living sacrifice. The imp's description of the rituals involved had made Taty queasy, and she stopped the tape when he began to go into detail. She looked at the skulls glowing like moons in the dark and threw up in the dust outside, remembering the things he had said. The image of Alphonse doing those things to children only cemented the decision she had made in the dragon rig.

She hunted around for the imp's collection of skulls, which were all neatly labeled, and selected one with a large emerald affixed to its forehead. She carried the bright skull out into the light, removed her boots, and began to scale the hillock of dust barefoot. It was difficult going, and she slipped many times trawling long sticky runnels back down to the bottom. Alphonse had explained that the interior of the dust cone was hollow, the dust slipping down into a well that sank many hundreds of meters into the subterranean core of the Necropolis: the postbox of the lost god. Taty crested the tip of this dust mountain on her stomach, careful not to slip into the volcano-like pit yawning within. Dust was perpetually swirling down the steep sides of this drop, down into the square hole at the center of the pit. The drain-like shaft dropped into grimy nether regions of darkness, a throat of edged stone reminiscent of the storm pipe leading to the Lost Quarter. Taty peered over the edge before rolling carefully over onto her back. She rested there for a moment staring up at the drifting underbelly of the pyramid and squinting each time the dust came ghosting down. She was by now completely grey and seemed to blend seamlessly into the dust upon which she lay. She reached into the hip pocket of her denim hot pants and pulled out the white scrap of Braille-typed paper. She folded this into the tiny metal case, which had been screwed into the interior of the cranial cavity, and hurled the skull over the edge. She turned just in time to see it bounce off the stone edge and down into the hole. It was swallowed instantly. She lay on her back waiting for the sound of impact, but nothing came.

LATER THAT DAY TATY SCALED a rickety ladder to the steps of one of the largest pyramids. She had selected the pyramid at random after discovering a garden of rope ladders hanging down against a burning dusk. These grand monoliths were suspended much higher than the other pyramids, and the ascent was at times frightful. Taty wasn't even sure if the ladder would hold, but the gravity of the act she had just committed incinerated her sense of self-worth. She knew that if she fell she would be done for but had somehow ceased to care. Taking a life did that to a person. It made them strong in unholy and irreversible ways. This pyramid was much more grandiose and labyrinthine in comparison to the one she had slept on the night before. A wide ledge of moss-eaten stone dropped at least twenty to thirty meters to the jagged roofing of broken temples. Wide ceremonial steps ascended to the summit interrupted by yawning portals to inner recesses and gloomy vaults lined with carvings. She glimpsed halls bordered by great pillars and enormous frescoes that caught the dying light as the vast structure turned on some arcane axis of energy. She stopped halfway up the pyramid, resting on a carved ledge as the light faded. The black summit still towered above her, ageless and unmovable against the sky. Her quest had ended in grey dust and the skulls of children. She listened bleakly to the last few minutes of the pink tape, staring out at a jungle sunset while Alphonse spoke. She had her six-gun out and twice put the barrel in her mouth to finish the job. Yet, despite her best intentions, she could do nothing but gag on the metal. She couldn't even cry anymore. There was nothing left to puke up. She rewound and replayed the tape until it stretched and the words slurred. She hadn't thought about her brother in ages. It was almost as if she had successfully managed to erase that part of her life. But like most drowned corpses, the memories had risen bloated and festering, forever a part of who she was. Alphonse's voice came to her like his ghost. It was almost as if the imp were already dead even though she knew that he couldn't be, yet. That last unseen act was still to come, when the god rose from its bower.

"You see, I'm a survivor, too, Cupcake. I've been in contact with Dr. Dali and have found a way to reverse the symbiotic transmutation. It's slow and painful, but I am sure I will enjoy it. Once you have done what I have asked, it will only be a matter of time before Mister Sister is screaming at my feet. The pendulum swings both ways, dear. It's just something you learn after a while. The pendulum swings both ways. It's a tarnished pearl I offer you, my cyanide cupcake, but a pearl nonetheless. The god you have summoned will rise from the sleeping city and by secret means bridge the gulf between its haunts and my house. Gods can do these things, you know, even dead ones [sniggering]. It will come from the jungle and tear delicately into the paralyzed face of Mister Sister with its fluted fingers. But he will remain conscious to witness his dismemberment. He will be forced to observe as the deity carves into the fabric of his sno-globe and begins to feast upon the very meat of his soul. They say that the material body is illusory. Imagine, then, the torment of having your true body consumed, of being sucked down into the throat of an ancient idol like a smoked oyster. The bloated reprobate will awaken inside the lightless soul of the god who never rests, among the many other devoured beings. And he will be trapped there until the day of reckoning when all the souls within this god are released as psychic ballast and the prophecies of that ancient and ridiculous people are fulfilled—when the temple rises and the god travels 'upon a road of souls to the moon.' How much more absurd an end could one wish upon their nemesis? He will be digested like some broken insect unable to escape the un-death of his predicament, lost among the legions of the devoured, compressed like a fruit cell inside the body of a monster."

Taty rose and climbed slowly while she listened, determined to reach the summit of the structure before darkness oozed over the shambolic city, saturating everything in the terminus of night. Alphonse continued like a ghost in her ears.

"But you know that you are killing someone by doing this for me—killing someone bad. You aren't a stupid-cupid. You don't fool me. I know your brother didn't just die. You killed him—if you even had a brother to begin with. You killed whatever you left behind, whatever you came into the Zone to forget about. You killed it. And now you are killing again. It's in your blood. Deep down, you are a cold little bitch—just like me [*cackling juicer sounds*]! I'm going to gloat now, Cupcake. I doubt you'll make it out of the Necropolis in one piece. Good luck, anyway, Tatum. I wish you all—"

She switched it off, tore out the tape, and hurled it off the edge. She watched the pink tape flutter off, a tiny speck of candy against a wilderness of decay. When it had vanished entirely, she continued up to the summit, intent on shooting herself when she reached the top.

DARKNESS CAME. THE MOON WAS stifled by wild cloud, choking the jungle in blackness. Nestled in her sleeping bag, cuddling her gleaming pistol like it was a teddy bear, she could see very little beyond the stone balustrades of the upper tier. A wind brewed out in the galaxy of vines and trees, skittering up through the Pyramids like a barrage of spiritual force. It was so long ago that she had lived like a normal girl caught up in school routines and domestic entombment. After months of fog, the windows were opening, letting in old ghosts. The numb comfort of entrapment that, for her, summed up the Lowlands rose in the back of her throat like bile. She felt for a moment the twin twangs of regret and nostalgia. Then, as though by alchemy, the trauma of her current situation harmonized with the memory of her troubled mother. The thought that she now shared a commonality with that screaming, desperate figure cut Taty clean to the bone. Visions of her life before passed like the reruns of some old television show, siphoning down various cracks to collect on the staring face of her brother. She could recall their shortcut home from school with perfect clarity—the metal track through long industrial backlots, down past the rusty billboard, across the monorail plot, and beneath the hover stations of the D'urban sky mall, which hung pale and heavy as a moon in the dusty air. She couldn't remember what she and her brother had argued about that day. The event, when it happened, was sudden and occurred in such a fit of anger that she didn't even register it until he was lying there like a pile of old washing. She had become furious over some triviality and lashed out reflexively with her mind. She stopped his heart as though it were a clock. It had all been so magical before. Being able to do secret things, perform secret miracles. She had lain in her bed and made things move just by looking at them. She had started fires with her mind. She could do things no one else could.

It had always made her feel special, but after what happened to her brother, she began to see it as a curse. Nobody else knew what had happened. Nobody knew that she was the one who had reached in and put a finger on his heart. Until then she had not realized that she was capable of evil. She had loved him. It was just a stupid fight. And all the people at the funeral crying and feeding her cake and commiserating. Her mother crying in the kitchen, popping pink pills as if they were Tic Tacs, her father, who was never home, away drinking with his substation colleagues. She in the corner—the household pet with a secret. Everybody knew about the Outzone. Everybody was always talking about it like it was fairyland. *In with the Outzone* was doing the rounds. The girls had all read Karolina K-Star's secret diaries, and everybody dreamed of running away into the jungle to become bounty hunters. She stuck it out for a couple of weeks, but in the end it wasn't hard making the decision to pull a vanishing act. She just got up one night, packed a bag, and walked into a dream. She broke her piggy bank and bought a bus ticket to the Zone. She had run into a brand new universe. But here she was again, lost and alone, with someone's blood on her hands.

She awoke in the wild, screaming night and thought she saw the god standing on a distant pyramid.

"I made a wish to my fairy godmother in a hotel room," she mouthed across the void to it, half-asleep and delirious. "I meant every word."

PART III

Paradise Discothèque

24
Merchandise

One Year Later

SHE SAT IN A DIM metal booth facing the video camera. The lights came on, white and surgical. In another dark room her face dominated a large screen. The past year had taken its toll. She stared full frontal into the whirring lens, an artificial smile painted across her face. Her fastidiously painted eyes were hollow with narcotics and lack of sleep. The blankness within them accentuated, revealing a wilderness that could never truly be erased. Glossy hair hung in a sculpted blow wave, makeup flawlessly executed by a team of professionals. The high Empress collar of her orchid print dress was visible on the screen, embroidered in metallic thread and crimson silk. The wall behind her was a lush tapestry of patterned wallpaper in green, gold, and purple. The hollow hiss of an open microphone filled the booth like a trapped wind. A deep voice emanated from a speaker system, projecting into both rooms simultaneously.

"She's a rock star, all right. She knows where everything goes. She knows how to pull the plug on the whole world if she wants to."

Figures shifted in the dark room as she smiled down on them, lights chipping in her black-hole eyes.

"She handles a belt OK. Maybe even cufflinks. But the rules say no scalpels."

"It's cool," she murmured blankly into the microphone. "Just no permanent scars."

There was some shuffling in the projection room. Exchanges occurred between shadows.

"Well, you heard the little lulu, but just remember, Paradise Discothèque has rules. Damage the Smile's merchandise and I'll get Florix to snip off your right ball. We have a nice collection down there in the catacombs, and I'm sure you don't want to add to it."

The voice cut out, and the camera stayed on. She stayed hanging in the hissing light, holding herself on display for a legion of strangers. A few seconds passed before the unseen speaker returned.

"She's all yours."

The video feed cut out, and she bowed her face slowly in the bright wash. Her fringe slipped, obscuring her face in shadow.

25
The Bad Seed

THE WALLS OF THE ONE-ROOM shack were constructed of faded flattened gas cans and pitched hardwood. The roofing was corrugated tin and banana trees cloistered round, brushing the metal loudly with their topmost leaves. The shack straddled the tree line, spilling out on the sand of a wild jungle beach. A withered old jungle Indian squatted on the sand outside toasting frogs over a paint tin fire. A wind-up turntable rested on the sand beside him, grating out Little Willie John's "My Love Is." The Indian warbled along to it, his eyes choked by cataracts, turning the stick upon which he had impaled his frogs. The stylus would reset clumsily each time the song ended, and the air was full of music. The Purple Clown was also there, some distance down the strand. He held his purple balloon on a long string. It whipped around maniacally in the offshore breeze. The panicked anxiety of the balloon was mirrored in his movements as though he could not bear what was happening.

There were no windows or lights inside the shack. The sunlight spilled in through a latticework of ragged cracks, creating jagged patterns of light hurling dusty bars of sunlight about. Strings of bones and cured fish dangled from loops screwed into the tin roof. A busted-up electrical generator occupied the center of the space. Smoke coiled in the light. There were several figures waiting quietly in the dimness of the shack. One was a heavy old Pierrot who went by the name of Florix. This fully costumed pantomime clown sat on a paint tin, slowly smoking a hand-rolled cigarette. Tiny blue tears had been carefully painted down his lined and powdered face. He wore the obligatory cone hat with three black pom-poms at a sensitive tilt while his baggy white sleeves and pantaloons disguised the physique of an aging soldier. Although Florix gave an impression of heaviness, there was clearly not an ounce of excess fat on his body. He had something of the acrobat about him, a springiness that ran contrary to his weighty muscle mass. It was a quality that highlighted the homicidal in him. A thin sullen man in his early thirties stood behind the Pierrot, hands crossed in an almost priestly fashion. He sported a black suit and tie, rose-tinted granny glasses, and he wore his shoulder-length hair in a middle parting. He went by the name of the Typhoid Surf and was the brother of the recently deceased Mary. There was a gangly loose-limbed aspect to the Typhoid Surf's movements that made him appear clumsy at times. A faint smattering of pimples rashed his face. He also smoked a cigarette while he waited. Something else occupied that side of the shack with them, something whose faceless head brushed against the roofing. The body of the dead god was pale, intricately marbled with fluid striations of musculature—as though comprised wholly of molten wax. Yet, there was a haphazard geometric quality to these many details, which lent its large body the textured delicacy of origami. The god was clearly an albino of sorts, and vestigial scales created pinkish patterns between its many bloodless folds. It was also possessed of an incredibly long spine comprised of hundreds of fine glassy vertebrae. These jutted from the skin in angular protrusions, enhancing the resemblance to ornamental paper and lending the god a sinuous, fluttery flexibility. Its ribs protruded in like manner, growing out of the skin in dense edged arcs. The god would have been far too tall for the shack had it not been squatted, its intricate back formations clustered to compact mass, limbs folded in unnatural articulations beneath. The god had spent so much time in the darkness of the subterranean realm wriggling on its long belly through underground passages and aqueducts that its body had acquired a translucent quality not unlike the centipedes you might unearth in long-sealed cellars. Its face was its most unnerving feature: a mask as featureless as a billiard ball gleaming at the end of an elongated skull. Frilly gills fluttered silently at its wide neck and sides, absorbing sensory information from the air around it. The unconscious person on the generator, the one for whom they all waited, was a character called Johnny Appleseed. He was slim and pale and had a sort of young unshaven Elvis look about him—dressed in fitted black chinos, shiny Cuban heels, and a white shirt that had been recently drenched with water. He was strapped stomach-up over the machine. His head hung upside down over the edge of the generator facing away from the spectators, arms fastened behind his head, ankles fixed apart to straddle the metal

casing. The trio waited patiently, filling the sun-lacerated air with smoke while the old Indian warbled over the perpetual song. Johnny awoke violently, breathing in large gulps like a landed fish.

"Johnny Appleseed," Florix smiled. "Welcome back on stage— we missed you."

The Typhoid Surf strolled around the side of the generator and looked down into Johnny's face without any discernible expression. He carefully placed a cigarette in Johnny's mouth and lit it for him.

Johnny inhaled, relaxing a little, trying to gather his thoughts. "Where's Sneezy? Sneezy Mac Kneel?" Johnny asked, focusing on the orange, cigarette glow above his upside down eyes.

"Oh, Sneezy's outside," Florix replied smoothly. "You know how he can't stand the sight of blood."

"No?" Johnny smoked, playing it icy.

"Not after what those soldiers did to him," the Typhoid Surf muttered.

"You know the Typhoid Surf?" Florix teased with a grin. "He knows you ..."

Florix let loose a deep-throated chuckle, and the other two ignored the dig, waiting for him to settle down. He did presently but was still smiling dangerously.

"How about Devoid?" Florix hissed. "You know him, too?"

You could see Johnny tense up as panic coursed through him.

"Devoid's in the room?" he breathed, wriggling against his bonds.

Florix started laughing again, big generous clown laughs that rocked the boards of the shack.

"Relax, my little ice cream cone," he cackled, slapping his knee. "Devoid's just along for the show."

Johnny started blinking in relief, dragging on his cigarette in three sharp puffs.

"You know what I'm here for, though, don't you?"

Johnny gulped, and his voice cracked when he spoke.

"I do."

Florix rose smoothly and kicked his paint tin seat up to the generator. He sat down between Johnny's spread legs with a sigh and started undoing his zipper.

"You know what the Good Lord said about seeds, don't you, Johnny?"

"No?" Johnny rasped.

"Well, He said that there's the good seeds that fall on good ground. Then there's the good seeds that fall on bad ground and are choked by weeds. And then there's the bad seeds ..."

He yanked Johnny's jeans down suddenly, exposing him.

"That's what you are, Johnny—a bad seed."

Johnny was gulping hard. The cigarette had fallen from his mouth, and it lay smoldering on the sand below his shaking head.

"Say, Johnny, you got a hard-on. Fancy that. Do you want me to put it in my mouth? I'll bet you'd like that, wouldn't you, my little girl? I'll bet you'll taste just like fresh ginger."

Johnny was sobbing now, sharp and angry.

Florix reached into his tunic and withdrew a pair of kitchen scissors. The Typhoid Surf took the hint and pulled out a roll of clear fishing gut and a bottle of antiseptic fluid. A needle swung from his hand in time to the song.

"Can you feel my fingers on your right testicle?" Florix asked.

"Yes," Johnny choked.

"Can you feel this?"

The piercing shrieks could be heard out on the beach. It didn't seem to affect the Indian, who went on toasting until his frogs were done, but the Purple Clown had both his hands clamped over his ears in agony. The balloon had come loose and billowed out to sea and was quickly lost against a galaxy of restless clouds.

26
A Favor for the Smile

Four Months Later

DADDY BAST'S SURGERY SHIP HAD traveled up the coast after
the invasion. It settled where there were always people in need of
medical attention: the wild shores some small distance from Paradise
Discothèque. The water there was turbulent and grey spiked with
drifts of brown murk stirred up by the churn. The sky was just as
grey as the sea—a sullen humid day. Shiny black-suited nurses were
hauling corpses overboard. On the other side of the ship, underfed
figures were being herded down a ladder into a yellow rubber boat
upon which the word "OUTPATIENTS" had been stenciled. Johnny
Appleseed was among this band of refugees, seated among partially
formed symbs whose development had been arrested, mutations,
victims of extreme violence, and quivering zombies. He looked a
little worse for wear after four months on the ship, huddled in his
denim jacket. He had Brylcreemed his hair for the occasion of his
release and wore shades the whole trip, refusing to speak to anyone.
The boat grumbled toward the distant shore, and as they drew in,
he caught a glimpse of the shack in which he had lost part of his
manhood. The shabby structure had been conveniently positioned
beside a small wooden pier, so that victims could be rushed to the ship
once their penalty had been inflicted. He found himself hypnotized,
barely noticing the pier until they were practically upon it. The pier
itself was a skeletal affair jutting from an otherwise deserted beach.
A dense tree line blotted into thick jungle, disguising a coast road.
Various people loitered on the boards of the pier, some holding up
placards with names on them. Most were bedraggled girlfriends
who had seen too much in too short a time, or taxi drivers in loud
shirts and bead necklaces. Johnny almost immediately picked out
the Typhoid Surf standing at the edge, holding up a sign with his

name on it. The boat eventually tethered, and a gangplank was thrown down. The passengers disembarked grimly, and the Typhoid Surf approached Johnny, tossing the placard over the edge. He wordlessly offered Johnny a cigarette from a crumpled black pack. Johnny regarded him for a second before taking one. People milled around them, exchanging greetings and slowly dispersing down the jetty. The Typhoid Surf took a cigarette for himself and lit both with a novelty hula-hula lighter, blowing smoke into the breeze.

"So, how's it hanging, Johnny?"

Johnny considered this.

"It's hanging just fine."

"Well, that's just funky."

The Typhoid Surf let out a long plume of smoke and glanced up the pier. The boat was pulling out, and they were the last ones left at the end.

"The Smile would like a word," he announced. "He's waiting in the limo."

"Let's go."

THE COAST ROAD RAN THROUGH the jungle worming toward the Outer Necropolis all the way back to Namanga Mori and the edge of the Zone. At its other end it led upland, skirting the coast for hundreds of miles until it reached the uppermost ends of the jungle. A wide dirt road branched off some small distance from the pier leading to Paradise Discothèque: last outpost of the party animal. Cars parked haphazardly, clustered around the path to the jetty. Most were large beat-up junks with fins and outrageous cone lights. Everybody souped up their rides, and most were resurrected crash victims or chop-shop specials. It was the frontier style of the place. A vendor was selling jungle chicken tacos fresh off the spit, and some of the outpatients were lining up for their first taste of landlubber chow. The clouds looked pregnant and electric, but somehow you got the sense that rain was still a way off. Bandaged victims filed into waiting cars that detached and creaked off down the highway like rusty tugs. A large white limousine brooded some distance down the road away from the hubbub. It stood out conspicuously from the other vehicles, and everybody gave it a wide berth. It was a well-known car around the area, and everyone was aware of who was

sitting inside. The smiley face embossed on the door gave it away in any case. Johnny Appleseed and the dour Typhoid Surf emerged from the tree line long after the last straggler. They strolled down through the slow-moving crowd, making a beeline for the bright shining limo. The Typhoid Surf opened the back door for Johnny, and Johnny climbed inside. The Surf waited outside, slouched against the minty paint job, lighting a fresh cigarette with his old one.

THE INTERIOR OF THE LIMO was spacious and decked out in white leather trim. It had a sparse retro sixties flavor to it—something medical, quasi-political. The astronaut from the Nebula Shell Sea Hotel was on a large semicircular couch, his harsh electronic breathing filling the cabin with a regular mechanical rasp. His suit was a little cleaner since the Shell Sea but otherwise unchanged bar one crucial detail: a classic smiley face had been engraved with lasers upon the reflective gold surface of his visor. He now turned this stylized face to Johnny, who sat on the opposite couch close to the door. For a few moments they simply regarded each other, the sound of artificial breathing filling the cabin. Johnny stared into the unnerving smiley face, which reflected his own within it, waiting for something to happen. Eventually, the astronaut broke the silence.

"Good to see you back on your feet, Johnny. How's the wound?"

Johnny coughed a few times into his hand, warming up.

"It still stings me some," he replied.

"Sad to hear it; sad to hear it. Must have freed up some space in the old blue jeans, though?"

"You bet."

"Well, there you go."

Johnny cleared his throat uncomfortably.

"Listen," he announced rather formally. "Thanks for getting me onto the sick freight 'fore the bleeding stopped my ticker."

"Well sure, Johnny. It's all part of the service. We don't like to see valued customers get all tangled and washed down the shower grate like that."

"Well, I 'preciate it."

"What you did to the girl was pretty awful, though."

"I guess."

"We usually take both gonads for that sort of stunt."

Johnny stiffened up visibly, half-expecting to be dragged down to the shack again. Instead, the astronaut merely continued in his monosyllabic robot voice.

"So, in a way, I figure you owe me that one remaining pinball."

"I guess," Johnny mumbled.

"I'm guessing you'd like to keep it, though?"

"You guessed right."

"Well then, you've got to earn it."

"No sweat."

The astronaut clapped his gloved hands together in a mockery of applause.

"That's the sort of attitude I like to see fresh off the banana boat. No group meetings for you, eh, boy?"

"None of that. No, sir."

"Top notch."

The astronaut flicked a toggle switch on his chest console, eliciting a chugging from a bulky piece of equipment on his torso. A glossy photograph emerged from a slit. He plucked it from his suit, handling it clumsily with oversized white gauntlets. Johnny reached over and took the picture, examining it behind his sunglasses. A portrait of Taty began unclouding slowly from the developing surface. She had been styled immaculately for the photograph, her hair up in an elegant chignon, makeup impeccable in the studio lighting. Her eyes, however, were as hollow and blank as bulletholes. The seductive smile clashed irreparably with those eyes, which told another story entirely. The effect would be nullifying to a person of any sensitivity. Yet, it was the sort of photograph sensitive people were unlikely to see. The image seemed like a catalog photo, an anonymous number picked from a brochure advertising many other hole-eyed girls who all smiled just as invitingly. A tapestry of lush patterned wallpaper was visible behind her halo of sculpted hair.

"I need the 'special talents' of your better half for this little one," the Astronaut explained.

"Right."

"This girl, she has a mother complex. Lost little dove, you know the sort?"

"Sure."

"I want you to become her Mommy."

Johnny blinked a few times.

"Uh huh," he acknowledged.

"When you have taken on this role in her mind, she'll become particularly impressionable and susceptible to suggestion."

"And then?"

"Instructions will follow."

"Right."

"Pop round to Paradise Discothèque later this evening and I'll make the necessary introductions."

"Fine."

"Of course, if you fuck this up, I'll send Florix round to finish the knob job."

"I won't be fucking up."

"That's a very commendable attitude, Johnny. The Typhoid Surf will be happy to drop you off at your shack. I'm sure you two have a lot to chat about."

Johnny grunted, pocketed the photograph, and exited the limousine. The highway was almost deserted. One or two haggard forms were bent over on the side of the road slowly eating their tacos. The owner of the stand was packing up shop, banging out pans of oil, and extinguishing his gas jets. The Typhoid Surf was waiting some distance down the stretch, watching Johnny step out of the door. He hooked his thumb down the road.

"Wagon's this way," he called out.

The Typhoid Surf drove an enormous large-finned hulk the Paradise Discothèque guards rather unimaginatively dubbed "The Shark." It had no top and sported the obligatory carnival cone lights so popular in the area. The surface was so badly battered and scarred that it was now impossible to tell what color it used to be. It hovered between an abused grey and a sort of vague rust color. The Typhoid Surf piloted the monster through a vegetation-choked back road while Johnny took the passenger side. He had that old Nina Simone number, "Good Bait," playing, wound past the piano intro until the drums and upright bass kicked in. They sat there wordlessly in the slow throb of the shuffle bashing through overhanging branches, hair flicking in the wind. The engine scrubbed loud and rude as it chewed up the foliage, and the Typhoid Surf removed his crumpled pack of cigarettes from his jacket pocket. He proffered the smokes to Johnny without taking his eyes off the road. Johnny slowly turned his head, jostled from side to side by the buffeting, and glanced down at the cigarettes. The Typhoid Surf also turned his head, and their eyes met behind their sunglasses. They shared an enigmatic unspoken exchange as the car raced madly down the cluttered vein of a road. Johnny didn't make a move for the cigarettes, and the Typhoid Surf did not retract the pack. They simply glared at each other as the foliage rushed madly past.

After a while they emerged onto a thin mangrove road where the car pulled up. Johnny climbed out and disappeared into the undergrowth without a word. The Shark screeched off down the road before Johnny had even vanished from sight.

27
The Lagoon Shack

JOHNNY LIVED IN A SHACK beside a mangrove lagoon. The black-shored water lay cloistered by dense banana trees and swamp vegetation fouled after years of run-off from Paradise Discothèque's sluice system. The water lay stagnant, polluted by trash and the bodies of poisoned fish. A tire and some other detritus drifted unmoored. A small fishing jetty reached into the water where it creaked continuously in the noxious ebb, a moldy old armchair balancing at the end of it. A small stool spindled beside this item of furniture, and Johnny would often place his beer and ashtrays upon it round sunset. His shack stood directly behind the jetty raised on spindly stilts. These foundation poles ran directly into the venomous black mud of the mangrove, finding purchase in the mesh of root systems, lifting it well above the surface. Johnny emerged from the trees, slowly skirted the lagoon, and mounted the squeaky bamboo ladder that rose up from the sodden earth, providing access to the shack. The door was still unlocked as he had left it. He flicked on a light switch and ignited the ring of neon tubing that encircled the floors. Light rose from below, illuminating a room whose walls and floor were upholstered with large sheets of relatively clean gold shag. A gloomy chandelier dangled from the moisture-sealed thatch. This item had been pilfered from a seafood restaurant that had long since closed down. It matched perfectly the large white wardrobe that stood alongside a boudoir dresser. A broad light bulb-framed mirror accompanied this dresser. A four-poster bed with mosquito netting occupied the opposite corner, flanked by a tiny red divan. There was a very definite atmosphere of femininity about the chamber, and perfume bottles and other womanly apparatus lined the various shelves. Tailored dresses and vintage furs hung like ghosts from a sequence of hangers, protected from the humidity in air-tight plastic sleeves. A rack of stylish women's shoes cascaded behind an assortment of hat boxes. Johnny stood surveying the

NIKHIL SINGH

interior of his shack for some moments before he noticed someone hiding behind the mosquito netting of the bed. A pygmy in a beaded grass skirt stumbled from the twisted sheeting. There was a bone pushed through his nose, and he was brandishing a spear. Despite his evident savagery, he seemed painfully embarrassed at having been caught.

"Johnny!" he uttered in a thick Brooklyn brogue. "You're alive, dude!"

"Get the fuck out, Donnie."

Donnie scuttled past him and down the ladder in the twinkling of an eye. He paused halfway to the tree line and looked up at Johnny over his feather shoulder sprays.

"How's the missus?" he inquired with some sincerity.

Johnny slammed the door behind him, ignoring the pygmy. He drifted over to the dresser and switched on the mirror lights, bathing the chamber in a bright stagy incandescence. He sat down before the mirror and removed his sunglasses, revealing those cinematic baby blues that the Paradise girls often commented on in admiration. He stared into his own reflection and did so for some time, studying every aspect of his unshaven face.

"Where are you, you bitch?" he muttered every now and then into the mirror.

The surface of the dresser upon which he leaned was cluttered with cosmetics, hairbrushes, and lipstick tubes. Three heavy-duty prescription bottles filled respectively with yellow, pink, and white pills loomed from the mess. There was also an ornate switchblade handled with bone and pearl inlay—an intricate pattern of double-twined roses on the hilt. A heavily thumbed paperback lay beside the knife. It was one of those old books that yellowed dramatically with exposure, puffing up like a French pastry in the humidity of the swamp. It was the sort of book you wanted to put your nose into and sniff deeply. A blue-skinned Tretchikoff face adorned the cracked and flaking cover. The title of the book lay above this face in a thick retro-orange font: *HOW TO COPE WITH A SPLIT PERSONALITY.*

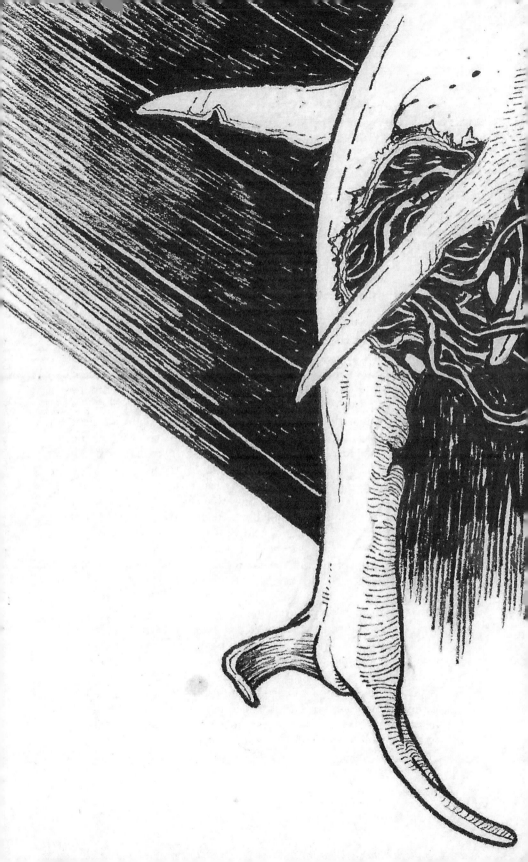

28
The Temple of the Far Axis

THE OUTER NECROPOLIS HAD FOR many years been thought of as the most sacred site of the enigmatic race that had so long ago inhabited the jungles of the Outzone. The grandeur of the Floating Pyramids and their arrested swastika formation, which spanned many hectares, was certainly grandiose enough to support this theory. Yet, there were intimations in the architecture of the Pyramids that suggested the entire layout of the Necropolis was mirrored by a smaller complex of structures that lay much deeper in the jungle. Numerous calculations were made over the years by academics and lunatics alike, theorizing the secret nature of the ruins. A popular theory postulated a sort of vast figure of eight suggested by the spiral movement inherent in the layout of the hovering pyramids. The geometric reasoning that postulated the figure-of-eight shape claimed that one loop of the form was larger than the other. If the Outer Necropolis was positioned at the apex of the larger loop, it would then follow that the lost complex would be located at the apex of the smaller. Expeditions were launched to find evidence of a fulcrum point for this immense ouroboros. If a fulcrum structure was discovered, it would support the figure-of-eight theory, and plans could be put in motion. Expeditions could be launched to locate the hypothetical pyramid temple of the opposing axis. After many months of searching, a thin spiral tower was uncovered in an uncharted region. It reached up from the canopy of trees, honeycombed by abandoned chambers and cellars. Frescoes depicting psychedelic highways to the moon and fire from the sky were found decorating these dusty chambers along with many of the other hieroglyphic displays common to the Outer Necropolis. Its positioning seemed to corroborate estimations regarding the placement of a fulcrum. And so, the hunt was on for the Temple of the Far Axis. This was discovered some years later in the unexplored western quadrants of the Outzone. This long-lost vegetation-wreathed megalith had also been constructed in a massive spiral not unlike what you would imagine the tower of Babel to look like. In appearance it was a vast stepped pyramid made up of concentric terraces all whirling upward toward an area of high pavilions. These sprawling circular terraces had been broken up into a complex of geometric hives that included innumerable vaults and chambers, corridors, balconies, and courtyards, both large and small. The superstructure was flanked by four large floating double pyramids, which had the appearance of massive eight-sided stone diamonds. These monoliths radiated out from the central structure and turned slowly in an opposing rotation to the gradual circumlocutions of the distant swastika. This opposition of movements indeed suggested some energy exchange between the sites: a movement of forces perpetuated by an arcane and indecipherable system of physics attenuated by the spiral tower at its fulcrum.

Dr. Dali was, of course, one of the first called in to examine the structures and deduce their function. It was rumored that he eventually solved the mystery of the flying Pyramids but disappeared underground long before anyone was able to question him about it. The coast road, which was then still under construction, was diverted to run within several miles of the temple. A wide dirt concourse was gouged out of the jungle to provide access, and a research station was established to be overseen by Dr. Dali. His quixotic experiments had led to construction in many of the ancient chambers and the development of awe-inspiring devices within the superstructure itself, which he claimed would unlock the potential of the temple as a "vessel for elevation and evolution." Nobody knew what he was talking about, and he had vanished into another dimension before his plans saw completion, searching for some mythical lost ingredient to complete his grand scheme. The research station was also eventually abandoned when the Outzone was declared lawless. When the doctor did eventually return, his head had "gone conceptual," his native atmosphere had become toxic to him, and he began to exist as an alien among his own kind.

Dr. Dali became increasingly lost in his work at the Clock Shop as the years drew on. He had, for a time, access to a means of wormhole teleportation, which allowed him to divide his time between radically diverse locations. His movements began to describe dense nodes of spaghetti tousled haphazardly across a whirling space–

time continuum. Nobody could keep track of him. His potentially insane agendas became the cause of much concern. Once engaged in conversation, the Temple of the Far Axis would inevitably come up and take hold of the doctor. He would refer to the temple as that lost cause or, stranger still, the unfinished quest for my perfect girlfriend. The Temple of the Far Axis, meanwhile, had gradually become a haunt of vagrants, vagabonds, and the interminably lost. Scenes of abominable vice were enacted within its many atriums, and bloodthirsty carnivals became the norm. The temple site was so distant and isolated that it became almost impossible to police even before the Zone became lawless. Of course, when the colonial systems of justice collapsed, the place went to the dogs.

The Temple of the Far Axis acquired a new name: Paradise Discothèque. It fell under the control of a long string of tyrants and gangs as the years slipped by and the Outzone grew steadily more uncivilized. The most sacred site hitherto discovered in the jungle had become utterly profaned, corrupted into a halfway house for hellish pleasure, taboo, and illicit trafficking. Of course, when Florix and the imp took over, they introduced a theatrical element and staged cabaret and pantomimes in and among the sex and grime. Florix had become a force to be reckoned with in his youth. His power had only grown. He ran gangs out of the jungle and pinned down the entire space-spice trade before he was even out of his twenties. Nobody knew who brokered the union between the clown and the imp. It all happened so long ago. But it was common knowledge that the pair were engaged in mutually beneficial dealings and had been for years. They made their debut by seizing control of Namanga Mori's vice trade at least a decade before Mister Sister sailed in with his cronies. It wasn't surprising when both made a play for Paradise some months after taking the city, rousting out the controlling gangs and coming up aces.

Later, of course, when Alphonse eventually tired of the frontier lifestyle, he retired to his mansion outside Namanga Mori to dally with sno-globes and energy manipulation at a spectral level. Florix and the old Paradise Discothèque floor boss, Papa Bang Bang, ran the show till someone dropped Papa out in the sticks with a ray gun and some machetes. The reign of the clown lasted for perhaps a decade with the support of the wrestlers, Daddy Bast, and Alphonse. But it was the symbiotes who eventually threw a spanner in that engine. After the invasion Paradise Discothèque saw a steady influx of refugees trawl from the cities and river settlements. Business was booming, and folks were flabbergasted when Florix up and handed the place over to the astronaut, a character who had apparently emerged out of nowhere, drifting in from the symbiote chaos. All of a sudden this suited stranger was running the whole Disco, ordering nonsensical construction work and generally letting the place go. Florix didn't seem to mind. When questioned, he would often say that the astronaut's running of things allowed him the space to concentrate on his clown shows and the management of the Paradise Theatre, which he had expanded to incorporate large musicals and obscene dance numbers starring kidnapped ballerinas and remote-controlled zombie dinosaurs. He still meted out punishment, ran the chain gangs, and remained the iron hand around the complex though it was clear he was taking orders from the astronaut, who later picked up the tag "Smiley," or simply "the Smile"—due to the gold of his visor. He must have thought he was being funny by carving a smiley face onto his bubble, but after the cruel and often absurd orders he was known to give, the nickname took on more sinister connotations. Everything was a peculiar joke to him, one only he seemed to understand. No one knew what he looked like or whether he was even human. Yet still, nobody dared argue with Florix's acceptance of him as captain of the whole damn plague ship. And so Paradise Discothèque began to drift into uncharted waters growing stranger by the day.

29

Champagne and Reefer

EVERY NIGHT WAS FRIDAY NIGHT at Paradise Discothèque. Sometimes a week of Sundays would coast past like a school of whales, but as soon as the sun went down behind the steaming trees, there it was again—Friday. Sometimes it felt like Saturday, but this far out, no one could tell the difference anyway. The calendar had gone up in flames, and the world was in a toothy mouth whose tongue had recently been torn out. A large portion of Paradise Discothèque cleared the high canopy of the rainforest, emerging like an enormous breast from the tumultuous green. Its ancient pyramid diamonds swiveled against the night like mountainous cliff faces falling in slow motion. Massive bonfires underlit the structures in a savage kaleidoscope of fire, and everywhere you looked you could see flaming torches in braziers and brackets. Rickety, makeshift bridges linked the Pyramids to jutting landings along the central structure of Paradise Discothèque, but nobody went out there unless they were drunk, crazy, or well-armed. The flat featureless sides of the Pyramids offered no means of purchase, and the pterodactyls had constructed nests in vile, mud-and-wattle terraces at the summit of each. Searchlights tracked the sky like a Hollymode premiere, catching the soaring underbellies of these flying beasts as they made mad passes at anything they felt they could eat. Wild music pumped out of various halls, and a hubbub of drunken voices spilled into the fragrant night air. Crashing and various machine sounds dribbled from jury-rigged vents. You could even hear the screams of monkeys who had invaded in gangs searching for fruit. Gunshots and fireworks bruised the air from high balconies, throwing out starbursts of shocking color and noise. Yellow-stoned colonnades yawned in massive arcs, enclosing vine-eaten plazas and twisting ramps. A sordid Babylon throbbed in what was once a silent mausoleum of abandoned holy spaces. Neon simmered in strokes and flashes through these prehistoric vaults, lighting up ancient panels of stone relief in strobe works of lurid color.

Prophylactic and cigarette vending machines illuminated the spaces between bird-headed statues and idol-haunted niches. Inebriated party-harders entwined on pagan altars, spilling like geese into chair-strewn catacombs while the distilleries steamed and bubbled all day and night to keep the place drowning in purple corn vodka and banana rum. Kitchens steamed and banged, throwing out chimneys of smoke like tentacles. Figures passed through the sweeping, upper chambers and rifts of smoke like characters in some Boschean pit: go-go girls, morf zombies, colonial hard currency refugees in silk suits and pith helmets, jungle Indians gone bad, half-symbs, quarter-symbs, bounty hunters, river runners, big game dinosaur jumpers—you name it. The whole carnival swilled and screamed against the jungle night, crowding the terraces, firing weapons, and feasting while the pterodactyls gathered like witches on the points of the Pyramids. You could see the beasts unfolding like umbrellas in the hellish smoke-haunted night sky, falling to earth and rising with the kicking form of some straggler who had loitered too long on the swaying bridges. Those networks of abandoned passages where no one dared stray without an automatic weapon.

A SLENDER WOMAN STEPPED FROM a mish-mash taxi and minced across a sequence of drawbridges, making a beeline for the awe-inspiring entrance arch. Meter-high burning letters spelled out the words "PARADISE DISCOTHÈQUE" in flaming characters, spilling sparks and embers down upon the gun-drunks beneath. There was something studied in her gait, an elegance that, although subtle, betrayed a certain over-attentiveness to poise. Her jet hair had been coiffed into an elaborate vintage do, and a long bare back moved sinuously above the low V-cut of her raw silk gown. A huge fur swung buoyantly about pale exposed shoulders as she glided past the long lines of people who waited to be processed for entrance. Surly guards in plastic smiley-face masks acknowledged her approach with waves of recognition—greetings she returned with vague gestures of her satin-gloved fingers. The masked men raised their pistols, allowing her access without even causing her to break her stride. Those who witnessed her effortless entrance and complained were treated to rifle butts and cudgels. She missed these violent reprisals, however, already sweeping down vast familiar passages, her ornamental heels

clicking out lazy tattoos to the rising volume of music. She passed
strobe-lanced halls crowded with drug-palsied bodies gyrating
to jungle drums and the shrieking of overheated electronics. The
crowded areas came and went, giving way to relatively deserted areas
haunted by stragglers. The atmosphere in these dim arcades was
wanton and savage, plagued by isolated scenes of surreal atrocity.
She saw masked men in tuxedos hack one of their own to pieces
with machetes, then later, a flaming animal galloping through an
empty hall. It screamed through the long galleries ahead of her,
lighting up the hieroglyphs as it moved.

The woman ascended broad, swirling terraces until she had
risen above the trees. She then entered smoke-clouded porticos
carved with the mythologies of plague and apocalypse. The noise
of a crowd swelled along with the metallic crashing of water in
large tanks. There was music, too—discordant wailing and bass-
heavy feedback that rattled the torches in their holders. A jungle
tamborine started and didn't stop, fading behind her. She entered
a large circular space whose high ceiling was hung with lengths of
thick chain. The entrance was on an elevated landing, and one could
look down upon the entire chamber when entering. The woman
did this, lighting a cigarette at the stone balustrade, scanning the
crowd below for familiar faces. Concentric moats circled the floor
of the chamber in wide rings, channeling clear water from springs
below. Walkways of stone griddled the waterways, emanating
outward like a mandala. A fire pit blazed in the center of the pattern,
surrounded by a bar and crowded with half-dressed figures who
splashed and frolicked in the water while large fish flickered to
and fro, vanishing down black drains that fed back into the spring
flow. Sometimes a small crocodile would wash in, and the people
would screech and flurry, firing their guns at it, creating havoc.
There were numerous altars in the niches around the edges of the
chamber, and people used these as platforms for fornication. You
could see them moving like pale ghosts throughout the shadowy
recesses. Monkey god idols squatted like gargoyles along the walls
clustered by real black monkeys from the jungle. They clung to
these effigies, screaming at everyone and staging raids on the hors
d'ouevres buffet, which had been laid out upon large sacrificial
stones. A giddy liquid tension permeated all areas of the monolith
lurking like a caged thing.

The Typhoid Surf was at the fire bar watching out for any potential trouble with an oversized smiley face badge on his lapel. He was there with a showgirl called Chirrup, whom he had been seeing for a couple of months. She was still in her glittery costume and makeup, fresh off the stage hovering like some fragile and exotic bird beside the bar. The Typhoid Surf was in the process of raising a banana cicada piña colada when he glimpsed Appleseed smoking at the railing above. He froze instantly, his entire focus shifting to her. She, too, had spotted him by now and observed him coolly from a distance. Their eyes remained linked as she descended to his level, becoming obscured by the crowd. It wasn't even uncanny how naturalistically feminine Johnny had become simply because it wasn't him anymore at all. His personality had submerged entirely, giving way to Appleseed—his other. And Appleseed was a different kettle of fish entirely. The Typhoid Surf abruptly set down his fruit-laden cocktail and knifed off through the crowd, leaving Chirrup in mid-sentence. The showgirl glanced up and spotted Appleseed across the room, realizing suddenly what was happening. An expression of bitter recognition flashed quickly over her face, but she retained her composure. The Typhoid Surf crossed stone walkways, took hold of Appleseed's arm, and guided her into a cloistered niche where they could speak unobserved. He pressed her bare back against the cool stone, their faces held close in the dancing flame light. He touched her cheek and forehead, and she watched him from between his fingers. He must have been drinking heavily because it seemed difficult for him to register her presence, let alone speak. "I thought I'd never see you again," he finally managed.

She slipped her face from his hands and discreetly lit another cigarette.

"I had to sink deep after what Johnny did. I had to sink deep and hide."

"We avenged you," he announced grimly, causing her to blink rapidly in discomfort.

She averted her eyes, turning her face from his stare.

"I can't talk about what you boys did," she whispered.

"I'm sorry; I'm so sorry, babe," he muttered, bowing his head. "You have to believe me, but we thought he'd destroyed you and taken your place."

She glanced about nervously, scanning the niche for hidden cameras.

"We can't let Smiley see us together. He knew that I wasn't gone; somehow he knew. He told Johnny to send me here. He wants me to do something for him."

"Did he say what it was?"

"I can't tell you," she implored, looking up into his eyes. "Johnny wrote me a note and said I wasn't to tell anyone."

"You can't trust Johnny, I've told you before. He's just no good."

"Well, it's my body, too," she muttered darkly, unable to meet the intensity of his gaze.

"I have to do what the Smile wants or risk more damage."

"We thought that you couldn't feel anything when he was ... when he is ..."

She went quiet for a moment, smoking and staring out at the debauchery of the chamber.

"He used to slip out sometimes at sea. You don't know what it's like. I suffered terribly on the ship."

He pulled her to him, his drunkenness beginning to show through at the edges. She laid her head delicately on his collarbone but found that the smiley face badge pushed uncomfortably into her throat.

"I'm sorry, babe. It's all so fucked up."

She looked out over his shoulder and glimpsed Chirrup. The showgirl had moved casually to the edge of the fire pit and was now watching them over her flute of champagne.

"We can't let the spaceman see us talking," she said quickly. "The Smile has eyes in the skies."

"He's out on the Western terraces," he deferred, moving away reluctantly.

"I have to go see him. I'll call you later."

"I'm glad you're back, Baby."

She smiled weakly and hurried off across a moat, vanishing down a dank throat of stone. He lingered in the flickering darkness, watching the tunnel mouth. You could see that she had put a spoon in his soup. Jagged cracks were showing up everywhere along the glacier of his inherent coldness. He looked up and unexpectedly met Chirrup's gaze from across the room. She glanced away, sauntering back to the bar. He left the niche, suddenly realizing how drunk he was. He crossed the room and joined Chirrup, avoiding her gaze.

"One look was all it took," she quipped, passing him his

abandoned cocktail.

He looked away bleakly, sipping at the ludicrous concoction.

THE BROAD TERRACES SPIRALED UP in wide avenues like a highway roofed over by vaulting and bordered by arches and out-bulging columns. The recessions of arches and curved stone pillars created a snake-like ribcage effect that was disorienting in its coiling repetition. Once above the gusting panoply of trees, it was easy to imagine that you were simply ascending into space. The placement of the four Pyramids at regular intervals created strange distortions of perception. Instead of seeing four, it often felt like you were seeing the same one. This warped the dimensions of the structure from the perspective of the terraces, making it seem longer and thinner, almost like a tower or a highway to the stars. Indeed, it felt as though you could climb and climb the terraces of Paradise Discothèque all the way to the moon, like the legends said. Toward the top the terraces thinned, convoluting like veins of stone. They delivered one to barren gardens of stone beneath the upper pavilions, places where the god was venerated in bygone days. It would be seen up there from time to time, squatting like some pale and monstrous dinosaur on the parapets, looking out over the jungle.

The Western terraces faced their pyramid. Fire blazed in brackets along the antiquated passage, highlighting the perspective in a glowing sequence. The sound of the jungle invaded harshly this close to the trees. The chaos and perpetual activity of the massive structure seemed to find chorus in the jungle without amplifying it. Monkeys and birds screamed while insects invaded every crevice, filling the night with their whistles and calls. Appleseed found the astronaut some distance from the access arch bathed in the shifting glare of fires below. He was facing the jungle, taking measurements on a complex brass instrument, looking up at the stars. He sensed Appleseed's proximity and turned his unnerving smiley to face her.

"You came!" he announced mechanically, folding up the collapsible instrument and placing it in a pouch on his suit.

"I had my suspicions that you might stay away just to ensure the loss of that other troublesome token of masculinity."

"Pain was never my game, Smiley. You know that."

"Oh, you shouldn't doubt yourself so. In fact, I would say that pain was one of your specialities."

She regarded him with a polite but bitter smile.

"You may know everything," she said. "But you don't know *everything.*"

"Well put," the Astronaut robot-voiced. "That sentiment describes perfectly the reason why you are still here bartering for your testicle."

"You mean bartering for Johnny's testicle."

"Oh, my poor little banana split. That's not what I mean at all. You see, I know the secret of you."

"Which is?"

He leaned in confidentially.

"That there is only one of you, after all."

"How can you say a thing like that?" she muttered in disgust. "The only reason Florix disfigured Johnny was because of what he did to me."

The astronaut suddenly whipped out a gauntlet and grabbed her injured genitals. He pulled her crudely to him as she gasped out in pain.

"Feels a little more realistic down there now, doesn't it?" he grated quietly.

"Stop it," she gritted.

"You can entrance the help with your little cobwebs, but your presence here proves that you are still looking out for your manhood."

"Please, stop ..." she sobbed.

He released her, and she stumbled back a few paces, unsteady on her heels.

"Come with me," he commanded, turning and striding up the winding terrace.

She followed him, limping for several meters as the pain faded. Together, they rose above the jungle, leaving behind the cacophony of insects and night howlers. A figure came into view along the curvature, gradually taking on character and form as they approached. Taty sat on the edge of the parapet, swinging her knee-high white stockings over the drop. She wore a powder blue schoolgirl's uniform in the old French style: straw hat and pleats. She had her back to them, gazing down upon a massive construction site that had eaten an ugly hole into the jungle below. Scaffolding had been erected some stories high, and what appeared to be enormous tanks or fuel canisters were being attached to the stone flanks of Paradise Discothèque. Gangs of workers toiled beneath the glare of powerful floodlights clad only in grime and loincloths, scuttling to and fro in the mud. White-faced Florix was visible in the tumult dressed in black leathers and wielding an enormous whip in his large gloved hands. He strode about like a painted bull, thrashing slaves and slave drivers alike, boss of it all. Occasionally he would bellow out orders and whip some unfortunate in an effort to punctuate his instructions. Taty was watching him lash a slave when she sensed the pair approaching. She turned to look back over her shoulder, and Appleseed saw that she was wearing glossy makeup that gave her the appearance of a porcelain doll. Her lips and eyes had been sharply defined and stood out like glistening candies. Her hair had been tinted a dark blonde and fell in large smoothly formed ribbon curls beneath her Madeline hat. A pair of perfect blue ribbons hung from her hatband, falling down her back like arrows. The floodlights lit her from beneath while occasional flurries of sparks detonated from the site.

"This is Appleseed," the astronaut said to her.

"Hi," Taty waved.

Appleseed smiled graciously, but the smile she received in return was vacant and automatic.

"Appleseed is joining us here at Paradise," the astronaut announced. "You two will no doubt work together at some stage, so it would be best if you made friends now."

He turned abruptly and marched off. The girls watched the suited figure recede down the slow gradient until he was out of earshot. Appleseed then drew up her gown and sat down beside Taty. Below them, Florix had drawn blood whipping merciless welts across the unfortunate slave's back and sides. The strangled screams rose up into the night becoming lost in the jungle noise.

"What are they building down there?" Appleseed asked.

"Dunno, but they've been at it for months now—there are more sites like this all round Paradise."

"They look like rockets."

Taty gazed wistfully down at the machines and tanks.

"I'd like to fly away on a rocket," she murmured.

"Maybe you will."

"Maybe."

Appleseed glanced around for signs of surveillance before looking Taty squarely in the eye.

"He wants me to spy on you, you know."

"I figured."

"Why is he so interested in you, anyhow?"

"I met him back in the city."

Taty paused suddenly, turning to Appleseed.

"You haven't come up from *Namangs*, have you?"

"No, I've been in the jungle for years."

"Oh," the girl nodded, losing interest.

"Wonder what it's like in the city now," she mused.

"I heard it was bad."

"Probably."

Some instinct caused Florix to look up at that point. He noticed Appleseed and went still, quivering. Appleseed quickly turned away, afraid to look into his distant blood-spotted moon face. His gaze lingered for a moment before he reached down and snapped the slave's neck. A hush descended followed by a wailing.

"So, you knew Smiley from Namanga?"

"I was working the Nebula Shell Sea, and he was my first pigeon. That was before he was what he is now, of course. I mean, back then he was just a nobody in a spacesuit. Anyway, according to him, I'm the only one who's ever been able to hit his trigger."

"You were a ghost girl?"

"Yeah. I was ghosting for the imp when the symbs hit."

"Ground zero, huh?"

"You could say that."

"Well, at least you got out."

"To this? I should have maybe stayed."

"Don't talk like that. You're alive; that's what counts."

Taty snorted. "Does it now?"

Appleseed hesitated, noticing Florix looking up at her again. Then he turned and strode into a dark passage. It was obvious that he was coming up to find her. She turned back to Taty, who was staring out into the blackness of the trees.

"I don't know, babe," she said, burying her skittishness beneath a veneer of casual conversation. "I'm just trying to put a perk on the quirk. Maybe it's all painted black, and we're fucked. Maybe not."

"Maybe," Taty mumbled.

"So, you hit the spaceman's trigger."

"Like a knife. He's been trying to recreate the act ever since, but Romeo the Dealer had all the ins and outs, so we could never get it right."

Appleseed sensed a veil but didn't pursue it.

"So, why spy on you?"

Taty sighed, as though she had explained this all before.

"He thinks that I can do it without the ins and outs. He thinks I'm lying."

"Are you?"

Taty twiddled her gleaming school shoes, studying them as though they were fish in a pond. For a moment she actually looked her age, Appleseed thought: sunny seventeen, clean, and un-preened.

"Well, actually ... After all, that lava lamp shit down at the Shell Sea, I've started seeing sno-globes. Out the corner of my eye, you know ..."

She stopped, raised her head, and gazed out at something Appleseed couldn't see. It was the sort of thing cats do sometimes.

"Sometimes I see a pigeon's trigger, and I think I could maybe flip it," she said, almost to herself.

"Just like that?"

"Just like that."

"Why don't you work it then? You could make a truck of bucks."

Taty shot her a look.

"We're in the jungle, and the world is burning. What good would a truck of bucks do me?"

"I suppose. Why are you working Paradise then?"

"It's what I deserve," she mumbled quietly, gazing back out into the darkness.

"Nobody deserves this," Appleseed said.

Taty looked at her out the corner of her eye. She could tell what Appleseed meant. It touched her in a way—concern always did.

"Wanna go get some champagne and reefer?" she offered.

"Sure," Appleseed nodded, eager to get off the terrace before Florix showed up.

They rose, and Taty led her down a nearby corridor. They had been gone only a few minutes when Florix appeared out of an archway. He sniffed around, jumpy as a hound, radiating adrenalin.

His bloody whip dragged along the stone behind him like a mutilated tail, leaving tracks and splatters as he ranged here and there for Appleseed. After a while he gave up, wiping blood from his white face and lighting a cigarette. He sucked into the darkness of an archway, heading back down to the slave pits.

TATY AND APPLESEED EMERGED INTO a long bar area cluttered with sprawling, interconnected couches. The couches were all cream leather lit by subdued neon running in tubes along the floor. Grottoes of candles bulged in the corners, vomiting out thick veins of incense. A rift of this cloying smoke hung in ghosts along the low stone ceiling reliefs, filling the air with the stench of flowers. Music leaked in from nearby chambers, oiling out into a mush of reverb and voices. A rash of gunshots in a nearby corridor caused everyone to look up at one point, but then things sank back down quickly enough. A group of girls were toying with an anaconda, putting its head in their mouths. A large pink cake lay savaged on the flagstones, and monkeys came in from the ventilation shafts, staging complex raids for it. Projected images of microbial forms played across a distant wall, catching the profile of a large fallen statue. Naked forms writhed in this reflected light, slumping inert in grimy corners or across banana leaf mats while inebriated patrons observed, lost in their own paralytic stupors. Taty stopped at an illuminated self-service bar and collected a bottle of champagne and a couple of dark-papered space-spice cigarillos. Appleseed picked up the champagne flutes, and they exited, moving down dark passages deeper into the heart of the ancient temple. They started smoking in the catacomb corridors, and Appleseed could feel that good Paradise spice start to hit her hard. Time tuned down, and all the colors started jangling at the edges. She stubbed the roll-up out before she was even a quarter of the way through, afraid to get too mangled. She watched Taty moving sure-footed in the dark, familiar with the twisted labyrinth, already on her second joint. She was swigging regularly from the bottle that dangled so carelessly in her fingers, seemingly unaffected by her intake. Appleseed wondered how much space-spice and champagne it would take to make her lose her balance down there. Nothing else to do probably, she thought, boredom breeds physical resistance— same old story. Sometimes they crossed through claustrophobic unlit passages, and Appleseed had to listen out for the crisp tapping of Taty's school shoes in the dark. She did not ask where the girl was taking her and simply followed as though caught in her wake. The champagne and reefer had taken an edge off the perpetual hysteria of the place, a quietude supplemented by the sullen darkness of the subterranean passages. It made her feel numb and cozy inside—as though she were already dead. This must be the little girl's world, Appleseed thought.

"Where you from?" Taty asked.

"Down the road, same as you."

"Are you happy?"

"No."

"Best question to test for liars, huh?"

Appleseed smiled in the dark, already beginning to warm to her.

THEY EMERGED INTO A LONG low chamber whose tiled floor cascaded into a myriad of angular pools and channels. Clear water gurgled darkly through these mazy waterways, flowing gradually from one end of the room to the other. It was placid and dim down here, illuminated by one or more distant light boxes that caused the water to luminesce and threw writhing patterns along the walls. Heavy fish hung suspended in this liquid, wafting amid delicate ribbons of greenery. Most of the ceramic-tiled pools were colonized by vegetation, and a multitude of leaves waved slowly in the shallow trenches. Despite the profusion of plants, the heavy mineral-rich water was kept clean and glassy by a spring-fed current. The girls were both quite inebriated by now, moving giddily on the tiled paths between pools, chuckling at inconsequential things. Taty threw her hat like a Frisbee, and it seemed to sail into the darkness without ever landing. Her long dark blonde hair bounced above her school uniform, lending her an unshakeable *Alice in Wonderland* quality. Appleseed followed her, observing her move across the tiled paths between the water. The old and regular envy had surfaced very distantly. The feeling she sometimes got around attractive girls. Real girls. How easy it was for them to be who they were. Taty giggled over her shoulder, oblivious to the grain of her companion's thoughts, setting the champagne bottle down on the tiles and wriggling clumsily out of her uniform. She stood, swaying, naked now save for her shiny shoes and white stockings, struggling to re-light a cigarillo stub. Appleseed watched as she took a drag and flicked it away, stepping clumsily into the heavy water. There were fading bruises along her white ribs and thighs. She watched Taty submerge and flicker about underwater, disturbing a gaggle of tiny red crabs. She still had her shoes on. Eventually, Appleseed folded up her gown and sat primly at the edge, re-lighting her own cigarillo, watching the girl swim. Taty surfaced after a while, scratched around for the bottle, and took a few gulps. She was staring at Appleseed with an unreadable expression on her face.

"Come swim," she commanded.

Appleseed hesitated. She took the joint from her lips, reached down, and placed it between Taty's to avoid wetting it.

"I don't want to get my underwear soaked," Appleseed murmured quietly.

"Take 'em off, then," Taty puffed.

Appleseed shifted uncomfortably. Eventually, she removed her elegant shoes and lowered her silk-stockinged feet into the cold water. She dabbled them around, avoiding Taty's gaze.

"Why won't you swim with me?"

"My body's all fucked up."

Taty finned to a tiled edge and leaned her head against it submerged to her chin, chewing at the smoldering cigarillo.

"What happened?" she asked, squinting in the wisps of smoke.

"My brother happened," Appleseed muttered.

She sighed, sipping carefully from the bottle of champagne.

"Some months ago he led me to this place along the river—you know, one of those little towns without people?"

"Uh huh."

"He had set up some kind of ambush for me. There were these … these river men there, rough diamonds all of them. They chained me up on the wharf and had a party … messed me up good."

"Why'd he do that to you?"

"I don't know. Some boys are born bad, unfathomable. I don't know why he wants to destroy me and take my place."

"What do you mean, take your place?"

"I … I'm not sure what I mean."

Taty watched her from the shadows, letting the cigarillo slip slowly from her mouth and fizzle in the water. She blew a last gust of smoke across the surface, letting her mouth fill with water.

"I killed my brother," she gurgled quietly.

Appleseed glanced up sharply.

"You did what?"

"I fed him to Devoid."

"Fuck."

Taty submerged slowly like a reptile. She remained there in the cool dimness, looking up at Appleseed who morphed in blurs above the quicksilver surface. She let out a slow string of bubbles and surfaced silently. Appleseed was studying her intently over the bottle. For a moment they simply regarded each other, weighing what had been said.

"It's all fucked up, babe," Appleseed eventually muttered, looking away.

"Uh huh."

"So, what's it like working the Paradise?"

The question caused Taty to become somewhat introspective. She fluttered back into the pool, rolling her hands and shoes to scare the fish.

"The men, they want to beat you more than they want anything else, like revenge for something, I dunno. They like to use blades, but management doesn't allow scars, so it's usually scalpels and shit."

"That bad?"

Taty stared at her blankly, non-comprehending.

"I still have some scars, though," she mentioned vaguely. "Wanna see?"

"I do."

"Most people say no," Taty said, studying her intently.

Appleseed averted her eyes awkwardly.

"Sorry," she mumbled.

"I'll show you later."

"If you like."

Taty swam over and took the bottle from her hands, drinking long draughts and belching bubbles into the water.

"Do you get any women?" Appleseed asked.

"Some," Taty nodded. "They can get fucking needy, and weird, but very few of them actually want to hurt me."

She finished the bottle off and let it float, watching it slowly flood and sink by degrees.

"It's the men who want to hurt, the fathers ..."

She looked up at Appleseed and smiled darkly—an echo of her video-ready seduction face.

"But they all melt under a smile," she pouted coyly. "You just act all sugar-sugar, and they melt—it shows that they're not real fathers ..."

The smile went away abruptly as though she had flicked some switch inside.

"I've never cried with any of them, though. I mean, tears come out sometimes, with the pain and stuff—they like that. But I'm not really crying."

She drifted on her back now, stilled and floating in the dark water.

"Sometimes I fantasize, I guess," she said quietly.

"I fantasize that this man comes, and ... he's a different kind of a man. He doesn't listen to the sex talk. He beats me till I cry for real ... Then he puts a knife to my throat while he ... Then ..."

"Then he holds you."

Taty lifted her head to look at her, capsizing gently out of her drift.

"No," she stared. "Then he cuts my throat."

Again they were watching each other for long crystallizing segments of drunken time. Taty broke abruptly from the moment, wading out to the edge. She climbed out dripping and shook like a dog, wetting everything around her. Appleseed lifted a glove to protect her makeup and noticed that Taty's gloss job was now an irreparable mess. She began to pull on her uniform roughly, suddenly cold and distant.

"I have to go. I have a date."

Appleseed rose uncomfortably, smoothing down her shimmery gown.

"OK," she replied, stoned and momentarily confused.

"Can you find your way back?" Taty asked, buttoning up her blouse.

"Sure, I think ... What? Are you going now?"

"I have to go," she said, scurrying down a tiled path toward a dark tunnel. She paused at the threshold and looked back over her shoulder.

"See you around, Appleseed," she called from the edge.

There was a strange, shocked expression on her face, visible even from that distance. Appleseed waved in confusion and watched as Taty disappeared into blackness. She could hear her shoes clattering as she began to run faster and faster as though fleeing the scene of an accident.

THE TYPHOID SURF WAS BY now very drunk. He had left the bar in a state and was hunting high and low for Appleseed. He wasn't sure what he wanted to say, but he suddenly knew that he had to see her. Some instinct drew him to the walkway over the entrance arch where he glimpsed a large finned mish-mash pulling into the mud lot outside the gate. The legend "TAXI" had been smeared in blood-red paint along its battered sides. He noticed too late that she was climbing into the mish-mash, pulling her heavy gown in like a predatory mollusk retracting into a crevice. He called out, but no one could hear at that distance—not above the noise. He pulled out his crumpled pack of smokes and stared at them in turmoil. It was ages before he could take one out and light it.

30
The Hidden Microphone

JOHNNY AWOKE IN THE HALF-DARK of his shack. Sunlight was seeping beneath the door, tinting everything on the floor with little halos of gold. He sat up and quickly discovered that alcohol had put some footprints in his butter. He was also annoyed to find himself still wearing Appleseed's clothes. Usually she would get undressed before slipping out to save him the embarrassment— timeshare, she called it. Bitch must have been wasted, he thought to himself. He crawled to the mirror and sat down heavily. Sensors in the chair activated the harsh bulbs around the mirror, causing him to squint in the glare. The sight of himself unshaven and wearing a dress made him sneer. He reached up and pulled the gown over his head, turning it inside out. He then slouched with it across his lap, running his hands through his greasy hair and pressing play on an old tape machine. Little Willie John's "My Love Is" bled quietly out of the speakers while he scratched around for the little stitch-picking device. The gown was heavy velvet lined with satin and embroidered in silver thread. He started unpicking a seam along the bottom and didn't stop until he could get his hand up into the lining, where he fiddled around unhitching something from a secret pocket. What came out was a long black wire attached to a tiny tape machine. He balanced it on his palm, smiling in triumph.

He washed in the outdoor shower, scrubbing himself raw to get the perfume off. When he was done, he quiffed his hair, pulled on a blazing white vest, black chinos, and his slim black alligator boots. He got his rings and silver crucifix off the hook where she had left them and slipped them on. When he was done removing nail polish, he sat out on the end of the jetty with a cup of gas-brewed joe and sunglasses. Trash skimmed the surface, and the water was speckled with belly-ups, but he didn't mind the stink. It was something you got used to, he would always say. He smoked a cigarette with one boot up over the arm of the couch, listening to what was on the tape machine via a pair of covert spy earplugs. The low-fidelity splashing of the tiled pools beneath Paradise Discothèque merged strangely with the stagnant lapping of the lagoon against the jetty. The juxtaposition of these watery acoustics seemed to sully the intimacy of the conversation he had so clandestinely captured.

"Sometimes I fantasize, I guess," Taty's voice spoke over the granular hiss of the tape.

There was a pause, and he listened to the sounds of her moving in still water.

"I fantasize that this man comes, and ... he's a different kind of a man. He doesn't listen to the sex talk. He beats me till I cry for real ... Then he puts a knife to my throat while he ... Then ..."

"Then he holds you."

"No. Then he cuts my throat."

Johnny stopped the tape and gazed out over the putrid lagoon. He sat like that for an hour or so, thinking. Rewinding the tape over and over.

THE LAGOON WAS DARK AT night, shadowed by overhanging trees. Moonlight infiltrated cracks, dappling across the surface. The light of a window in the raised shack threw pale highlights over the black water while glowflies created curious patterns in the foliage. The repetitive groove of "My Love Is" drifted out through the window, carrying eerily across the swamp. Johnny sat before the illuminated mirror preparing himself. He had on black clothes under a heavy tan trench coat, winding bandages around his head and face. When he was done, he buckled on a large pair of industrial goggles and a fedora. Claude Rains was on the tiny monochrome television set in the background, playing the invisible man in James Whale's old picture. Johnny thought he looked just like him. After a while, a pair of headlights crept up through the trees, shining in from the road, illuminating ghostly creepers and monstrous veils of cobweb. When Johnny saw that his mish-mash had arrived, he deactivated the music, mirror, and TV, plunging the shack into sudden silent darkness. He passed by the lagoon, heading for the light, which gleamed in shafts through the Spanish moss. Donnie was up in a swamp creeper, and so Johnny didn't see him. The headlights illuminated his bandaged, goggled face while Donnie frowned down

in concern, sensing something ominous in the air. The taxi pulled off, and the moonlight seeped back in a luminous shimmer. Donnie stayed in the branches, puzzled. After a while, he scampered down toward the shack to try on clothes.

31
Daddy

THERE WERE TWO PUBLIC ACCESS points in Paradise Discothèque. The first was the main entrance whose flaming characters could be seen for miles at night. It was always busy, and the queues and procedures there could be long and exhausting if you were not a member or a regular from around the area. The second way in was via a small shambled archway set into a wall on the other side. It was a bleak little back door cloistered by dark mango trees leading directly into the "hive"—or what the locals called the "cathouse." The hive was accessible from the rest of Paradise Discothèque, but this separate more private entrance had been provided for those who wished simply to do their business and leave. A large orange photo booth luminesced near the archway, looking distinctly out of place against the old masonry. Its glow backlit a pair of surly bouncers in luminous smiley-face masks who guarded the doorway. Johnny appeared out of nowhere in his *Invisible Man* get-up only to have machine guns leveled at him. The guards barked threats in guttural jungle dialect, but he stepped into the light wordlessly holding up the astronaut's photograph of Taty. The men went quiet and lowered their guns, recognizing the print quality of the Smile's suit.

"Looking for the whippersnapper, huh?" one of them asked.

Johnny nodded.

"Been to Paradise before?"

Again, Johnny nodded.

"Well, I guess you know the jingle-jangle."

He led Johnny to the photo booth. A bucket of dimes had been placed beside the booth, and the guard selected one, dropping it into the slot. He ushered Johnny behind the faded curtain and pressed a silver stud. There came a click, a hum, and a flash of white light from within the cubicle. Four passport-sized portraits of Claude Rains fed out in a single sheet. The bouncer took up the newly developed print, examined the masked face momentarily, and then dropped it into a large wicker basket of similar passportsized photos. The words "HIVE WEEK 89" had been spray-painted on the half-full basket. Johnny stepped out of the box, and they let him pass. He vanished into the darkness of the passageway without a word.

TATY AND CHIRRUP SHARED A large room on one of the upper wings. It was common practice for wranglers to lodge girls together—for the sake of company and practicality. That deep in the jungle, it really was a kind of paradise for some of the poor, lost things: a room with furniture and running water in exchange for your body—infinitely better than the nightmare towns along the river. Taty and Chirrup's room was vaguely circular, carved eons ago out of the yellowish interlocking stone that made up most of the monument—a hard stone quarried from great depths to ensure strength and heat resistance. Nobody could say how the structure had been built (and no one was particularly interested anymore, anyway). Taty would often sit on the balcony looking out over the steaming expanse of the jungle, imagining that it filled up the whole world with its dream of green. It wasn't a hard thing to visualize. Large double doors gave out onto this half-moon balcony. A hand-carved mahogany table took center stage on the spacious platform—pilfered no doubt from some sacked mansion. Paradise Discothèque, lest we forget, was incredibly well furnished. After so many years harboring pirates and cross zone smugglers, the place had become a fairy castle. A bedtime story left to rot like a cake at the edge of nowhere. Empty champagne bottles cluttered the corners of their balcony. Overflowing ashtrays and glossy magazines tumbled over stacks of old vinyl. A machine gun balanced precariously against the balustrade trailing colored paper ribbons that had been wound around its magazine. Chirrup had on her "Good Bait" record, and the loose heavy piano chords were about to tinkle into the smoky drum shuffle. It was one of her favorite tunes, and she used to do a little dance number to it when she started out working the floor in Paradise. It wasn't too long before her act caught the eye of the Typhoid Surf. In fact, later, after they had gotten together, he would often refer to it as "their song." Two large beds occupied the room placed at skewed angles and shrouded in spray-painted mosquito netting. A pair of large mahogany wardrobes adjoined these along

with matching vanity bureaus. Taty's side of the room was relatively sparse in terms of decoration while Chirrup's had become plastered ceiling-to-wall with photographs of stage performances, yellowed newspaper clippings, and all manner of memorabilia. It was neat. In contrast, Taty's clothes and belongings spilled out all over the place. The showgirl was half-dressed, standing at the floor-length mirror, arranging feathers in an enormous flamingo headdress. Taty sprawled over her unmade bed with a baggy T-shirt over her gold bikini. She was flicking through a magazine and had a joint in her hand. A shrine dominated the side of her bed adorned with glittery items she had magpied over the last few months: colored glass, glowing isopods, Christmas streamers, plastic hearts, and polystyrene angels. The sacred niche bore a resemblance to certain shrines of the Virgin Mary as re-imagined by a nursery school class. The walkie-talkie took pride of place on the small religious altar, replacing the customary statuette of the Holy Virgin. Daisy chains draped this communications device. Glitter and confetti decorated it. Number Nun's voice came through abruptly, causing Taty to perk up sharply. The action spilled greasy ash all down her T-shirt.

"Come in, Childbride."

There was a long stoned pause while the girls stared at the glowing shrine. Taty eventually brushed off the ash and rolled over onto her back. She let her head hang off the edge of the bed and stared out at the upside down jungle, blowing dysfunctional smoke rings into the night.

"Very well," Number Nun clipped. "You may ignore the messenger of the Lord for only so long—I'll call back later—over and out."

"How come you never answer her?" Chirrup asked, brushing out her long chestnut hair.

Taty went quiet, thinking of her low lean days in the Necropolis, surviving off nothing and wanting to die.

"I dunno," she replied thickly.

Chirrup fussed over her spangled costume, arranging feathers and sequins with a fastidious attention to detail.

"Sooner or later you are going to pick up that walkie-talkie and spill your soup," she tut-tutted to Taty.

"I guess."

"Yeah, yeah. Dam walls don't give a damn. I know that song."

"I want to tell her everything. I just ... I just can't, not yet."

"It's been over a year."

Taty sat up, stubbing out the space-spice.

"Wonder where she's washed up ..." she mused nostalgically.

The intercom came on with a buzz, and a robotic voice invaded the chamber.

"Hook up for the little lady—Chamber 99 in fifteen. No specifications."

Taty slumped over the edge of the bed and stared down at her pigeon-toed feet.

"Shit," she muttered thickly. "What should I wear?"

"Pity you trashed the schoolgirl number."

"School is for losers."

ROOM 99 WAS AN OLD tomb reinterpreted as a love nest. A wooden door had been jerry-rigged to give the low-ceilinged chamber some privacy. A bed had been installed upon the sarcophagus stone. Black candles guttered, and the area swarmed with shadows. It was one of the smaller cheaper rooms in the hive—a far cry from the glowing mirror suites lining the upper levels but far more isolated. Taty sat on the edge of the bed counting pulses on the big flashing panic button. There was one in every room, and you could use them to call the guards. It was a necessary precaution, and if the girl pushed it, the visitor was usually dead within minutes. Her makeup was clumsy that night—with only a quarter of an hour to be ready, she had skipped the long jaunt down to the slinky salon and smeared on kohl and cherry lip gloss like it was jam and peanut butter. She wore a long black evening dress with matching satin gloves and had her hair up in a frayed chignon. Pearls were draped carelessly around her neck, and she might have gotten away with it were it not for her dirty bare feet, which swung impatiently against the stone. A dog collar hung off her thin neck, attached to an iron ring by means of a stout chain. When the masked man came in, she found herself going quiet and still. There was something familiar about the figure that immediately caused her to experience a wave of danger. But the recognition was in the wrong area, a displacement that threw her off and manifested a shadow being—a shadow of someone she instinctively recognized. He stood at the door for long seconds, emanating a vibration of contained violence. She reacted to this with watchful silence, trying to spot eyes behind the impenetrable goggles. Eventually she stood up, scrunching her toes uncomfortably on the cool stone.

"So, what's your flavor, Mister Man?"

He ignored her, and she shifted around some more.

"You gonna take off that mummy get-up or what?"

He took a step forward, deliberating something, and she flinched.

"Listen, you either start talking, or I call for the big guys with guns."

Then it was as if someone had thrown a brake inside the masked figure. She went cold a heartbeat before he hurtled forward, scrabbling madly for the panic button. He managed to reach the chain before she could press it and yanked sharply on the leash, bringing her down to her knees. She spluttered in the collar, struggling as she was hefted back onto the bed. He twisted her around and pinioned her arms while she squealed and hissed and bit. But this resistance was quelled by a sudden onslaught of blows to her face and gut. Bright blossoms of pain-light burst behind her eyes, growing like flowers and sucking out into sharp hollows of a neural blackness. Her head rang as it caught his fist again and again, shooting her vision down into the blur of pillows. She took three more sharp blows to her stomach before she threw up. The light caught in tiny blood droplets hanging like crystals in her hair, and the sight of them fascinated her for a moment. Then the flurry of fists ceased, and she was suddenly lying on her back, panting and sobbing with shock. One of her teeth felt loose and the world had suddenly become very numb and shiny. Her hand fingered the panic button, but something inside her had cracked open—a jar filled with putrid mental remains. Was she being punished for being a murderer? She was tired of playing hide-and-seek with the torturous truth and was more than ready, she realized, to escape the dungeons of guilt and self-annihilation. She was crying raggedly, blood streaming from her nose as she forced her hand from the button. Perhaps now things would finally end, she thought, in a mad sort of mania. He loomed over her, blocking the light, somehow placated, as though he knew she would not call for help. She heard the clean click of a switchblade and gulped back hysteria, staring up at him as though hypnotized. Her vision kept switching into a perceptual mode where she could glimpse energy moving in currents throughout the room.

A deafening hum resonated in her head—the sensation of large, lazy insects trapped within her chest and throat. She gazed up and saw that the bandaged figure had not one sno-globe but two. Twin orbs of intricate light gave the impression of a cell perpetually splitting. One of the orbs was greenish, patterned in intricate convolutions while the other was a turbulent blue laced with flashes of hot white light. The pair meshed violently along the center, creating a storm of decaying light—an ellipse in which the shadowy form of the man lay trapped. Taty stared up at this strange vision, entranced by the play of light. Her hypnotic reverie was broken only when he flipped her over onto her stomach and wrenched up her gown. Her vision reverted instantly to normality as she felt him enter her body. It was like jerking the cable on a faulty television down there, she thought, one second a signal, one second noise. She felt her head being jerked up, and everything went slow and sickening. She started to cry as the knife came up to her arched throat—struggling against a primal urge to defend her own life. She squirmed and shook then went stiff as a board while he hesitated. When she started to scream, he hit her again above the kidneys. She went quiet and limp, and he jerked her up by the hair. It was fear that stopped him at all the crucial moments, not basic humanity. Sudden thoughts of the Smile came to him and played with his mind like cats toying with an injured thing. His hand was shaking visibly, and a whirlwind of rage seemed contained between the blade and the skin of her throat. His desire to end her life was so great that he almost went through with it several times before hurling the knife into the door where it lodged fast. He began to tear her gown to strips in the sort of hideous anger that usually follows an act of personal cowardice. Taty lay limply beneath this fury, trying not to move as the storm broke down upon her.

SHE REALIZED THAT PARTS OF her were stuck to the pillow and sheets. It seemed hours had passed. Then she felt the adrenalized suppleness of trauma assert itself, that looseness that comes after a beating. She realized then that she must have slipped into unconsciousness for only a few seconds. The man was adjusting his coat before the door. A lozenge of blurry light winked, and he was in the corridors receding like a reckless automobile.

θθθ

CLOUDS OF ENERGY, SLOWLY COAGULATING like candy around an element, moved through the haze. She felt she was falling at great speed through this glowing nebula until a pinhole opened. Sound sucked in, blasting everything away. She was on her bed, and Chirrup was shouting at the pair of guards who had brought her back up to the room. Taty blinked painfully, and the whole universe fluttered, shifting casually back and forth into another visual range. Their sno-globes luminesced like distant neon planets pulsing across the universe of the room.

"Find the freak and shoot him! Jesus!" Chirrup was yelling.

"But she didn't press the panic button; that's consent."

Chirrup's globe was a storm of golden birds shifting in flocks. The guard to the left had a fast food luster to his. The other guard lay obscured, glinting between the two like an eclipse.

"Well, I'm pressing the panic button!" Chirrup shouted from across the void. "Wipe that gimp on my command!"

"I can't! I'll lose my job, man. She didn't press the button ..."

"Ah, get out, you fucking hot dog."

She slammed the door, and the world shifted in Taty's eyes. She blinked, attracting Chirrup's attention. The dancer sat on the bed, and Taty could see all the mechanisms of her sno-globe in close-up. They immersed her, gleaming from within, growing and shifting in patterns of cellular distribution. A strangely tendon-like formation drew her attention for some reason, shimmering in accordance to the mechanics of her own sphere. She realized she had, quite by chance, located Chirrup's trigger.

"Doll, what the fuck? Why didn't you blow for the kamikazes? You can't let the Jolly Rogers peck you to shit like this!"

Taty tried to move her arm and instead jolted a tentacle of ectoplasm up into Chirrup's globe. The tendril coiled like a vine around Chirrup's shimmering trigger as though magnetically attracted to it.

"Babe! Are you reading me? I'm going to get the Typhoid Surf on the horn and get him to dig up that twisted mister. Then ..."

She experimentally flicked her tentacle, causing Chirrup's formation to unfurl in a detonation of ghostly origami. Then it was as if a bomb went off, and Taty watched her whole globe jiggle like a pudding. Chirrup was about as unprepared for orgasm as a person could be and collapsed across the bed as though suddenly electrocuted. She lay like dead weight across Taty's legs, spasming for a moment before letting out a shriek. Taty struggled up, cradling Chirrup's face despite the pain in her own arms.

"Sorry," she rasped.

Chirrup slowly pulled herself back into focus, her chest heaving and eyes rolling. She was clammy with sweat as Taty helped her to sit up.

"What ... what the fuck was that?"

"I shook your sno-globe. Sorry."

"Do it again," Chirrup sobbed through a grin.

The med-bots found them crying and laughing at the same time.

32
The Man Eater

THE RAPTORS IN THE SURROUNDING jungle were pack hunters who usually moved in prides of about seven females to one male. These numbers excluded the young who trailed behind as the adults made sweeps along the river's edge. The packs were constantly bickering with one another, and you could hear them hissing and squealing for miles when territorial disputes broke out. These predators stuck to the waterline and subsisted mainly off the calves of the larger herbivores that grazed in shallow waters. When a litter of pups matured, one of the young males would inevitably challenge the alpha male of a pack for dominance. If the pack leader was toppled from his perch, he was not killed—merely humiliated publicly in front of the females before being hounded into permanent exile. Usually, it was the former alpha male who lost out to the young blood. Unable to turn to his former mates who now spurned him, the emasculated ex-dominant would flee into the jungle to lick his wounds. These exiled males would survive for a time—how long depended on their own personal strength—becoming scavengers, existing without fixed migratory or nesting patterns. Unable to feed on the prey available to packs, they had to resort to smaller specimens for food. Sometimes one would stray too close to a village along the river, and people would start disappearing. It happened rarely, but when it did, the people on the river would naturally turn to the strongest and most feared for assistance. Messengers would come to Paradise Discothèque at all hours asking for Florix when a maneater was loose. Florix had been born and raised in the Outzone. In his youth he had loaded guns for the big game hunters and ridden out in gunboats as a colonial soldier. He knew the ways of most of the varmints in the wood and how to kill them.

θθθ

PARADISE DISCOTHÈQUE HAD RECEIVED A transmission regarding a rogue raptor that had been taking children from a settlement down the river over the last couple of weeks. Florix cracked out his machine guns and a boxful of grenades. He called the Typhoid Surf to drive him out in the Shark, and they took along old Gus Henry and a slapper for backup. The ride out to the settlement took about an hour and a half in the pitch black. The headlights scrubbed illuminated vegetation through the blinders, but even then it was pretty much zero visibility. The slapper had a working knowledge of the area and kept them out of gullies and sinkholes with deft efficiency. He used a psychic slap-back method that was not unlike sonar and often had a look on his face like someone had made him chew up a lemon. He called it concentration, but people still laughed behind his back. They reached the settlement just before midnight—a few shanty cabins and a small loading dock on the river with no name. The people spotted the headlights and started coming out of the 'shine shack to take a gander at what was happening. Old folks, jungle Indians, and crying mothers started trying to put flower garlands around Florix's neck when they saw that he had come. He took it all in his stride like the stage performer that he was with a gruff courtesy that always seemed old fashioned. It was strange seeing him act like that, particularly since he never wore his whiteface makeup out on hunts. Seeing him without makeup was rare, and it gave his face a deeply lined humanity that never failed to invoke a hideous sadness in those few that knew him. The Typhoid Surf had brought this up with Florix one day in conversation, but the Boss Pierrot simply laughed at him. "Show me a clown that doesn't do sad," he said dismissively. The Typhoid Surf and the boys didn't say much now while Florix was talking with the villagers. They just stayed in the car, smoking cigarettes and checking the guns. A woman brought them cold fruit punch, and they thanked her, spiking it with monkey rum from Gus's hip flask. Florix refused the drink, and when he was done questioning the villagers about the beast, he got out his night vision goggles and scanned the tree line for heat signatures. Then he saddled up the guns and explosives and set out into the jungle alone. He had put down sixty raptors over the years and was familiar with their nature and nocturnal habits. He was always able to bag the monster without so much as a scratch—even though he only ever carried short-range

firearms and knives. The boys stayed frosty in the Shark, waiting for a possible distress signal, measuring out their rum punch to avoid getting too bleached. The Surf had one of Appleseed's old tapes, the one with "My Love Is" on repeat. Appleseed had started out as a conversationalist in the neon pits, and it was the song she always used for backdrops and kissing episodes. He listened to it from time to time when the memories came back at him, making him either crazy or stupid.

CHIRRUP WAS DANCING CHORUS LINE in one of the big shows that night and couldn't take off her massive headdress to use the walkie-talkie. She managed to find time between scenes to get to the public access videophone and put in a call to the Typhoid Surf. It was total chaos backstage with curtain calls every few seconds due to the insane level of elaboration that Florix now insisted upon in all his productions. The music from the orchestra pit was driving her up the wall, invading through the door of the glass booth in waves of deafening brass. She watched men in dungarees disassemble stage sets while she told the Typhoid Surf what had happened to Taty.

"Why didn't she just press the panic button?" he spoke into his wristwatch, watching her tiny face pixelate in the bad pick-up.

"Chick's a Section 8, babe. Fuck knows why she does anything. But the guards won't lift a finger, and I want to help a sister out."

"So, where's she at now?"

A stage manager with a clipboard came past and started banging on the booth, gesticulating wildly at the stage. Chirrup shooed him off in exasperation, yanking closed the tattered velvet curtain.

"Robots trucked her off to med bay," she replied testily. "Probably out by morning."

The Typhoid Surf pinched at his stubble as he sometimes did when he was pondering.

"Listen, Chirrup," he said, "the Smile can't get wind of this little event."

Gus and the slapper both went quiet when they overheard him say this. They stepped discreetly out for a cigarette to avoid hearing anymore.

"He has a special hard-on for that piece of tail. And if he hears about this, he'll do a tap dance routine for sure. I'll pull the photo booth record of this eight ball and go pay him a visit. How's that sound?"

"Kiss kiss, sailor. That'd be just peachy."

"Right, then. I'll see you after the show. We're eating dino steaks tonight. Over and angst."

He tweaked off his wristwatch and got out the car to join the boys.

"Trouble in Paradise?" Gus quipped.

"Just another doughnut asking to get bit."

He lit up a cigarette, and they observed the trees for any sign of movement. The situation on the phone had created a delayed reaction irritation in the Typhoid Surf, and he turned to Gus.

"You know that chick Smiley found living out in the Necs?"

"The whippersnapper. Sure, sure."

Gus stood expectantly, but the Typhoid Surf went quiet and surly again. They all went back to watching trees while villagers mooched around, waiting for gunshots.

"Wonder what Smiley sees in that fucking cupcake," the Surf muttered after a while, almost to himself. "She's heading straight for the wall, if you ask me."

33
Trouble in Paradise

IT WAS SWELTERING OUT ON the pool decks. These large piazzas topped the upper platforms of Paradise Discothèque, radiating outward in geometric terraces. Massive stepped pits channeled water up from the springs, creating sparkling pools amid the hot stone. A cascade of tables scattered beside one of these glittering bathing areas. Half-finished meals abandoned the night before leered across the white tablecloths, spoiling quickly in the sun. The feast had been an opulent one with excessively garnished courses served in silver tureens. Now the broiled river fish stared sightlessly into the sun while the remains of roasted piglets gleamed within a haze of sparkling flies. Toucans and parrots scavenged among the leftovers muttering nonsensically to themselves, pecking at the monstrous red ants twisting lines around their feet. The Purple Clown balanced on a high parapet, his balloon whipping around in the steamy wind while the tip of a pyramid floated just beyond the edge of the deck, garbled up by its clutter of pterodactyl nests. Taty lay on a deck chair smoking space-spice under a beach umbrella and listening to that once-popular single, "Sneezy Mac Kneel." She had ingeniously managed to create vinyl versions of this and other tracks on the ever-evolving *In with the Outzone* by using an old spare parts printer she had discovered in the engine shop. The track now looped grainily off a wind-up record player. A wide-brimmed straw hat, massive brown sunglasses, and pancake makeup did little to hide her injuries. The bikini didn't help either, and ugly purple flowered beneath her otherwise even tan. Champagne frosted in an ice bucket near her hand alongside a ravaged cherry-red lobster and a bowl of electric-blue lollipops. Appleseed lay on the deck chair beside her, her legs folded in exactly the same manner as Taty's. In contrast to Taty's lack of modesty, however, Appleseed obscured her form in a padded kimono. Cat's-eye sunglasses, copious makeup, and a swathed turban completed her ensemble of physical camouflage.

She had been to the salon that morning, and they had given her long red fingernails. She now used these to manipulate an oyster shell cigarette holder while drinking flute after flute of bubbly.

"I don't know how to answer that," Taty eventually replied after much thought.

She hesitated again, taking a couple more drags of space-spice.

"I can't say exactly how it felt. I suppose I felt sick. He hit me so many times in my stomach."

"Did he make you cry 'for real?'" Appleseed asked in a vaguely predatory tone.

When the girl didn't answer, Appleseed repeated the question in a softer voice.

Taty turned to regard her, removing her sunglasses in order to see better. Crimson lightning licked at the white of her left eye while both sported black and purple bruising.

"Are you trying to be my mommy?"

Appleseed looked at her through dark glasses.

"I suppose I am."

Taty glanced away, flicking the smoldering joint end into the pool.

"My mom was just like me. A drugged-up drunk. A total fuck-up. I always wanted a better one. Miss Muppet tried to be my mommy in the backseat of a car, but that was just pheromones, I guess," Taty slurred, swigging deeply from the icy bottle of champagne.

She wiped her bruised mouth gently with the back of her hand, daubing at her swollen lips with a tissue when the sweat began to sting. The damage had given her a faint lisp when she spoke.

"Then there was my fairy godmother in that hotel room—though she was jiving me for sweats, so I can hardly even count her. Number Nun got shot full of holes and washed out to sea. Everybody else is dead."

Appleseed nodded absently, by now quite tipsy. She was in a foul mood and could not, for the life of her, understand why. Taty's state had shocked her, but that was somehow not the primary reason for her detached sense of unease. A poisonous atmosphere had drifted in and cauterized her sense of pity. Something was incongruous—a bone lay shattered beneath untroubled skin.

"Well, then I'm lucky number three. If you don't count the hotel fairy," she smiled at Taty.

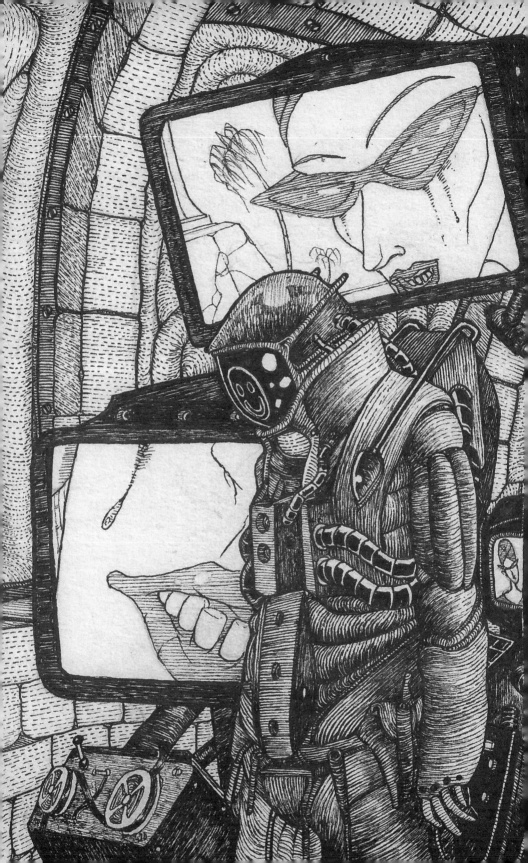

Taty regarded her companion with the seriousness of a child. Something vital inside her had been broken, and she needed a branch, any stem of support to grow around in order to maintain balance.

"OK, Appleseed," she said in the same vein of seriousness. "You can be my mommy."

"Come lie by me."

Taty obeyed. She set down the champagne bottle, removed her hat, and carefully crawled onto the other deck chair. There she placed her head delicately upon Appleseed's collarbone. Appleseed drew her loose-sleeved arms around Taty. They lay like that for a while.

SOMEWHERE IN A DARK CHAMBER, the astronaut watched. The room was foam-padded and heavily insulated despite the heat. Exterior piping along the walls made a submarine bridge out of the grotto. Banks of television monitors glowed in the dimness, displaying various views of Paradise Discothèque and the surrounding jungle. The long chamber had been constructed on several levels with metal steps and ladders leading up to various platforms and niches—all lit up with screens and displays. The lights twinkled in patterns, a comforting reminder of well-maintained machinery. The far end of this Santa's grotto splayed out into what looked like the spacious cockpit of a zeppelin. Vast bubbles of reinforced glass plumed above banked consoles and a pilot's crash couch. Futuristic metal shutters enclosed the curved glass, allowing little or no light to enter. The astronaut had seated himself at the bank of monitors, toggling grainy close-ups of Appleseed captured from various angles. Her face dominated the wall of screens while her high-res breathing came through the speaker systems, captured by strategically placed long-range microphones.

"Yes," Appleseed eventually replied, her voice ringing with multiple-source tap delay. "I want you to call me Mommy."

Taty snuggled under Appleseed's chin, and the two of them lay like that, baking slowly in their slice of umbrella shade. The astronaut watched them for a moment before flicking a switch on his chest panel. A dial tone opened up, emanating audibly from his external speaker grille. After a moment, a heavy male voice came online.

"Yes, Boss?"

"Get the Typhoid Surf in here."

"Twenty-twenty, Mister Boss."

The astronaut tacked two or three cam feeds to his inner helmet display and left the chamber via one of the three heavy-gauge airlocks, still listening in on the quietness of the girls. He entered a stone corridor in one of the highest enclaves of the old temple, watching the tiny images of Taty and Appleseed out of the corner of his eye. The passage he had entered was a long sloped channel that led upward toward a gleaming slit of sunlight. Stone relief friezes lined the walls on either side depicting various mythological scenes. Strip lighting illuminated these wall panels from above and below as in a museum. Geometric notes and photostats were pasted everywhere along with topographical readouts and the odd wall-mounted instrument. Stylized scenes of Paradise Discothèque in its heyday adorned the lower walls of the corridor. The bottoms of the diamond pyramids were still touching the ground in the old images, their lower tips pirouetting like stylus points. Crowds of reptile people formed concentric circles around the central superstructure in many of these lower scenes. Their god was also present in the majority of these reliefs twined about a small pavilion at the very top of the temple, arms outstretched toward an ever-present moon. As the corridor progressed, so did the ascent of the four double pyramids in the carved images. The crowds disappeared, and the Pyramids rose fractionally higher. The god also began changing position, moving here and there, sometimes atop a floating pyramid, sometimes coiled on the ground. In later friezes the god was absent entirely. The episodic history of the structure ceased midway down the corridor, replaced by the more psychedelic visions familiar from many of the Outzone ruins. Indeed, colorful "end of days" descriptions adorned so many old structures in the Zone as to render them commonplace. The most recognizable hieroglyphs included, of course, the eventual fall of the Pyramids and the destruction of cities by pillars of fire that radiated from the sky. The friezes also displayed many images of the moon and a road leading to it through space. Perhaps the strangest were the high final friezes, which showed the simplistic figure of a suited spaceman entwined with the god. Someone had scrawled a smiley face over the stone of the astronaut's face here and in other depictions. Perhaps it was in jest, but a few had indeed accorded the Smile something of a quasi-religious status. To many he was part of the stoneworked prophecies of the place, a sign of end times. Some felt that this was the reasoning behind Florix handing over total control to the astronaut. The controversy merely added to the peculiar atmosphere that now infested Paradise Discothèque. "Nothing like an inside line on apocalypse to bring in the big money," the Smile was heard to remark. Whatever the case, he passed through the corridor and reached the shining slit at the end. A mechanism of stone panels grated open smoothly, admitting the suited figure into bright sunlight. He stepped out onto the highest point of Paradise Discothèque: a small globular pavilion with a pedestal at its center affectionately dubbed "the moon verandah" for as long as anyone could remember. The "holy balcony" was another name ascribed to the high pavilion, chiefly because the god had been depicted upon it in so many of the ancient carvings. The 360-degree view was staggering at that height. Aside from the vertiginous panorama of the jungle canopy, it was also the only point on the structure where one could view all four pyramids simultaneously. The pristine mathematics of the place became easily appreciable when viewed from the perspective of the moon verandah. The chaotic arrangement of certain terraces suddenly made sense as did the unusual juxtapositions of pillars, pedestals, and piazzas. The pavilion was, after all, at the zenith of the entire structure, and the pedestal rising from the middle of the carved floor was its centerpiece. Yet, this stone pedestal was blank and featureless, its purpose impossible to divine through casual observation. The astronaut would stand for hours simply staring at it as though attempting to accomplish something using only the power of his mind.

THE TYPHOID SURF WAS MOVING cautiously through the undergrowth surrounding Johnny's lagoon when his wristwatch began to crackle. He squatted in the rushes and held it to his ear, watching trash ebb around.

"Ten-ten, Surf, this is the Disco Commander. Are you reading me? Over."

"This is the Surf. Come in, Disco."

"Roger, Typhoid. Smile wants you over double time. Some beef in the mix-up."

"Copy that, Disco. I'll be along squarely. Over and angst."

He tweaked his watch to cut transmission before rising again. The sullen shack loomed over the water, stinking of memory.

It was dark inside the shack. Something stirred in the mosquito netting of the bed, and the Typhoid Surf was able to catch a glimpse of Donnie, half-in/half-out of a Victorian corset. The door opening had him spooked, and he bolted for the light, spear in hand, lingerie trailing. The Surf caught him easily enough, scooping him against the door by the scruff of his neck.

"Relax, Donnie. You know I don't have anything against a man in ladies' underthings."

"Typhoid Surf! Fuck, dude—I thought for sure you was Johnny."

"Johnny's out to lunch. His better half is catching rays in Paradise."

Donnie relaxed, and the Typhoid Surf let him down.

"Listen," Donnie mumbled with some discomfort, "you won't tell the lady I was in her stuff, will ya?"

"Forget about it."

Donnie grinned up at him.

"I don't care what the old folks say, Surf, you're a prince. And your sister, she was a princess—before that imp turned her into a zombie, of course."

The Typhoid Surf extracted the hive's photo booth prints of the "invisible man" and waved them at Donnie.

"This is Johnny, right?"

"That's him," Donnie answered darkly.

The Typhoid Surf leaned against the shack and stared out at the lagoon.

"Fuck a duck," he muttered bitterly.

"He messin' with the missus again?"

"Some other little chicken."

The Typhoid Surf descended the ladder and strolled along the muddy shore.

"Stay out of trouble, Donnie," he threw over his shoulder.

"Likewise," Donnie called, looking grim.

The pygmy drifted back into the shack, emotionally affected by what the Typhoid Surf had revealed to him. Donnie hated pain of any kind, and the injury Johnny liked to cause often made him sad and fidgety. He looked over at the message that Johnny had scrawled across the mirror in lipstick and sighed gloomily. The note had clearly been left for Appleseed: *When you least expect it, bitch.*

APPLESEED HAD GONE IN SEARCH of a bathroom in order to throw up. She felt truly awful and could still not fathom why. That morning she had awoken aching and languid as though she had run miles the previous night. Some dirt was stuck under the fingernail of her day, and it had become impossible to dislodge. Now she was drunk and in one of the long bathrooms that haunted the upper plazas like miniature train terminals. No one was ever able to interpret the function of these long stone cul-de-sacs that needled the level beneath the upper terraces in random profusion. Many of these areas had been fitted with plumbing and turned into toilets or sex dormitories. Glass- and mirror-finish cubicles created a train station atmosphere where stone niche toilets and public shower areas brooded in gloomy recessions like railway platforms going nowhere. The excessive use of mirrors in the upper regions of Paradise Discothèque further complicated the already mazy interiors. Infinity illusions doubled spaces, creating confusion in many of the newer visitors. Appleseed, however, was familiar with the layout of the upper levels. She had worked plenty of the mirror tunnels in her day and knew the jingle-jangle inside out. She went into one of these bathroom cul-de-sacs and threw up in a corner. The place was deserted, and the echoes of her retching multiplied disturbingly throughout the long tunnel. She went to one of the stone basins and rinsed out her mouth, feeling profoundly unbalanced. Johnny was in the mirror when she looked up, far away, loitering in a cubicle door somewhere down the intestinal warp of an infinity reflection. She saw him in the mirrors sometimes, usually when she felt weak or ill at ease. He would always be in the distance warping like a light reflection, saying nothing and staring intensely at her. She thought of him as a bird at times like that, some vulture or eagle ready to swoop down upon her in a moment of weakness. She splashed her face with water and adjusted her makeup while he watched from the shadows. Her hands were trembling, and she had to fix her eye lines twice. For some reason her knuckles were faintly bruised. The tendons had a post-adrenal looseness and quivered when she strained them. She took Johnny's manifestation as a sign of terrible things laying ahead.

θθθ

SHE WAS STROLLING BACK TOWARD the pool when an arm reached out of a doorway and pulled her into another corridor. She felt herself swiftly maneuvered into a deeply shadowed niche behind the pedestal of a towering statue. Her back was pressed firmly against the cool stone while the sunglasses fell away. She recognized the smell of the Typhoid Surf before she felt his teeth scraping through her freshly applied lipstick. The sharp fear subsided, and she opened her mouth as though drowning, melting quickly in the half-dark. Her arms twined like vines, of their own accord, around his throat. The shock of such long-anticipated physical contact went through them both like a blast radius, knocking up a tidal wave that blew all the way out to the past. When they paused for breath, panting like animals with their foreheads pressed together, they could still feel the tidal wave of future events sweeping around them, annihilating everything. It was the sort of kiss that cost lives—impossible to disguise.

"Spaceman has cameras everywhere, but this is a blind spot," he whispered raggedly.

"I hate this place," she answered, pushing her mouth forward only to fall back at the last moment when she saw the look of distress in his eyes.

He took her face suddenly and held it up, staring madly at her.

"Listen, you have to leave with me right now. Johnny's gone and raped that girl."

He could feel her fossilize—something moist suddenly exposed to scorching heat. She went brittle in an instant as though suffering a mortal blow.

"You mean that I—" she mouthed sickeningly, unable to finish.

"If we leave now, we can make it to Namanga Mori before Florix gets wind. I can maybe even get us a boat."

"Namanga's gone. Maybe the spaceman doesn't know what happened yet, maybe he—"

"I found out. He will, too. There's no other way. He'll set Devoid on you for sure."

"And what about that little dancing doll of yours?" she asked, suddenly caustic, pulling back like a cat. "Are we taking her with us?" she smiled bitterly.

"No. Just you and me, babe."

She seemed to consider this, leaning her head back against the dusty stone. Her face had fallen into shadow, and it became difficult to see where she was looking. He soon realized that she was studying him intently, her eyes glittering with champagne and danger.

"There is another way," he heard her say.

"There isn't."

"You also know how to call up Devoid for a death jinx."

"So?"

"Set Devoid on the Smile."

He stared at her shining eyes for a while, counting out all the seconds he had to pretend that he had not heard her proposition. When he slapped her, it was vicious and abrupt. Her face was turned instantly by the blow, now almost completely swallowed by the line of shade. Only her throat remained in view, pale and heaving. Her smile, when it returned, was laced with blood from a leaking nostril.

"You always did hit like a little pussycat," she giggled.

He struck her face again and watched her head loll like a wilting flower. She was still smiling when she came up, but the blood had become electrified with dissent.

"You think I would go anywhere with someone too chicken to kill for his missus? Fuck you, boy."

She wiped blood off on her hand and flicked it imperiously across his face.

"Even after what you did to him, Johnny still has more balls than you ever will. Go play with your go-go girl. I can take care of myself."

She broke suddenly from the dark, swooping into the corridor like an escaping bird. He went after her but stopped at the edge of the pedestal, afraid of being seen.

"Wait!" he hissed, but she was already gone.

THE ASTRONAUT STOOD LIKE A statue of himself in his control room. The shutters on the bubble windows had been retracted and unscrolled. Sunlight flooded the previously lightless chamber while air conditioning units brought the temperature back down to a tolerable level. Through the glass, one could view the awe-inspiring vistas of the jungle canopy as well as a scattering of high terraces and flat roofing. An expanse of yellow crenelated stone lay pierced by the various clear pools. If you knew where to look, you could easily find Taty's candy apple-red beach umbrella and perhaps make out the miniaturized outline of her body beneath. Cameras tracked the equally tiny figure of Appleseed as she made her way across baking terraces and wide staircases toward her distant companion. It was very much like watching an ant traverse the surfaces of an enormous golden cake. Monochrome images of Appleseed's grim face danced shakily on screens around the chamber, visible from various angles. She eventually reached the umbrella and lay on the empty deck chair. Their voices wafted through the speakers as though originating in the same high room.

"You have blood on your face ..." Taty murmured.

"Battery is contagious, baby doll."

"Have some more champagne; it's better than Band-Aids. Here, let me roll you a reefer."

A klaxon sounded in the control room, announcing a visitor. The astronaut flicked a switch on his wrist gauntlet, muting the girls' conversation instantly. He crossed to one of the airlocks and began to crank an enormous hydraulic wheel. Heavy tumblers rolled, and a pressure seal sucked open the bank vault door. The Typhoid Surf loped into the metal room looking a little worse for wear.

"I need a drink," he muttered, pushing up his rose-tinted spectacles.

He moved to the mini bar while the astronaut sealed the air lock behind him. He mixed himself a stiff Martini, stealing painful glimpses of Appleseed on the various screens.

"Where the fucking olives at?" he found himself snapping.

The astronaut, meanwhile, had moved back to the screens.

"Before I get to what I'm going to get to," the Smile began, "I thought you should see this."

The Typhoid Surf joined him as a pre-recorded tape cut off the camera views of the pool deck. Together they watched while grainy noise resolved into a field-recorded telecast. Black helicopters swarmed across the jungle, descending on the house of Alphonse Guava like hungry children. The screen showed fast edits of the pool area strafed by machine-gun fire intercut with images of the private cinema torched by flamethrowers. Twenty wrestlers hung off the graffiti-heavy battle robot, bringing its rusty machinery down through the sheer power of their biceps. Then they saw the hideously obese figure of Mister Sister taken down by a sweaty knife-wielding Bronski Glass. The whole clip had a retrospective action movie flavor compounded by a soft-porn electronic soundtrack and flickering wah-wah guitar. The face of Karolina K-Star filled the screen along with a digital graphic of her name. She held up a wind-protected microphone and began to speak in the tones of a professional news anchor.

"Soft House top man, Bronski Glass, seen here apprehending the malicious mastermind behind the invasion of symbiotes from Protoverse X. The showdown took place in a decadent villa deep in the jungle. This old colonial villa—once the property of infamous imp Alphonse Guava—had become the stronghold of rival vice lord, Mister Sister—otherwise known as the Big Buddha."

Heroic propaganda shots of Bronski Glass flashed in quick succession accompanied by synthesized orchestra hits: Bronski holding a massive ray gun silhouetted against a jungle sunset, kicking down doors and so forth. Michelle followed him in adoration throughout this kaleidoscope of mayhem. She was finally off the cross and dressed in army fatigues, which seemed to suit her. Once the burden of crucifixion had been lifted, Michelle had taken to Bronski's specialized form of genetically enhanced Pilates with a vengeance. It took months of hard work, but she had finally been able to restore strength to her atrophied arms and to lose the slouch. Her new life as an action movie sidekick saw to all that troublesome excess weight, and she was trimmed down to combat readiness. She discovered mirrors and got a snappy crew cut to match her new sporty physique. All those troublesome Christ complexes and manias were transmuted to the healthy vigors of fascism under the eagle wing of Bronski Glass's elite division. Shots of this new Michelle booting the corpses of the Buddhist Punks strewn across the blood-splattered lawns zoomed in and out of focus on the newsreel. Wrestlers swarmed like prize bulls through the house, captured on shaky hand-held news footage.

"I thought Mister Sister and Bronski Glass were allies," the Typhoid Surf said, chewing neurotically at an olive pit.

"The Big Buddha is powerless now," the Smile replied. "Bloated like a tick. This was all inevitable."

Karolina K-Star's voice came back in over more hero propaganda shots, this time of Michelle looking fierce in her brand new black fatigues and beret.

"Bronski's aide-de-camp, Michelle, the illegitimate daughter of God, has aided him in the purging of these interdimensional swine. Let's go to her now for an exclusive on their future missions."

Cut to Michelle, poolside, badly lit by roving halogen spots. A microphone is thrust into her face, maneuvered deftly by Karolina's manicured purple-nailed hand.

"Now that you have quashed the sinister Mister Sister and his minions, what are your plans?"

Michelle, obviously very excited to be on television, began to babble hysterically. ("Who would have thought she was so prone to flamboyant hand gestures?" Karolina was later heard to remark.)

"Well, since we can't destroy the bugs, we plan to go all out and blitz every one of the fuckers we hold personally responsible for the deviation in general!"

"And who would that be?"

"Um, well, since we got Mister Sister already ... and Alphonse has been torn to lasagne, I dunno, maybe Daddy Bast?"

"But the Voodoo Surgery is one of the only medical facilities left in the Outzone."

"Shit, yeah, that's true. Um, well, then I guess we have to move straight to Plan Zero."

"And what would that be?"

"Paradise Discothèque! It's the last outpost of vice in the fuckedup zone. We're gonna go in there and nuke it to shit!"

"But can't you do something to help the thousands who have fled the coastal cities? Or even attempt a mission to stop or at least contain the escalating number of symbiotes?"

"Ah, fuck 'em. We feel that getting even is more important right now."

"But how has Paradise Discotheque contributed to this invasion?"

"Well, I'm not sure ... at this precise moment in time. But I'm sure I'll have a reason by the next time you broadcast! Anyway, if you'll excuse me, I gotta go watch my boyfriend blow some shit up!"

"Well, thanks for that, Michelle."

The astronaut abruptly cut the tape, and all the screens reverted to close-ups of Appleseed and Taty. The Typhoid Surf caught a glimpse of Appleseed's mouth and suffered a boiling pang of emotion. He moved quickly back to the mini bar, shaking up another martini.

"Are they serious?" he asked, pouring out a double measure of vodka.

"My sources confirmed it," the astronaut replied. "We have about two weeks before the strike force gets here."

"Fuck a duck, what are we going to do, Boss?"

"Not much."

The Typhoid Surf looked up in disbelief while the astronaut calmly toggled close-ups of Taty's face and body, zooming in on her bruises.

"We can't survive an attack," the Typhoid Surf protested. "Our workforce is fucked from all these rockets you've been attaching to the outer walls—I mean, what are they even there for?"

"That's my little secret," the spaceman replied. "In any case, I don't really have a problem with everyone dying."

He turned to face the Typhoid Surf.

"You are welcome to take my steamboat if you want to leave," he offered magnanimously.

"But we have to evacuate!"

"Negative. Not a word about this to anyone."

"But—"

"I just found out that some piece of grot had the gumption to rough up my special little ghost girl. Now I have to put cameras in her room, and you know how much I hate invading the privacy of my girls. I need you to find this maniac and set Devoid on him. You won't be able to do that if there's a mass evacuation."

"But, Boss, Bronski Glass will nuke this place and land helicopters on the burning bones."

"That's the least of my concerns. Right now I need you to find out who assaulted my little lady."

The Typhoid Surf stared at him in exasperation before turning to his martini. He finished mixing it, quaffed it in a single draught, and then looked back at the spaceman as though he had reached a decision of some kind. Too late, he realized that he had forgotten the olive.

"There a problem of some kind?" the astronaut asked.

"No, nothing's wrong, Boss. I'm on it."

"Good. Find me this bad seed, so I can watch Devoid squash him. Then maybe we can talk about an evacuation."

"Sure," the Typhoid Surf answered grimly.

He set down his cocktail glass and moved back to the airlock where he operated the hydraulic seal, glancing back one final time. The astronaut had returned to his close-ups of the girls sunning themselves. He unmuted their conversation, and Appleseed's voice came through in sharp focus.

"Sex is no communion, babe. Not here in the jungle. Here we are all just fucking animals eating each other in the filth of creation. Every embrace is just a mouth full of teeth, and the mouths chew and chew and chew at each other until we're all pulp. Till we are all scream dreaming, hip-deep in broken teeth."

"Don't cry, Appleseed," Taty whispered.

The Typhoid Surf sealed off the airlock as the pixelated monochrome figures embraced onscreen. His face was dark, and his mind was set. It was going to be a busy afternoon.

34
Sugar-Coated Tapeworm Eggs

LATE AFTERNOON WAS TEETERING ON the brink of dusk. The sky over the jungle was melon yellow, turning red at the rims. Pterodactyls circled lazily, turning like wheels against this luminescent void. Chirrup was out on the balcony in her favorite leopard print dressing gown, hair parceled up in a white post-bath towel. She was painting her toenails cherry red, one pale leg up on the table, cotton puffs pinched between each toe. A fluff-tipped heelless slipper lingered on the other foot, its counterpart placed daintily on the tabletop like a piece of confectionery. A small tray accompanied the slipper, laden with a china cup and saucer, silver coffee pot, and a bowl of exotic fruit. A bottle of globular white pills also sat conspicuously before her along with a vintage cream-colored rotary dial telephone. *Ma Jeunesse Fout L'Camp* was playing quietly on the turntable while a halo of pterodactyls circled the nearby pyramid, letting out mournful squalls that carried out across the haze of trees. The dying light bathed the nest-ridden tip of the pyramid, catching on the occasional remains of those unlucky enough to be snatched. A baby pterodactyl had drifted in from the turning flock, circling the balcony out of curiosity. Now it sat on the balustrade, cocking its head quizzically at Chirrup, who tossed it the occasional fragment of fruit, watching with amusement as it was snapped out of the air. The balcony doors were wide open, and white gauze curtains gusted in the fragrant breeze. Taty was on her bed also freshly bathed, one arm behind her head. She was still somewhat inebriated from her poolside experience and gnawed at a crimson apple in a half-hearted attempt to replenish nutrients. She crunched through the flesh and accidentally crushed a seed between her molars. The pungent taste of bitter almonds flowered across her damaged mouth.

"Apple seeds taste like marzipan," she announced drunkenly.

Chirrup glanced back at her and winked.

"That's because there's cyanide in them."

"Am I going to die?" Taty blurted incredulously.

"Oh, we're all going to die, Cupcake."

"So, why does marzipan taste like cyanide?"

"Because it's made from almonds."

"Oh."

Chirrup finished off her right baby toe and emptied a generous dose of globular pills onto her palm. She swallowed about six, washing them down with coffee, staining the rim of the cup with lipstick. She even tossed a pill to the baby pterodactyl who gobbled it up without hesitation. An adult pterodactyl noticed Chirrup feeding the infant and began to waft closer to the balcony, clacking its toothy snout in a display of territoriality.

"What are those pills?" Taty squinted against the languid honey light.

"Sugar-coated tapeworm eggs."

Taty raised an eyebrow, impressed.

"Why are you taking so many? You took about thirty yesterday."

Chirrup reached back and lazily scooped up the machine gun.

"My motto is: You can never have enough tapeworms."

She fired a burst and managed to wing the approaching creature. The baby scrabbled in fright. Spooked by the noise, it detached and swooped quickly out of sight. The injured beast let out a series of squawks as it began to spiral limply down toward a mud-stricken construction site. A pair of roving opportunists spotted their injured flock mate and managed to tear it to pieces before it even hit the ground. Chirrup set down the machine gun and started slipping cotton balls between the toes of her left foot. Taty's eye unexpectedly alighted on the switchblade laying across her bedside table. The knife had been recovered from the door of Room 99 by hive guards, and she had decided to keep it as some kind of morbid souvenir. Now she flicked it open, using it to slice off a crystalline sliver of apple, which she then held up near her face. The close-up fragment glowed white-green against the sun while pterodactyls swirled in the sleepy distances beyond. A single black seed hung like a drop of ink from the luminous shard. She plucked it and placed it beneath her eye like a tear.

"Taty and Appleseed, sitting in a tree, F-A-L-L-I-N-G," she sang out softly.

The dancer glanced over her shoulder with an expression of concern.

"You must love the taste of poison," she said quietly, returning to her toes.

"She's like a mother ..."

"And if you eat too much of her, you'll go blue and die. She's trouble."

"Maybe," Taty mused after a thoughtful pause.

Chirrup sighed, capped the nail polish, and fiddled around for a smoke. When she finally managed to light a cigarette, she turned to regard Taty with an expression of sisterly complicity.

"Don't you think it's time you left Paradise, babe?"

"And go where?" Taty laughed, incredulous.

Chirrup shrugged.

"I dunno. Back to the Lowlands maybe—same as everybody else."

Taty shook her head.

"If I'm going to crash my car, I'm going to do it out here, where the air is jungle fresh."

"You need a boyfriend," Chirrup surrendered, slinging her leg back up onto the table.

"I'd rather have a mother."

"Whatever roasts your red thang."

Taty touched the apple seed on her face lightly, feeling it press against the bruised skin.

"Are you happy, Chirrup?" she asked unexpectedly.

The question caught the showgirl off guard, and she paused to pour out a fresh cup.

"Well, I tell you, the road was hard," she mused after some thought. "But time here is ... different."

She pinched her cigarette up from the ashtray, sipping at the steaming black coffee.

"It's all kind of slowed down," she cooed dreamily, wriggling her half-painted toes against the sun.

After a few drags she glanced over at Taty with a wry expression on her face.

"I dunno, kiddo," she smiled. "I never really thought about it."

"How can you not think of happiness?" Taty protested.

"I watch a lot of movies," Chirrup replied neatly, pivoting the nail polish dispenser above her agile toes.

Just then, the telephone began to ring. Chirrup snagged it up and held it between face and shoulder, so that she could continue applying cherry red without hindering her conversation.

NOT MANY PEOPLE HAD SEEN the interior of Florix's apartment and lived. His quarters were relatively modest in size but exquisitely furnished. Heavily draped bay windows stood at tree level, and it was possible to gaze deeply into the jungle as well as survey the sky and ground below. The walls were all deep maroon trimmed with actual gold leaf piping. The colors created a sense of austere majesty especially when combined with a lifelong accumulation of priceless furnishings. In addition to furniture, Florix also collected fine oil paintings whose subject matter consisted of Pierrots and nothing else. These were the only images adorning the walls—each piece lit from above by a brace of tiny gold spotlights. The lights were on now despite the fact that it was still only late afternoon and the chamber was flooded with natural light. The artificial illumination curdled in a rift of gun smoke, which hung bleakly around the main lounge area.

The Typhoid Surf sat panting in a Louis XVI chair, his collar and face lightly dusted with fresh blood. The stench of gunpowder still clung to him, a smoking pistol dangling from his fingers while his wristwatch hand hovered beside his mouth. A rash of bullet holes decorated the lush wall behind him, extending across a particularly baroque painting of the archetypal white clown chasing a sickle moon across a tower-stricken hamlet. Florix was across the room from the Typhoid Surf, on the floor, crawling painfully across a patterned rug. Blood seeped from the many holes in his body each time he moved. The fluid was everywhere around him, showing up on his white face in radiant slashes. Despite the extensive physical damage, he was still trying with all his might to close the gap between him and his assailant. The Typhoid Surf spoke into his wristwatch, watching Florix as one would watch a poisonous snake.

"Hey, Sugarplum," he said casually across the line to Chirrup. "In the mood for a sunset drive?"

"Sure, Babe ... You're breathing awful heavy; have you been running or fucking?"

"Nothing like that. Meet you at the lava lounge in half an hour?"

"Is this an 'I'm going to break up with you' sunset drive? Is that Appleseed bitch with you? She listening in?"

"No, no, nothing like that. Listen, I thought we could spend a night or two on Smiley's steamboat, maybe hit the cities. Wanna pack an overnight?"

"What about my show? I have two nights booked and—"

Florix was already halfway across the rug and now had his blade out.

"Just fucking do it!" the Typhoid Surf barked. "Half an hour in the lounge."

"Jesus, lover, since you put it that way ..."

"See you then. Over and angst."

He tweaked off the watch and cocked his gun, leveling it square at Florix's left eye.

"OK, that's far enough," he warned. "Just lie down already."

Florix smiled, chuckling up some bubbles of blood. He lowered himself slowly down to the rug where the dark puddles began to collect and fan out like fungal forms.

"You're doing the right thing, son," Florix spluttered. "I would have gutted you if I'd caught wind of what you're planning."

The Typhoid Surf tipped up his rose-tinted granny glasses and pinched the bridge of his nose. He seemed genuinely saddened by this turn of events.

"Well, I'm sorry it came to this, man," he apologized with sincerity.

Florix nodded, gazing thoughtfully into space as though imagining something dim and distant.

"I would have enjoyed facing off with Bronski Glass, I suppose," he mused. "That preening ass."

"You would have eaten him like a cocktail olive," the Typhoid Surf acknowledged, eliciting a modest shrug from the aging soldier.

"Still," the Typhoid Surf pushed. "No way Paradise could survive an all-out attack ... everyone would die."

"That's true. They have those fancy-ass helicopters."

"So, you really think I'm doing the right thing?"

Florix seemed to break from his reverie. He looked up at his former right-hand man with an expression of undisguised mirth before letting loose a deep belly chuckle. Gouts of blood fell from his mouth, blotting across the fine weave of the carpet.

"There is no 'right thing' out here, Sonny. Not in the jungle."

"But Smiley's crazy. We'll all fucking die! If I give him to Devoid, at least I can pass the order to evacuate once he's out of the way."

Florix considered this, weighing it carefully despite his situation. After a moment he regarded the Typhoid Surf in a parental sort of way.

"He's still the boss," he stated firmly. "And he has a plan, you know."

"Yeah, yeah right, all that space cadet bullshit about Paradise Discothèque being a UFO and how it's all written in stone and whatnot. Dude, I don't fucking care! I just want off the rock with my nuts and sluts intact."

Florix smirked at this outburst.

"Well, then, like I said, you're doing the right thing."

The Typhoid Surf met the slave driver's sharp sarcastic glare and could not help but crack a rare smile.

"Tough old buzzard, aren't you?" he drawled. "I must have put about seven showstoppers in you—how come you're still able to debate the finer points?"

"It's a quirk—happens after you butcher and disfigure enough innocent people. Kind of like a perk."

"Well, do you think you could hurry it up?" the gunman joked. "I have a date, you know."

"Sorry to inconvenience you, son. Maybe you should just finish it."

"I guess," the Typhoid Surf replied, his smile slipping and then vanishing entirely.

"Adieu," bade the Pierrot with stately decorum.

"Ciao."

The Typhoid Surf shot Florix in the face and then swiftly approached the corpse, firing a few rounds into the back of the head and chest area. When he was done, he checked his wristwatch and crossed into the ornate black marble bathroom to wash up. He unwrapped a fresh slab of the Pierrot's homemade glycerine soap and spent a good fifteen minutes erasing every drop of blood from his person.

IT TOOK SOME DOING, BUT he managed to get Chirrup out of the lounge and on the road in less than ten minutes. It usually took a few hours to reach the Outer Necropolis, but the Typhoid Surf had been riding the jungle with slappers for years and knew one or two shortcuts. It was close to sunset when he sensed that they were almost there. There didn't seem to be any road whatsoever where they were. The Shark was just barreling head-on through dense vegetation, making a beeline for where he thought the Pyramids were supposed to be. Succulent leaves smacked and buckled against the windscreen in a ceaseless onslaught. Chirrup was in the front passenger seat with huge sunglasses on, her hair held back with a checker-print handkerchief. She was smoking, digesting all the radical new developments with paranoid grace.

"This is not what it seems," said the Typhoid Surf. "Well ... maybe it is," he added after a pause.

"How long till Devoid eats his globe?" she asked pensively.

"If we get it done now, then probably around morning."

"I think we should turn back and pick up the 'snapper.'"

"We're not turning back now, Chirrup, no way. Not for that little minx. Smiley will raise bright blue hell if his trophy budgie walks the plank before prom night. Especially if they find Florix."

"I don't know why you didn't just chop him up and feed him to the 'dactyls."

"No cameras in his quarters but plenty outside. His place is also soundproofed, so don't be sweating it. Nobody is going to disturb Florix when his door is shut."

Chirrup spat out her lipstick-stained cigarette stub and lit another, dodging a large cluster of leaves. She folded her arms in something like distress.

"We can't just abandon Taty," she repeated, shaking her head.

"Besides," she added, "aren't you going back to evacuate everyone?"

"Forget about them! We're out safe, and that's what counts! Suicide to go back now."

The car burst unexpectedly through a screen of leaves and out into open space. The Floating Pyramids spanned before them in awe-inspiring recessions as they skidded across a wide stone platform, skittering stones off the edge. They slewed to a halt, and the ruins sprawled out below them, glazed dramatically in the haze of approaching sunset. Shadows brooded everywhere, creating rich purple masses whose growth threatened their plans. It was not possible to perform a death jinx at night, so they would have to hurry. A wide ramp led off the platform and down into the old thoroughfares. He drove like a maniac through the silent city, trying to beat the light. Chirrup had forgotten how beautiful the flying stone cubes were—especially when silhouetted against a scarlet sky. Nevertheless, despite the distractions, she could not get her mind off Taty. She thought about calling to warn her but knew that the Typhoid Surf would prohibit such an action. Perhaps in a few days she would be able to talk him into allowing her to get a message across. The immense grinding of the gnashing pyramid became audible, growing louder and louder as they raced through the dilapidated structures. When they finally stopped, the Typhoid Surf seemed to relax, sensing that they would make it with some time to spare. Below them, across a broad, partially obscured plaza, they could see the fantastic spectacle of the gnashing pyramid and its collection of calcified towers. They climbed out of the Shark and headed quickly into the network of crumbling passages which led down to the plaza.

"So, this is where old Devoid lives," Chirrup nodded.

"He can't refuse a death jinx if it's accompanied by the appropriate sacrifice," the Typhoid Surf explained. "It's just the way things have been for thousands of years, so I guess he must keep a nest somewhere underneath those towers."

"I thought Devoid was the spaceman's friend. What if he won't kill him?"

"Well, see, there's all these ancient stone panels with Devoid and some character who looks like he's in a spacesuit. Old Devoid probably just hangs round him because of that. Personally, I think Smiley is just milking the resemblance."

"Creepy."

"Devoid used to follow Florix around like a dog, just watching him carve people up. Was Florix who first found him, you know? It was on an expedition into the buried cities. He used to go down there all the time with the imp and Doc Dali."

"Listen, I don't want to be around here too long. This place weirds me out."

"Florix caught wind of the death jinx circuit from the jungle Injuns and decided to make friends with what was doing all the killing. Just like old Florix, huh?"

"I didn't know him," Chirrup snipped, uncomfortable with this sudden outpouring of nostalgia for the man he had just murdered.

Perhaps nostalgia was how he dealt with pressure, she thought.

"He wasn't all that bad," the Typhoid Surf nodded.

By now, the scraping of the staggering stone faces had grown uncomfortably loud. The entrance to the kasbah of passages beneath the towers loomed ahead. A recent windstorm had disrupted the dunes of ground stone, creating strange swells and clefts in the uniformity of grey. When they reached the postbox of the god, they saw that the wind had destroyed the steep hillock of powder, revealing the cubic pit amid creamy scallops of fine dust. Chirrup was by now quite irritated, constantly brushing the perpetually falling powder from her hair and prized angora sweater. She eyed the dark pit with a look of disdain.

"You aren't seriously expecting me to go down there?"

"Of course not; it's a sheer drop of about 150 meters."

"Wow, that's deep," she muttered drily.

"Deeper than Smiley's hip pocket," he nodded appreciatively, temporarily oblivious to sarcasm.

She presumed that it was stress causing him to act like such a dolt, and so she attempted patience. The Typhoid Surf jumped up, disappearing into the grotto that held the sacrificial materials only to re-emerge a moment later carrying a jeweled skull, blunt syringe, and a pocket-size Braille/English dictionary. He sat with his legs dangling over the hole, looking up letters and tattooing their equivalent onto the card with the syringe. Chirrup paced up and down, bored and agitated. Eventually, she sat beside him, placing her sunglasses gingerly on a patch of dusty stone.

"Why do we have to come all the way out to the Necs to summon Devoid?" she asked. "I mean, I thought he could pop up anywhere with all those tunnels of his ... Wasn't he up on the roof yesterday?"

"Dropping a rock down the postbox on a head bone sinker is the only way to jam a jinx. It's tradition."

"What's with the dots?"

"Gotta print the name in blind-speak. The Injuns used to talk to Devoid in touch, but Florix and the Doc taught him Braille. He can't read by sight—no eyes, y'know."

"I know why he's called Devoid, Typhoid."

"Difficult," he muttered, sticking out his tongue in concentration. "Gotta print it backward, so he can read the bumps on the other side."

Somehow, the sight of his tongue sticking out like that aggravated her. Chirrup let out a sigh and attempted to locate a relatively shaded spot that wasn't full of skulls. He finished the card just as the bloody half-dark of sunset began to infiltrate the mazy passages. She glanced up at one point shielding her eyes against the rain of debris to see the entire flank of the massive pyramid stained a luminescent red. Despite the grandeur, she couldn't help thinking that it resembled an enormous quarter-slice of watermelon. The Typhoid Surf rose to his feet, crammed the card into the skull, and then seemed to hesitate as though the full weight of his actions had only just occurred to him. The moment of indecision passed quickly enough, though, and he flipped the skull down into the hole without a second thought. He was like that when it came to irreversible decisions.

"Let's quit this boneyard," she called, already walking away.

He followed her out of the labyrinth and across the plaza. Neither of them had any idea that they were being watched. The tall spindly jungle Indian, painted canary yellow and wearing a gigantic wooden bird mask over his head, observed from a discrete distance. He watched the couple recede, moving soundlessly from pillar to pillar to keep them in view. He was not alone. Hundreds of these bird people hid behind every available structure, statue, or plant. Each was painted head to toe though no two colors were alike. Where similarities in hue occurred, there was always some subtle distinction of tone or shade. Their bird masks were equally unique: each beautifully chiseled and patterned in a kaleidoscope of garish pigments. The result was an energetic army of human rainbows.

In truth, the notion that the Necropolis was deserted was a false one. These vivid bird people lived among the crumbling structures in a state of supernatural wariness. Nobody who came from outside the jungle had ever seen them, let alone knew of their existence. They were only a little less obscure among the local tribes due to their painstaking avoidance of people. As soon as the visitors had departed, the multitude of bright bird people flooded back into the plaza. They brought with them countless items of furniture that the tribe had pilfered over the years, hoisting in a veritable river of chairs, lampshades, sofas, coffee tables, and other assorted bric-a-brac. Perhaps it was some strange nesting instinct that drove them to steal and hoard these domestic items, a trait picked up from the birds they so flawlessly emulated. Whatever the case, they chittered and tweeted excitedly to one another as they transformed the previously deserted plaza into a bustling center of social activity complete with furnishings, dancing, and ecstatic bird noises. Couches arranged peculiarly against the backdrop of shambolic ruins, accessorized tastefully with rugs, low tables, divans, and a gratuitous assortment of similarly plundered household décor. A twelve-chaired dining table stood amid a colorful crowd of painted figures who danced and twirled to their own orchestra of cheeps and whistles. Within moments, it was as if the plaza had always been this way.

THE GUNMAN AND HIS SHOWGIRL could hear the bird-like cacophony start as they reached the Shark, but like so many before them, they simply assumed it to be another vibrant jungle chorus. They were about to climb into the car when Chirrup slapped her forehead.

"Hot damn, I left my shades down at the death pit."

She spun on her heel and crossed down into passages while the Surf took a smoke break, pleased as punch that they had made it before dark. Chirrup hurried back down through the passages and across the deserted plaza. She arrived at the tower maze, which was by now quite dim, and found her sunglasses exactly where she had left them. She was eager to be clear of the place and scampered quickly from the towers. She reentered the desolate plaza and froze. Some meters away in the middle of the empty space, she spotted a rather chic chamois-upholstered settee. She approached it cautiously and saw that the item came complete with tasseled brass lampshade and mahogany coffee table atop a handwoven rug. She raised an eyebrow, vaguely amused.

APPLESEED STILL KEPT HER OLD locker at Paradise Discothèque. It made life easier if she needed a quick change of clothes or to hide something. She had staggered there after the episode at the pool, lying to Taty and telling her she was going back home. She needed some privacy to clear her head, to get her mind around what Johnny had done. She showered in a private booth before changing into her two-piece navy Chanel. It was difficult to accomplish this without looking into any mirrors. She did look at a mirror once by mistake while pulling up her stockings.

Johnny was still on the other side of the looking glass, only much closer now. She realized that she was sobering up and decided to head to a lounge that she knew would be quiet. The suit came with matching purse and hat. A tiny veil of netting crimped out over the brim, and she pulled this down to hide her eyes when she reached the lounge. Long airport-sized windows gazed out into the bloody cutlet of sunset. The red light was everywhere spilling over the jungle, invading every room. She drank half a bottle of champagne before she remembered that she needed to make a call. Luckily, there were phone booths facing the windows from across the lounge. She limped over to one and collapsed onto the enamel seat, fumbling for the receiver. She attempted to dial several times before the phone started ringing of its own accord.

"Hello?" she answered in confusion.

"I'm so glad you tried to call," the Smile said graciously. "I've been watching you."

"You have? Of course, you have ... silly me."

The crimson glare infiltrated the massive bubble glass of his control room. Almost every screen showed a close-up of Appleseed in the phone booth. Others replayed shots from the afternoon at the pool: Taty swimming in reverse, the pair walking away from the pool deck, entering corridors, a close-up of Taty's fingers moving inside the broken lobster. The spaceman was at his console, the entire chamber reflected red and warped in his laser-etched smiley face.

"She's already calling you Mommy," he mentioned proudly. "You are good, aren't you?"

"No, I'm bad, remember? A real bad seed."

"Well, even bad seeds can be good sometimes."

"No, of course they can't. Bad seeds stay bad forever. They breed flowers of evil."

"I suppose so. In any case, I want you to go up to her room tonight, late tonight. Wake her and ask her if she will ghost you. She has a real talent for shaking a globe."

"A real good seed, huh?" Appleseed sneered.

"The best I've seen."

"All right, sure, what the fuck. I'll do what you want, Captain Cunt. You going to be watching?"

He flicked another switch, and some of the screens flooded over with images of Taty on her bed watching the sunset, toying with the switchblade in her hands.

"You know me and my spies in the pies of the eyes in the skies," he joked.

"Well, I'll try to put on a nice show for you then," she whispered snidely just before hanging up.

She swigged from the near-empty bottle and crossed the lounge, headed for the long windows, and entered the apocalyptic glare, tracking large pterodactyls as they wheeled above the hazy pyramid. Some instinct of morbid fascination kept her eyes riveted on the flying creatures. She leaned her hand on the clean glass, leaving marks against the red light. One of the pterodactyls had snagged a laborer. The creature was flapping heavily toward the nests atop the floating monolith as its prey kicked and struggled in a mesh of hook-like teeth. She observed as the wriggling figure was dumped into the cascade of filthy nests. The laborer tumbled, suspended in space for the briefest of moments before the beast tore one of his legs off. Another pterodactyl began to invade his kettle of guts, unraveling him like a ball of string. She watched the event unfold in heat-shivering silhouettes, which seemed unreal against the nuclear sky. She soon realized that Johnny was also watching. She could see him reflected in the glass, standing just beside her. No, wait, she thought, he wasn't watching the killing at all. He was looking at her. He had always just been looking at her.

35
Switchblade

TATY HAD BEEN IN BED since late afternoon. The heavy-duty painkillers had made her drowsy, and she had felt herself drifting in and out ever since darkness fell. Dreams invaded, filling her head with pungent smoke. Visions caught in her mind's eye then broke apart, dissipating like water down a grate. She awoke in confusion to find that it was already night. Chirrup had still not returned, and the room was silent and dark. The only light came from the full moon that poured in through the open balcony doors, throwing great golden ponds of luminescence about the chamber. The light also created quivering slicks of impenetrable shadow, which seemed to distort the space, making it larger and smaller in turn. She felt as though she were still dreaming and turned on her side, so that she could look out over the moon-bright balcony. Enormous cumulonimbus formations curdled in the skies beyond the pyramid. Despite its beauty, the vision only added to the atmosphere of unreality that the jagged dreams had invoked. She felt her bruised eyelids slipping as she was sucked back down the well of drug-induced slumber. She was almost asleep when her fingers strayed against a cold metal object in the bed. The sensation roused her, and she found that it was the switchblade. She flicked its release, and the sharp steel report was stark against the ambiguous liquidity of moonlight. The sound woke her instantly, and she inched to her elbows, flicking the blade in and out. A distant shuffling outside the door made her perk up her ears. Light knocking emitted into the chamber, and she rose unsteadily. She crossed the room as though her joints had been pumped full of helium, unbolting the door to discover Appleseed swaying in the blackness of the corridor. She was drunk and weary, wearing a netted veil with a cigarette dying in her hands. Taty slipped effortlessly into her arms, and the pair embraced quietly in the dark.

"Mommy," Taty moaned, feeling long curved nails drift into her hair.

They eventually separated—like globules of molten wax. Taty dragged her across the threshold through golden pools toward the bed. Appleseed slouched heavily on the edge, half-in/half-out of a wan shaft of light while Taty coiled in beside her. She had slid her head onto Appleseed's lap and now lay quite still like some kind of woodland animal, breathing shallow as though in hiding. Appleseed glanced down, parting her lips to allow glowing coils of smoke to tumble gracefully from her mouth. The stink of liquor was heavy upon her, and it was impossible to say how far gone she was at that point. Her back slumped, and her limbs seemed dislocated, lined with lead and promises. Taty blinked slowly, reaching up into the black hole of Appleseed's face to lightly touch at her mouth.

"I'm scared I've gone mad," Taty breathed.

Appleseed's breathing hushed over when she heard this.

"You're not mad," she told Taty. "Trust me."

Her veil shifted as the hat came off. The light caught Appleseed's heavily made-up face like a painted mask as it drifted down toward Taty. Cold waxy lips smudged clumsily, and she felt her own hot mouth open like a wound. The grimy flavors of cigarette tar and sour booze blossomed into her with an almost unreal clarity, instantly resurrecting the recklessness of their afternoon by the pool. The kiss became slow and feverish, exploring a tidal pool in the dark. Then Appleseed pulled back abruptly, and they were staring at each other like cats.

"I want to show you something special ..." Taty whispered, burrowing her elbows and knees as deeply as she could into the amorphous fabric of the woman beside her.

"Show me," Appleseed murmured, stroking the girl's hair apart with her dragon nails.

She felt Taty's fingers clench tightly against her body, watching as the girl's eyes grew wide in the ghostly light. Their color seemed to drain beneath the rinse of moonwash, her pupils dilating. The golden moonlight spilled in, filling her eyes. A palpable current radiated out of her, sinking its charge into the body beneath, causing Appleseed to break out in gooseflesh. It was an unexpectedly pleasurable sensation, and she leaned down hungrily, physically drawn to this display of supernatural electricity. A tingling expansion bloated throughout Taty as their open mouths merged. Her eyelids fluttered closed, and she could feel the features rearranging in her face, eating into the kiss as one would eat into overripe fruit. An aurora of psychic illumination flashed through the bone above her nose, collecting in places like static. Taty opened her eyes to a universe of deafening light. Appleseed's face broke from hers, and her form receded, revealing the curious double sno-globe from Room 99. Whiplash currents were surging between the two of them, flooding down through the ellipse between the twin globes. It fed down into Taty like fluid moving through a delicate root system. She gazed up to see that the ellipse had elongated, penetrating deeply into her energy body like the hunting tongue of a cuttlefish. A severe jolt of recognition throbbed between her legs, traveling up her body in a shockwave.

"Daddy," she blurted.

Her hand found the switchblade reflexively. She raised it, pressed the hilt to Appleseed's throat, and released the blade. There was a dream-like quality to this action, and for a brief instant, it seemed as though nothing had even happened. Taty's vision trailed back to normality like a dissipation of fairy dust. Within moments, the vision of the twin globes was erased from her sight forever.

Appleseed was staring down into Taty's flickering eyes, only now beginning to register what had just occurred. Black ribbons flowed down like glistening oil traveling along her neck, engulfing stray sprays of hair. Some drops even kissed warmly against Taty's face, a dark flowering leaking down into her hairline. Appleseed shifted slowly, and Taty rolled gently off her legs. Appleseed rose, drifting up into the moonlight with the hilt of the switchblade still protruding from her rigid neck.

Taty watched, entranced, as the figure ghosted through the breathing curtains and out onto the luminous balcony. Appleseed was observing the moon enter a cloud, leaning drunkenly against the low stone balustrade while blood spouted quietly from her mouth, splashing on the stones around her. When she toppled off the balcony, it was still within that eerie spell of unbroken silence. Taty found herself following her out onto the balcony in confusion, her vision still stammering between this world and that. It was a straight drop, and Appleseed plummeted like a weighted doll down into the luminescent night. Her clothing buffeted up as she tumbled, her intoxicated mind struggling to make sense of what was happening. The entire jungle was rising madly as the ancient wall rushed past beside her. A gulf of shadow yawned, and she was suddenly plunged into blackness. A leathery flapping sounded near her face, and the slipstream became interrupted by a violent meaty thud. She found herself knocked sideways with a force so intense that it seemed as though a car had hit her. Something had clamped itself tightly around her body, shattering several ribs and bringing with it the hideous stench of abattoirs. The overpowering smell disappeared temporarily as she was jerked upward like a landed fish. The wind blasted her hair back, instantly destroying all sense of up or down in a flurry of vertigo. Gravity upended, hurling her back up into the sky. Once again, she entered the vivid fields of moonlight where she began to utter gurgling shrieks, realizing suddenly the depth of her predicament. The bony snout of the pterodactyl had locked into her, crushing her right hip and part of her ribcage. She studied the filthy crosshatch of barbed teeth perforating her stomach in helpless panic. Blood flickered off into the lunar void as the majestic wings beat against the night. They billowed like monstrous umbrellas, sails of meat that caught the blinding sheen of moonlight, and created giddy moments of weightlessness each time they pumped. A wide hairless face snorted beside her shoulder. A pair of piggy eyes, set wide apart, large as eggs. Hot breath was heaving beneath her shirt as the creature's tongue moved wetly against her bare skin. She felt the jaws crush down into her to release more blood into the panting gullet. The pressure of the bite winded her, creating a peculiar cocktail of claustrophobia and vertigo. She felt that she was about to pass out; but then the wings expanded and the whole beast tilted like a kite. She felt herself wrenched sideways into the void as the upside-down pyramid hurtled frantically up to meet her.

Taty was at the balustrade, staring at the rising form of the winged dinosaur in disbelief. It climbed like a glider passing out of shadow and into silhouette, soaring against the milky canyons of cloud. She watched as the beast described a lazy arc, circling toward the corpse-ridden pinnacle of the pyramid with the broken puppet in its snout. She let out a choked sob, feeling her hands slide across the railing only to then discover that they were filmed in blood.

θθθ

THE EGGY STENCH OF THE nests was overpowering, fecund, and prehistoric. The air was pregnant with the heavy magnetic humming of the pyramid. The haphazard terraces of jungle mud, guano, and bones formed a scale work of nests along the tip of the monolith. These nests created cup-like crevices wherein roosted the leathery, screaming hatchlings wallowing in the mess of last season's shells. The adults were swooping, scrabbling, and squabbling about their colony of festering forms. Human remains lay everywhere, sometimes even incorporated into nests as structural support. A man in a soiled tuxedo was miraculously still alive in one of these pockets of filth. He nursed a severed arm, fighting off a brace of starving infants and desperately trying to commit suicide by leaping from the nest. Appleseed flickered above him for a moment, caught in the pendulous cloaks of wing skin. The teeth slid from her body, and she toppled out into space. She hit the tilted stone hard, sliding several meters down the greasy layer of secretions while the blood left her body from a hundred holes. Yet, despite these various wounds, the only thing she still clutched at was the switchblade protruding from her throat. She hit a nest, crashing deep into the layers of rotting eggshells and bones. Glutinous debris clung to her hands as she floundered for the edge. She managed to get her head over the side only to be struck unexpectedly by the colossal splendor of Paradise Discothèque.

It suddenly seemed such a fantastical place rich with mystery, saturated with life. She began to cry. Was Johnny also crying, she wondered as she struggled to drag her damaged body over the lip of the nest. There was blood everywhere, and she felt as though she was sinking into quicksand. Yet, she still turned back to gaze at the spectacle of Paradise Discothèque. She knew the layout well enough to locate the balcony. She saw the pale figure of Taty at its edge and realized that she had been there only a few moments ago. She opened her mouth to call out, but there was too much blood to utter anything but a faint gurgle. A scraping and screeching made her suddenly whip her head up. The action caused the embedded blade to sever vital tendons in her throat. Half of her jaw fell uncontrollably slack as the pterodactyl scuttled down the stoneface, its folded wings flapping like a stall of leather coats. It fell upon her, crushing her into the detritus. She began to struggle and howl, smothered by the musky flanks of the heaving beast. Taty was watching and witnessed the struggling human figure make it to the edge of the nest one more time before the creature closed its jaws around the pale smudge of a face. It twitched its long snout, wrenching off Appleseed's head along with most of her spine. Then it absently flicked these out of the nest and proceeded to gouge into the chest cavity. Even from that distance, Taty could see the switchblade dislodge and glint silver as it fell away. The tadpole shape of the head and spine followed, rolling down the monolithic plane of the pyramid until they vanished into darkness. Taty didn't even realize she was screaming until the guards broke down the door and dragged her away.

36
Shower Scene

THEY TOOK HER UP LONG stone corridors all the way to the top. She was gulping in shock, bare feet trailing across the stone while the blood dried across her pajamas. The higher they got, the more cluttered the passages became. Equipment and hardware had been set up everywhere. Hastily erected light banks illuminated chugging fan units, fat cable stations, and miles and miles of foil tubing. She stumbled over whirring valve casings and spaghetti braids of hot electrical wire, guided inexorably toward the zenith: a massive hydraulic airlock situated at the end of a sealed corridor. They came to a halt, and one of the guards slammed a large metal button. Klaxons sounded while a red light began whirling above the door. She looked down to see her bare feet pigeon-toed against a scuffed welcome mat. Seals ruptured with a hiss of pressurized gas, and the circular vault door cracked. The astronaut reached out and pulled her into the chamber beyond without a word, slamming the airlock shut behind him. The guards regarded each other wearily, shrugged, and blundered off.

TATY FOUND HERSELF IN A claustrophobic metal space between the first airlock door and another. A red light pulsed above while metal pipes shook and throbbed around her, rattling with pressure. Each airlock door had two levers marked PURGE and RELEASE respectively. The astronaut yanked down the RELEASE on the second lock, and they emerged into the control room. Taty gazed around, stupefied, taking in all the screens, glass, and consoles while he sealed the door behind them.

"I wasn't expecting you to stab a mother figure in the windpipe," he mentioned conversationally.

"How did you see?" she burst out hysterically. "You promised no cameras in my room!"

"That was before someone used you as a birthday cake. Come with me, I have a bathroom you can use."

He turned abruptly, clumping down a spiral staircase. Taty rubbed her tearful eyes, shaking, following him because there was nothing else for her to do under the circumstances. The case wound down into a luxurious circular lounge. Long windows gazed down over the jungle and some illuminated portions of the roof terraces. The curved walls and ceiling had been stitched over with soft cream diamonds of dinosaur leather. It lent the place the air of a padded cell. Which, under the circumstances, seemed perversely fitting to Taty. Dense blonde shag occurred infrequently along the soft leather floor, collecting like pubic hair between an arc of couches. These couches were of a curious design. They blended ergonomically into the leather of the walls, curling up into a long tube with open sides. You had to crawl in as though you were entering a tunnel. Pale illumination lit the soft leather tube from within. The astronaut noticed her gawking and cleared his throat. The sound emerged somewhat robotically from his chest-mounted speaker, distorting whatever tact it might have held.

"The couches have seatbelts as well," he explained. "But, of course, you can't see them from this angle."

Taty sneered at him, kicking over a nearby light box. She wanted it to break, but the box turned out to be rubbery. It just bounced, rolling over undamaged. It made her want to cry. There seemed to be no sharp edges in the lounge. Even the large recreational monitor was oval. A door led to what she assumed was a galley while plastic urns overflowed with enormous tropical orchids. The strangest detail, however, was the long line of retro fridges secured to the far wall with heavy straps. A golf bag was similarly strapped to the wall alongside them. By the time she recognized the function of these items, the astronaut had already begun to move down the wide black-tile corridor that ramped downward from behind the stairs.

The corridor descended in zigzags comprised of long stretches and asymmetrical turns. The tiling was uniform, covering walls, floor, and ceiling without break or detail, creating a peculiar lack of dimension. This made the approaching turns manifest as optical distortions, coagulating at the end of a gleaming recession of perspective. A substance bearing a resemblance to tooth enamel ran between these tiles, emitting an even, white illumination throughout the shaft. The result was quite shadowless, further enhancing the starkness of the corridor. Taty limped after the striding astronaut, trailing blood along the walls as she leaned against them for support. She felt as though she were about to collapse at any point, the stress manifesting as an inexplicable rage toward the astronaut. Perhaps she would have been angry with anyone who had been there. Thinking about what she had just done made her want to smash her head against the tiles.

"The corridor has to be long," the astronaut grated in the manner of a tour guide, "in case there is a breach in the hydro system and we need to seal it off. A long bent corridor gives us some extra seconds to maintain structural integrity."

"What the fuck?" she shouted in fatigue.

"Of course, you haven't been briefed, yet," he mentioned.

She padded sullenly in his wake, wishing she could just die.

The corridor terminated in a landing emerging into the raised center of a dark spherical vault about twenty meters in diameter. The landing and walls of this globe room were of the same tiling except that, inside the chamber, the enamel's luminous properties had been deactivated. This changed quickly, however, when the astronaut approached a simplified panel with four glowing buttons: red, green, yellow, and white. He pressed the white button, instantly flooding the spherical vault with light from between the thousands of tiles. Taty threw a hand over her face, smudging a line of blood over her nose. Smiley twisted the button like a dial, adjusting the intensity to a bearable level and allowing her to take in the details of the huge peculiar area. The chamber was relatively featureless except for openings at the top and bottom. The evenly spaced tile created a smooth swirling effect, highlighting the disparity of the upper and lower regions. The top was a flat chromium grille, spanning over five meters, neatly punctured with hundreds of square holes arranged in circles. The bottom of the chamber boasted a slightly smaller circular feature about two meters across. This was a chrome-lined hole that fed into a shiny sloping pipe of equal diameter. Various objects and utilities surrounded the edge of the opening: buckle stirrups, a lever, and a thin tap rising from the chrome along with two manholes that had been set into the curvature of the tiles. Discrete metal rungs led down from the landing to this hole area. The acoustics were strange in the room, lending their voices a flat submerged sense of distance.

"This turns on the water," the astronaut told her, indicating the green button. "It's tuned to a heavy slow flow to avoid excessive inhalation of water vapor—you could easily drown like that."

"No, you can't, silly!"

"Things are different in orbit," he replied.

"Where's the toilet?" Taty asked, becoming disturbed by all of this.

"There's one upstairs that doubles as an escape pod. Down here you have to squat at the edge of the hole."

"I'm not a fucking kangaroo!"

"It's all part of the system," he explained curtly. "Come along."

He began to descend the rungs toward the chromium-lipped hole, and Taty followed sulkily. The tiles leveled out, and she slipped off the rungs, shuffling down the curvature to the edge where she stood staring down the wide shiny pipe. He clumped down in his own time and indicated the shiny lever and white rubber stirrups.

"Stirrups go around your ankles, so you don't drift off during business. Lever activates the suction fans. Turn them on when you want to use the toilet—it pulls waste and water down. Can't have excrement floating around like thought bubbles, can we?"

She pulled a face. "Call this a bathroom?" she shouted.

He ignored her outburst and strolled casually around the circumference of the hole.

"Water and waste gets filtered down to the indoor forest. So, every time you shower, the forest gets watered and overflow gets cycled. Waste is siphoned off and turned into fertilizer. Paradise Discothèque does hold large basement tanks if things get disastrous. The entire structure from tower to cellar will uproot and ascend. You see, the whole of the temple was designed to be a self-contained vessel. So, if worse comes to worst, we can also scavenge the jacuzzis, pools, and floors below for ice. After a while, though, we will need to replenish the supply from a natural source. That's when you press the red button ..."

"Why the fuck are you telling me all this?"

She glowered at him, pacing while he waited patiently for her to calm down. Despite her show of aggravation, he could see that she was becoming curious. Displacement into a new environment was aiding her well-tuned capacity for denial. He had observed her closely now for some time and was expert in the kind of tactful manipulation required to ground her.

"What's an indoor forest?" she asked eventually.

He crossed around and raised one of the two circular manholes. Each had a word engraved across it. The one he had just lifted sported the legend FOREST while the closed manhole cover read LAUNDRY. She approached cautiously and stared down into the opening. A spiral staircase led down through thick stone to an unseen lower area. He beckoned to the stairs, and she gingerly descended, shooting him a "no funny business" look as she passed beneath the stone. The area into which she emerged was vast. It actually seemed to span an entire floor of Paradise Discothèque, receding in all directions to distant walls and windows. She had emerged onto a small metal landing close to the high stone ceiling, gazing down upon thousands of evenly spaced Christmas trees and coconut palms. The trees were set out in alternating checkerboard squares interrupted occasionally by a vine trellis holding either runner beans or dusky black grapes. The trees grew out of a thigh-deep layer of specialized hydroponic jelly, which rendered their root systems visible as though viewed through clear water. Sun lamps had been embedded beneath these root networks and along the ceilings. The light they emitted refracted evenly throughout the glutinous jelly pods, saturating the massive space in a warm glow. Beside her, she could see the silver waste chute coiling sideways into a barrage of pipes and filtration systems that ran all the way out to the distant walls. Various contraptions and consoles gurgled at the opposite side of the landing, controlling aspects of the filtration. Thousands of tiny sprinkler heads speckled the ceiling, and she twisted at the nearest, feeling her fingertips become moist. Crusted blood dissolved, running down her wrist, filling her with wretched melancholy. No stairs or ladders led down to the trees, so she dragged herself back into the globe chamber above. The astronaut had climbed back to the mouth of the corridor and was holding up a fluffy white towel. It was a comical image, but she couldn't imagine finding anything funny while she was covered in blood.

"Why do you have a forest in your basement?" she demanded.

"To produce oxygen and grow food, obviously," he replied.

"How do you get down to the trees?"

"You float, of course."

"You what?"

He unexpectedly reached down and activated the green button. A heavy fall of warm water rained down from the ceiling grille in a broad circumference, instantly creating a pillow of steam. Taty was caught in the center of it and became instantly drenched. She was about to protest when she realized how soothing and welcome the warm water was to her bruised and battered body. She stood for a moment watching the blood wash off and spiral away. She wandered slowly to the edge of the pit, feeling as though she were walking outside in the rain.

"I'll be up in the control booth if you want to undress," the astronaut called, amplifying his voice to penetrate through the rush of water. "There's a soap tap, and you can toss your clothes down the laundry hatch."

"Well, it's nothing you haven't seen before, Mister Cameraman!" she yelled.

He disappeared back down the corridor without comment, leaving Taty alone in the tingling downpour. All the tension of the night seemed to detonate somewhere within, and she began to cry, slowly peeling her clothes off, finally lying sobbing on the tiles, feeling the water wash everything away in a steady gush of warmth. Below her, the filtration systems had activated. Gauges began to dance as pipes clanked and shook. The sprinkler system came online after an allotted processing period, and a light rain began to shower down softly over the quietly rustling leaves.

37
Escape Velocity

DAWN SIFTED THROUGH THE HORIZON. It wept pale yellow over the galaxy of trees, touching lightly at the flanks of Paradise Discothèque. The astronaut was in his control room observing various views of the slumbering leviathan while light crept slowly into his parlor. He saw sleeping guards and vacant tombs. He shuffled between visions of dog kennels, pyramids, and flocks of flamingos. He turned huge batteries of floodlights off and on for no reason. He ran schematics on all his slave gang rocket thrusters, plotting vectors on a wrist-mounted holographic calculator. Taty, meanwhile, had risen to her elbows, lying in the hot rain of the huge shower like a little sphinx. She had dozed off in the delicious onslaught and awoken feeling somehow purged. Last night's events had begun to feel more like an exorcism. The thought crossed her mind that this was simply what she was telling herself to eradicate guilt. But there was no doubt of her guilt. She had tortured herself for years upon the altar of her brother's death. Perhaps now, she was simply aware and, indeed, weary of the uselessness of it. She found her mind returning to Miss Muppet. How cold that predatory woman had seemed to her. Now she could clearly imagine the pair of them sharing a smoke, bantering like old cronies: true sisters of the Zone. What had begun with her brother and peaked in the lonely reaches of the Necropolis had by now reached its zenith. She was transformed entirely. But into what? If I look into a mirror, she thought, would I see the face of a psychopath? The thought evolved further: would something have changed or had she always been like this? All of a sudden, the stupidly innocent face of her brother seemed to bulge out at her. Could she really continue to blame herself for what was essentially an accident? After Appleseed, her view of murder had altered irreparably. The wildcard of secret power, which had mocked her for years, now fell silent. She was the tiger who, by simply attempting to swat away a hand, had only succeeded in mauling weaker creatures. She had done all she could to deny her nature, but now this was no longer possible. Beneath the flimsy covering, a wellspring of uncontainable power had asserted itself.

SHE CRAWLED SLOWLY OUT OF the water and climbed to the landing where she shut off the roaring flow. The pearly dripping of a hundred droplets pinged and echoed throughout the great tiled globe as she stood realigning herself. There were two towels, and she wrapped her hair up in the smaller one, swaddling the large one about her like a cloak. When she felt ready, she headed back up the corridor.

The pale flare of dawn illuminated the cream leather lounge, gleaming in through a stereoscopic array of windows. She noticed that a pile of her things lay neatly across the floor, draped beside and across one of the couches. She approached to find that all the items from her room, closets, and lockers were present: all her shoes and dresses and costumes, her suitcase and blankets, her wigs, cosmetics and jewelry, her walkie-talkie, and even its shrine. Everything except her machine gun, she noted wryly. Somehow, she found herself unoffended by this invasion of privacy or the liberties taken. She felt that she could not return to that room now, no matter what. It was a pattern with her, she realized: kill and run away. So, she stood there dripping in the gathering light, surveying her entire life gathered inconsequentially across a weird couch and a patch of blonde shag. Everything had changed, and she was on the move again. There was nothing for it but to pad up the stairs to the control booth and try to find out where they were going. She found the spaceman at his world of television screens watching over his perverse little kingdom just like the insane dictator that he had pretended to be. The sight of him amused her, and she came up beside his chair, sitting down heavily on what looked to her like the most delicate piece of apparatus. He noticed her trying to crush the device and unzipped a pouch on his suit. She watched as he withdrew a can of cola, which he tossed over to her. She caught it and almost dropped it again due to its surprising weight.

"This soda weighs a ton!" she exclaimed, discovering a bizarre reinforced pressure seal at the top complete with a pulsing LED.

"I designed the cans to withstand the void. They are radiation-proof as well."

"Space cola—fab," she clucked, cracking the can and taking a long swig.

He turned in his chair, regarding her as seriously as one could with a reflective smiley over his face.

"Let's you and me get out of here," he proposed.

"Get out of where?" she frowned, wiping her mouth on the back of her hand.

"I don't know. This planet, for starters."

She looked at him for a few moments, realizing that his helmet was the only mirror she had seen since the shower. She leaned forward, brushing her hair back with her fingers and inspecting her teeth.

"Sure, why not?" she murmured, engrossed in her own reflection.

"I'm so glad that you have decided to join me on my fantastic trip to the dark side of the moon," he declared in his robot voice.

"I'm like one of those sharks. If I stop moving, I die."

"Don't let a little homicide get you down."

She leaned back, unimpressed.

"And how exactly are we supposed to get to the moon, Mister Crazy Spaceman?"

"That's what this place was built for," he declared grandly, sweeping his arm around to encompass the entirety of Paradise Discothèque. "The old people constructed it to ferry their god to the moon. It was the sole purpose of their entire civilization."

"Isn't it a bit mean of you to jack his ride then?"

"I find it rather funny, actually."

She sucked cola grimly at this.

"I suppose it is."

She finished off the heavy can and hurled it at a small screen, managing to crack the glass. This little act of destruction seemed to cheer her up, and she turned to him with some satisfaction.

"So," she burped. "When do you want to go?"

"How about right now?"

She blinked at him for a few moments, a tiny smile beginning to flicker at the edges of her mouth.

"That sounds good," she mumbled softly.

He slapped his kneepad and rose triumphantly, crossing the room toward the upper airlock. Taty followed, waiting as he unsealed the massive door. He led her through the long corridor of stone reliefs toward the distant light while she goggled at the many notes and intricate stone carvings.

THEY ARRIVED AT THE HIGH pavilion, where dawn had begun to paint the reeling vista with its clean palette of yellows and blues. The birds were cheeping in their universe of trees while a fragrant breeze gusted against her moist skin. She moved from pillar to pillar, gazing out over Paradise Discothèque in wonder, staggered by the view. Cloud banks were rolling in from the west, threatening rain later that day. The astronaut walked to the center of the pavilion and loomed over the pedestal.

"There's your ticket off this rock," he declared.

"But, it's just a stone *thing* ..."

He drifted toward the edge where he leaned against a pillar.

"Not to someone like you," he said.

She stood blinking at him, unsure of his meaning.

"Alphonse, Florix, and I had Jennerators everywhere scanning for just the right ghost girl, ready to amplify her talents when she came in out of the cold. We needed one special enough, one who had the ability to do this. You have no idea how long we had been beachcombing, trying to find that one last piece of our beautiful jigsaw. Perhaps Alphonse got sick of it all, distracted by his cookie jars. He was always easily distracted ..."

Taty had gone quiet, unbalanced by this sudden confession.

"What are you talking about?" she murmured.

"Well, this is what he was training you for. This, exactly."

"You mean Alphonse sent me out here for this?"

"How did you think I knew to find you in the Necropolis? Or why I was the first to test drive your abilities at the Shell Sea?"

"I thought you just ... I thought he ..."

She sank down suddenly, leaning against a pillar. He watched as she retched, vomiting quietly over the edge. When she was done, she wiped her hand carefully over her mouth, sobbing on the ground. Tears were spilling down her shivering cheeks, catching the dawn.

"You mean, he was trying to save me?" she groaned.

He walked over and kneeled down beside her.

"Your capabilities were foreseen thousands of years ago by an ancient race. That is how special you are. Perhaps you doubt yourself, but I understand your true purpose."

She was crying heavily now, and her voice stammered when she spoke.

"You mean this is why you wanted me to ghost a globe without an operator? This!" she exclaimed, pointing at the pedestal.

"The old reptiles had perceptive faculties similar to yours. Only one with their abilities can operate the incredible device that they have left behind. And you, my dear, are able to do just that—aren't you?"

She pawed at her bruised face, swabbing away the tears, so that she could fix her gaze upon the pedestal. She held her concentration like a breath, feeling a tiny surge of pressure behind her sinuses. All of a sudden the world inverted, coalescing into a familiar miasma of spectral currents—that secret mysterious anti-world she had seen in glimpses throughout her entire life. Beyond the cusp of the astronaut's brilliantly shining sno-globe, the jungle teemed with protoplasmic energy. She gazed out across this microbial orgy of forms to witness highways of energy, gloaming in across a flickering sky. These bands of force traveled over the jungle in a massive ribbon, twining and pulsing around Paradise Discothèque to create a circuit of power which looped back out toward the horizon again. Taty recognized now that this highway of power originated from the Pyramids in the Necropolis. A massive exchange of energies swelled constantly between the two complexes, gathering force from the jungle with each circuit. Rivers of natural psychic energy, the very same she had once used to move objects with her mind, had been tapped and channeled, directed by these ancient structures. It was this concentrated telekinetic force that had kept them suspended in the air with such dependable constancy all these centuries. She understood now why the ancient people had not been able to activate their creation themselves. The monoliths had required millennia to accumulate enough ectoplasmic force to rise above the ground, storing psychic charge in their links to one another.

"It's what killed them off," she whispered.

"Yes," the astronaut answered, holding her arm to steady her. "It was their intention for the Pyramids to drain and channel their energy, siphoning off their sno-globes one by one, compressing an entire race into a river of spiritual fuel that would exist in perpetuation, strengthening itself over time."

"What I'm seeing is ... *them*?" she whispered incredulously, gazing out at the gleaming loop of spectral force that raged around the structure and back out again, moving at a speed that was not speed.

"In a way, yes," he answered. "They have transcended entirely into a single form—still living, yet existing as pure energy, developing itself slowly toward that moment when their great plan would finally come to fruition."

"They're still alive!"

"Yes, but their consciousness is not as ours, not anymore—they have become some kind of cosmic exercise bike pedaling onward across the centuries, swelling in ectoplasmic mass, charge, and speed—a sentient telekinetic engine manifested for one purpose only ..."

"Gasoline for a god ..."

"A one-way ticket to the outer dark."

Taty gazed down, observing the bands of energy as they snaked up the flanks of Paradise Discothèque woven together by the loom of the four Pyramids. These bands grew smaller the higher they went, more concentrated and tightly woven, spinning up toward the uppermost area. Dizzy, she turned around to see them coalescing in a blinding vortex around the pedestal of the high pavilion. Just above, hovering at about chest height was a flower-like form of energy that billowed and turned: the focal point for the entire circuit.

"My spectral filters allow me to see it," the astronaut said. "It is the collective soul of the old people, the activation area where they wait—the flower of the moon ..."

"It's so beautiful ..."

Taty rose, entranced, and the towel slipped off her shoulders. The astronaut managed to catch it as she advanced naked toward the pedestal. She did not seem to notice her nudity and continued forward like a sleepwalker, an unclothed psychic priestess atop an ancient temple at dawn about to fulfill a centuries-old prophecy. He had occasionally suspected the ancient collective of saturating the consciousness of the surrounding jungle and its people somehow manipulating events to their own end. Such a moment smacked of orchestration, and he could not shake the sense that the temple itself had manifested this sequence of events. Taty seemed to have entered a trance state, and through his spectral filter, he saw the energy of the pedestal reacting favorably to her strangely pulsating, oversized sno-globe. It swathed her with a billion tendrils of speeding light, drawing her perceptive faculties into this age-old network of power. She felt the ecstatic presence of a thousand people a second, and it made her sick with wonder. Taty had now entered the vortex and could feel the currents of the gargantuan circuit infiltrating her. She was lifted bodily off the ground, much to the surprise of the astronaut who observed her levitating before the pedestal, hair swirling about as though buffeted by powerful aquatic currents. It was a phenomenon compounded by the stitches of static electricity, which occasionally gathered and broke across her skin in discharges of white and blue. The vortex swirled her gently around the pedestal in a spiral, a movement that brought her within the aureole of the revolving flower form, a translucent manifestation, pinkish and unfathomably dimensioned. She sensed a benign yet undeniably alien influence guiding her into an advanced understanding of what she had to do in order to unlock the ancient mechanism. Tentacles of her own energy swirled from her hands, and when she brought her wrists together, these tendrils twined into a caduceus that entered the alien flower in the same way as would the proboscis of a butterfly. The contained force of the ancient form caught her emanations like ink in a whirlpool, and she cried out in shock, feeling her energy reeled into a tremendous maelstrom.

The astronaut saw her go rigid in the air, arms held out as though casting a spell. His spectral filter was unable to process the vast amounts of energy and now only showed white. He was forced to switch to a standard view of reality only to find that Taty was spasming violently in the air, back arching as her eyes rolled to the whites. He was unsure of whether or not to interfere though some instinct reassured him that she was still somehow in control of the situation. Taty felt her consciousness expand as tentacles of her energy sucked recklessly out into the Great Grand Prix of the energy circuit, elongating into fine filaments that spanned hundreds of miles in an instant, whipping around the spiral tower through every floating pyramid and back to Paradise Discothèque in a heartbeat. She sensed her perception following this course, riding out in heart-stopping velocities over the jungle through the pinball machine of the Necropolis to plug back into her. Every stone of every pyramid felt, for a moment, like her very own flesh. She could track the subtlest movement of each plant along the path of the energy band, the awareness of each animal, the placement of each stone. From somewhere far above this vortex of sensory data, her mind knocked frantically at the door of herself. She sensed that, unless she broke the circuit immediately, her sno-globe would be upended like a thimble in this fast-forward river. She concentrated what attention she could on the flowery shape, feeling her minute filaments wrap and weave into every aspect of its form with each turn of the circuit. It was easy for her to twist it all apart after that, dropping a spanner into a machine that had been running smoothly for countless millennia. The flower form froze, describing for an instant a star before separating into a million petals that instantly severed her connection with the circuit. Her cosmic consciousness of the jungle and Pyramids was lost. She felt herself shuddering back into her sno-globe with a jolt, watching as the highway of energy snapped like some gargantuan rubber band. It whipped off over the horizon, reeling back toward the Necropolis in an instant.

Taty awoke from her trance state realizing that the whiplash would strike Paradise Discothèque at any moment. She tumbled to the ground as gravity reinstated itself. The shock of reality hit her with the ground. It was dawn, and she was naked on the stone floor of the high pavilion, covered in goose pimples. The featureless pedestal had begun to retract into the floor, filling the air with a dull grating. Without it, the globular confines of the high pavilion began to take on the qualities of a birdcage. The astronaut came up behind her and draped the towel around her shoulders, helping her to her feet.

"Are you all right?" he asked.

She glanced up at him in confusion, her eyes shining, her vision flipping back and forth. The interaction with the ancient circuit had transmuted something inside her, lending a new metallic luster to her irises.

"Hold on to something," she warned, just as the sirens began to boom.

Perimeter alarms had been tripped by seismic tremors. Flocks of birds and pterodactyls poured out into the morning light, spooked by the noise. Their panicky forms scattered through the air as they fled the structures. A low rumble sounded from far below, and the astronaut backed off to the pillars, feeling the entire structure shiver beneath his boots. The ever present hum of the Pyramids suddenly intensified to a low frequency din. The sound caused Taty to clap her hands to her ears in reflex, an action that did little to numb the deep buzzing that traveled through stone and flesh alike. The sound passed quickly, vanishing entirely, leaving a massive gap in the familiar acoustics of the place. The astronaut turned to see one of the pyramids shudder against the dawn. The system of pterodactyl nests adorning its summit began to crumble and slide down the sides, prompting mass panic among the flying beasts. The pyramid had lost its telekinetic buoyancy and hung sickeningly in the air for a moment before falling in a sort of slow motion, trailing shafts of dust and debris. They saw it crash into the outer courtyards, cleaving in half as it struck the trees and broke apart. Taty watched, mesmerized, as a cloud of dust began to fountain from the crash site, swarming up the walls, swallowing balconies and terraces. She braced for the impact of the dust cloud but found herself pulled to the floor as the entire mass of Paradise Discothèque uprooted like a tooth, jerking up above the trees. The displacement of air sucked the dust cloud back down, and she glimpsed the massive entrance sign falling, slipping into the churn.

People and animals screamed as the next pyramid unmoored and plunged into the chaos below. Its fall boosted Paradise Discothèque even higher; the horizon slipped, and the jungle fell away. Taty crawled to the edge and observed a staggering airborne view of the destruction. The bottom parts of the sprawling structure trailed soil and debris into the gaping chasm as distant figures rushed across rooftop plazas and balconies in panic. The remaining Pyramids fell together, lifting the temple to a frightening height. The people in the surrounding jungle heard the noise from miles around and came from their dwellings to see the spiral structure lifted high above the trees, its function as a gigantic, mythical airship finally revealed. The underside was an inverted stone spiral made up of causeway walls dark with dirt and tapering to a rounded point. Water vented from severed pipelines, showering the area below with a rain of muddy effluvium. It was a great golden beehive in the sky shining brightly in the rays of dawn, which had not yet reached the canopy of trees.

Stricken people clung to the walls of fractured passages, falling occasionally to the receding canopy. Couches and cars spilled out into the sunlight. All manner of objects rained down in a bizarre slow motion, entering the cloud of dust spiked with the rubble of the Pyramids, now proved to be nothing more than telekinetic ballast for the central structure. A crocodile tumbled above the trees, falling through the upper layers of a hardwood and entangling itself in vines halfway down. Below, in the festering subterranean barracks, guards had awoken in their bunk beds, roused by the deafening reports of breaking masonry. They fled as the flagstones in the floor loosened, letting in shafts of sunlight. Some made it to the door, where they glimpsed the long room breaking apart, spilling stone cubes down into the forest like children's toys. Riot and calamity rampaged through the area, and Taty clung to a pillar above it all, wild-eyed, with the sun in her hair. Once the four Pyramids had fallen, the ascension leveled out. Paradise Discothèque rose as smoothly as a balloon, gathering strength from the Necropolis, which had only now begun to disintegrate.

The bird people had sensed a gathering hum in the Pyramids and fled to the upper tree line where they witnessed the first of the structures begin to tumble. Cubes of weathered stone rolled like dice through the decayed boulevards, smashing arches and colonnades, instantly leveling structures that had stood for a thousand years or more. One by one, the Pyramids dislodged and fell, radiating outward from the center of their swastika formation in a corona of destruction. Some of the larger structures even punched abyssal clefts through to the subterranean labyrinths of the Lost Quarter, letting in sun where before there had been none. A biblical cloud of dust was raised, distributing outwardly through the ruins like the viscous ink of a squid. This wall of obscurity reached the bird-masked people like a ghostly pall. It invaded the jungle in a fast-moving rift within whose depth could be discerned the distant echoes of calamity.

TATY CLUNG TO HER PILLAR, staring in disbelief at the jungle, which had now flattened out to a verdant sheet. She could not grasp how they had risen so quickly into the silences of the upper reaches. Here the air was clean and dry, the light piercingly bright. Gusts of wind traveled through the pavilion, forcing her to keep a tight hold on her towel. The astronaut came up beside her and handed her a bulky pair of combat binoculars, pointing out a faraway patch of paleness against the endless green. She gazed through the device and saw that it was the Necropolis. Many pyramids were still afloat piercing through a veil of dust that was slowly rising. She observed the Pyramids drop one by one into this fugue, transferring their energy to Paradise Discothèque. She was watching the spectacle unfold when a chilly whiteness stole across the lenses to blind her. She removed the binoculars from her face only to discover that they had passed into a low cloud. It was cold and soundless within the nebulous mass. The acoustics took on a cotton wool closeness that made everything seem to reduce in size. She could barely see the opposite end of the pavilion where the astronaut stood, his gold visor catching the light through the murk.

DOWN ON THE POOL DECKS a lifeguard was panicking, running through the misty cloud while bikini-clad girls screeched indecipherable jungle lingo insults at him from across the patios. The water in all the pools lurched in synchrony, splashing everywhere and sliding off the distant edges into space. On the tables some of the hardier luncheon lobsters had begun to move, revived by the moistness of the cloud. Within the lounges, cinematic windows gazed out onto glowing whiteness. Gamblers and hangover harpies stood speechless against the glass while waiters in full livery ran about like headless chickens. A peacock fluttered, squawking through the rooms. Then suddenly, without any warning whatsoever, the whiteness fell away, and the chambers were flooded with a crystalline high-altitude light.

A dramatic vista of blinding white clouds revealed itself, leaving those who observed staggered and silent. A rush of stratospheric wind unexpectedly rocked the structure. Up on the roof, Taty had to catch her balance. Entire bar areas smashed apart as hundreds of bottles toppled and fell, filling the air with the pungent fragrance of a thousand cocktails. A swarm of bright parakeets spilled through the lounges and hallways, escaping into the clouds via broken windows and ruined walls. All the open doors swung drunkenly as the temple tilted again, swayed by sudden surges of wind.

θθθ

TATY WATCHED AS TOWERS OF cloud rushed past as though viewed from a rapidly ascending elevator. It was icy in the open air despite the bright sunlight. The astronaut had grabbed hold of her as the winds began to bluster, and she clung awkwardly to his arm while cumulonimbus giants rose and fell. They wafted eerily through stray areas of cloud, her feet and hands long since numbed. She felt her teeth begin to chatter uncontrollably.

"You should put some clothes on," the astronaut pointed out. "It's already below zero."

"I can't leave now!" she clattered, gesturing excitedly at the clouds.

Yet, it was frightening to see those puffy leviathans beginning to shrink slowly beneath them. She gazed out over the cotton wool mindscapes of the cloud layer, watching the polystyrene magic of it all slip away as they climbed steadily higher into frigid space.

"Go back to the bathroom and press the yellow button," the astronaut said. "A pressure lock will unseal. It leads to a storage facility. You'll find your spacesuit in there—I had it made up some time ago."

"Fucking A!" she whooped, shivering uncontrollably and grinning despite the fact that she had turned a subtle shade of blue.

She rose and crossed the pavilion, huddled ineffectively in her soft towel.

"Back in a tic-tac-toe!" she called, yanking open the airlock and scampering down into the corridor of reliefs.

She ran all the way, scooting down staircases in a mad frenzy, sprinting down the black tiles with her towel trailing from her upraised hand like a flag of triumph. She emerged into the bathroom panting heavily and thumbed the yellow button. A rectangular section of the wall protruded with a clank and hum, revealing a similarly tiled walk-in closet. She entered and poked around gleefully. Several spacesuits identical to the one the astronaut wore hung like inanimate versions of himself. Only one of these spares had a smiley face etched onto its visor, and she guessed that most of them were as yet unused. Oxygen tanks hung beside silk dressing gowns, and Turkish slippers were lined up, preserved in airtight glass capsules. White linen suits, leather shoes, striped flannel pajamas, and a pith helmet all offered tantalizing glimpses into the man behind the suit. It was strange for her even to imagine that there was a person in there. She walked deeper into the closet and found four smaller spacesuits hanging at the back. She was delighted to see that these suits had been designed differently to the astronaut's, plated with an alloy that had been given a sugary glitter-pink finish. Large fishbowl helmets dangled like bright candy pearls, their glass gleaming with a reflective coating. The metallic green of the bubble visors contrasted with the shimmery candy of the suits, and she found herself nodding in approval. He had obviously wanted to make her happy with her suit, and the gesture made an impression. Perhaps she had been wrong to mistrust his motives. She pondered this, clambering naked into the heavy shell of the nearest suit. Webbing adhered to her form within, holding her in place and offering plenty of mobility. The suit sensed that she was inside it and activated automatically. Lights began to flash along the inner and outer lining. She had to attach the gauntlets separately once the suit was in place. The locking sockets seemed self-explanatory, and all one had to do was draw them on to activate the power relays. Mechanisms locked them in place as soon as her hands were inside the comfortable inner gloves. Digital readouts began to flutter along wrist panels, showing the status of various life support units.

She grabbed one of the helmets and crossed back to the door. She found out very quickly how ridiculously heavy the suit was. She emerged from the closet like a pink beetle and pressed the yellow button again, sealing the closet with a hiss of pressurized gas. She then hit the white button and doused the spherical vault in gloom. She was about to exit when a tinny scratching made her stop in her tracks. The shower globe was a remarkably quiet chamber, and the sound felt immediately foreign to her. She stepped back out onto the ledge and looked down, sensing that the sound had emanated from the chrome-lipped hole. More scratching and scuffling leaked up at her, and she quickly pressed the white button, turning it up to full capacity to flood the tiled sphere in a galactic light. She realized then that something was moving in the pipe. A long pale arm snaked unexpectedly from the sloping tube clutching at the lip with long needle-tipped digits. She let out a piercing shriek as the distorted blank-faced head of the dead god emerged from the chromium hole. It began to coil out quickly across the tiles, its segmented spine flexing in the surgical glare. Taty turned and fled up the shaft, hopelessly hampered by the restrictive bubble gum spacesuit. The helmet slipped from her grasp, bouncing and skittering across the tiles ahead of her as she struggled to heave her titanium-soled boots. At that point she turned her head and saw the god emerging into the corridor. It was so massive that it took up half the passage and had to remain crouched to avoid scraping the ceiling. The sight of it jolted her into a nightmare of adrenaline, and she yelled out in fear as it hunched down low, galloping fluidly toward her. She stumbled and fell in panic, sliding across the tiles with her arms thrown over her head. Horrible visions of Appleseed's pterodactyl-mutilated body filled her mind as she skittered and scrabbled for purchase. She was still screaming when she felt the god pass above her like a wind. It sidestepped her neatly and accelerated on down the passage. She lay where she was, sobbing in an absurd combination of relief and confusion, watching the deity recede until it had vanished entirely around a far corner. She scrabbled up, suddenly aware of what was happening. Then she began shouting uselessly for the astronaut as she ran, scooping up her helmet as she fought to bridge the gap.

It took her a few minutes to reach the lounge where she paused for breath, perspiring profusely from her efforts inside the suit. Ice caked the massive windows in fractal formations, and she could see that they had already ascended beyond the feathery cirrus formations and into the immeasurable blue distances of the upper stratosphere. She did not tarry but rushed up the spiral stairs as quickly as she could. In the screens of the control booth, she glimpsed scenes of ice ravaging the interiors of Paradise Discothèque. Freezing winds blew crockery and furniture out into the void. Already she could see the blue outside deepening to the indigo of the ionosphere, those great bands of terminal distance where no wind ever blew. The airlock leading to the corridor of stone reliefs had closed automatically, and she pulled it open without thinking. A blast of icy pressure sucked her out and almost a quarter of the way up the corridor. Her helmet flew out of her hands again, traveling ahead of her. She tried to scream but found that she was unable to draw breath. The air was too thin and hurt her throat with its merciless chill. The entire corridor was sparkling white with frozen condensation, and she slid and skittered across this glittering shaft clutching at her throat in panic with clumsy metal fingers. Light attachments hung like frost-blasted branches overhead while she struggled against the inrush. Ice flakes were already beginning to form across the suit, and her skin grew numb. The blinding overture to an ice cream headache had begun to blossom, aided by oxygen deprivation.

She glimpsed the airlock slamming behind her and flailed for it. Luckily, the sealing of the lock equalized the pressure, and her helmet came bouncing back down the slope. She grabbed it and rammed it over her head, struggling to get all her hair in, so that it could seal properly. She was running out of breath when the helmet clicked satisfactorily into place. It was a peculiarly unnatural sensation to enclose her head when she felt that she was suffocating, but she had learned to hold it together in a car crash and pressed on. A green light flashed, and warm air began to gush reassuringly into the glass bubble. Her skin started to tingle ferociously as it thawed, and she could hear herself gasping and gulping in confinement. Demisting vents cleared the condensation in an instant while digital readouts began to flicker across the interior of the glass. A speaker system kicked in, and she found herself listening to her surroundings in stereoscopic clarity: the distant hiss of escaping air, the grinding of frozen stone, and the sound of metal objects striking one another in the chaos without. She pulled herself to her knees as her breathing evened, struggling to raise herself up. Once on her feet, she began to lope up the long passage, trying as best as she could not to slip on the ice particles, which had frosted over everything in a shimmering patina.

She heard them smashing against the pillars before she even emerged through the lock. The god was whipping about its sacred chamber, attempting to gain a hold on the astronaut whose defense mechanisms delivered powerful psychotronic shocks wherever contact with the suit was made. The results left them hopelessly entangled with blinding rainbow discharges issuing constantly from the suit. The shielding seemed to create an electromagnetic force field that repelled the clutches of the pale reptilian claws and spines much the same way as two opposing magnets repel each other. The astronaut slipped chaotically between the whipping coils. It was maddening to see and obviously damaging to him. He was attempting to fight back with concentrated bolts of psychotronic energy delivered from his palms, but the god was too quick and massive: a vast writhing hydra of pale musculature. It was clear that the astronaut would not last long despite his clever mechanisms. Outside, the vista of pure blue was already darkening into the radiant blackness of outer space. The frozen battlements of Paradise Discothèque had tuned into that high-resolution clarity peculiar to a lack of atmosphere. They stood out in cut-glass detail against the hazy glow of the planet below, seeming almost hyperreal in their crispness of form. Clouds roiled across the luminous span of the world beneath much like the milkshakes of energy she had seen in sno-globes except far slower as though existing within a larger time frame. Iced beach umbrellas, deck chairs, freeze-dried waiters, pets, sofas, champagne bottles, and countless other objects joined the crusts of ice scaling from the rising leviathan. This debris fell like glitter, flowering back into the ionosphere like pollen from a monstrous orchid. The astronaut's voice came unexpectedly into her helmet cut with crackling and strained with effort.

"Get back inside!" he was yelling. "I can't hold it off for long!"

A magical moment followed where the gravity lessened noticeably. The god's coils spooled outward, relaxing and filling the space like an art nouveau detailing. Their struggle seemed to pause as both figures acclimatized to their new sphere of balance. Taty felt herself float above the ground, and she scrambled for the air lock handle. Her flailing arm only tipped her into a graceful somersault, and she would have sailed off the pavilion entirely had it not been for a nearby carving of the god, whose blank face she was able to grab hold of. She reoriented herself as the figures began clashing once more, their exchanges spinning them faster and faster within the globular space. They began to create a slippery maelstrom of forms as though trapped in a whirlpool. The blue without had become deep purple, and a kaleidoscope of stars was visible.

The vastness of this upper stratum calmed her, lending her a moment of perspective. She knew what she had to do almost the instant they entered the vacuum. She drew her perceptive faculties back toward the spectral realm, and the blackness of space suddenly transmuted into a rainbow-hued nebula. Immense planes of color struck and melted into one another across the galactic distances, chiming out neon starbursts, saturating the vaults with celestial iridescence. She was awestruck but had the good sense to concentrate her attention on the figures before her. Their sno-globes had distorted like white blood cells attempting to devour one another. The astronaut's was relatively normal in comparison to the many spheres of energy she had seen, but the sno-globe of the dead god was an entirely different affair. It was massive and frothed with countless bubbles of energy.

She drifted closer and was able to discern tiny humanoid forms encapsulated within each of these cells. She was startled by the realization that the bubbles were, in fact, all the sno-globes upon which the god had feasted over the centuries. The energy bodies had not been consumed after all, merely compressed and stored in miniature form bereft of their long-dead physical frames. Taty did not allow herself to be distracted and instead scanned through the cellular formations to the ectoplasmic infrastructure of the god's own globe. She found what she was looking for and reached out her hand, throwing a pseudopod of extended energy deep into the clusters of compressed sno-globes. She wrapped her tendril about a spongy, frilled formation and in one sharp movement, decapitated it. The effect was instant and explosive. The entire sno-globe retracted, a collapsing star before a supernova. The physical form of the god rapidly untangled, whipping itself into a perfect circle. Its tail twined about its upper regions to create a spiny ouroboros that fit perfectly within the globular confines of the high pavilion. It was a display that demonstrated the design of the chamber clearly. It had been constructed with the precise intention of containing the god in this form. Taty and the astronaut had stopped moving, stilled by the vision of the god in this state.

When the deity began to spin within its chamber, the astronaut immediately reached out for Taty, but he was too late. The curve of the god ring struck her unexpectedly, knocking her past the pillars and out into space. Her screams were deafening within the claustrophobic confines of the helmet, further intensified by the sheer lack of sound feeding back through the external speakers. Space was like being locked in a tiny room forced to watch herself on the largest screen in the universe. Now she watched in panic as the pavilion slewed away from her kicking boots at crazy gradients, her confined breathing harshly amplified. She was tumbling erratically high above the roof terraces. These platforms rapidly fell away, and she saw the walls stretching down in a moment of suicidal perspective before spinning out over the far edge and into the void. She flailed helplessly above the vivid surface of the planet, watching in horror as Paradise Discothèque drew farther and farther away.

The astronaut, meanwhile, had escaped the pavilion in an

attempt to avoid the god, who had now begun to whirl—an uncontrollable centrifuge. Its external features blurred together into a sort of pale sphere as it accelerated faster and faster within the fitted form of the stone pavilion. The astronaut turned and saw that Taty had diminished to a tiny flailing form, thrashing against the glowing fields above the planet. He acted quickly, unlatching a slim metal cable from a ratchet loom in his waist rig and locking it around a nearby pillar by means of a titanium carabiner. He quickly threw up a map of vectors, which calculated a flurry of gradients projected along the inner glass of his visor. Once a course locked, he diverted the coordinates to his pressure booster unit and felt an array of nozzles swivel and orient about him. The blast jolted his entire body, and he was propelled outward at high velocity with the metal cable unreeling neatly behind. The stony parapets of Paradise Discothèque wafted dreamily underfoot as he passed quickly above them, entering the space beyond. He hadn't had enough time to calculate the necessary boost and simply pushed the mini-thrusters to their limit. It was far more important to get the launch trajectory correct and that had taken up more time than he was comfortable with under the circumstances. It was difficult estimating speed in space as there was no way to tell how fast you were moving without nearby objects to gauge against. His only hope was that he would not overshoot her as he had burned all his fuel in an attempt to catch up. The suit thrusters had been designed for minimal movement in a vacuum, not for launching out after high-speed objects. The astronaut quickly uncapped the opposite end of the metal cable and armed its magnetic catch lock. Thus prepared, he readied himself for the flailing pink form, which grew closer and closer in his line of sight.

NEITHER OF THEM SAW THE moon verandah's roofing begin to open. The velocity of the spinning god had created a force that activated an ancient architectural mechanism. The roofing and pillars all began to blossom outward at equidistant gradients. The pieces of masonry separated from one another and continued to extend outward into space, detaching entirely to leave the platform bare save for the pillar supports and the sunken entrance to the corridor of reliefs. The god, meanwhile, had become an almost solid sphere of velocity. Spectral light radiated, saturating its form in a halo of pale fire that gathered steadily in intensity. This build-up of energy seemed to attain critical mass at a certain point, and ghostly humanoid figures spewed out of it in riotous flurries. The spinning was somehow decompressing the sno-globes contained within the god, releasing them as ectoplasmic doubles of their former selves. These translucent ghost forms comprised people of every possible description who had been harvested over the ages by the dead god: colonial explorers, sacrificial victims, reptile people, warrior chieftains of long-extinct tribes, cat people, lost children, bird-headed jungle Indians, and a plethora of others—some whose species were too ancient to even recognize. The figures flooded out in streams tumbling in spectral profusion collecting in a growing cloud high above the turning god. The ghosts pivoted almost in unison when they saw the great moon shining through them. They all faced it, separating and then linking wrists and ankles to create a formation out of their cloud of protoplasmic chaos. Gradually, they began to describe a type of ordered geometry.

THE ASTRONAUT CAME UP TOWARD Taty much faster than he had anticipated. He slammed the magnetic cable lock against her abdominal plate and activated the reel-back mechanism with a flick of his thumb. Unfortunately, the disparate velocities tore the belt rig that secured the cable device to him. Without anything to hold him in place, the inertia caused him to overshoot before he had time to react. Taty had just enough time to glimpse herself reflected in his smiley face before he was gliding away from her at tremendous speed. She reached out her hands to him only to feel herself jerked backward by the metal cable. She was being reeled back toward the safety of Paradise Discothèque, held fast by the magnetic lock.

"Don't leave me!" she shrieked at the shrinking, turning figure.

Despite her wails, the reel-back had already lengthened the gap between them. He was already nothing more than a glinting speck, vanishing into the luminous curvature of the planet.

THE SPINNING AND STEADY LOSS of souls had caused the god to shrink rapidly. Spectral figures still fountained out of it at a seemingly unstoppable rate, and within this self-perpetuated vortex, the god was already only about half its previous size. Above the pavilion the ghosts had begun to extrude a tendril of their linked bodies. This structure of wrist- and ankle-bound ghosts stretched ten figures across, unfolding a strange highway out toward the distant moon that formed rapidly from the gathering nebula of souls and shocked Taty into silence. She saw the moon shining through their jelly-like cloud of transparent bodies. The rate of bodies spewing out of the god had by now attained a white-water velocity. They jetted out like bubbles from a jacuzzi, expanding into their full forms like popcorn on a hot plate.

She found herself reeled in toward this boiling cluster at an alarming rate. Already the cloud above Paradise Discothèque had attained gigantic proportions, shadowing most of the roof terraces in an underwater play of shifting shadows. The ancient stone walls loomed up to meet her, and she was suddenly soaring over the pool decks into the outer corona of floating bodies. She stared in fascination as a glassy hunter in feathers drifted by. Their eyes made contact, and Taty realized that they were all still conscious only somehow programmed like drones to fulfill their celestial roadwork. All manner of these jelly-like characters began to pass her like enormous fairground balloons. She went straight through an old man and was surprised to find that they were semi-solid, comprised of ectoplasmic jelly. She glanced back to see the man reforming in her wake, oblivious to his temporary dismemberment. She entered the gushing rapids of this river of souls, and the sounds and sensation of their many impacts across her suit was like being pelted with a hundred water balloons a second. The cable wound her inexorably through this tumult locking back into itself at the pillar. She unlocked the release mechanism after a moment of fiddling but kept the magnetic lock engaged and the cable secured around the pillar lest she lose her footing and blow back out into space. She began to lean into this waterfall of gelatinous bodies, trying to penetrate the center of vortex to catch a glimpse of the god. Fate came to her unexpectedly, and she saw the face of Alphonse. Their eyes met only for the briefest instant before he was lost in the writhing mass of forms. Yet, despite this, the impact upon her was huge. Guilt struck her a blow, but this was quickly replaced by a glimmer of possible salvation. The fact that some sort of forgiveness might manifest for her treatment of the imp only served to renew her vigor.

THE ONSLAUGHT OF SOULS WAS diminishing. Already it was more like being in a shoal of jellyfish than river rapids. Within moments the outpour dissipated altogether, floating upward like helium balloons to gather in their mass refracting the gold of the moon within the silver of their bodies. The god was turning slowly in the geometric center of the empty pavilion. It had shrunk to the dimensions of a large kitten as the last remaining souls oozed from it, popping out into shape and ascending, leaving it dazed and spinning. Taty bounced up toward the creature and took it in her hands. It felt loose and sleepy, half-conscious after its ordeal.

"When did *you* get so cute?" she clucked, tucking it under her arm and swimming for the corridor entrance.

THE AIRLOCK WAS STILL OPEN, and it was chaos inside the corridor. Tablets of stone had dislodged, knocking soundlessly against loose instruments and dysfunctional flurries of debris. She struggled down the passage, pushing aside bobbing blocks of masonry and paraphernalia, squeezing past obstructions in a peculiar underwater miasma of flotation. It took her several minutes, but she finally made it to the opposite airlock. She "put down" the god in midair and opened the WARNING panel to reveal PURGE and RELEASE levers. Without thinking, she pulled down on the RELEASE control. An explosion of escaping pressure blasted her backward violently as loose items began to suck out after her: bottles from the mini bar, papers, and pencils all swarmed out of the airlock, smashing against her with the intensity of arrows. Frozen air also gushed out in blinding shafts of vapor. Luckily, there was so much heavy debris in the passage that the large stone fragments quickly created a jam at the far end much like a clog in a drain. The pressure equalized momentarily, and Taty was able to scuffle back toward the automatically closing air lock. She snagged Devoid, who was still spinning in a dazed fashion, and pulled herself along the railing with all her might. Some chairs had jammed in the airlock, preventing it from closing properly. She managed to squeeze past to find that an emergency seal had closed just beyond preventing any further loss of cabin pressure.

SHE FOUND A WAY TO disengage the magnetic cablehead, cleared the chairs, and climbed into the narrow space between the air lock and the metal seal, breathing heavily from her exertions. She was eventually able to close the air lock from the inside and found herself crunched into the sardine-can space between. This time she pulled the PURGE lever. A red light came on as the area depressurized. Within moments the light burned green, and the emergency seal overrode. It cranked up, and she floated back into the control booth in triumph, her little god still under her arm. Outside, the stone tablets relaxed their vicious clog. The pressure dropped, and everything in the corridor reverted to a dreamy flotation.

THE NIMBUS OF SOULS ABOVE Paradise Discothèque had shrunk visibly as their highway knitted outward. The clarified diamond light illuminated the figures as each soundlessly pivoted to grasp one another's wrists and ankles. Within a few hours, their work was complete, and a shining quilted road stretched from the head of Paradise Discothèque, reaching a finger into the unknown.

PART IV

Girl with the Golden Eyes

38
The Haunted Castle

Three Weeks Later

SHE WOULD FLOAT IN THE center of the shower sphere ten meters above the hole for hours watching the heavy flow at work with her brand new golden eyes. The water would emerge like hot glass toothpaste separating into steaming amebas, which tumbled down gracefully and broke over her scattering an array of morphing globules into the air. Once, she forgot the suction fan and dozed off in the soothing warmth. She opened her eyes later to see the entire sphere layered with strata of coagulating water formations. She spent hours somersaulting through them with Devoid, who would scamper up and down the walls clinging to the tiles like a gecko. The god's telepathic faculties seemed effectively to replace any need for sensory organs. It would probably still need to read in Braille, but there was very little danger of it running into a wall. The god rarely left Taty's side in any case. A bond had formed since she had manipulated the god's ancient sno-globe, activating its metamorphosis. She was curious as to where this would all lead.

Taty would often tune the shower to a light rain. It drifted down as flat and soft as petals while she tumbled in the middle with her Walkman® drifting somewhere above on a coiling headphone cord. *In with the Outzone* was still haunting her Walkman® with love letters from the planet's surface. A narcoleptic highway tune called "Dead Starz" became her new number-one outer space song. She rewound and replayed the track till the tape had stretched out to a crackly seaweedy ribbon. Eventually she had to recapture the song, wearing the mutilated original recording as a choker. She sported this accessory at all times until it finally came apart one day in the slow motion shower. The soft little petals of water would be sucked down easily, forming glass balloons around the lower drain, which

Taty would stare at for hours. It was amazing seeing these forms crawl down the pipe like living things. The shower sphere was definitely her favorite place in what she started to call the "haunted castle." She could watch the shapes the water made all day spinning through the great crystal flowerets in slow motion.

AT FIRST, SHE WAS AFRAID to explore the haunted castle. The camera views showed corpses whose chests and eyes had exploded in the vacuum. The bodies she saw had all been freeze-dried, and radiation baked into flattened sculptures that resembled metal and ice more than flesh. She was terrified that she would see someone she knew, but boredom diluted her fear after a couple of weeks. Now that she had grasped the PURGE and RELEASE system, she began using the lower air lock, which led into the sealed corridor the guards had first brought her through. It was on her first jaunt out that she nicknamed the place HAUNTED. In many ways it was exactly that. It was darkest in the areas without windows, and the shadows had a purity of blackness impossible to achieve under any other circumstances. It was the lack of air that created such clarity. The vacuum wiped the screen clear to show the true color and form of each thing. Except that inside the castle things were mostly monochrome—either shadow-infested or covered in a dense layer of compressed ice. Frozen corridors stretched shakily in the glare of her suit lamp, inhabited by encrusted furniture and other slowly revolving detritus. She once found an imploded crocodile hovering in a lavish bedchamber in and among solidified pillows, clothing, and hairbrushes. Mummified waiters drifted like embalmed Egyptian princes. The water of an entire koi pond floated down corridors—a crystalline flying saucer decorated with preserved fish and petrified lotus blossoms. Anything with the slightest amount of air trapped within it had detonated violently, flattened out, and frozen solid. Sometimes it was difficult even telling what things had been. Sunlight passed through the peripheral spaces in solid straight razor beams. These patches of edged light instantly scorched whatever they touched, leaving nothing but frozen ash in their wake. Her suit was impervious, and she found she could track how stable the castle's spin was by studying the slewing tracks of the shadows. Some rooms were only touched in corners by this unearthly sunlight that never diffused and by doing so, preserved an atmosphere of night in all areas left untouched. In the instances where a room had been subjected to this light, it was as though that part of the room had been dipped into black ink. Whatever loose items she touched in these areas would inevitably crumble to flakes and powder—a blackened lampshade expanded slowly into a cloud of fine particles, Martini glasses drifted slowly out into the blackness of space.

She took to wearing jumpsuits in the pressurized areas because she thought it went with the whole outer space thing—jumpsuits and pajamas. She also liked that she could be barefoot the whole day without getting her feet dirty. She was surprised how quickly she got the hang of anti-gravity and how much fun it was. It was all a question of not getting stuck in the middle of a room, she figured. You were dead in the water without anything to push against and had to start performing cartwheels and all sorts of acrobatics to get anywhere. Once she got her launching and somersaulting right, she was whizzing around like a bee with Devoid chasing her everywhere like a faceless puppy. Once, she smashed a jar of cocktail olives by mistake and spent an hour eating them out of the air, blowing aside shards of glass. The lounge also had a killer sound system, and when she grew weary of "Dead Starz," she graduated to a number called "Icepunk," which she would blast at high volume. This track had allegedly been recorded in orbit on an older space tour. All the instrumentation seemed suited to a zero-G environment and lacked the heat of the jungle to which she had grown accustomed. Taty was under Mister Sister's thumb at the besieged house when she first heard the song on a stolen radio. At that time the icy aesthetic had escaped her entirely, lacking the candied meatiness of tropical motifs. Now that she was actually in space surrounded by frozen extraterrestrial vistas, she was dancing upside down screaming along to the words at the top of her lungs and bouncing off the padded walls with Devoid, who would always get overexcited whenever there was loud music playing.

SHE WOULD BUCKLE HERSELF INTO the pilot's chair every now and then. She had the soft harness tight, so she wouldn't float off. This way it could at least feel like she was sitting down. She missed sitting down sometimes—lying down, too. It was weird waking up against the ceiling on the far side of a room. Her hair refused to behave, clouding like an anemone. She liked it and took hundreds of shampoo commercial snapshots of herself on the security cameras wearing crazy makeup and dresses that billowed like flowers, focusing in close on her brand new gold eyes. A huge green blob of fizzy cream soda floated beside her head as she sat, connected to her mouth via a stripy straw. She sucked on this, gradually diminishing the blob while scanning the distant continent below through a long-range viewer. After a few minutes she located an opening in the cloud layer and was able to zoom in on a small coastal city some small distance from Namanga Mori. Shaky building tops moved around in her view as though she were staring down on a circuit board through a magnifying glass. She zoomed in closer to witness the cityscape swarming with symbs. These greenish creatures slithered and roosted almost everywhere she looked, and for a moment it seemed as though she were looking at a microscopic slide infested with emerald bacteria. She heard a scratching sound and turned her head to investigate. Devoid was clawing at the upper airlock like a kitten asking to be let out.

"No, baby," Taty scolded. "That's OW-TAH space out there. Come here to Mama."

The little god gave up and sailed nimbly across the room, landing on her shoulder like some bizarre parrot. It nestled there, chittering to itself as a tiny white speck caught Taty's eye. The object grew slowly larger approaching above the subtle curvature of the massive planet.

"Here he comes again," she murmured.

She quickly toggled the viewfinder matrix and spotted the figure of the astronaut silhouetted against the glowing plane of the world below. He drew closer, flailing his arms as he passed some distance before the enormous stone structure, shooting off quickly in the opposite direction as his inertia carried him around the planet again. She watched him recede, sucking thoughtfully at her floating blob.

"He does seem to get closer each time, don't you think?" she mused.

Devoid twittered incomprehensibly, nuzzling at her crazy hair before hurtling off down the stairs.

θθθ

THE TREES IN THE INDOOR forest waved around like toys in an aquarium. Coconuts floated through the air, and the jelly occasionally rose up in glowing clumps like aliens from a B movie. She was floating between the Christmas trees, ankles crossed, talking on her walkie-talkie.

"So, where you now?" Taty quizzed, twiddling her toes against a sprig of evergreen.

Number Nun was on her back drifting in the black water between enormous icebergs. Cracked ice caked her inside and out while shawls of snagged kelp trailed in her wake.

"Somewhere bright and cold," she answered pertly.

"Like a fridge. Ha ha."

"Your lack of wit has always been a great source of comfort to me."

"Happy to help."

"So, tell me, Childbride, do you ever feel remorse for your great sins?"

Taty rolled slowly until her bare feet faced the ceiling. Strands of her hair caught in the jelly below and trailed along after her.

"I dunno," she answered after a while.

"You must have done, to avoid speaking to me for so long."

"I guess."

Number Nun observed the passage of great blue shards of crystal and sighed.

"Well, let us not talk of repentance just now," she said to Taty. "You have suffered greatly. True, you are a filthy little sinner and probably deserved it, but I am not without mercy."

"Whoop-di-doo. Vomit. Whatever."

"Jest not in the face of our synthetic savior, Childbride."

Taty chewed her lip and flipped right side up, crashing softly into a tree.

"Sorry," she said.

"Saying sorry is an acceptable first step."

"I wish you were here. You wouldn't miss your legs in space."

"Extraterrestrial missionary work has always been a long-cherished dream of mine."

"Being up here is kind of like swimming and snoozing at the same time."

"There's more to life than lounging by the pool, Childbride."

"Yeah, right!"

"What an unforgivable little sinner you are."

A loud beeping sounded from far above, and Taty kicked up like a dolphin flicking high above the trees in a smooth motion.

"Gotta go," she announced. "Spin cycle's done—I'm finally washing the bloodstains out of my stuff."

"Try not to destroy anything."

"I won't. Bye."

SHE HAD FALLEN ASLEEP UPSIDE down in the cramped galley, her feet bumping lightly against the ceiling. The galley had been decorated in varnished wood and brass fittings like a sailing vessel. A tiny breakfast table with seatbelts nestled snugly beneath a large porthole. Half-eaten hamburger fragments disintegrated slowly in the air before her. Ketchup expanded in tentacles while a bun flowered open in the manner of a time-lapse seedpod. Devoid was at the porthole scratching lightly at the glass again. She was only asleep for an hour or so like this before the nightmares returned. She was awake in moments, choking back screams.

DESPITE HER AFFECTION FOR NUMBER Nun, she found that she was still unable to discuss the entirety of her experiences with the android. She would begin to talk about Appleseed and Alphonse and then reflexively begin to paint herself as the victim of circumstance. Perhaps, if she had been surrounded by people as she had been in the jungle, she may have been able to plaster over the events for a few more years at least. But in the haunted castle alone in space with an alien god, she found herself living in full view of the starkness of her acts. She would stare at herself in mirrors, studying her new eyes in silent fascination. She could remember a time when such an entrancing cosmetic change would have thrilled her to the core. Now the transmutation, however spectacular, seemed nothing more than a benchmark of her growing inhumanity. Murder had sealed this covenant with divinity. Somehow the pale gold of her eyes reminded her that, no matter how cruelly she had suffered at the hands of Johnny Appleseed, she was still the one responsible for ending his tortured existence. The sight of his barbaric death was

fuel enough for a lifetime of nightmares. She found herself driven
to distraction aboard the floating stationary temple haunted by this
and other things. The structure had not moved since ascension,
hovering in a static position just above the upper atmosphere. The
isolation, coupled with the feeling of being dead in the water, bred
a kind of mania in her that found expression in unexpected outlets.
She discovered herself testing the limits of her confinement with
unchecked recklessness, sipping drinks on the highest balcony in
existence, looking down at a world she was still desperately trying
to leave behind.

39
Pushing Buttons

TATY WAS STRAPPED INTO THE pilot's chair, half-in/half-out of her spacesuit. The endless sunny midnight of outer space often had her ragged with sleeplessness and morbid boredom. Her space helmet floated somewhere above, accessorized with unused stickers she had originally saved for her previous machine gun. At first she had tip-toed around the controls, not wanting to upset the delicate balance of any life support system, but after the fourth week, she was so bored she had ceased to care. Perhaps a life-threatening emergency was all she needed to get her mind off the brain-numbing lifelessness of the haunted castle. She was chewing bubble gum, sealing off the pink balloons with her tongue and then spitting them around the control booth where they would stick on things. She stabbed randomly at buttons while she did this. Various unalarming things occurred with each button combination: monitors changed views, external lights activated, shutters opened and closed. Then she spied a pulsing red button, which seemed vaguely dangerous, and pushed it on impulse. A blinding crimson laser beam fired from directly below the control booth all the way down to the surface of the planet. She jumped in delight and began pressing it repeatedly, discovering a nearby toggle that allowed her to wave it around like a wand, making crazy patterns as one does with a flashlight at night. She wasn't watching the surface of the planet with her binoculars, but if she had been, she would have seen the beam cleaving through whatever it touched. At one point, the red line sliced randomly through the clouds above one of the dingy cities, slicing off sections of old decaying buildings and concrete bridges that crashed to the symbiote-infested areas below. Halved cars tumbled while the green creatures observed. The beam did not harm them for some reason. Instead, they seemed to absorb its intense heat, drawing strength from it.

She had an idea while playing with the high-powered laser and scampered down to the retro fridges in the lounge beneath. She was grinning in manic excitement as she pulled out armfuls of paint-filled milk bottles that she then ferried to the trash ejector. She loaded as many of the rainbow bottles into the trash receptacle as would fit and sealed the hatch. A handle had been placed alongside the containment unit, and she jerked it down, watching the colored bottles flush out into space. As soon as she could see them tumbling outside the glass of the lounge, she bounced back up and buckled herself in. The bottles had just begun to tumble past the control booth, and she chuckled at the sight of them spilling out into space. She rubbed her hands together with glee and began togging the laser at them. The bottles detonated just as she had imagined. Ameboid forms of vacuum-pure color flashed and froze, spreading and extending into one another in delicate sprays of frozen particles brightly lit against the luminous blackness of outer space. Taty began dancing around with glee screaming, "Pollock! Pollock!," overjoyed with her invention of a new form of painting. To celebrate, she used a precious tube of liquid eyeliner to scribble a swirly moustache beneath her nose. She then pulled on a beret and scarf and set about using up almost half the supply of paint bottles creating her Fauvist jellyfish bonanzas and watching them morph slowly away into the void of orbit, their colors too frozen to mix. She would rig up the external security cameras to track them and take hundreds of holographic snapshots that she had no idea how to view. All the same, it was the highlight of her week. Yet, despite the levity the paintings had aroused, her recklessness was escalating unchecked.

SHE WAS IN THE SPHERICAL bathroom switching the floodlights on and off for no reason. She had also been eyeing the red button for some time. She bit her lip. She chewed her finger. Eventually, she just pressed it. Somewhere along the scarred underside of the vast megalith an area of flagstones jettisoned, leaving a space about the width of two cars. A metal casing extended into the sharp light and began to extend down toward the surface of the planet at the end of a collapsible metal tube. It bore an unmistakable resemblance to a vacuum cleaner and was, in fact, something of the sort. The segmented tube unreeled down through the great planes of the upper atmosphere, dropping into the clouds. It trailed through dense formations of vapor and emerged shining above the ocean.

It fell like a comet, crashing magnificently into the waves. Large machine parts activated along its head, and the device began to suck up great quantities of water trawling its load up beyond the clouds into space. Once beyond the upper atmosphere, the pleats in the tube began glowing red as they superheated the interior. This kept the water from freezing before it reached its destination. It also sterilized it to some degree.

If Taty had been up in the control booth she would have been amazed to see the glowing red coils of the pipe snaking down into the churn of clouds below. The pipe led to a large empty vault in the basement regions. The root of the suction device was located in a large construction site set into the stone floor, which resembled a large electric generator, lit by floodlights and surrounded by a halo of floating barbed wire fences. Danger signs wafted placidly about like tropical fish in and among the loose rubble of the site and one or two stray statues. A klaxon activated, rendered soundless in the vacuum while warning lights began to strobe. Shortly, a vast fountain of heated seawater began to gush into the vault, freezing instantly as it left the pump. Parboiled sharks exploded like balloons in the drift of glacial matter as the boulders of fresh sea ice began to collect, slowly filling up the chamber like an explosion of gigantic polystyrene. Taty, meanwhile, was turning her head this way and that looking around the shower sphere, waiting for something dramatic to happen. She hummed to herself. She tapped her foot against the wall. After a while, she deactivated the red button in disappointment. Down in the ocean, the device abruptly shut down with a clank, retracting quickly up into the sky. By the time she reached the control booth, it was as though nothing had ever happened.

A STRAY COMBINATION OF BUTTONS and levers opened a secret panel in the control booth. Taty watched with shiny eyes as a glowing pedestal emerged, crowned with a pulsing smiley face button. Meanwhile, some distance away, the astronaut was completing his 168th orbit of the globe. Paradise Discothèque was still only a tiny golden speck, and he was ready to put his plan into action. He had to wait until this particular circuit because his orbit was growing steadily more elliptical. Each pass brought him nearer to the stone leviathan, but unless he acted within the next three orbits, he would begin to pass beneath the temple and then drift farther and farther out. His radio had been broken in the tussle, and he was unable to ask Taty for assistance or reach the computers of his control booth. He was also running out of water, nutri-feed, and concentrated oxygen tablets. His suit was able to release vast amounts of oxygen from those tiny tablets, and he would have been able to survive for another two months had he stocked his suit fully. But, alas, the Boy Scout motto had again not been applied.

Now he had to act swiftly if he was to survive his predicament. The plan came about while he was cataloguing supplies on his sixty-fourth orbit. He had no fuel, but he did have three vacuum-resistant cans of cola. Theoretically, if he were able to open them at precisely the correct vectors, he would be able to use their fizzy outpouring to launch himself back to Paradise Discothèque and thus avoid a tedious death in space. All that was required was a little push to get him on course, and this would do the trick if he shook the cans enough. To this effect he had calculated and recalculated distances and geometries, throwing a wire-frame alignment of his own hands onto the digital display, so that he would know exactly where to position the can in relation to the giant stone structure. He also had a countdown clock running, which was ticking down fifteen minutes to cola launch. Luckily, he had three cans and therefore three chances. Even if he were way off with his first two, they would still make things easier for him on his third try. Unless, of course, he was drastically unlucky and managed to throw himself on an even more disastrous orbit. He was readying himself for this first attempt when he began to notice large nuclear eruptions occurring in and around the vast dark sprawl that was the Outzone. The mushroom clouds swelled beautifully through the cloud layer, blowing circular whirlpools through the vanilla milkshake clouds, annihilating everything around them.

"I wonder how she found that secret button ..." he chuckled in amusement.

A flicker of color caught his eye, and he turned his head to see a rapidly approaching Fauvist painting spread out in the void like some psychedelic jellyfish.

"Art!" he cried. "What the hell?"

He threw up his arms to protect his visor as he smacked through the warps of color. The curtains of frozen particles succeeded in instantly spray painting his dirty white suit. He passed through several successive paintings and emerged lashed with bright hazy rainbows, utterly bewildered.

TATY WATCHED IN HORROR AS the detonations spread below. She snatched her hand from the button and tried to kick the secret panel back into its niche.

"Oh, shit!"

She fumbled for the long-range viewer control and saw buildings and sprawling quadrants of jungle erased by expanding rings of atomic fire. The walkie-talkie crackled, and Number Nun's voice came through.

"I'm registering large-scale nuclear impacts on the other side of the globe. Can you see what's happening?"

"Er! Uh, it's nothing, I think—oh, shit!"

"Childbride, what have you done?"

"Nothing! Fuck! I have to go!"

She turned off the walkie-talkie and held her head in shock, watching the blast waves spread through the Outzone while Devoid bounced around her in playful obliviousness.

THE RAINBOW-SPRAYED ASTRONAUT POSITIONED himself according to his onscreen coordinates, aiming his can of salvation cola, looking very much like a prog rock album cover in motion. He waited until the various digital contours aligned themselves before cracking the soft drink. An ejaculation of frozen soda plumed out in a jet of crystal, propelling him off on a tangential course toward the great golden beehive. He had to hold onto the can with magnetic finger pads to avoid it rocketing away, but when the can had spent itself, he released it. It traveled beside him like a pilot fish carried along at the same velocity. He watched as the great stone walls of the lower courtyards approached, growing more and more megalithic until they towered before him, dwarfing him with their great height. The spiral terraces loomed above, their perspective realigning as he felt himself shrinking against the mass of ancient stone. It was so strange, he thought, how so much time in orbit had distorted his sense of scale. He had begun to feel at times that he was gigantic—a titan caught between the glowing plane of the planet and the lightless void of space. Now the shocking immensity of the temple reminded him of the true state of things. Dark frozen windows grew larger—like spiracles along the patterned flanks of some monstrous sea creature. Junk floated past at intervals. An entire dining table passed him by as he entered the proximity of the slowly turning building. He shot over the angular walls of the lower courtyard areas and passages, narrowly missing a watchtower and ricocheting off a terrace pillar. The impact was heavy, and he rebounded into a wide colonnade. He entered the edged shadows of the structure, spinning into a far wall and finally coming to rest in a wide statuary niche. He quickly scanned for damage and was relieved to find that he had made it in one piece. He then pulled himself out of the shallow depression and into a nearby archway, activating a line of lights along his helmet. He passed through the shock void of the passages and rooms, floating up staircases and down long swooping galleries until he finally reached the first set of airlocks. He entered the sealed corridor and released the PURGE control. The doors sealed while massive fans began to blast oxygen into the passage. Thermal plating kicked in, and all the ice began to melt, releasing twists of liquid into the air. The passage depressurized within minutes. He was finally able to reach up and blow the locks around his throat, removing his smiley-face helmet for the first time in an age.

A TEAR ARCHED HORIZONTALLY OFF Taty's eye like the delicate eye-stalk of a snail. It reached out into the air, questing off her saturated eyelashes where it swelled and separated into floating globules. She had curled up in a corner of the walk-in closet floor, weeping beneath a screwed-down bench. Through the blurry bubbles of her tears, she saw the closet open. A pair of spray-painted spacesuit legs floated into her field of vision and came slowly into focus. The figure knelt down and gathered her in his arms. She burrowed into the defaced suit, rubbing at her eyes while she sobbed. The shifting face of Dr. Dali gazed down upon her, rearranging constantly like some multidimensional painting.

"That's some rash you got there," she sniffed, staring at the absurd shifting of his head.

"Inside, I'm smiling."

She broke into a fresh bout of tears, which lifted from her face like the tangled tendrils of a bluebottle.

"I blew up the world!" she exclaimed hoarsely.

"It's all right, it was just the Outzone really, and I was planning to do it anyway."

"But ... but why? All those people ..."

He sighed from a mouth that traveled slowly into an inverting cheekbone only to emerge inside out from the warping tunnel of an ear.

"It's the rancid stink of reality, ma chérie. It deviates in, contaminating every secret dream like rotting food in the next room. I grew tired of the twists, all the tiny pockets of dirt that made up a staggering portrait of filth. I wasn't vain enough to save the world. I only wanted to make things clean and uncomplicated for a moment. Just a wipe of the window, so that we could see some light again."

"But everyone's dead! No one will see the light."

"You will, one day."

"You're mad!"

"Oh, we're all mad here," he smiled, his teeth flipping and unzipping to reveal a pair of amused eyes moving slowly up the hairline tunnel of a throat.

She grew still, sniffing occasionally up at him.

"I suppose," she admitted. "At least those symbs are nuke food."

"Au contraire, they shall probably be the only things to survive in the Zone—in a way, at least. I designed them that way."

"What?! What do you mean, you designed them?"

"You didn't think they were really from another dimension, did you? I mean, the sexual compatibility with humanoids, the carrots ..."

"The carrots were your idea?"

"My idea of a joke, yes. I originally thought of genetically encoding them to react to something more arcane and thematically suitable—like a rare crushed beetle perhaps. But at the end of the day, carrots were far more amusing."

"But why?"

"The symbs are able to absorb vast amounts of heat and transmute this into physical matter; in other words, extreme heat adds to their mass. Once they had enough time to root, I planned to feed them on thermonuclear fodder. Now they will start growing in long lines that will reach into the sky and curve back down in vast arcs, intersecting and meshing with one another to create an emerald city from the ashes. They will quickly decontaminate the soil and air by feeding off the radiation, and nature will reclaim itself within a few years. They are my seeds of Eden."

"And the Protoverse? A friend of mine found the door."

"Ah, yes, their navels, the umbilical portal, yes. The Protoverse is where I grew, incubated, and cultured my little building blocks of the new world. It is a fluid universe, an amniotic realm capable of supporting any number of experiments that require large-scale wombing.

"As much as I would like to continue this discussion now, I would like to draw your attention to the fact that I haven't bathed for a month. Be a dear and wait for me upstairs."

IT DIDN'T TAKE THE DOCTOR long to get things shipshape. Taty would hover cuddling her pet god, watching the ex-spaceman flit about adjusting dials and moving things around with a blank expression on her face. She half-expected Devoid to go for him again, considering the epic quality of their last tussle. But the god now seemed to display more interest in the loose threads on her clothing than it did Dr. Dali. The doctor couldn't care less, it seemed. It was weird for her to see him without a spacesuit. He was so much smaller and more intense. He wore white suits beneath an extravagant silk dressing gown and pointed Turkish slippers. His ties were often holographic, and he always wore spotless white magician's gloves. His head was a riot. She wanted to get stoned and just look at his head. He showed her a food store she had not discovered, and she started eating candy bars like there was no tomorrow.

"If you keep eating candy bars like that, we'll run out before we reach the moon," he told her.

"If I keep eating candy bars like this, I'll probably need to diet by then anyway," she munched, her mouth full of nuts and chocolate.

"When do we leave, anyway?" she asked. "We've been parked in the same place since we came out of the jungle."

"I need to batten down the hatches, my dear. Once we let our little monster out of his cage, he should start dragging us along his homemade highway. With any luck we'll make it to the moon in a couple of months."

"It doesn't look that far."

"Believe me, it's a long way to walk with a castle-sized backpack."

After a day or two, things calmed down. Dr. Dali said that he needed to recoup his strength before they "set sail" and set about drinking a lot of tea.

DR. DALI WAS FLOATING UPSIDE down in the lotus position, his silk gown aswirl, holding a china cup and saucer in his white gloves. An ameboid tea form jellied out of the cup, and he nibbled delicately at it whenever his mouth slid into alignment. She was at the window watching the world in denim shorts and cuddling her little god. A dark cloud of ash now obscured most of the equator, creating a nuclear winter that was gradually spreading outward toward the poles, around one of which Number Nun was presumably bobbing.

"You sure know how to make a mess," she muttered darkly.

He glanced up absently.

"It took me years to construct and discretely plant all those bombs throughout the Zone."

She floated grimly, observing the movement of many dark clouds while he continued with his tea.

"How did you meet Alphonse?" she asked out of the blue.

Dr. Dali chewed on a cube of sugar, enjoying the sensation as it crunched through his forehead.

"He was one of the first things I snagged in my interdimensional Venus Flytrap so many decades ago," he replied. "I'm not sure exactly where that imp came from—some strange hole, no doubt. I offered to send him back, but he said that this reality was too much fun. Now look at him—butter on the toast of a toasted world."

"He's right outside," Taty confessed quietly.

The doctor raised an eyebrow—a somewhat ridiculous thing to behold.

"What? Do you mean to say Alphonse Guava is outside? Where?"

"He's holding hands with the other ghosts," she said. "Devoid coughed him up like a hairball."

"Gosh, I wonder who hated him enough to throw him to the gods? I suppose a creature like that accumulates many enemies."

She frowned miserably and chewed her lip, kicking the glass in inner turmoil.

"Are they really ghosts?" she asked.

"In a way, yes; in a way, no. Devoid over there is not a physical being like you or me. It is a god. Its mass comprises a special ectoplasm which, for some reason, is corporeal on this plane as well as some others."

"Huh?"

"It is, for example, just as physical in dreams."

"What?"

"The god is also able to compress and expand its substance at will, so when it 'eats' a sno-globe, it is really just storing that person's consciousness—or soul—in a part of its body. So, in a way, you could say that these ghosts were, in fact, still alive. Definitely more so than when they were stored in a cellular formation throughout the god's body. Now, when you did what you did to the god, which was very impressive, by the way ..."

"Thanks, Doc."

"Don't mention it. But when that happened, Devoid shed each sno-globe along with a part of its own substance, which then expanded to mimic the devoured person's original form."

"You're confusing me!"

"Those ghosts out there are physicalized ectoplasm and maintain all of the characteristics and memories of their old selves except that their original bodies are dead and these new bodies are really just borrowed fragments of Devoid here—bodies that are subject to the will of the god—hence the 'holding hands highway.' Maybe when Devoid has no more need of them, it will release them and then they will really be dead ... or perhaps even alive again in some ectoplasmically sustained, independent form of consciousness! Who knows?"

Taty lifted up the little creature and shook it lovingly, rubbing her nose against its featureless face. It responded by clawing sleepily at her and snuggling under her chin.

"My little super pet," she coochi-cooed.

Dr. Dali smiled wryly.

"You are a messiah to the reptiles who built this place, you know," he said. "Their psychically elevated bloodlines have disseminated through our species for centuries, evolving within and seeking expression, culminating, finally, in you. You fulfilled a destiny and released their god from bondage. For millennia Devoid was trapped in the Outzone, confined to broken cities and a galaxy of worm tunnels. The only way to release the psychic ballast of all those devoured souls was to twiddle his globe in the star chamber just as it reached the stratosphere—which you did! Well done!"

"I should get a reward or something."

Dr. Dali shook his head and chuckled.

"Devie keeps trying to get out into space," she mentioned, spinning impulsively into a backflip. "He's always scratching at the locks."

"It wants to get onto its highway and begin the voyage to the dark side of the moon. All part of the plan, my dear."

"OK."

"We'll sail as soon as I've got things up to scratch."

"Hey, Doc, listen. My friend Number Nun is down there by the icebergs. Please, can you bring her up here? I'll bust up as many fridges as you want in my swimming costume if you do."

He blushed heavily and coughed into his glove, suddenly embarrassed.

"I, er, I'm sorry about that, it's just that I … damn," he mumbled.

"Please!" she whined, stamping her foot on the ceiling.

"She's the one on the walkie-talkie?"

"Yup."

"I'm not very fond of robot nuns, you know. I've had very bad experiences with robot nuns."

"Pleeeease! She's my only friend—apart from Devie here!"

"Well, I suppose I can always deactivate her if she gets on my nerves. All right, give me the walkie-talkie and I'll see what I can do."

Taty dropped the god and sailed over to the doctor, throwing her arms around his neck. The impact threw both of them into a mad spin, and he flinched to avoid the milky comet of tea. He frowned, disentangling and brushing a spot of liquid from the lapel of his silk dressing gown.

"Now, now," he chided. "I only have three of these fellows left, you know."

40
Calling Number Nun

DR. DALI SAT BUCKLED INTO his pilot's chair. He was wearing his Captain Nemo uniform and consulting various holographic schematics of the planet below. He had used the rocket thrusts affixed to the outer walls to take them out of their stationary orbit and into the area above one of the poles. Gradients flickered on screen, tracking the massive structure as it crawled slowly through the glowing void. A green target light pulsed on one of the maps, and a small counter ticked down the diminishing distance between it and the yellow blip of the flying temple. When the lights had aligned, Dr. Dali pulled down the brass horn of the intercom.

"Are you in position?" he asked.

Taty perked up when she heard and leaned over to the button console intercom of the shower sphere.

"Aye, aye, Captain!" she shouted enthusiastically.

She was in her spacesuit minus helmet and gauntlets, hovering over the red button and waiting for the command to push. The doctor could, of course, have activated the mechanism from his control booth, but he recognized that Taty would need to feel as though she had played some vital part in the rescue operation. Otherwise, she would most certainly get in the way, possibly even destroy them all. So, to avoid tantrums and mass destruction, he assigned her the role for which she had been rehearsing all month: that of button pusher. Needless to say, she was pleased with her job description.

"Wait for my signal," his voice boomed back.

"Roger!" she replied.

Back in the command booth, he raised the heavily accessorized walkie-talkie to his cubist face and cleared his multiform throat.

"Calling Number Nun," he radioed.

Number Nun, who was adrift in a haunting seascape of shattered ice, received something of a fright at the sound of the strange voice in her head.

"Who is this?" she demanded. "What have you done with the girl?"

"This is Dr. Dali. Perhaps you have heard of me? In any case, I can assure you that I have done nothing sinister to the young lady."

"You are the one responsible for the destruction of all those sinners, aren't you?"

"Why, yes I am, as a matter of fact."

Number Nun nodded to herself, processing this information.

"A most effective purging," she conceded.

"A compliment?"

"My morality circuitry is still in debate."

"Well, I'll just have to do something about that circuitry. Forgive my curtness but the young lady has asked that I bring you aboard. Are you in favor?"

"Thank you for the invitation. That would be lovely, yes."

"Top notch. Look over to your right, would you?"

Number Nun turned her sensor sweep starboard and detected the enormous tube falling from the skies. It was some miles distant and fell like a great silver snake crashing into the distant waters. She observed as it began to approach at great speed, trawling through the air like a badly scribbled ballpoint line. Icebergs battered against the machine as its persistent grinding grew steadily louder. She zoomed in closer to find that the head was dragging some meters above the water sucking up sea spray. Its suction tube hung too high to draw in water, and the waves became distorted into vortices as it passed.

"I have your device in my sights," she reported.

"As an Excelsior Missionary Model, I assume that you come equipped with standard retractable chest-mounted catch line?" Dr. Dali enquired.

"Of course."

"Well then, fire your line when the suction device is within range and catch a ride up the tube. I have deactivated the post-atmospheric heating coils, so it should be a relatively smooth trip."

Ice fractured between the glass breasts of Number Nun. A portal along her sternum opened as a tiny transparent torpedo extruded, protected by a sliver of casing.

"See you on the other side, Dr. Dali," she signed off, readying herself.

The pipe was by now almost upon her, towering up into the turbulent sky. She fired her torpedo at the appropriate moment and watched as a glassy line unspooled from her inner core like a glistening spider's web. It pierced the weathered metal casing of the vacuum pump at an oblique angle and extruded grappling claws that held fast. She locked the spool and was instantly dredged from the surge. Seaweed trailed from her flying form like ragged wings as she curved above the churning water, smacking through the tops of waves. She pulled in the line, managing to maneuver herself perfectly into the yawning mouth of the encrusted pipe. She disengaged the torpedo head as the powerful inrush caught her, sucking her quickly up the undulating subway to the sky. Above her, the dark pipe receded like a flexible train tunnel that whipped about with violent grace. She rode the artificial wind with a rather smug look upon her face almost as if she had known all along that something like this would happen.

WHEN DR. DALI WAS CERTAIN that the android Madonna was in the tube, he sent word to Taty. "All right, you can retract it," he called. "I'll keep the suction going till she's aboard."

Taty slammed the red button in triumph, knocking herself horizontal with the force of the blow.

"You can go meet her in the chamber I showed you on the map," Dr. Dali said, signing off.

Taty squealed with delight, pulling on her helmet and gauntlets before launching herself up the corridor. She flustered through the lounge and control booth, rushing out of the air lock before the doctor had time to turn. She purged the passage and entered the icicle-blasted corridors of the haunted castle in a fizz of joy. Light strips along her gauntlets; helmet and chest console illuminated her like a deep-sea jellyfish as she passed through the massive honeycomb of desolation, dodging tables, chairs, and other weightless obstacles.

When she finally emerged into the sunken lot, the pump site was gushing out a majestic plume of frozen air. This geyser fluffed out into the yawning, floodlit space in a detonation of glittery vapor crystals. The pipe was evidently still in the process of clearing the atmosphere, and frozen gases gushed steadily, knocking about the weighty boulders of sea ice as though they were nothing more than soap bubbles. Taty soared down from the ceiling trap and swirled happily into the twinkling mist, searching this way and that for a sign of her long-lost friend. The silver plume abruptly died as the pipe left the atmosphere, venting its last dregs of shimmering effluvium into the clutter of ice. When the torso of Number Nun eventually sailed from the hole trailing fluid dynamics and frozen seaweed, Taty was waiting above like a candy-colored angel. She caught the limbless torso of the robot and held her helmet against the translucent collarbone as they both twirled into a spin, pinballing off the various glacial masses. Number Nun scanned for frequency and all of a sudden could hear Taty crying out in her head.

"Mother Superior!" she was shouting, clinging to the nun as though she were the raft of salvation itself.

"Oh, Childbride," Number Nun tut-tutted down at her with a smile. "No need for sentimental formalities."

"I'm so happy now," Taty sobbed as they spun slower and slower, drifting through the sparkling fields and ice blocks finally en route to the moon.

DR. DALI WAS AT HIS monitors, watching images of the pair turning in the mist. He switched camera angles as though at the ballet before finally losing interest. He flicked a switch and killed the engines of the suction device, steepling his white gloves in deep thought. He turned to Devoid, who was playing with a bundle of wires.

"We have plenty of sex droids down in storage that I can cannibalize for parts," he mused rhetorically to the god. "Get some arms and legs for this nun."

Devoid finally managed to un-snag the wires, and a series of monitors went blank. It twittered to itself clawing away at something else, utterly oblivious to the doctor's prattling. Dr. Dali turned happily to the little god and regarded it with academic seriousness.

"Soon, we will let you out, my little friend," he confided grandly. "Soon, you will be fulfilling your great and sacred quest—all those centuries you waited in the dark! Soon it will all be over."

Devoid tumbled off the table, fighting with a paper clip.

41
Ghosts

DR. DALI SURPRISED TATY BY rigging her spacesuit to interface with the old Walkman® she carried around everywhere. When she found that she was able to play tapes in space and adjust the controls through her wrist module, she ascended to a new plateau of happiness and self-sufficiency. Although she was unable to change tapes while actually inside the suit, it was enough for her just to be able to listen to music in outer space. They had finally let Devoid out after attaching a long leash to it. The leash, which was a tacky fuchsia and covered in a sort of "bones-for-cartoon-dogs" motif, turned into a length of junkyard chain a hundred meters long. The heavy chain ended in a stout ring sunk into the walls outside the control booth. The contraption enabled the entire temple to be towed by the pint-sized god like some gargantuan carnival balloon. Devoid was out on the road of souls, running to the moon happy as a clam, and it couldn't have cared less what was attached to its neck. The ghosts beneath held each other tirelessly by their wrists and ankles, watching as the god scampered from body to body like a household cat heading unerringly for the great golden coin that hung suspended in the darkness ahead. Taty was skipping along, singing that old "If You're Going to San Francisco" song quietly to herself. The ghostly humanoid hammock stretched out before them, still and strange, receding to the faraway lunar satellite while each ghost wordlessly performed its service. Once traversed, the ghosts would wait until the pair had reached the center of their highway. They would then unclasp their spectral hands and flit, fast as swallows, toward the distant head of the highway. There they would rejoin one another as before, perpetuating the distance, reaching ever outward toward the moon. Ghostly forms were wisping overhead and underfoot constantly, shooting like forlorn comets down the highway while

Taty sang along and Devoid pounced energetically onward. At one point Taty stopped, balancing on the thigh of a jungle warrior, looking back at the great beehive of the castle. The flurry of ghosts above and below dwindled and then ceased altogether as the chorus of suspension waited for her to continue. She was gazing back at the large bubble windows of the control booth where she could just make out Dr. Dali at his wall of monitors. Number Nun hovered beside him, now complete with long, somewhat mismatched arms and legs. They both noticed her watching and waved. She lifted her arm and waved back across the gulf.

"Hi, Mom! Hi, Dad!" Taty cackled to herself.

She returned to the activity of bouncing from body to body, and the flow of ghosts resumed overhead, figures flashing onward, toward a faraway apex. Some instinct made her stop again after a few meters when she realized that she was standing atop the chest of Alphonse Guava. He lay spread-eagled beneath her, regarding her with a world-weary expression upon his translucent face. She switched off the tape with trembling fingers and began to rewind it, gazing down at his almond eyes with a surge of mixed emotions. The entire universe was behind him and below her boots, but somehow the vista gave her a peculiar sense of confinement. He said something then, and she heard the words in her head—a far-off voice speaking in a locked room, a tiny room, in the deepest basement of a haunted castle.

"I see," said the blind man. "How can it be? My eyes are blind, but I can see."

She smiled softly down at the ghost of the imp while he sort of shrugged casually as though to say, "C'est la vie." After a moment or two, she stepped lightly off his chest, continuing after the receding god with a new and intoxicating sense of liberation. She pressed play as she glided from shape to shape, starting the song from the beginning again.

Acknowledgements

This book was written in Zululand on a balcony overlooking the Umhlanga Mangrove Reserve.

Thanks to Carmen Incarnadine—for endless psychic safaris and the secret of the Siamese Inside. Thanks to Rosie (Roseblood) Hastings for the 0800-TATY hotline. Thanks to John Harris Dunning, pulp prince of the "Hampstead Underground." Thanks to Karolina Nevia and all her influential transmissions from planet K-Star. Thanks to Mika Mae Jones for countless depth readings from the lost universe of Hollywood phone booth land. Thanks to my literary agent Sarah Such for disentangling the mangles and reminding me to keep a spangle on the bangle. Thanks to my editor Ellah Allfrey for her generous support and laser-point attention to detail. Thanks to Joe Royster and Danny (Bunny) KayTraynor at Aural Sects for keeping it unreal. Thanks to everyone at Kwani? Trust, particularly Kate Haines and Billy Kahora, for supporting Taty—and also for all their efforts to champion new voices of the African diaspora. Thanks to Caitlin Pearson and the folks at the Royal Africa Society for bringing Taty to the Africa Writes Festival. Thanks too, to the people at the Africa Utopia Festival. Thanks to Geoff Ryman and Zahrah Nesbitt-Ahmed for their sterling support of Taty and African sci-fi in general. Thanks to my UK publisher, Valerie Brandes, Laure Deprez, and everyone at Jacaranda. And lastly, a cosmic high-five and great thanks to Bill Campbell, for bringing Taty to the US, and also, for coralling together so many rare and strange voices from the sci-fi underground.

Please make sure to check out the *Taty* original soundtrack:

https://cococarbomb.bandcamp.com/album/siamese-inside